HALF-BUILT HOUSES

Eric Keller

Copyright © 2012 by Eric Keller.
E P Keller Publishing Ltd.
kellepc@hotmail.com

For my mom.

PART ONE

CHAPTER 1

As the massive house came into sight of her drink-blurred eyes, Natalie thought the wide porch with its white columns and bright lights was something out of a movie. Her shy escort parked the car, killed the engine, and silently got out, leaving Natalie with no choice but to follow.

It was one of those clear winter nights of all-encompassing cold that only occur in northern climates. The sky was full of stars and no wind stirred, but it was so completely frozen that the snow on the driveway gave out squeaky creaks beneath Natalie's light steps, and her chest ached sharply from breathing in the frigid air. Thankfully, Natalie was wearing a vintage man's dress coat. People often took the dated coat for retro stylish, but she had bought it at a thrift store because it was warm and inexpensive. Now, moving towards the hulking mansion, she wrapped the long, bulky coat around her in a vain attempt to ward off the painful cold.

At the huge double doors, her unnamed date nervously fumbled with his keys. The delay allowed Natalie to ponder her situation. She did not think of herself as a prostitute. She was a waitress who also worked part time as a party girl. But she had taken money for sex a handful of times. She had never actively sought this type of attention out, but when an attractive girl took her clothes off at drunken parties, it was likely someone would make such an offer. Almost always she politely declined, but if she was drunk enough, the guy seemed safe enough, and the money was good enough, she would accept. Tonight she had drunk heavily at the bachelor party, the man seemed too nervous to be dangerous, and he had offered her two thousand dollars, which was more money than she had ever had at one time. There was really no question whether she would accept, and when the man finally managed to open the door of the house, Natalie dutifully stepped inside.

She had barely shed the overcoat when he roughly grabbed her from behind and started pulling at her clothes. Natalie thought he was merely eager, which was fine with her as it meant the night would be over quickly, but when she stopped his hands to keep them from ripping her shirt, he threw her to the hardwood floor. Looking up at him, she saw that his mannerism had drastically changed; the nervousness was gone and a hateful lusting now filled his eyes.

*

Charley pulled off his work gloves. They were not the kind of gloves with linings for winter, and the left one had a large hole in the palm, but they were the only pair he had. He took the twenty-dollar bill being handed to him through the truck's window as the man behind the wheel said, "Good work today."

He merely nodded without looking up as he knew his thick glasses gave his eyes a bulged look that made people uncomfortable.

The man asked, "Can I give you a lift? Looks like it might be about to storm."

Charley knew that this kind of offer from a boss to a day labourer was an extraordinary courtesy, but he shook his head and stepped away.

"Ok, well, if these clouds open up like it looks like they want to, we'll have lots of shovelling tomorrow. If you're at the corner early in the morning, I'll be able to give you a full day's pay for a full day's work."

With that, the truck pulled away. The three labourers he had shovelled snow with all afternoon were lingering down the way he wanted to go. They were probably discussing what bar they would spend their day's pay in. Worried they would either ridicule him or, worse, invite him to join them, Charley waited until they wandered off before beginning his familiar trek.

His first stop was a fast food restaurant. The place was dirty and the food poor, but that meant it was usually deserted. Tonight was no exception, so Charley was able to move quickly past the empty tables to the counter and mutter, "Six cheeseburgers."

The bored teenage girl behind the counter was used to dealing with the less-than-affluent and did not ask Charley if he wanted fries or a drink. She merely took his money, set his change down on the counter to ensure she would not have to touch him, and after a short wait, handed him his food in a paper sack. The place was completely empty and he considered sitting at a table to eat, but he was worried others might come in, so he headed back outside.

As he walked down the dark backstreets, Charley ate. He did not like mustard, but the burgers came with mustard and he could not ask for anything special. He had not eaten anything all day, and by the time he had covered the two blocks, he had finished four of the small sandwiches, stowing the remaining two in his coat for tomorrow's breakfast.

His second stop, a discount liquor store, was crowded, so he loitered outside for a few minutes. When only one old lady remained in the store, Charley went inside, kept his head down, and moved briskly to the cooler, where he took out two large bottles of malt liquor. The clerk tried to engage him in small talk about the impending storm but received only non-committal shrugs in response.

With his errands done, Charley commenced the long march to where he slept. The corner where the day labourers were picked up and dropped off by those with menial work to be done was, understandably, in a rough neighborhood south of the downtown core. This was far from the rich area on top of the hill north of downtown where he spent his nights. Still, Charley regularly made the trip to the corner because that was the only place he knew he could find work. At first he had been picked because he was big and white and looked relatively healthy compared to the others waiting to be hired, and then, after a time, he was hired because bosses came to know him as a hard worker who never complained or loitered with co-workers on jobs.

As he walked, the bitter cold made him thankful he had a decent coat, a heavy ski-parka he had lucked into at a shelter last winter. Unfortunately, his large feet made it impossible for him to find donated boots, so he was wearing worn-out sneakers, and his feet were perpetually frozen. As he trod across the ornate bridge over the ice-covered Bow River, the wind picked up so that the icy snow stung his face. The harsh weather and the exhaustion of the long day weighed on him, so he allowed his mind to wallow in its favorite daydream in order to ignore his misery as he walked.

*

Slowly waking, Natalie smelled a mix of her perfume and stale sex. Much of her ached, with her neck throbbing the worst, as if the muscles had been torn. Through half-opened eyes she could see darkness outside the window. She recalled being drowsily awake for a moment when it was light out, so she must have slept through the entire day, making it Sunday night now.

Her mind struggled to remember what had happened. At first she could only manage blurred, fragmented memories, but as she lay in the strange bed, partial recollection eventually came. The bachelor party had been usual enough: about a dozen men in their late twenties aggressively drinking in the back room of a bar. Her friend Shelia and one other girl from the agency had arrived at eight o'clock, changed into lingerie, and spent about an hour serving drinks and fake flirtations. Then the music was turned up and the lingerie came off as wads of cash came out. The men were relatively well behaved; there were a few misplaced fingers and some overly hard groping, but there were always misplaced fingers and overly hard groping at the parties.

He had come in late. By then she was quite drunk, but she still got the impression that he did not know the others. The other men stayed with the group, wanting their acts of minor debauchery to be witnessed by their friends, while the newcomer had each girl come with him off to the side.

She vaguely recalled sitting on his lap as he lightly stroked her thighs and back. She tried to flirt with him, but he seemed uneasy about talking. After about ten minutes of the light petting and stilted conversation, he slipped a pair of twenty-dollar bills into her stocking, and she returned to the others.

When the party was breaking up, the newcomer approached her as she was pulling on her jeans and whispered in her ear, "Two thousand if you spend the night with me."

Despite his ravenous look, when they got inside his house the man had proved to be impotent. Unfortunately, his inability did not stop him from repeatedly trying as he slapped her, twisted her breasts, dug his nails into her ass, and for a terrible moment, choked her to near unconsciousness. She was bent over and he was thrusting at her in vain when he grabbed her long hair and yanked backwards. It felt like her neck might break, and she had screamed with a combination of pain and fear. It was then that he finally became excited enough to perform the act and, in a minute, it was done.

He had left her alone for a few moments and then returned with a glass of water. The man muttered something that sounded apologetic. Confusion filled her. She was both furious and humiliated. Without looking at her, the man held the glass towards her. She was worried he might get angry again, so she took it and drank. That was the last she remembered.

Now lying in the plush bed, afraid to move, she strained to hear if he was in the room. After minutes of no sound, she dared to slowly roll over. She looked cautiously around the wide, largely empty room. It was difficult to tell if he was in one of the shadow-filled corners, but she needed to chance it. Trying to be as quiet as possible, she forced her drugged and battered body to slip from the bed.

At first she could only stand unsteadily, as she felt groggy and dizzy. For a moment she thought she was going to vomit, but she forced herself to take a deep breath and then managed a few steps towards the door. Then she tripped and crashed back to the floor.

Lying on the floor, she heard movement behind her and turned to see the man stepping out of a corner cast in darkness. He was only wearing boxer shorts, with his white belly hanging over the waist band. Reaching into a dresser drawer, he produced a pair of handcuffs. He seemed to have returned to the odd nervousness as he mumbled, "Sorry, I can't let you leave."

She glanced at the bedroom door; it was too far to reach before he would catch her. Looking around for anything she could use as a weapon, she found nothing. She pondered attacking the asshole with her bare hands. He was not large, but she was tiny, not even five feet tall and barely a hundred pounds. It would be futile.

Desperation overwhelmed her and she merely cringed away from his advance.

*

Charley had found his current residence by pure luck six months ago. He had been picked up at the labourer's corner to work for a lawn care company which mowed many of the yards of the wealthy neighbourhood on the north bank of the Bow River overlooking downtown. They had been unloading their equipment, preparing to cut the grass and weeds that had grown up around a large half-built house when the boss mentioned to one of the men that his brother-in law had been the general contractor building the mansion. Laughing, the boss told the other worker that his smug brother-in-law had lost his shirt when the owner went broke in the stock market collapse and could not pay to finish the house. Through his eavesdropping, Charley learned that the construction site was essentially abandoned as its future was being fought over in a never ending court battle.

After finishing work that day, he had made the hike back up to the ridge to scout out the house. Staying upstairs would not work because, despite the fact that the house was on a large lot surrounded by high hedges and trees, it would only be a matter of time before a neighbour would notice the gangly stranger behind the uncovered windows. But the basement windows had been covered with plywood, making it a secure, cement cave. For a man seeking simple, private shelter, it was perfect.

Over the months, Charley had actually made a decent residence for himself. There was no heating, but he had built a sleeping pad out of scavenged cardboard to keep him off the cold cement and had collected numerous blankets. The power was off, but a few flashlights served as his lamps. Two plastic milk crates were his shelving. He had found an old wobbly kitchen chair with a bright yellow seat. He had managed to decorate the dim space with various items he had found abandoned: a light blue vase, a number of framed landscapes, a remnant of carpet, and a collection of throw pillows. The decorations were constantly changing, as whenever he found some discarded item he thought might make the place more livable, he'd bring it back with him. Also, since he did not need to haul all his possessions around with him anymore, he was able to keep some extra clothes, a collection of books, and some food. Most importantly, he had put a cheap padlock on the door at the top of the basement stairs that he could lock when he was inside. Being able to sleep behind a locked door was taken for granted by most people, but it was a priceless luxury to a person who had lived on the streets.

Sitting on the shaky chair in the dim light of a flashlight, he gratefully pulled his wet shoes and socks off his frozen feet before burrowing into his nest of blankets. He pulled one of the malt liquor bottles from the bag and felt a moment of joy when he twisted the cap and heard the familiar, satisfying crack. He took a long drink of the harsh liquid, then took a breath followed by another long drink before pulling a paperback off the pile of books. These couple of hours before going to sleep were his favorite part of any day. The basic comforts were nice, but mainly he enjoyed this time because it was the longest period until he would need to interact with anyone again.

An hour later the first bottle was empty, and the novel had been replaced by one of the dirty magazines he had found last summer behind a convenience store. He could hear that the storm had picked up as the wind was now howling outside. There would be a lot of snow shoveling to do early in the morning, and he knew he could make a good deal of money. Looking at the second bottle peeking out from the bag, Charley figured he should leave it alone and go to sleep so that he could be on the day labourer corner first thing. Regardless, without any real, conscious thought, he grabbed the bottle and cracked it open.

*

The dealer flipped over the last card. Nine of clubs. The man across the table in sunglasses and oversized headphones whom Brian had played with numerous times but had never heard speak tapped the felt, indicating he was checking the bet. Brian figured that his opponent had been on a diamond flush draw that was now busted, and he barely hesitated before putting four five-dollar chips over the line, making a standard half-pot bet. Expecting a fold, he was surprised when the man slid a pile of chips forward, silently raising him a hundred dollars.

The other players at the table had all folded pre-flop and had been engaged in the familiar discussion about the latest hockey trades, but with some real money now in the pot, they stopped talking to watch the action. Brian looked at his hole cards; he only had middle pair with a low kicker. Not long ago he would have called the bet out of a combination of pride and curiosity. Now he barely hesitated before tossing his cards into the muck. The dealer swept all the chips over to his opponent.

On another night of the week, the other player might have shown his hand, letting people see if he was bluffing or not. But this was Sunday night. On Thursday, Friday, and Saturday nights, the regular players spent endless hours taking pots off of the amateurs who wandered in from the blackjack or roulette tables. Sunday nights the amateurs were all at home getting a good night's sleep before another week of work, and the poker pros used the opportunity to prove their skills against one another by fighting over the spoils from the weekend.

The dealer shuffled and dealt a new hand. Brian instantly folded a three of hearts and six of spades before checking his watch. It was five minutes to midnight. He got up and moved towards the loosely forming line. It was dinnertime.

Brian always thought anyone interested in studying human behavior should observe a poker room late at night. There was an abundant mixture of camaraderie, aggression, desperation, addiction, competition, flirting, and bargaining, all in an isolated habitat with its own particular rules and abundant drinks. To Brian the oddest phenomenon of the very odd place was the free dinner. Every night, at midnight, the casino would provide all poker players with a meal. Normally it was pizza or some sort of overcooked pasta, but on Sunday nights, since only the regulars were there, the dinner was a spread of decent Chinese food. Players who thought nothing of betting hundreds of dollars on an open-ended straight draw would line up like eager school children, paper plates in hand, to get five dollars' worth of free food. And they would complain loudly and continually if the substandard meal was late or cold.

Brian, done gambling for the night, was planning to go home right after eating a pile of ginger beef in order to justify his minor losses. He was waiting in the line when someone tapped him on the shoulder. He turned to see a rotund young man named Raj, whom he knew to be a decent player who liked to bluff out of the big blind.

"Hey, Brian."

"Hi, Raj, how's it going?"

"Alright. Would've been way up for the weekend but got rivered by a donkey late last night at fifteen-thirty. How are you making out?"

"I don't play that much anymore." He gestured to the steam trays. "I just come in for a shitty dinner once in a while."

With the necessary small talk done, Raj moved to the point and asked, "You still doing the lawyer thing?"

This question came up often in the poker room, and each time it made Brian realize how different his life was now. Two years ago, he had been working at a national law firm with a nice office, a high salary, a cute assistant, an expense account, and a number of senior partners bringing him high-end corporate files to work on. However, like a number of young lawyers, he had a difficult time making the transition from impoverished student to well-paid professional. With a steady stream of cash coming in, he was able to indulge the vices he had not been able to afford while he was struggling to make ends meet in school.

Predictably, drinking, gambling, and womanizing ran out of control, getting worse each time his salary or line of credit was increased. He began making mistakes at work, and more importantly, his number of billable hours dropped, however, Brian had managed to keep his job despite these problems. This was partly because national law firms made money off even subpar associates, as they billed them out at exorbitant rates; but more importantly, he was fun to go out with and to have along on firm retreats or golf trips. This meant they overlooked his professional deficiencies, as the partners viewed him as an entertainment expense for the firm—not that different than having golf club memberships or the luxury box at the Saddledome. However, when the recession hit, the firm moved to reduce overhead, which meant letting underperforming lawyers like him go, no matter how much the higher ups liked hitting on cocktail waitresses with him. Despite this cost cutting, Brian did note that the firm kept the luxury box.

With everyone having abundant concerns over the economy, no one was hiring junior attorneys, and his only experience was in corporate litigation, which is not an area that lends itself to making money as a sole practitioner. While many areas of legal practice had dried up, people still committed crimes during a recession, so Brian reluctantly hung up his own shingle and joined the ranks of criminal defence lawyers in an attempt to pay his bills.

Understandably, his infant practice did not pay well so, with the extremely generous, bi-monthly influx of cash gone, Brian was forced to get his vices under control. He curtailed his drinking, partying, and gambling. However, he had found that continuing to visit the poker room on occasion was a decent source of clients. And, now that he wasn't playing drunk, he could even make a moderate profit most nights.

Brian scooped some of the deep-fried beef onto his plate as he answered Raj, "Yeah, I'm still practicing law. You need help with something?"

"I got a goddamn DUI on Wednesday."

Drunk driving was the criminal defence bar's bread and butter, so it was the first area Brian had needed to teach himself. He answered confidently, "I can help you with that."

"What's it going to cost me?"

"This your first DUI?"

"Yeah. I've got no record."

"For you? Five hundred down with another thousand if we need to go to court."

Raj reached into his pocket, dug out a handful of poker chips, and handed over five black ones. "Sounds good to me."

Brian wondered what the law society would say about having a retainer paid in poker chips. Regardless, he took the chips and handed over a business card in exchange, as he said, "Thanks. Give me a call tomorrow and we'll discuss your options."

*

A loud screeching sound shocked Charley awake. He was slumped against the wall, the magazine upside down on his lap and a flashlight glowing weakly beside him. Confused, he worked his way through the maze of unfinished walls to the back of the basement where a vent hole for the dryer had been cut. Always afraid someone would find his shelter, he had learned that by sticking his eye right against the hole, he could see much of the backyard with minimal risk of being seen himself.

The storm had picked up, so the snow was now blowing sideways across the yard, but Charley barely noticed the intense weather. It was the fact that he could see the weather at all that worried him. Headlights. A car's bright headlights had lit up the yard.

A sports car was stuck at an odd angle off of the alley, its back tires spinning in the snow. Charley instantly knew what had happened. There was a slight ditch between the yard and alley which had a cement retaining wall. The driver probably put a wheel into that snow-filled ditch, which made him crash along the wall. Charley's fear lessened. This was not someone coming to the house; it was a simple accident.

Checking his watch, Charley saw that it was four in the morning. It was odd for someone to be out driving a sports car at four in the morning in a blizzard, but he had long since given up on trying to understand why people did the things they did. After another minute of trying to drive the car out of the snow, the driver seemed to realize it was pointless and got out. The short man scurried around the back of the car and frantically looked at the buried tires from different angles. Even from his peephole, Charley, with his rural upbringing, figured the fool had spun the tires so much that the car had dug itself into a deep hole it would have to be towed out of. The bad driver moved back towards the car door, but as soon as he put his hand on the handle, it exploded open.

The door smashed into the driver, sending him falling back

into the snow. Someone climbed out of the car and moved awkwardly through the storm towards the unfinished house. As the person stumbled closer, Charley realized it was a woman. A small woman. A small woman in a long black coat. A small woman in a black coat with her hands tied behind her. She was twenty feet away when the driver recovered and came running after her.

Too stunned by what he was witnessing to move, Charley mutely watched as the man grabbed her by her long, black hair. He was not large, but she was tiny. Her feet shot out from under her, and for an instant she dangled in his grasp before he threw her down. The edge of the vent hole obscured Charley's view of the ground, so all he could do was watch the snow blowing across the yard, unsure what was occurring until a bright light came on in an upper-story window of the house across the alley. The driver must have seen the light come on as well, as he immediately popped back up into Charley's line of vision. He hesitated for a second, looking back down at where the woman was lying before darting off into the blackness.

Panic filled Charley. Moving in his usual clumsy way, he tripped and stumbled his way back to his blankets. Certainly people would come when someone called about the stuck car. They might look around, find the girl, and then they would find his home. Or they might not; it was merely a car stuck in the snow, probably one of hundreds of minor accidents that would be reported on a night like this. He sat in the darkness, surrounded by his meager possessions and worrying about what fresh horror was about to befall him. Then, through the fear, liquor, and confusion, he realized that a woman was lying outside in the storm. It was not a dream. It was actually happening.

CHAPTER 2

The familiar sound of his Blackberry ringing on the nightstand woke Hugh from his uneasy sleep. It was four in the morning. This would not be good. It was probably someone in an Eastern time zone with bad news about the takeover.

He picked up the phone and answered, "Hugh Young speaking."

"Dad, it's Jason. I, uh, messed up."

Hugh was relieved that it was only his son with another of his problems rather than a business crisis, but he did not let his voice reveal the relief as he angrily growled, "What the hell did you do this time?"

"I need to get someone to tow my car."

"Fuck, Jason. It's four in the morning. You're twenty-five years old. Certainly you can call for a goddamn tow truck without waking me up."

"I can, but there's a problem. There was a girl."

Hugh was waking up and could now hear the panic in his son's voice. He sat up, swinging his legs over the edge of his plush bed, and asked, "What did you fucking do?"

*

The girl was dead. There was nothing he could do for her now. Yet remnants of the dream fogged his mind, and as much as he wanted to, he knew he could not simply leave her there to be buried in the snow. Charley moved across the alley, slipping into the yard where the upstairs light was still on. For a long time he stood and stared at the window. Knocking on a stranger's door in the middle of the night was a nightmare for Charley, but with the image of the poor girl's corpse filling his mind, he managed to force himself to ring the doorbell.

After a long time, an older man dressed in a bathrobe and carrying a golf club like a weapon came to the door. He glared at Charley through the window and loudly asked through the glass, "Yes?"

What Charley had carefully planned to say disappeared and his words came out in a cascading stutter. "A woman. A woman across the alley."

Confusion crossed the old man's face. "What? What are you saying?"

He thought the man was going to get mad at him, and he took a step back as he rapidly said, "A dead woman, across the alley."

"Son, slow down. What has happened?"

He got even more flustered and his fragile composure completely failed, but as he ran away, he managed to blurt out over his shoulder, "Call for help."

As he headed back to his basement, Charley was cursing his inability to have a normal conversation, but he was soon distracted by the rumble of an engine. Turning, he was able to make out a large vehicle coming down the alley, moving fast through the snow with its headlights off. Charley quickly hid behind nearby garbage bins.

Peering from the shadows, he could see the heavy-duty pickup stop in front of the stuck car. A big man in a parka jumped out of the driver side while a scrawny man in a jean jacket got out of the passenger side. With the efficiency of men used to working together, a chain was produced from the truck box, and not even a minute after arriving, they had pulled the sports car out of the ditch and both vehicles were quickly driven off, leaving Charley alone.

*

It was mornings like this that made Randall Jenkins think longingly about his impending retirement. It was six in the morning; the wind had died down but it was at least thirty below. Jenkins had been a cop for almost thirty years, the last ten as a homicide detective. He had a full pension, numerous grandchildren, and multiple ulcers. He could not help but think that there had to be a better way to be spending his later years than standing over the frozen corpse of a young woman in the pre-dawn hours.

Jenkins asked, "Who called it in?"

Stephen Wilson, a rookie detective who had been Jenkins's partner for the last year, pointed across the back alley with his thumb as he answered, "Older guy who lives back there. Says he woke up at four in the morning, and while he was in the can his doorbell rang. There was a strange guy at his back door who told him there was a dead woman over here."

"He see anything else?"

"Nope. He called 911 and headed back to the bathroom. You know, you old guys can't pass up the chance for a bowel movement."

"Trust me, I know. What have we got?"

Wilson pointed his pen at the body and rattled off the details, "Woman, aged eighteen to twenty-five, dead for less than eight hours. Various contusions. A nasty cut on the cheek. Cause of death appears to be strangulation. Can't confirm sexual assault out here, but given the bruising it looks likely. Hands are cuffed behind her with standard issue porn shop gear. Only wearing the coat and the boots. Nothing in the pockets. No ID."

Jenkins sighed. Murders were rare in Calgary. In his ten years as a detective, he had only dealt with a couple dozen, and of those, most solved themselves with the victim being identified as a gang member or a rueful husband quickly confessing or some other obvious explanation immediately presenting itself. He had, however, handled a handful of stone-cold whodunits which required lengthy, inventive detective work to solve. Two of those cases remained on his desk, festering like lingering sores on his career. Unfortunately, this crime scene reminded him of those sores.

He asked, "Any sign of how she got here?"

Wilson waved his hands to indicate the falling snow and said, "No. Hell the cops who answered the 911 call would not have even found the body if one of them had not tripped over it."

"Who owns the house?"

"Will have to check the title. The old guy said that the construction has stalled. He hasn't seen any activity over here in almost a year."

Jenkins began slowly walking around the yard, carefully examining the scene. Tall fences, along with hedges and trees, largely blocked any view the neighbours would have. Flood lights had been set up by the crime scene techs, but without them it would be pitch black, the hulking house blocking any light from the street lamps out front. With the heavily falling snow and the empty home, it would be a smart place to dump a body. Except for the mysterious stranger telling the old man to call the cops, the corpse could have stayed unnoticed until spring. But Jenkins figured a person would have to be either very cunning or very desperate to dump a body in the middle of a wealthy residential neighbourhood.

Wilson interrupted Jenkins's thoughts, calling out, "Randy, we found something in the house."

Climbing into the shell of a house, he pulled plastic slippers on over his wet shoes and asked Wilson, "What'd we find?"

"Looks like someone's been squatting in the basement."

Jenkins took out his flashlight and followed him to the staircase, where Wilson silently pointed out the padlock hanging on the inside of the door before leading him down. A lock on the outside of the door could have indicated someone being imprisoned. A lock on the inside indicated someone living there. As Jenkins reached the dark basement, his flashlight revealed that a living area had been set up in one corner.

Numerous mismatched blankets were piled on top of a stack of what appeared to be unfolded cardboard boxes. Next to an old kitchen chair that tilted badly, shelving had been constructed out of milk crates. Two flashlights lay on the floor beside a few items of clothing, two empty bottles, an overturned paperback, and some magazines. It was a dreary and dark place to live, but Jenkins figured that, while it would not be overly comfortable, the cardboard bed would be warm enough with all its blankets. And the resident would be a lot safer sleeping behind the locked door than out on the streets. Sadly, in his years on the police force, he had seen far worse living arrangements.

Wilson touched one of the socks hanging off the milk crate shelf and said, "Still wet. Someone must have been here pretty recently."

Jenkins nodded as he carefully pulled a receipt from a liquor store bag. "The beer was bought at six-thirteen last night."

"What are you thinking?"

Wilson always asked him this question early on in an investigation, and he always answered the same way, "Not thinking anything yet."

"Well, you want to know what I think?"

Jenkins had learned long ago not to engage in speculation, so he ignored the question, but Wilson continued regardless as they picked through the possessions. "Our urban camper picks up the dead girl from hooker stroll and brings her back to his little love nest. She balks on seeing his bizarre living arrangement. He gets rough and decides to keep her down here. She gets away but he catches her in the yard and makes her dead. Then he panics or gets a case of the guilts. He sees the light on across the alley and tells the old guy across to call the cops before he disappears. Sounds about right, right?"

Ignoring the question, Jenkins handed Wilson a book from the shelf and said, "Why don't you start by visiting the library and see who borrowed this book."

Wilson took the book with a grin, "And what are you going to be doing while I'm flirting with librarians?"

"Drinking coffee somewhere warm."

*

Hugh Young strode into the main boardroom of the law firm Rainer Hopkins LLP, his no-good son following behind him. It was not quite seven in the morning, but a spread of muffins and coffee had been laid out for them on a sideboard. When Jason, looking like he was still asleep, moved to help himself to the food, Hugh grabbed his elbow and shoved him towards a chair saying, "We aren't here for you to eat fucking breakfast."

The room was massive and designed to not only show off the affluence of the firm, but to intimidate. One wall was floor-to-ceiling windows with a breathtaking view across the still-dark city. A huge table of highly polished stone filled the space; the type of table that most people were afraid to even put their papers on, the type of table used to make people uneasy. Hugh was not easily intimidated and had spent many long nights aggressively negotiating deals over the expanse of marble, so he casually dumped his briefcase on it as if it were a plywood desk. Father and son only had to sit in pained silence for a minute before they were joined by two lawyers in dark suits, both trying to look happy to be there despite the early hour.

The round man with the bald dome was Larry Wellington, a successful corporate lawyer who had made a fortune over the years billing Hugh's various oil and gas exploration companies five hundred dollars an hour. He eagerly shook Hugh's hand and said, "Good to see you."

"Morning, Larry. This is my son Jason."

Larry and Jason exchanged nods before Larry turned to introduce the other lawyer, "This is Jacob Poetker, our firm's criminal specialist."

Jacob was a tall, thin man of about fifty with designer glasses and a coif of thick silver hair. He shook their hands and said, "Nice to meet both of you. Hopefully we can help with whatever your problem is this morning."

"Hopefully. We've got a hell of a problem on our hands." Hugh turned to Larry, "Before we get into this, Larry, do you recommend Jacob as our guy for dealing with a serious criminal matter?"

"Oh, yes, he does very good work on such things. He recently got one of my clients off on an insider trading—"

He held up his hand to interrupt, "Fine, if you say he's the guy, he's the guy. You don't need to be here for this meeting."

Even though he was familiar with Hugh's abrupt manner, Larry still seemed surprised by being rudely asked to immediately leave the early morning meeting he had been requested to urgently set up. "Oh, well, if it's a question of cost, I don't need to bill for this, but I should be in the meeting—"

"It's not the fucking cost, Larry. The less people who hear this, the better."

Larry glanced at Poetker, who nodded slightly. The round lawyer shrugged, grabbed two muffins off the sideboard, and walked out of the boardroom. The remaining men all sat down around one corner of the massive table, and Jacob started, "Ok, first the technical stuff. I'm assuming you are concerned that a crime has occurred and that one or both of you may be charged. You are now both my clients, but you need to understand that your interests may be in conflict and you are both advised to get your own lawyers. But that being said, I am willing to act for both of you at this time. Based on this, anything said between us will be protected by the lawyer-client privilege. Are we all in agreement?"

Father and son both nodded. Poetker continued, "Fine, what's the problem?"

Hugh had never been the type to mince words, but he found himself having a hard time saying what needed to be said in this situation. However, as he hesitated, Jason, still looking at the floor muttered, "I kidnapped a stripper."

It took a moment for that to settle in with Poetker. Hugh figured that the upscale law firm of Rainer Hopkins LLP did not have many violent criminals sitting in their main boardroom. To his credit, the lawyer regained himself quickly, pulled a pen out of his jacket, and started writing on the notepad in front of him as he said, "Tell me what happened."

Listening to his son describe picking up the girl at a stranger's bachelor party, bringing her back to his house, attacking her, and then drugging her, Hugh could not help but wonder if maybe he should not be helping him. This was the worst trouble he had been in but there had been many other incidents: totaling two cars while drunk driving and drug possession charges—not to mention flunking out of three separate universities. Maybe it was time to let him get the punishment he deserved.

Back then Hugh figured his wife had wanted a child mainly because her friends and sisters were mothers, and he was fine with giving her the distraction. His business was taking off at the time, and he had taken only enough interest in the pregnancy to keep his wife content, assuming that when the child was born, he would feel some sort of connection. However, when the nurse handed him the newborn, wrapped in a soft blue blanket, all he could think was that he had been given another obligation. For a long moment, he wondered why any man would want such a thing, something costly and time consuming that he could not eat, fuck, drink or sell.

He wanted to blame his wife for their son's behaviour, but he had to admit that he had contributed as well. He had very little to do with the raising of his son, so his sense of responsibility for Jason's behavior came from the fact that he perpetually ignored the stupidity of his wife's parenting. Jason's mother ensured her only child wanted for nothing. If there was a toy he desired, he got three of them. If there was an activity he showed even a slight interest in, private classes were promptly arranged. Even though his wife did not work, a full-time nanny was hired in case the infant needed attention while his mother was away for an instant.

Jason had actually been a decent athlete in junior high and high school but lacked the discipline necessary for normal team sports like hockey or basketball. Plus, his mother disliked anyone being rough with her baby. As a result, he became involved in more obscure sports such as squash and skeet shooting, where he could excel by only beating the handful of other kids who did not make the cut in normal sports and could afford such odd pursuits. Regardless, all of these minor athletic achievements were touted and praised along with any other simple accomplishment, no matter how insignificant.

All of this combined to make Jason a spoiled, arrogant brat, but he was not truly a troublemaker until he moved out. Thanks to his tutors basically doing his homework, Jason's high school grades were good enough to get into university. However, with no work ethic and a healthy allowance to spend on debauchery, Jason was put on academic probation after his first semester. Then he was caught with pot, and by the end of his second semester, a complaint had been filed by a female student and he was promptly expelled. A similar story played out at two more schools, but still, his delusional mother would not admit that he was not going to become a doctor or, at least, a lawyer.

Through his business contacts, Hugh got Jason a good job at a technology company because he had mentioned he liked computers. That lasted about a month before Hugh received a call informing him that Jason continually failed to show up for work, and when he did show up, he was a problem with the women in the office. Not wanting to have his reputation ruined, Hugh gave Jason a job at his company, but due partly to Hugh not wanting to spend time with him and partly to Jason not wanting to work, he was mainly paid to stay home.

As they tend to do, Jason's few high school friends had been dispersed by life. Since he had not lasted long at any university, he had made no friends there. And with no real job, he had no professional colleagues. His mother, tired of the Alberta winters and her disappointing child, essentially moved to the family villa in the south of France. As a result, Jason became isolated. Hugh figured his social life now consisted of online video games, drinking alone in bars, and hiring escorts.

Hugh had never been friendly with Jason, and now he only heard from him when he needed money, wandered into the office to harass the secretaries, or was in trouble. Dealing with his son's issues was an annoyance, but he also saw it as an obligation, a payment of penance for his failed parenting. Despite this sense of obligation, Hugh realized he really did not care if Jason went to jail or not. What he could not handle was having the reputation he had built up ruined by his son's deficiencies. The threat of this scandal in the papers made him both ill and furious.

Jason was explaining to the lawyer that he had drugged the woman with roofies after he had sex with her and had kept her in a drugged state until late Sunday night. His plan was to drive her around town to disorientate her and then drop her off at the bus depot, knowing that she would be relatively safe and unnoticed there until she came to her senses. He was certain she had been sufficiently drugged to have a limited memory at best.

Poetker looked up from his notes; his gaze settled on Jason

and then shifted to Hugh. Jason did not understand the silent question being asked, but Hugh did. The experienced lawyer realized that Jason was too specific and too confident in his plan, a sign that he had probably done this before, and was asking if he should be concerned about other women coming forward. Hugh answered by nodding slightly, and Jacob returned his attention to the notepad.

Hugh knew that Jason enjoyed controlling women; it had gotten him into trouble before. Plus, given his own predilections, it was probably genetic. He had set Jason up with the specialty escort company he used himself, hoping that would solve the problem of women making assault claims. He had paid the outlandish bills, so he knew he had been using their services regularly, but apparently that had not been enough for the idiot.

Jason continued his story, "I figured I would go down the back alley, you know so people wouldn't see my car. But it was snowing hard and the road was a mess and I ended up getting stuck. While I was trying to get it out, she ran from the car, and when I was trying to stop her from getting away I knocked her around, you know to get her back in the car. Then a light came on in a house across the alley, so I took off."

The lawyer scanned his scribbled notes and tapped his pen on the pad. Finally he looked up. "Does anyone else know about this?"

Hugh answered. "The idiot couldn't get the car unstuck so he called me. I phoned a couple of guys that work for me from time to time and told them to go get the car as quickly and discreetly as possible."

"Will they talk?"

He shrugged. "If they get pressured by the cops they might. But I pay them well and know where their skeletons are buried, so I doubt they will give anything up willingly."

Poetker returned his attention to Jason. "What about the people at the bachelor party?"

Concern crossed Jason's face as if this were the first time he was thinking about the possibility of someone at the party identifying him. "I didn't know any of them. I went to that bar because this woman I know sometimes works there and I wanted to talk to her. She never showed up, but I got a glimpse of the strippers in the back room. It looked like a good party, so I gave one of the guys five hundred bucks to let me join. I told them my name was Jay, and they basically ignored me, as the strippers were more interesting."

"How many girls were at the party?"

"Three."

"Did you talk to all of them?"

"Yes, we chatted for a few minutes."

"So they would remember you?"

A juvenile smirk crossed Jason's lips as he said, "Oh, yeah, I tip well."

Hugh slapped the table and glared at him. The smirk disappeared and he sheepishly responded, "Yes, they would probably remember me being there."

"Fine. Would people at the bar know who you were if the police came asking around?"

"I've been there a bit. Some of the staff would know me as Jay. I avoid using my full name at bars."

"Anyone else who might know about this or be able to put the girl with you?"

Hugh and Jason both shook their heads, and Poetker scanned his notes again before asking, "Do we know anything about this unfinished house that she was left at?"

Jason answered, "I drive by it all the time. It's been under construction for over a year, but nothing has happened on it for six months or more."

"What state was the girl in when you left her?"

Jason seemed confused. "What do you mean?"

"Was she unconscious?"

"Um, I'm not really sure. Like I said, she ran away, I got her by the hair and pulled her down. Then I hit her a couple of times and was shaking her before the light came on. She was lying in the snow when I ran off."

Jason had only told Hugh that she had gotten away at the house, so he was shocked and enraged by this new information. "So maybe she's fucking dead? Maybe you fucking killed her?

"No, I didn't kill her." Jason's voice was adamant, but when Hugh's hard gaze focused on him, he lowered his head and said into his lap, "I'm, well, I'm uh, sure she was alive when I left. Pretty sure. I got scared someone was coming and ran off."

Hugh asked, "But she was in the snow, beaten and drugged on a freezing night, right? What was she wearing?"

"She had a long coat on and boots." He looked back down. "And her hands were cuffed behind her. But I think she was alive. I think she was moaning when I left."

The lawyer sighed, "But maybe she is still out there and we are talking about murder."

Jason opened his mouth to protest, but Hugh let out a stream of curses and Jason merely looked back down at his lap. Poetker continued, "Anything on the body that could be used to identify you? Fingerprints? Fluids?"

"No, I was careful. Even washed her down before we left."

Next, Poetker asked about Jason's record, and Hugh had to sit patiently while Jason went through the lengthy details of his troubled past. Finally, Poekter checked his notes one more time and then looked up. "Those are all of the questions I have for now."

Hugh asked, "So, what are our options?"

"Right now there are only two choices. The first is that Jason turns himself in and throws himself on the mercy of the court. Bearing in mind that we would need to explain how the car got removed from the scene, which would implicate you as well, Hugh—"

He interrupted the lawyer. "What do you mean, 'implicate

me'? I didn't fucking do anything."

"Unfortunately a prosecutor would not view it that way. By calling in your employees to remove the vehicle from the scene, you were obstructing justice and possibly aiding and abetting in the commission of a violent crime, maybe even a murder. These would not be minor charges and my guess is, given your stature in the community, it would become fodder for the press, which would mean no prosecutor could take the matter lightly."

Now, beyond the idea of protecting his son to avoid a scandal, he was suddenly worried about the prospect of getting in trouble himself. "Can't we just lie about that part? Jason tells about the girl and then says he got the car out on his own?"

"Sure, but if they think the confession is at all doubtful, the first thing the cops will do is check Jason's cell phone records. It's practically protocol now. That will lead them to you and a certain phone call you made at four in the morning to the impromptu tow truck drivers. One simple lie and you are headed down an extremely slippery slope."

He glared at his foolish son, his already sizable hatred growing as he asked, "And the other option?"

"The other option, the one I recommend, is to do nothing. Given the nature of this crime, Jason's previous troubles, and the desire to keep you out of this, I don't think there is any benefit to talking to the police at this point."

Hugh leaned forward. "Your professional advice is to do nothing?"

"If the woman is alive, according to Jason she'll have a very flawed memory at best. She might make a claim but will likely have a hard time piecing it together, so her story will be riddled with holes. Even if the police suspect Jason, it could get messy, but we could probably get by with simply saying nothing. Plus, we might get lucky and she may not talk at all. There are a number of reasons victims don't want to report attacks: she might be embarrassed about stripping or she might have a sordid past or a clueless boyfriend."

"And if she's dead?"

"If she did not have any close friends or family who will report her missing, then maybe no one will be looking for her. With all the snow last night and the house being abandoned, the body might not be found until spring. It could be months before the cops start looking into this. Even if they can identify the body, by then the memories of the people at the bachelor party will be faded and it might be impossible for the police to link Jason to the stripper."

Jason interjected, "And, I mean, she is just some hooker. Even if the cops do find her body, I doubt they're going to look too hard for the killer."

Poetker shook his head. "No, if a body is found in Calgary, they won't care who she is. Murders are not that common, and they'll look long and hard until they find someone to charge."

Hugh asked, "And if she does have a family and they start looking for this girl right away?"

"The police will quickly figure out that she was last seen at the bar. From there they will learn that Jason was the stranger at the bachelor party and they will come to speak with him."

"What does he do then?"

Poetker slid his business card across the table and glared seriously at Jason, "You say nothing, and I mean absolutely nothing, and hand them this. Neither of you will discuss this matter in any way with any person." The lawyer looked back down at his legal pad as he said, "And I can't counsel you to destroy evidence, but it may not be a bad idea to do some house and car cleaning when you get home."

CHAPTER 3

After the car had been towed away, Charley had gone back to the basement, but he heard sirens and had to flee before he could collect his belongings. Knowing he would stand out as an oddity wandering about in a rich residential area as people started leaving their homes for work, he headed back across the river to the downtown core where the homeless merely blended into the cement. There he numbly walked the icy streets before settling into an ATM kiosk to warm up and rest.

Sitting on the wet floor, he did a quick inventory. He still had his good coat, two cheeseburgers, four dollars, and shoes but no socks, gloves, or hat. It was thirty below and he had nowhere to go, and he could already feel the dirty slush on the floor soaking through his jeans. Over all the years he had been in Calgary, Charley had been in some extremely difficult spots, but this was one of the worst situations he had faced.

As he pulled one of the slightly squashed cheeseburgers out of his pocket, the key to the cheap padlock he had put on the basement door fell onto the floor. He picked it up. Despite being twenty-five years old, this was the only key he had ever owned. He remembered the joy he felt when he closed the lock for the first time. It was more than simply having a place of his own; it was a sense of survivor's pride because he could look past making it through each day and ponder a future for himself. Now he realized he could not be found carrying the key, so he slipped it into the slot in the bank machine, the slot where people threw away their receipts showing how much money they had in their account.

He was only able to stay in the kiosk for an hour before a security guard found him. The guard clearly did not want to send the pathetic man out into the exceptionally harsh cold, but he sheepishly said that the bank employees would be showing up soon and they would give him grief if they found someone sleeping next to the bank machine. Charley left without a word.

Having nowhere else to go, he instinctively walked to the day labourer corner. Because the weather was so bad and he was there so early, he got picked up right away to shovel snow. Charley had worked for the boss before, and the man took pity on him, giving him a good pair of gloves and a toque.

*

Jenkins was checking missing person reports when Wilson strutted into the office and dropped an enlarged printout of a library card on his desk. The picture on the card was of a thin, unsmiling young man with thick glasses and messy hair. It matched the description the neighbor at the crime scene had given them. Wilson sat down and said, "Our basement squatter has a name. Charley Ewanuschuk. The address and phone number he gave are fakes though."

"Did anyone at the library know him?"

"Sort of. One of the librarians said the guy's been coming in about once a week for years, but she doesn't think he's ever said a word to anybody. She did say he was cleaner than the other homeless people and never had a late book, so he has that going for him."

"A name and a picture. We've found people with less." Jenkins, now feeling hopeful this would be a quicker case than he had anticipated, stood up and grabbed his coat. "Let's go check the usual spots."

*

Even though he had been extremely tired and his feet had screamed with cold, Charley had been content to push a shovel all day as the mundane, physical work was relaxing and allowed him to ponder his situation. By the end of the day, he had forced himself to conclude that it was not hopeless. He could not go back to the house he had been using, but that did not mean he could not find another abandoned construction site to use. It would take some time, but he had time; he had little else, but he had time. When the work was done, he was driven back to the corner, given sixty dollars, and told to keep the gloves and the hat. It was enough money to get a room at the hostel for the night. Life would continue to be hard, but it would not be impossible.

As he started walking away, a truck pulled up, unloading another crew of day labourers, and one of the workers called out to him, "Hey, you. Guy who never talks."

He recognized the man as a regular at the corner whom he had worked with a few times. He pointed at himself questioningly.

"Yeah, you. Just thought you should know that the cops were out here this morning showing your picture around. You may want to lay low for a few days."

The man knew Charley well enough not to expect a response, so he turned to jog after his friends, leaving Charley alone on the frozen sidewalk. Renewed panic struck at him, easily pushing away the optimism he had gained throughout the day. He had not even considered that the police would look for him. He had always seen himself as a mere visitor moving about beneath the notice of the real inhabitants of the city, so the thought that someone would look for him never occurred to him. Charley had never been to jail but he had overheard much about the place from day labourers, and being locked up was one of his greatest fears among an impressive list of fears. It was not actually being deprived of his freedom so much as being constantly surrounded by people with no privacy or reprieve that he knew would be an unimaginable hell for him. He could not go to jail.

*

It was nights like these that made Brian miss his job at the law firm. He was sitting under the harsh, fluorescent lights of the Legal Aid office at nine at night drafting a brief for a shoplifting case involving a five-dollar bottle of mouthwash. After the firm fired him, he had put his name on the list of lawyers willing to take Legal Aid cases and had discovered that, while these files paid badly, they did provide valuable experience as senior lawyers volunteered to help younger lawyers. Plus, with no salary, he had come to fully understand the meaning of beggars not being choosers.

Tonight he was working at the Legal Aid office instead of at home because his laptop had crashed. The reason he was still there so late was that his block heater had quit, so his car would not start, and he had to wait for his girlfriend to give him a boost. He had not had dinner, but the idea of walking through the bad neighbourhood in the freezing cold to get some greasy fast food did not appeal to him, so he was starving. Pondering his hunger, he realized it was Monday. Italian night. If he were still at the firm, he would be eating the gourmet lasagne they served on Mondays for the daily free dinner brought in for lawyers working late. While he ate the gourmet food and joked with the other associates, the all-night word processing department would be typing up his brief. When the food, jokes, and brief were done, he would have taken the firm's complimentary car service home. With a sigh, he took a long drink of bad coffee and told himself that those days were long gone.

As much as he wanted someone else to blame, Brian knew there was no one but himself responsible for his situation. His father was killed in a car accident when Brian was an infant, leaving his mother to raise him and his brother alone. However, a substantial life insurance policy ensured that, while they were far from wealthy, they lived comfortably with his mother working as a bookkeeper to pay for much of their education. Using his ingrained charisma, Brian had gotten his undergrad degree in business without having to work very hard. On graduating, the idea of entering the labour force with its forty-hour workweeks seemed daunting, so he decided to try law school. As usual, he easily made friends, and through these contacts, he received the best class notes and was invited into the best study groups. As a result, he graduated with decent enough grades to get interviews for good articling positions, through which he was able to charm his way into a top-level job offer with a national firm.

Once at the firm, he relied on what had worked in the past and tried to befriend his way through the job. That worked to a degree, but he got the impression that his nonchalant attitude annoyed those who diligently devoted their weekends and evenings to their careers. Despite getting that impression, Brian continued to shirk his duties and get by on exploiting his popularity because that was easier than working. When the recession came and it was time for the firm to cut expenses, he learned the harsh lesson: dollars dictate.

After being fired, he became desperate and tried calling his mother to get a loan, but each time he picked up the phone, he remembered all she had done for him and his brother. He knew she had prudently saved enough that she could afford a well-earned retirement of modest comfort. He could not ask her to risk that after she had given him every opportunity, opportunities he could now see he had squandered.

He figured he would get a couple of clients who would allow him to cover his living expenses for a while. Soon a position would open up at another firm, where one of his many law school buddies could pull some strings to get him hired. However, when he started practicing on his own, he learned his second harsh lesson: your reputation is determined by those who are not your friends.

Those diligent co-workers he had annoyed with his cavalier attitude had spread the word that Brian was more interested in using expense accounts than billing hours. That's all it took. Occasional job openings came up, but with a large number of junior lawyers out of work, Brian's reputation ensured he was easily passed over. Further, most of his contacts were not even willing to refer decent clients to him, as presumably they were worried he would do a half-assed job, which would then reflect badly on them.

Alone with no prospects, he considered giving up, getting a job serving drinks or selling insurance, but the thought of having to tell his mother he had floundered away all of that tuition money forced him to give the practice of law a real try. It was a struggle, spending all of his time trying to find clients or working on files he did not understand as he learned new areas of the law. But he provided excellent service to his initial shoplifting, drug dealing, and drunk driving clients, so while his lawyer friends had largely forgotten him, those people gladly referred him to their criminal colleagues, and his business increased. After a while, despite his usual cynicism about such things, he found himself taking pride in the small practice he had developed.

Reading over the stolen mouthwash brief one last time, Brian decided it was done, hit print, got another cup of bad coffee, added lots of cream in hope that it would stem his hunger, and settled in to read the sports section.

*

Stamping his feet to try and get some feeling back in them, Charley saw the young man inside the office put his feet up on a desk. Like most of his information, he had learned about Legal Aid by listening in on day labourers while waiting on the corner. While a few men complained that they had been screwed over by the free lawyers, all of them agreed it was far better than trying to deal with the complicated court system by yourself. When Charley had first arrived at the office earlier that evening, it had been too busy for him to even consider going inside, so he had loitered outside the office in the harsh cold, watching people leave, waiting for a chance to go in. For the last hour, only the young man appeared to be left at the office, but he seemed to be busy working, so Charley used that as an excuse not to interrupt him. Now, however, it appeared the apparent lawyer was only killing time. With great effort, he forced himself to leave the shadow he had been hiding in and approach the door.

*

Brian was dozing off and almost fell out of his seat when the loud doorbell sounded. He checked his watch. Nine thirteen. Too late. The official closing time of the office was seven o'clock, although the doors often did not actually get shut until after eight. Brian considered simply ignoring whoever it was, but then he remembered that, at some point tonight, he would need to leave, and this was a rough enough neighborhood without having a pissed-off criminal waiting for him outside.

 Through the bars on the office door, he saw a gangly man with a ski cap and extremely thick glasses staring down at the sidewalk. Despite the unthreatening appearance of his visitor, Brian was not foolish enough to open the door, so he had to call through it, "Sorry, we're closed. You'll have to come back tomorrow."

 For a brief moment, the man looked up and met Brian's eye, then the visitor returned his gaze to his shoes before giving a slight nod to the sidewalk and walking off down the street. Brian was surprised by this reaction. He had expected anger or at least some form of bargaining, not a desolate shrug. Regardless, he was off the hook and headed back to his reading.

As he walked back to his desk, Brian could not help but think of that one second when the man looked at him. His face had been the perfect picture of fear. Not the usual fear he sometimes saw in people who had done something wrong and were worried about their future; this was immediate terror, as if he were currently in a crisis merely by being at the office. He checked his watch: he had at least another half hour before Anna would be there to start his car. It couldn't hurt to listen to the guy. Brian opened the door and called out, "Hey, on second thought I've got a few minutes if you want to come in and at least warm up?"

The gangly man turned, nodded again at the ground, and trotted a few long strides back to the office, mumbling, "Thank you."

Brian sat his visitor down at one of the intake desks and said, "My name is Brian Cox."

Staring at the desktop, the visitor muttered, "Charley."

He immediately thought his reconsideration had been a mistake. "Ok, can I get you a bad cup of coffee, Charley?"

A nod.

"Cream and sugar?"

A slight shake of the head. Pouring the coffee, Brian pondered the young man. He had removed the ski cap, showing a mess of greasy brown hair, but he still had not looked up as he wrung the hat in his hands. While tall and broad, the man was thin but not emaciated. Brian figured he was probably a regular drug user but not yet a hardcore addict. Walking back to the desk, he bet with himself that he was going to hear about a crack cocaine possession charge.

"So, Charley, what can I help you with tonight?"

There was a painfully long pause before he said in barely more than whisper, "Last night. A woman was killed."

Brian leaned back in his chair. Unconsciously his mind did the math of what the Legal Aid tariff would pay for handling a murder charge. Even if there was a guilty plea, it could be thousands of dollars. Dollars he desperately needed. Technically the file would have to be assigned by the Legal Aid director, but as a matter of practice, if a lawyer who took in the file wanted the case, he would get it. The idea of trying a murder case made him extremely nervous, but he took refuge in the knowledge that, because he had never handled anything nearly as serious as a murder case before, a volunteer mentor would be assigned to the file to help him. Still, ultimate responsibility for the matter, and the government-paid fees, would belong solely to him.

He tried to sound calm and sure as he replied, "Ok, Charley, I can help you with that. First, though, we need to do some paperwork."

A nod.

He pulled out the standard intake form. "Full name?"

"Charley Ewanuschuk."

"Phone number?"

Shake of the head. Brian wrote down "None".

"Address?"

A hesitation followed by a shake of the head. He merely wrote down "Calgary".

"Age?"

"Twenty-five."

"In order for us to help you for free, we need to ensure that you do not have the means to pay for your own defence. Do you work, Charley?"

A nod.

"Where?"

"Day labour."

"Ok, how much money do you make?"

A shrug.

"What assets do you have?"

"Sixty-four dollars."

"Any other significant assets? A car or a truck?"

Shake of the head.

"Do you have any family or friends who would be able help you out with legal bills?"

Shake of the head.

"Have you ever received social assistance?"

Charley hesitated, apparently unsure of the question, so Brian clarified, "Have you ever been on welfare or received unemployment insurance or gotten disability payments?"

Shake of the head.

"Have you ever been arrested?"

Shake of the head.

"You sure? Not for anything?"

Another shake of the head. Surprised, Brian crossed out the last two pages of the form that dealt with prior charges.

"Alright, that's enough of that." He set the form aside and pulled out a pad of notepaper. "Tell me what happened last night."

Without looking up, Charley asked quietly, "What do you want to know?"

"Just tell me what happened from the beginning, and then I'll ask you questions afterwards."

Brian's new client whispered to the desk, "I was sleeping in the basement of a house. The house isn't finished yet; it's abandoned. I woke up when I heard a crash. I looked outside, through a hole in the wall, and saw that a car had gotten stuck in the alley. A man got out and then a woman. She tried to run away but her hands were cuffed behind her and the man caught her and threw her on the ground. I couldn't see them then but I think he hurt her. A light came on across the alley, in a window in a house. Then the man, he ran off, leaving his car stuck in the snow."

Brian waited, assuming that this was only a pause in the story. When he realized that nothing more was coming, he inwardly cringed. It was obviously a memorized lie. A poorly conceived lie at that. He would never understand why clients felt the need to lie to their lawyer, but often they did and the best thing to do was to wait silently. They would eventually start talking again to fill the silence, and their rambling would cause them to unravel the lie on their own.

The two young men sat across the desk, Brian slowly sipping his coffee while Charley stared at the mangled toque in his hands. The only sound was the annoying buzzing of the lights. After a long minute, he watched as Charley cautiously reached out a thin hand and pulled his coffee cup to him. Without looking up, he drank the cup of bitter coffee in two long swallows. At this point, Brian assumed that the story would continue, but instead his new client merely resumed staring at his lap.

Finally, Brian gave in, asking, "Ok, what happened next?"

"I stayed inside the basement for a while because I was scared, but then I went outside to where the woman was in the snow. I knelt there for a while, I guess. She was hurt, bleeding badly. I didn't know what to do."

"That's understandable. I mean how often do you find a body in your backyard?"

Charley lifted his head slightly and looked at Brian. The thick glasses made his eyes look far too large and bulged. He appeared to have noted the twinge of sarcasm and was pondering him, perhaps trying to determine if Brian knew he was lying. Charley began to stand, saying, "I think I should go—"

Brian interrupted, "No, no, I'm sorry. It's been a long day. Please sit and tell me what happened next."

Charley obediently sat back down, returned his gaze to his lap, and continued, "I couldn't leave the woman to be buried in the snow. I went across the alley. I, uh, well, I don't like talking to strangers, but I went over there and knocked on the door of the house where the light had come on. A man came and I told him to call 911."

"Did you wait for the police to arrive?"

A shake of the head.

"Ok, well then the police don't even know you were there. The neighbour saw you but he would not have your name."

A more aggressive head shake as he said, "No, they were showing my picture to guys at the corner, the corner where we wait for work, looking for me. That's why I came here."

"How did they know you were there?"

"The library."

"The library?"

"I went back to the basement but the sirens came and I ran before I could get my things. My library books were in there. You need to get your picture taken to put on the card if you want to get books without a driver's license."

He was a little surprised at Charley's intelligent deduction, but he supposed if you only got your picture taken once in a blue moon, you would probably remember the normally mundane event. He said, "Fine, well, you did nothing wrong. Maybe the police just want to talk to you as a witness."

A shake of the head. "They won't believe me."

"Why not? They would have found the car stuck in the snow. Whoever it's registered to will be their suspect. At least you can claim a reason for being there; the driver of the car won't have that."

"No, they took it."

"Who took it? The police?"

"No, two men."

"Who?"

"Two men came right after I told the neighbour to call the police. I hid. They had a truck. They pulled the car out of the ditch and one of them drove it away."

Brian looked at Charley. It was obviously a fabricated story but something seemed off. If he were lying, he would not have added this especially unbelievable part about the car getting towed. He could have said that the killer got his car out and drove off on his own. Still, it was a bizarre tale and, true or not, Charley needed help.

CHAPTER 4

Randall Jenkins was staring at a sketch of a young woman. She was attractive, with long, black hair, but her almond-shaped eyes stared lifelessly, straight ahead. It was a reconstructed picture of their victim, without the split lip, cut cheek, or swollen eye. They had run her fingerprints but got nothing and no one had reported her missing. He hated using the media to find victims as it was a horrible way for a family to be informed, but they had no other option in this case because a murderer was running free. He handed the picture back to Wilson and said, "Ok, it looks good. Get it to the TV stations, but tell them to downplay why we are looking for her."

"I'll do my best. What about our buddy Chuck?"

He was even more wary of using the media to try to find suspects, so he answered, "No, let's spend one more day beating the bushes for him. Get copies of his picture to the bus depot and airport though."

"The old guy across the alley fingered him as the guy at his door. He's gotta be our killer. Why don't we just drop the net on him tonight?"

"Experience. I doubt a guy who lives in an abandoned construction site far away from the normal places the homeless hang out will be known by anyone willing to call us. And even if someone does know him and calls us, I doubt they'll be much help in finding him." He was tired but he knew that part of his job was teaching the younger detectives, so he explained further, "If you put out a suspect's picture, more often than not, one of their buddies will see it and warn the suspect rather than call us. It's much easier to find someone who is going through their usual routine than trying to find someone who is fleeing for the hills or laying low."

Wilson, still full of energy despite being at work for the last fifteen hours, popped out of his chair, saying, "Makes sense."

Jenkins checked the clock. Nine-thirty, only half an hour to the first newscast. For some reason they had ordered in burritos for dinner, and his stomach was now roiling. He wanted to head home and rest, but he knew that if their picture of the girl was going to lead anywhere, it would likely happen quickly after it hit the airwaves. He took another antacid tablet and through his chewing said, "Alright, I'll do some paper work and wait to see if we get any calls."

Wilson was halfway out of the office when he turned back and said, "Oh, and I'll make sure the patrol cops get a copy of Charley's picture, starting with the night shift. Maybe one of the cruisers will be able to pick him up."

"Oh, yeah, good idea," Jenkins answered, feeling foolish for forgetting something so basic. The older he got, the more he noticed he was missing the simple things. It was frustrating that just when he had learned most of what there was to know about this job, he began forgetting what he had learned. Another good reason to make sure the young guys were well trained before he retired.

*

One of Hugh's assistants placed a plate with a porterhouse steak and a baked potato on his desk. "Thanks Amber, you can head home if you want."

Despite him making her stay late, the stunning woman still managed to flash Hugh her pretty smile and say, "Thanks Mr. Young, have a good night."

His assistant sashayed out of the office. He delayed eating his dinner for a pleasant minute to watch the tight black skirt walk away. It had been a long day, a long day at the end of a string of long days. After the painful meeting with the lawyer about his jackass of a son, he had spent the rest of the day negotiating terms for the impending takeover of his company. For twelve years, he had been working tirelessly on growing Young Exploration. Starting from an exploration company with only some cheap oil and gas rights to moose pasture in northern Saskatchewan, it had become a fifteen-thousand-barrel-a-day operation with fifty employees. Two weeks ago, he had received a signed a letter of intent from a Korean conglomerate in which they offered to buy the company. The purchase price was subject to negotiation, but he was confident it would be close to two hundred million. Hugh had founded and sold four other companies over his professional life, but this sale would be the crowning achievement of his illustrious career. Plus, he had lived lavishly and made some overly aggressive investment choices that had not panned out, so he was eager to get his portion of the purchase price. However, the takeover was far from complete, and the never-ending list of details involved in such a complex deal required all of his time and energy.

As usual on weeknights, he had dinner brought in from Caesar's Steakhouse and ate alone at his desk as he watched the evening news on the TV in his office. The first story was about an apartment building fire followed by a report about an increase to parking prices. Then the sketch of a young woman popped up on the screen with the words Police Search underneath it, and Hugh stopped eating mid-chew. Thoughts of Jason's problem had been in the back of his mind all day, but he had been too busy to focus on anything but the takeover and there was nothing to do since the lawyer had said they should do nothing but wait. It appeared that the wait was going to be much shorter than they anticipated.

The pretty, blonde anchor used her best serious tone as she reported, "The Calgary Police are looking for information anyone may have regarding this woman. She is in her early twenties, five feet tall, one hundred and ten pounds."

That was it. No information as to why the police were looking for her. But Hugh knew. They had found the body and were now trying to figure out who she was. He turned off the TV as the sports reporter began talking about hockey, and picked up his phone.

Jacob Poetker answered on the third ring, "Hello?"

"They found her."

A brief pause before the lawyer asked, "How do you know?"

"It was on the fucking news. They had a sketch of some young broad and said the cops were looking for information on her. I highly doubt two hot bitches got killed last night."

Another annoying pause before he responded, "Ok, well, it's not all bad news. If someone had reported her missing, they would not need to put her picture on the news. Maybe nobody will recognize her—"

"Enough of your fucking maybes. I think it's time for Jason to get his useless ass on a plane to some far-off country."

"That might not be a bad idea for Jason, but I doubt you'll be as willing to do the same thing."

"Why the hell would I need to run? I haven't fucking killed anyone."

"I know that, but if the cops figure out Jason is involved but has fled the country, they won't simply give up. They'll keep investigating to try and get anyone who helped him. That will lead to you."

Hugh rubbed his face with his hand. He had some money stashed away in offshore accounts—not as much as he should have and not nearly enough to maintain him in the lifestyle he deserved. Then he saw the simple four-page document that dominated his desk, the letter of intent from the Koreans for the takeover. He could not flee everything he had built in Calgary to live a life of anonymity because of his son's stupidity. He said, "Ok, she's dead, Jason must have killed her, I helped Jason get away—I get the picture. What now? You're saying we're fucked?"

"Not necessarily. The cops finding the body so quickly is not good. Not only does it mean they have a better chance of finding someone who remembers her being with Jason, but it could mean that they have some sort of witness that led them to the abandoned house in the first place. Still, I don't think it's time to give up. Even if they do link her to Jason, if he's smart enough to keep his mouth shut, they don't have much of a case against him."

"So your legal advice is that we should keep on doing nothing?"

"Yes, I think that—"

Without another word, Hugh hung up the phone. His mind was racing and he was feeling twinges of panic, but he managed to keep his thoughts under control. He had spent his life conducting successful deals in the cutthroat oil and gas industry where survival often required quick, creative thinking under duress. Long ago he had learned that you wanted to be the aggressor in chaotic situations, to be the one acting rather than reacting. It was clear to him that it would be a mistake to assume the police were too stupid or lazy to figure this simple case out. They would easily make the connection to Jason, and with his troubled past, he would look like a good suspect. Especially if he was the only suspect.

*

The lawyer had gone to refill their coffee cups, giving Charley a chance to look around the Legal Aid office. The furniture appeared well used and the space was crowded, but everything seemed neatly organized and professional, at least out front. Peering into the back, he could see movie posters on walls, bobble head dolls on messy desks, and a number of bulletins for a charity fundraiser. Charley figured it was a place staffed by younger people. For an instant he thought wistfully that it might be a fun place to work.

He knew he would never actually be able to work in such a place, but Charley was pleasantly shocked with himself regardless. He had been able to talk with the lawyer for longer than he had spoken with anyone in many years, and he had actually been able to make sense. He had expected the lawyer would laugh at him or get mad at him, but he had only listened and asked questions. Charley understood that he was not brilliant, yet he was smart enough to know that his story was hard to believe. Regardless, Brian had not called him a liar.

The lawyer returned, setting the coffee down on the desk. Charley would have actually preferred his with cream, but he had not wanted to impose any further. He wrapped his hands around the hot mug and tried to force himself to look at the man who was helping him, but could only manage a quick glance before staring back down.

"Alright Charley, I have to get going soon, so we should discuss your options. As I understand it, you have done nothing wrong, except maybe trespassing at night by squatting in the construction site, but I doubt the police would seriously pursue that. However, as I think you appreciate, what happened last night is pretty strange."

The lawyer paused and Charley figured he was waiting for

him to say something. He was going to only nod, but given Brian's pleasantness, he felt a confidence he was unaccustomed to and managed to say, "I know."

"Ok, to be frank, I think the police will have a hard time believing you if they don't find any other suspects. That being said, one of your options is to go to the police and tell them what you saw. The benefit of coming in on your own is that you look less guilty than if they find you and haul you in. However, the risk is that they will not believe you and you could easily end up charged with the murder. I'm not sure if a jury would find you guilty or not based on what you've told me, but it is quite possible. Does that make sense?"

"Yes."

"Alright, the only other option I can think of is to do nothing but wait and see if the police are able to find the killer. The risk with this option is that if the cops find you on their own, then we are deep in the mess all the same but without the benefit of you having gone to them first. Do you understand that option?"

Charley's eyes actually lifted up when Brian referred to them being in the mess together. He had been alone for so long he could not recall the last time someone had used the word "we" when referring to him. He was horribly afraid, but he did feel better not having to face this nightmare on his own, especially since he had been enduring nightmares on his own for as long as he could remember. He answered, "Yes."

"If you want to go to the police, I can help arrange things with them and I will go with you to be interviewed, but I think you had better be prepared to be arrested at that time."

Charley surprised himself by firmly saying, "I can't go to jail."

"I understand. I really do, Charley. If you don't want to go to the police, I can't help you evade them, but if you were ever thinking of leaving the city for a short vacation, this might be the time to do that."

The thought of leaving the city had crossed his mind, but the idea was too daunting. He had nowhere familiar to go, so it would mean learning a new place. He had arrived in Calgary seven years ago, and after being roughly mugged the second night he was in town, he immediately found himself penniless in a massive city full of strangers. His upbringing left him with no sense of how to make money, how to get food, or how to find a place to sleep, and his crippling mistrust of everyone made it nearly impossible for him to ask for help. By fearfully wandering about, he found a largely deserted park with some thick trees where he could hide, having to venture out only to hunt through garbage for food. However, when winter came he was forced to use the shelters, where his inability to befriend anyone made him an easy target for thieves or other attackers. Finally, one of the shelter administrators, perhaps worried Charley would be killed, told him about the day labourer corner so at least he could earn some money.

With that income, he had been able to rent a room at a hostel on really cold nights and get proper clothes that allowed him to sleep in the park on not-so-cold nights. Over the years, through much painful trial and error, he had learned, and that education had allowed him to have a life that, while far from enjoyable, had become tolerable. Going through that horrific learning process again in a new city was not an option.

He muttered, "I've got nowhere to go."

"Well, then I think we should prepare ourselves for you being picked up." Brian pulled an envelope out of a drawer and wrote "Confidential Legal Communications" on the back.

Brian then slid the envelope across the desk and said, "What I want you to do, tonight if possible, is write out what you saw last night. Then put it in this envelope, seal it, sign your name over the flap, and then mail it to me. If the police do start asking questions we can show them that you did not come up with this story because you were worried about being charged. It might not do much good, but every bit helps. Can you do that?"

Embarrassed, he shook his head as he cautiously picked up the envelope.

Brian opened a desk drawer and began fumbling as he said,

"Well if you can't write it out, I can maybe lend you a tape recorder and—"

Understanding the misunderstanding, Charley answered, "I can write. I just don't have a pen or paper."

"Of course, sorry."

Brian slid a few sheets of paper and a pen across the desk along with his business card. With a serious tone he said, "If the police do bring you in, then don't tell them anything. Don't say a word. Not a word. Give them my card and I'll come right away. You understand?"

Charley nodded.

Brian let out a quick laugh that startled him into looking up as the lawyer said with a grin, "You know, Charley, I've given that piece of advice to many, many clients, but I think you will be the first one to actually follow it."

*

"We got one."

As Wilson walked in, Jenkins was numbly filling out expense reports while he waited to hear if the news report on their victim would get any response. He eagerly sat up and asked, "Who is it?"

"Carrie Rasmus. Says she thinks the girl is her roommate."

He pointed to his phone. "Put her on."

Wilson pressed a few buttons and then spoke into the speakerphone, "Hello, Carrie?"

A nervous voice came from the phone, "Yes, I'm here."

"Hi, Carrie. I'm Detective Jenkins and I'm here with my partner Detective Wilson. I understand you may have recognized the picture on the news tonight?"

"Um, well, no. I didn't see it, but my friend did and she thought it was my roommate, Natalie."

"Is your roommate missing?"

"She hasn't been home for a couple of nights now. I've

texted her but she hasn't gotten back to me."

"Is that unusual? For you not to hear from her for a few days."

"She might, you know, not come home one night and we aren't like close friends or anything so she might not call to tell me, but normally she texts me back. Plus, all her makeup and stuff is still in the bathroom."

"Can you describe her?"

"Why? I mean, what has happened?"

"Well, Carrie, unfortunately the girl from the picture was found dead early this morning."

"Dead? How? I mean, was she murdered?"

"Carrie, perhaps you can give us a description of your roommate first?"

"Um, well, she's very short and petite. Long, straight black hair and dark brown eyes. She's pretty with sort of mocha skin. Does that help?"

The description matched. "Yes, it does. Does she have any piercings or tattoos?

"No tattoos. Not sure about piercings. I mean, I know her ears are pierced because she always wears these silver hoop earrings, but I don't know if she has anything else pierced."

Jenkins looked at Wilson, silently asking if the body had been found with silver earrings. Wilson nodded. The general description matched, the earrings were right, and these days, a girl with no tattoos or body piercings was a rarity. He was certain the absent roommate was their victim.

"Ok, Carrie, I'm very sorry but I do think that your roommate is the woman who has been killed."

With far too much experience with these types of conversations, he knew the best thing to do was to wait silently and let the person come to grips with the tragic news on her own. After a few moments, Carrie's tearful voice came back, "Was she killed? I mean murdered? Who would do that to her?"

"I was hoping that you might be able to help us figure that out. Can you answer some questions about your roommate?"

She sniffled but answered, "Sure, of course."

"Thanks, Carrie. I know this is not easy. What is her full name?"

"Natalie Peterson. I don't know her middle name."

"When was the last time you saw Natalie?"

"Um, I saw her Thursday at about four in the afternoon. She was heading to work."

"Ok, did she say anything to you at that time that may have been odd?"

"No, I don't think so. Like I said, we weren't really close but she was, you know, easygoing and nice. She said there was some leftover pasta in the fridge if I wanted it and then she was gone."

"Where did she work?"

"At that sports bar Shanks, downtown. To be clear, she didn't actually say that she was going there, but they have to wear these skanky tank tops and that's what she had on, so I assumed she was going for the evening shift."

"And that was the last you heard from her?"

"Yeah, but when I got up to go to class on Friday morning—I'm taking nursing at Mount Royal—her keys were on the counter and her bedroom door was closed. She normally leaves it open unless she's in there, so I thought she was still sleeping. She would often be at work until at least two in the morning and would then sleep most of the next day." There was a pause and then Carrie added, more quietly, as if speaking to herself, "I used to joke that was what made her such a good roommate."

Jenkins asked, "What time did you get home on Friday?"

"Um, I didn't. I went to my boyfriend's after school. I didn't come home until around noon on Saturday. Her bedroom door was open then and I don't think she's been home since."

Jenkins quickly checked his notes. The medical examiner

put the time of death as late Sunday night. Not only did they have a name for the victim, they now had a time window from Friday morning until Sunday night. Jenkins asked, "Are you aware of anyone who may have had a problem with Natalie? An angry ex-boyfriend? Someone who had threatened her? Anything like that?"

"No, nothing like that, at least not that I knew about. I mean she had only been living with me for a few months after I met her through a friend of a friend. We did talk about a bit about boys and things, so I think she would have told me if something nasty like that was going on."

"Ok, any drug abuse or money problems?"

"No, nothing like that. At least I don't think so. I mean, she was broke like the rest of us. I know that she was upset last week because she had to put a new part in her car and had to use the money she was saving for Christmas presents to pay for it, but it wasn't like she owed money to a gangster or anything, just to Visa."

"What about drugs?"

"No. She'd smoke pot but wasn't like a pothead. She'd only smoke at parties, you know, when other people brought it. Nothing harder than that."

"Thanks, all of that helps us out. Is there anyone else you know of that we can contact who may also be helpful? Any family members or close friends she may have been in touch with?"

"Um, not that I know. She talked to her mom a couple of times a week on the phone, but she lives in Manitoba. I think she has a sister who is a bit messed up that she hears from once in a while. Her dad's not around. Sorry, I don't know her friends very well, but I know she hung out with a couple of other waitress from the bar."

"Alight, Carrie, thanks very much for calling. You have been a big help and I'm very sorry for having to deliver this awful news. Can I ask one more favour?"

"Sure, if it will help catch whoever did this."

"Can you come in tomorrow and identify the body?"

A whimpering gasp was followed by her saying weakly, "I suppose, yes I could do that if someone has to."

"Thank you very much, it is appreciated. My partner here will give you the details of where you need to go and who you need to see."

Wilson picked up the receiver as Jenkins slowly lifted his heavy frame out of his chair. It was coming up on midnight, but he knew the best chance of finding anyone who knew the victim at the bar where she waitressed was to go there at the time she usually worked. He considered calling home to let his wife know he was going to be late, but she was asleep by now, knowing from years of experience that it was foolish to wait up for a detective working a homicide case. Wearily he pulled his coat off the hook and took his sidearm out from the desk drawer.

CHAPTER 5

The blank paper stared up at Charley. Every time he tried to start, the pen froze as he realized how hard to believe the story was. He picked up his coffee but only took a small sip, he needed to make it last for as long as possible. With nowhere to sleep and being afraid to go to the shelters—and without even a blanket or socks—he had been forced to resort to what he thought of as "Coffee Shop Surfing" to get through the bitterly cold night. Basically, by buying a cup of coffee at an all-night café he could buy himself an hour or two of warmth. When the staff started giving him dirty looks, he would move on to another coffee shop and then another. This was painfully boring and did not allow him to sleep, but the main reason Charley hated it was because it required being amongst people far too much. Tonight, however, the horrible weather ensured that most places were largely empty, and the deserted coffee shops gave him a place to work on his letter to Brian.

Finally, to make the task easier, he decided to write out the events as a numbered list rather than trying to create a narration, focussing on one point at a time rather than contemplating the entire horrific scene. It had been years since Charley had written anything, so his penmanship looked awkward and childlike, which was embarrassing but he figured it could not be helped. He became so engrossed in his task that he did not notice the approaching woman until she was right next to him saying, "Excuse me, we are tossing out some of the older donuts—"

Charley jumped in his chair, banging his knees into the table. The middle-aged cashier, holding out a plate of donuts, was startled but she smiled at him. However, Charley knew a smile did not mean she was friendly. He tried to speak but his tongue would not work, and he merely stammered. The woman looked confused for a moment and then set the plate down on his table and said, "Well, if you want them, go ahead. No charge."

She paused for a second to see if he would at least say thank you, but Charley, his face hot with embarrassment, could only stare at his lap. As soon as the woman turned to leave, he gathered up the paper and darted from the coffee shop, silently cursing how pathetic he was.

The air outside was so cold that it struck him like a physical blow as he stepped from the warmth. It was hard to breath and his face instantly began to ache in the freezing wind. After just a few steps, his feet, protected only by the old sneakers, were frozen. Before he had gone a block, he knew he needed to find heated shelter or he would not survive the night.

He knew there was an office building nearby with an underground parking lot that he had snuck into before when he was desperate. The garage was not well heated, so it would be cold but at least he would not freeze to death. As he was about to turn down an alley, a police car drove by and Charley had to fight off the urge to sprint away.

When the cruiser passed without incident and he was able to breathe again, he was struck by an overwhelming despair. His home, as sad as it was, had been taken away. He could no longer work for fear of being arrested. And he was about to spend the night huddled in a freezing parking garage, waiting fearfully until some security guard threw him out. All because he was too damn cowardly to sit in a coffee shop after a woman politely offered him free pastry.

Even if he made it through this night, then what? Wander the streets until the cops found him and threw him jail? He had sixty-four dollars in his pocket and the liquor store on Fifth Avenue was open late. Maybe it was time. Maybe, with this last heaping of unfair misfortune upon him, it had gotten too hard. He could buy a bottle of whatever he wanted, find a nice spot in the park by the frozen river to sit and drink himself unconscious. He would simply fall asleep under the stars and that would be that. A nice peaceful end in fresh fallen snow. It was that thought which brought the image of the dead woman to his mind and reminded him of the half-written letter in his coat pocket. He had been struggling to describe finding her when he had fled the coffee shop.

The young lawyer had been willing to help him. Charley had expected him to say that he was a liar or was retarded or was hopeless and kick him out of the office. Instead, they had sat and talked, talked like normal people over cups of coffee. At the end he had even said they were in this together and joked with him. The man had offered to help and hadn't asked Charley for anything but that he write the letter.

Buoyed by the memory of his normal encounter, Charley remembered he was not some animal struggling thoughtlessly through life; he was a human. Animals did not have meetings with lawyers and humans did not go off into the woods to die. He forced himself to dismiss the embarrassment in the coffee shop as a minor mistake, something to be forgotten. He would go to another coffee shop and finish the letter. No, he decided he was hungry. He would go to the pizza-by-the-slice place on Eighth Avenue, order a meal, sit at a table and eat a meal like a person while he worked on the letter. Stamping some feeling back into his feet, Charley moved on.

*

Drinking a glass of red wine while leaning against the counter in their small kitchen had become a pre-bedtime habit of Brian and his girlfriend, Anna. They had been living together for six months now and had discovered that, with her busy studying while waitressing part-time and Brian needing every spare minute to drum up clients—not to mention the time he needed to actually practice law—often the only opportunity when they could talk was right before bed. The glasses of cheap wine had been added to the conversation as a pleasant sleep aid.

Their apartment was cramped, with only a nook for a kitchen, a tiny living room, and a narrow bedroom. Brian used to have a studio-style lofted condo downtown, but he could not afford the mortgage when he got laid off, so had been forced to sell into the down market and revert to renting the simple apartment. When Anna moved in, their combined possessions overwhelmed the limited space. Over time, however, they had managed to whittle down the clutter substantially as their comfort with one another grew and they became more and more willing to let go of the duplicate items they each needed as individuals but not as part of a couple. The resulting home was far from luxurious, but by carefully combining the best of the two sets of possessions, they had made the basic apartment remarkably comfortable.

Anna, with her blonde hair pulled back in a ponytail, still

wearing the white top and black pants of her waitress uniform, was telling him a funny story about a very rude man at the restaurant who had sent his steak back three times. She poured a little more wine into their glasses and continued, "The guy's date—apparently realizing how obnoxious he was after he complained about the freshness of the oysters, berated me about the wine being at the wrong temperature, and sent his steak back twice—she reached into her purse, gave me a hundred dollars in cash and said, 'Sorry for the way he's acting. This should cover my meal; the rest is for you.'"

Brian asked, "What did her date do?"

"He could only stare stunned as the woman got up, slipped on her jacket, and politely shook his hand. She said something like, 'Goodbye, I'm sorry to leave like this but life is simply too short to spend time with someone who is that rude,' and then she walked out." Anna laughed a bit before continuing, "I mean, the guy had been a real piece of work. He was bragging his ass off and trying super hard to be impressive, letting her know repeatedly he could afford to buy her whatever she wanted and then belittling me over everything, but you still had to feel a little sorry for him. Anyway, I got a big tip out of it and she left her chicken, so I put it in the fridge for your breakfast."

He snorted out a tight laugh, saying, "Good deal."

Anna apparently noticed that his response to her story was more stilted than she had expected and asked, "What's wrong?"

"Sorry, just a long day, plus I had a weird intake at Legal Aid."

"Aren't all of those weird?"

"Yeah, but this one was a different kind of weird. It was after the office was closed and this young, gangly, homeless guy with ridiculously thick glasses knocked on the door. I told him we were closed, expecting the usual swear-laden protest, but he just slinked off down the street. I wasn't doing anything but waiting for you, so I called him back."

"You have to be more careful. I don't like you dealing with strange street people all by yourself at night."

Anna had never talked of wanting children, but she was nearing thirty and her mothering instincts seeped out from time to time, normally directed at him. For not the first time, he considered getting her a cat. Brian let a small, conciliatory smirk onto his lips as he explained, "I know, but this guy seemed more sad or shy than dangerous. Anyway, we sat down and he wouldn't even look at me; he stared at his lap the whole time. I really had to prompt him to tell me why he was there."

"What did he do?"

Brian gave her a look over his wine glass. She pantomimed zipping her lips. She knew the rule. He wasn't supposed to tell her about clients, but he disliked keeping such a big part of his life from her, so he greatly relaxed the confidentiality requirements with her.

"He said he was squatting in the basement of an abandoned house up on the ridge when someone crashed a car in the backyard. A man got out to check the car and then a woman fled from the car. The driver caught her and apparently killed her with his bare hands. All while my guy watched from a hole in the basement wall."

"Sounds like his story needs a bit of work."

"It gets worse. The killer flees on foot so my guy goes out and tells a neighbor to call 911, but before the cops get there two men in a pickup truck show up and pull the killer's car out of the ditch and then drive it away."

"Convenient. I'm guessing that he didn't stick around to talk to the police either?"

"Nope."

"So, what actually happened was that your Legal Aid guy killed this girl and made up this crazy story to cover his tracks?"

"Probably, but it doesn't really make sense unless there is a piece he's not telling me about, which is very possible. The murder was in the middle of the night, at an abandoned house with a heavy snow falling. He could have packed up whatever he had in the house and left. Hell, it might have taken months for them to find the body and they'd have no link to him. If he killed her, why go and get someone to call 911 and then flee?"

Anna answered quickly, "Remorse? Stupidity? A combination of both."

"I thought of that, but remorseful people normally confess to their lawyer rather than tell them made-up stories. And he didn't really strike me as a dummy. He was really strange, practically mute, but when he did talk he seemed smart enough. He had figured out that the reason the cops knew he was there was because he left his library books in the basement." Brian sipped some wine before continuing, "Plus, he's an ugly homeless guy without a car. How did he get a young woman to come back to this construction site with him?"

"Who knows? Maybe he'd been saving up to buy himself some fun for his birthday. It sounds to me like you've got yourself a murderer for a client."

"Maybe, maybe not."

Anna gave him a smirk of her own, "You believe this guy?"

He returned her smile with a shrug.

She drained her wine and walked past him, slapping him gently on the ass. "You're getting soft in your old age."

*

Despite his new found confidence, Charley was still thankful to find the pizza place empty. It had taken him weeks of repeat visits to become even slightly comfortable ordering his cheeseburgers at his usual place. When the tired clerk asked what he wanted, he could only point mutely at the greasy pizza in the glass cabinet. The man took out one slice; Charley managed to hold up two fingers so the clerk took out another. When the man asked if there was anything else, he wanted to order a drink but could not make his mouth work, so he shook his head.

Regardless of the not-completely-successful meal ordering, he felt good that he had gotten himself back inside and had managed to get something to eat. While he had not had any food all day except for a cold cheeseburger, he made himself eat ridiculously slowly as he was sure the man at the counter would kick him back outside the moment he was finished.

Pulling the letter back out, Charley carefully smoothed it out on the grimy table. The last line he had written was about how he had left the basement. He was about to describe finding her but the memory stopped him. She had been so small and completely helpless with her coat flung open, exposing her to the harsh cold. He wondered what her life had been like. Did she laugh? Was she nice to people? Did she have family? Did she have friends? Was she alone like him? Was anyone missing her? How had she ended up there?

A sudden pang of guilt stabbed at him. He knew that he should go talk to the police, but the thought of prison was too terrifying to face. He picked the pen back up.

*

Four young men in loosened ties were at one table loudly talking over pint glasses, but the rest of the large sports bar was empty. Wilson and Jenkins opened their overcoats to let the warm air in as it was so cold outside that even the short walk from the car had chilled them. They stepped up to the bar, and the bartender, a tired looking man in his forties, came over. "Sorry guys, already did last call."

Jenkins knew that Wilson loved this part of the job, so he kept his mouth shut and let his partner have his fun. Wilson sighed dramatically as he reached into his jacket and dropped his badge onto the bar. "Sorry, you're gonna have to stay open a bit later than usual tonight."

The bartender muttered a curse under his breath before he leaned on the bar and asked, "Alright, what can I do for you officers?"

Jenkins showed him the sketch of Natalie Peterson. "Do you know this woman?"

Concern crossed the man's face. "Yeah, that's Natalie. She works here. What's happened?"

Experience had taught Jenkins that there was no point in mincing words in these situations, so he said, "She was killed last night."

"You're kidding? Jesus Christ." It took a moment for the man to compose himself, and then he asked the questions Jenkins had learned to expect: "What was it? A car accident?"

"No, we think she was murdered."

"Really? By who? I mean she was a sweet kid, straight off some farm in Manitoba."

Wilson intervened, "Don't know yet. That's why we are out here so late. When did she work last?"

The bartender opened a small fridge and pulled out a beer bottle. He pointed into the fridge, silently asking if they wanted one. Wilson glanced at Jenkins to see if he would accept. Technically they weren't supposed to drink on duty, but it was almost midnight and Jenkins figured it might help him digest the burrito dinner, so he nodded. As he opened the beers, the bartender answered, "She worked Friday night."

Jenkins took a drink of beer and then pulled out his notepad, happy that their time window was shrinking, "Until when?"

"Um, I left around midnight and she was still here. I'd guess she stayed until closing at two."

"Anything unusual happen?"

The bartender took a drink as he thought back before saying, "No, don't think it was very busy. I mean, it was busy but not as busy as most Fridays because it was so goddamn cold."

"Was she supposed to work Saturday?"

He went over to a calendar next to the cash register and checked it before answering as he walked back, "Nope, she had it off."

"How well did you know Natalie?"

"She's worked here about a year and we all sit around shooting the shit, the group of us, when it's slow or after closing, so I knew her fairly well."

Wilson was apparently getting impatient with the preliminaries because he intervened, "Can you think of anyone who might want to hurt her?"

"No, she got along well with everyone as far as I could tell." The bartender took another drink as he thought before continuing, "But she and another girl did scale back their weekend shifts starting a few months ago. It's odd for a waitress to give up weekend shifts and I got the impression from overhearing their giggling and shit that they might have gotten involved in something on the side."

Wilson asked, "Something? Like what?"

"I don't know for sure, they were secretive about it and I didn't ask. But you know how girls are: what fun is having a secret if no one knows you've got a secret? I heard them joking about how annoying it was to have to buy new work clothes when they didn't really wear them for work."

"Call girls?"

"Maybe, but I've been in the bar business for a long time and have known a lot of young waitresses looking for extra cash, and these ones don't seem the hooking type to me. My guess would be stripping."

Jenkins pulled out his notepad and asked, "Do you know where we can find this other waitress?"

CHAPTER 6

Although it would be polite to ring the doorbell, Hugh owned the house and was there because of the stupidity of its resident, so he used his key and marched in. The living room contained only a leather recliner, a huge TV, and a variety of video game equipment. The expensive parquet hardwood floor was littered with empty pop cans and candy wrappers. Annoyingly, the scene looked not all that different than the room in the basement Jason spent a most of his time in as a teenager. Back then Hugh figured it was what kids did; now he thought it was a pathetic way for a grown man to live.

He had bought this house for Jason when he got engaged a couple of years back as he thought his son was finally growing up, even if his fiancé was a nineteen-year-old bimbo who waitressed in a nightclub. Predictably, the engagement had been short lived once the woman learned about Jason's peculiar tastes, and Hugh actually had to write the woman a check to keep her from suing. It was ridiculous for Jason to live alone in a million-dollar mansion, but the real estate market had gone down, there was a significant mortgage in place, and Hugh had never gotten around to putting the house up for sale.

Now, as he walked through the house that Jason lived in for free but could not even be troubled to furnish or clean, he felt his powerful temper rise. It was easy to be mad at Jason: he was lazy, irresponsible, and immoral, but looking back it was obvious how he had become that way. His mother had done everything for him and still gave him everything he wanted even before he asked for it, while praising his every move and excusing away every fault. She had ensured Jason never felt any stress and inflated his ego to the point of absurdity, so it was no wonder that he was incapable of managing in the real world.

It was seven in the morning on Tuesday, so there was no way Jason would be awake. Hugh strode through the massive, gourmet kitchen with its permanent pile of pizza boxes on the floor, past the marble-tiled bathroom littered with laundry, and into the master bedroom. Jason was sprawled out on his bed, snoring softly.

"Jason, wake up," Hugh said as he shook the bed with his

foot.

There was only a murmur in response.

He shook harder and yelled, "Get the fuck up!"

Jason startled. He stumbled out of the bed. His too-long hair was a tangled mess. He wore boxer shorts and a t-shirt with a stain on the chest. Struggling to wake up, he asked, "Dad? What are you doing here?"

"We need to talk. Get some clothes on and meet me in the kitchen in one minute."

Father, dressed in a neatly pressed suit, and son, shoeless in sweat pants and stained t-shirt, sat on stools at the Italian marble kitchen counter, next to a sink full of dirty dishes. Jason looked extra haggard with especially blurry eyes.

"Are you hung over or high?"

"Just hung over. What's wrong dad? Why are you here so early?"

"What's wrong? You killed a fucking girl, remember?"

"I didn't kill her. I'm sure didn't."

Hugh just glared at this feeble protest causing Jason to continue meekly, "And, uh, anyway. We talked to the lawyer. He said there's nothing we can do."

"Shit's changed. They found her body. The cops had her fucking picture on TV last night."

It took a moment and then panic lit up Jason's face as he asked, "What does that mean? What do we do?"

Hugh bristled at the use of the word "we". This was all his son's fault and now, like every problem he had ever created in the past, he was expecting to have it fixed for him. Regardless of this annoyance, the reality was that Hugh was in this mess as deeply as Jason, so this was not the time to cut the idiot loose to flounder on his own.

All night Hugh had been contemplating the situation. The lawyer was right that the police would not give up and Jason had left an easy trail to follow. They needed to muddy that trail as much as possible and hopefully send the police looking in a different direction. Hugh was confident that he could concoct a believable story for the authorities and set things up in a manner that would lead them away. He did, however, have a problem believing his son would be able to maintain his composure long enough to pull off a complicated deception. That's why he had come, to try to fortify Jason and make him understand that he needed to deal with this like a man.

Hugh used his most serious business negotiation tone as he calmly spoke: "Jason, this is a perilous matter, for both of us. We are going to have to work together to get out of this, so I am going to need you to be strong. You will need to focus and make smart, mature decisions under pressure—"

He stopped, noticing that Jason's eyes were already tearing up. After a moment he began sniveling, "I didn't kill her, Dad, I didn't. I mean I acted badly, sure, but I didn't kill her, I'm sure I didn't. I wouldn't do something like that, Dad, you have to believe me..."

As he watched his adult son blubbering through his desperate lies like a young child caught stealing candy, Hugh realized he would need to handle this all on his own.

*

Exhaustion was making Charley's head ache. He had spent most of the night in the back corner of the pizza place working on the letter, but at six in the morning, the guy behind the counter told him he had to go before his boss showed up. After dropping the finished letter in a mailbox, he aimlessly wandered the frozen streets for an hour until the donation center at the shelter opened.

It was unlikely that they would have anything good this time of year, but sometimes you could get lucky and find a decent blanket. The plan was to get a blanket, buy a bottle of malt liquor, huddle up in a secluded park, drink the edge off the cold, and try to get some rest. He knew he should stay away from the shelter as the cops might be there, but it would be hours before any stores would be open where he could buy a blanket. He was exhausted and he needed a blanket before he could go to sleep, so he convinced himself the police would not bother with the shelter this early.

Normally Charley was nervous walking into the donation center but this morning he was too tired to worry about having to deal with a stranger. The room smelled of laundry soap and moth balls with that slight hint of body odour which lingered in the places homeless people frequented. An overly cheerful lady was working behind the counter. "Why hello. You're up early. What can I get you?"

Charley mumbled, "A blanket. Please."

She disappeared in the back for a moment and returned with a thin blanket. "There's only a couple of blankets back there. This one is not very good but it's the best of the bunch. Anything else you need?"

This struck him as an odd question as he had nothing, but he shook his head and muttered, "No, thanks."

He was stepping down the stairs, cursing himself for not also getting socks, when he heard the brief whoop of a siren. He spun to see two huge police officers stepping out of their cruiser. One of them firmly said, "Don't move, sir; we want to talk to you."

Charley was unable to force his mind to work as the two policemen walked towards him. He numbly dropped the thin blanket onto the snow and raised his hands slightly. The nightmare was happening.

Brian's cell phone bounced to life on the kitchen table as he shoveled cereal into his mouth, "Hello."

"Brian Cox?"

"Yes, who's this?"

"Sergeant Reynolds with the Calgary Police Service. Is Charley Ewanuschuk a client of yours?"

A wave of stress crashed through him. They had already arrested Charley. His day was about to get much more complicated.

"Yeah, he's a client of mine through Legal Aid."

"We have him in central booking at remand. He won't say anything but he mumbled 'lawyer' and gave me your card."

Brian grinned slightly. The cops made their living off criminals who were too cocky or too scared or too stupid to merely keep their mouths shut. He suspected that Charley's insistent silence was driving them insane. It was that thought which gave Brian an interesting but risky idea for how he could keep Charley from being held in the general population.

"You know the drill. Any interrogation you had planned is over."

Abandoning the half eaten bowl of cereal, Brian donned his only decent suit and, after willing his car to start, he made it to the police station less than half an hour after the phone call. He was led to a cramped lawyer interview room where Charley was waiting. "Good morning, Charley. You alright?"

Charley did not look up from the metal table, but he did nod his head slightly. Brian took the seat on the other side of the table and pulled a notepad out of his brief case as he asked, "Have you said anything to anyone?"

"They said I had to tell them my name."

"That's all you told them?"

A nod.

"Good. You know you've been charged with trespassing at night for squatting in the basement?"

A nod.

"Ok, they are probably using that charge to keep you in custody until they can decide how to proceed on the murder."

Charley looked up and the oddly bulged gaze from behind the thick glasses actually met Brian's eye for a moment as he said, "I can't go to jail."

The fear in his magnified eyes was palpable and Brian thought the young man was near tears. He had spent some time in the remand center meeting with clients and helping inmates who had been charged with breaking prison rules. The people he had met and the stories he had been told made Brian certain that a person like Charley would be cruelly tortured in jail.

"I understand but it is not possible to keep you out."

Charley looked back down at the table and muttered, "I can't survive trapped with so many people."

Brian figured Charley would survive as murders were actually rare in prison. Then he realized what his client was saying. Murders were rare in jail. Suicides were not.

On the way over, he had contemplated a plan that might keep Charley out of the general population for a couple of days. It was somewhat risky as it would involve misleading the prosecutor, so Brian could get in trouble. Ultimately he had decided it was not worthwhile as Charley would almost certainly end up in the general population eventually. But now, seeing his client's despair, he figured he needed to do everything possible, no matter how ridiculous.

"Look, I will do whatever I can to help but you have to promise me that you won't quit. We have a lot of work to do to prove your innocence and I don't want to put all that time in if you aren't going to stick it out with me. You promise to not bail?"

Charley only nodded.

"Fine, I have an idea that might help. From this moment on you are unable to communicate. You don't speak, you don't nod, you don't write notes, nothing."

Charley looked up with a confused look on his face.

Brian smiled at him. "That's perfect. I'm going to tell the prosecutor that I need a psychological review and that I think you may lack mental capacity. They can't put you in general population if they think you are mentally challenged."

Without looking up Charley defiantly stated, "I'm not a retard."

"I know that, Charley. But if we don't at least try this they'll have you in a group cell with some very unfriendly men before lunch. It might not work; hell, it probably won't work. But I think this is worth a try, don't you?"

A nod.

"Ok, if you are able to play this out and I drag my feet and make things difficult, you may be able to stay out of the general population altogether if they don't come up with enough evidence to charge you with murder." As soon as he said this, Brian wished he could pull the words back as he knew this was a false hope; they would not be letting Charley go any time soon.

Regardless, Brian had no choice but to carry on and explain to Charley what to expect next, knowing he was treading a fine ethical line by advising his client to act out this charade. As far as he knew he was breaking no ethics rules. Still, if this strange man told anyone that Brian had counseled him this way, his reputation as an upstanding lawyer would be roundly sullied among the Crown prosecutors. He would just have to trust that his new client would follow the plan.

CHAPTER 7

"Why are the hallways in apartments always so goddamn hot?" Wilson asked Jenkins as they climbed the stairs to apartment 302.

Through heavy breaths, Jenkins answered, "Makes the overcooked cabbage smell linger longer."

Although it had been a short night's sleep, Jenkins was feeling well rested and eager to work. There were many parts of the job he did not think he would miss, but there would be no replacement for the rush of working a case where the pieces were rapidly coming together. Last night the bartender had told them Shelia Tatum was the waitress who had taken the side job with Natalie, and he was hopeful that she would help pinpoint where the victim had disappeared from.

They reached the door and Wilson wordlessly paused to let Jenkins catch his breath, something that took longer and longer with each passing year. It was highly unlikely that they would encounter any sort of problems as they were simply questioning a waitress, but it was a homicide investigation so it was always smart to be cautious. Not to mention that it was embarrassing for a police officer to talk to a member of the public while huffing and puffing from walking up three flights of stairs.

Wilson knocked on the door. Nothing. He banged on the door. The faint sound of rustling; someone was moving inside. He banged again.

A woman's annoyed voice, "Ok, ok. Who is it?"

"Ms. Tatum. It's the police, we would like to ask you a few questions."

"Um, ok, just a second."

There was the sound of frantic movement inside the apartment. Wilson and Jenkins grinned at each other. They had heard this rapid clean-up being conducted numerous times before as people quickly hide illicit substances before letting them in. Finally, the door was opened a crack, revealing a young woman with blonde hair with wide purple streaks. She asked, "What's going on?"

Wilson flashed his badge. "I'm Stephen Wilson and this is

my partner Randall Jenkins. We are detectives with the Calgary Police. May we come in and ask you a few questions?"

Jenkins had decided he would have Wilson run this interview. They had discussed what information they were looking for during the car ride over, and with Wilson asking the questions, he would be free to gauge the responses. Also, it would be good practice for him. The woman reluctantly opened the door.

The apartment was fairly standard for a young woman working in the service industry. Obviously not a lot of money had been spent, but she had imparted her apparently colorful style. The couch was ugly, faded brown corduroy, but she had laid a bright blue blanket with a bizarre pattern over the back. The coffee table was cheap, but it had a funky piece of red painted driftwood on top of it. A large map of the world done in neon shades covered one beige wall, while a green throw rug hid much of the grimy, thinning grey carpet. The not-so-subtle smell of pot smoke being masked by incense filled the space, and he wondered where she had hidden the bong as he sat down on the worn out couch.

Wilson took a seat on one of the stools by the kitchen counter and said, "Please take a seat. Sorry for barging in so early but we have some important questions to ask you."

The politeness of the words did not match Wilson's stern face or his serious tone and the girl promptly obeyed, sitting on the arm of the couch. They figured that this waitress had nothing to do with the murder, but she had valuable information that they needed, and innocent people lied to the police all the time for reasons that had nothing to do with committing crimes. With a murderer on the loose they did not have time to deal with her fabricating stories so her parents would not find out she was stripping or because she was worried people would think she was a bad friend. Wilson was making her think she was in trouble and asking questions quickly so her only concern would be to prove she had done nothing wrong by telling the truth. He smiled to himself as he thought that it was the same tact he would have taken.

"Do you know Natalie Peterson?"

Shelia answered immediately, "Yes. What's wrong? Has

something happened to Nata—"

Wilson interrupted, "Do you know where she is?"

A shocked shake of the head. "No. Is she missing?"

"When were you last with her?"

"Saturday, well, actually I guess it was early Sunday morning."

"What did the two of you do on Saturday before you separated?"

Jenkins was again impressed by Wilson's questioning technique. The natural impulse would be to focus in on where Natalie was last seen, but it was important to fill in as much of the story as possible, and if you changed the chronology on witnesses they often got confused or missed things. Fill in all the gaps before moving on was a mantra of Jenkins's, and apparently Wilson had learned it.

"Nat stayed overnight here on Friday after work. We slept in until like noon, then went to the mall. We got back here around five. We made fajitas, had some drinks, and listened to music as we got ready to go out."

"Ready to go out where?"

The abrupt shock of the interview apparently faded as realization of what they were discussing came through and tears started to fill her eyes, but Shelia's voice came out hard, "I'll tell you everything I know but, first, tell me what happened to her?"

He guessed this girl had been scratching out an existence on her own for some time and that had made her tougher than she looked. Wilson remained unfazed, ignored her question, and asked, "Where did the two of you go on Saturday night?"

"Look, I'm not going to tell you anything else until you tell me what happened. You have me worried."

"Natalie was murdered Sunday night. Now tell me where the two of you were."

Wilson's first mistake. Predictably, the girl covered her face with her hands and began sobbing. Wilson should have kept her in the dark a little longer, as Jenkins now figured they would not be able to get any information until she was consoled, and even then, her mind could be so overwhelmed with grief and guilt it would muddy her answers.

Surprisingly, however, after a few moments she wiped her eyes and glared at Wilson, her hard voice cutting through her crying, "What do you need to know?"

"Tell us where you were on Saturday night."

"We went to a bachelor party. We were both working as party girls."

Wilson questioned, "Party girls?"

"Yeah, we put on lingerie and high heels and go to bachelor parties or whatever, serve drinks, flirt with the guys, and liven the place up."

"Alright, so where was the party Saturday night?"

"Beckham's Bar downtown, in the backroom."

"What time did the party start?"

"We showed up around nine. The guys were there before that."

"How did you get there?"

"Cab."

"Anything unusual happen at the party?"

She looked up at Wilson with puffy eyes. "Unusual?"

"You know, anyone get too grabby or aggressive?"

"They always get too grabby but this one was no worse than any other party. Actually, it was better than most. The guys were pretty nice, we all drank a lot, and they tipped well."

"Whose party was it?"

"Not really sure. I think the guy organizing it was named David and the bachelor had an old man name like Arthur or Edward or something."

"Do you have a last name or a phone number or anything

that would help us find this David?"

"No, it was all set up through the agency. They just tell us where to go and who to ask for when we get there."

"Were you and Natalie the only girls there?"

"Um, no, there were three of us. This other girl from the company, Ashley, was there too."

"Ashley her real name?"

A shrug. "I doubt it."

"Ok, did you and Natalie leave together?"

Shelia put her face in her hands but maintained enough composure to mumble, "We were always supposed to stick together; that was our deal. I should have stayed with her."

"You did not leave together?"

"No, no I, um, was with a guy for a while and when we came back out everyone was gone."

"Any idea where she went?"

"No, I texted her but she never texted me back. I thought she went home and passed out. I mean, her purse and stuff was gone. I jumped in a cab and came back here." She looked up with her red eyes and asked with a serious tone, "Do you think one of the guys at the party did this?"

*

It took three tries for Brian to get through to Clay Matthews, the senior Crown prosecutor who would be dealing with the Natalie Peterson murder. He had only dealt with Matthews a couple of times on minor matters. He had been difficult to deal with even on those small cases, so Brian was not thrilled that he had been assigned to this file.

It was coming up on nine in the morning, and he knew he had to be quick, as Matthews was likely headed to court. "Hi Clay, this Brian Cox. I represent Charley Ewanuschuk."

"Hi Brian. Who's Charley Ewanuschuk?"

"The man you have in custody for allegedly squatting in a

house, a crime that apparently warrants having a senior prosecutor assigned to it."

"Right, him. What do you want to discuss?"

"I've met with Charley and he is practically mute. I need a psych review before we can talk bail."

"Shit, Cox. I'm really busy. Is he actually crazy or are you jerking me around?

"Clay, the guy barely talks."

"So? Is he nuts or just quiet?"

"That's not for us to decide, now is it?"

There was a minor hesitation, then the prosecutor asked, "How long would you be willing to delay a bail hearing in order to get a review done?"

The rule was that a person under arrest had to be brought before a Justice of the Peace for a bail hearing within twenty four hours of his arrest. If bail was set too high or denied, the accused could appeal that decision to a judge, and that appeal had to be heard as soon as possible. Brian was guessing that the authorities were still getting their ducks in a row on the homicide or they would have charged Charley with the murder right away. As a result, Matthews would likely want as much time as possible before getting this mess into a bail hearing as a justice of the peace may let a vagrant with no record go on a trespassing charge.

Brian answered, "Look we both know there's some extenuating circumstances on this, so let's waive the JP and go right before a judge for bail. If you promise to keep him out of the general population until he is reviewed so he can get the help he needs, we can wait on a bail hearing for a while."

"Fine. I'll try and get him reviewed as soon as possible but if you are screwing around on this I'll make sure you never get another favor out of this office until ten years after you retire, you got me?

"Got it."

Matthews hung up and Brian simply stared at his phone for a

moment, hoping Charley was really good at keeping his mouth shut.

*

The corporate offices of Steamy Nights Incorporated were located in a beige, cookie-cutter house in suburbia. Wilson and Jenkins got the name of the stripper agency from Shelia and a corporate records search had lead them to this suburban address.

"Why are we freezing our asses off way out here?" Wilson asked as they trudged up the driveway. "Our killer's in a holding cell downtown."

Dispatch had called to let them know Charley Ewanuschuk had been brought in by the patrol car Wilson had sent to sit outside the shelter. Wilson was eager to interrogate him, but Jenkins was wary about leaving leads dangling.

"He's not going anywhere. Let's fill in the last time gap we have."

"The guy's probably just waiting for someone to show up so he can confess, but I'll defer to your lengthy experience."

Wilson rang the doorbell twice. There was the sound of a woman scolding a child before the heavy door was opened a crack. A thin woman in her forties with dyed blonde hair and heavy make-up asked coldly, "Can I help you?"

Jenkins held up his badge and asked, "Are you Suzanne Millerson of Steamy Nights Incorporated?"

The woman responded with a firmness that he did not expect from a housewife in suburbia, "I don't run a brothel. If one of the girls decided to give a customer something extra after a party, she did that on her own. And I don't talk to the police without a warrant and my lawyer present."

With that the door was closed. Wilson gave him an annoyed look, silently telling him that he had been right about this being a waste of their time. Jenkins merely shook his head. He had dealt with innumerable uncooperative witnesses in his time and he doubted this woman would actually require a warrant in order to get her to answer questions.

He knocked and called loudly through door, "Ms. Millerson, we are not concerned with prostitution. We are homicide detectives and have some questions about one of your employees who was killed last night."

The door remained closed, so he continued, "If you are unwilling to talk with us perhaps we will visit your neighbors to see if they saw any lingerie-clad teenage girls hanging around your house who may be able to help us. Sorry for bothering you and thank you for your time."

Before he could even take a step back, the door opened and Millerson snarled, "Ok, get in here and ask your goddamn questions."

The house was the standard, pre-packaged, upper-middle-class family dwelling: an open space concept with dark hardwood floors, a large kitchen with marble counter tops, and matching furniture made to looked aged when it was bought new from some mid-price boutique. A boy, about five years old, ran by making engine noises while waving a plastic airplane through the air. He was trailed by a yipping dog and a diaper-clad toddler.

The woman seemed ambivalent to the chaos and pointed to the kitchen table. Jenkins and Wilson chose not to sit, instead standing as their host leaned back against the counter and asked, "Ok, what is this all about?"

"One of your employees, Natalie Peterson, was killed early Sunday morning after working at a party you sent her to."

The woman seemed unfazed by this information, her harsh, overly tight face not even wavering. She did, however, reach for a half-full glass of white wine that was tucked back on the counter and took a long drink. Jenkins noticed Wilson checking his watch. It was just after ten in the morning.

After taking a swallow, she asked, "What happened?"

"That's what we are trying to find out. We know the last time she was seen was at a bachelor party organized through your company by a man named David for Saturday night at Beckham's bar. Does that ring any bells?"

"First, let's get something clear. All my company does is get the girls to the parties and take a management fee from the host. The girls aren't employees. They get paid by the customers directly, so they are more like contractors—"

Wilson stepped forward and intervened, "Ms. Millerson, we are investigating a murder. We don't care about your grab-ass business. Do you remember setting up the party or not?"

She glared at Wilson for a moment but she still answered, "Yes, I remember."

Jenkins asked, "Who booked the girls?"

"That I won't tell you. I have built up a very successful business and I will not have you jackbooted thugs ruining that by harassing my clients."

For a long moment he merely stared at the woman. She was too thin, her face drawn and pinched under a coat of expensive makeup. Her hair looked wiry, as if it had been treated a few too many times. There was a defiant arrogance in her composure that did not quite make it into her eyes. Jenkins had seen this bitter and contemptuous attitude before from women who were once revered for their beauty but now had to face that this reverence faded with age. He figured she still thought she was better than everyone else but was worried that no one else realized it anymore because of the situations an unfair life had put her in. He knew he could patiently stroke her sizable ego to get her to play along, but today his stomach hurt and he could not help but think of the battered woman lying in the snow because this woman collected a fee to send her out to be a party favor. He let the control over his normally manageable temper slip as he stepped forward. "You took advantage of this young girl to earn a few fucking bucks so you could buy another handbag and now she's fucking dead—"

She pointed her wine glass at him like a weapon. "You listen here, no one comes into my home and talks to me that way."

Jenkins took another step forward and put a finger in the skinny, shrunken face. "I will talk to you however I fucking like and if you piss me off one more time I'll drag your drunk ass out of this house in cuffs and call every reporter in town to tell them about the dried-up hooker turned madam we arrested. We understand each other?"

She stepped back and the arrogance faltered a moment, but she managed to respond, "My brother-in-law is a lawyer at a big firm. I think it's time I gave him a call."

On cue, Wilson casually reached into the case on his belt and pulled out his hand cuffs as he said, "You can tell him you are being charged with living off the avails of prostitution, obstruction of justice, and being a bitch."

The woman hesitated in her move towards the phone, and Jenkins decided it was time to play the humanity card, so he placed his hand on her arm and calmly said, "Ms. Millerson, we don't worry with niceties when there's a murderer on the loose. If you want to mess around we have no problem being extremely harsh with you regardless of the consequences, but frankly, I only want to catch this killer and don't want to waste our time. Now, save everyone some pain, including yourself, and give us the name and phone number of your client so we can be on our way."

Stepping out the house, the name and phone number of the party organizer safely in his notebook, Wilson slapped Jenkins on the back, "Nice work, partner."

Opening the car's door, he asked, "You have any buddies working in vice?"

"Sure."

"Get them out here with a search warrant. I'm sure they'll find enough to shut her ass down."

CHAPTER 8

Although he was near sick with fear, Charley could not pass up a meal. After Brian had left the interview room, a policeman had come in and explained that he was supposed to go to booking but the prosecutor wanted to talk to him first. He got the impression this was supposed to scare him but he was content to sit in the room by himself. The policeman gave him a ham sandwich, a bag of chips, and a bottle of water. With nothing else to do but worry about his unknown situation, Charley ate slowly, trying to appreciate the simple joy of eating alone at a table.

He was almost done eating when the door opened. The policeman came in followed by an older man and a younger woman, both dressed in dark grey suits. As the other two took seats across from the table, the policeman took the tray, saying, "Lunch is over."

Instinctively, Charley grabbed the remaining crust of sandwich and crammed it into his mouth. The policeman laughed at this as he walked out, which made Charley painfully embarrassed, but someone who had lived on garbage could not leave any edible scrap uneaten. Plus, his mother had taught him to never waste food.

The man in the grey suit opened a file on the table and appeared to be reading while the woman began writing on a yellow note pad. That was all he could see as he kept his eyes on his lap. Brian had told him that he would be interviewed and that idea caused panic to rise, his control slipping, but then he remembered the instructions. He was not to speak, not even nod. While having normal conversations was not something he had much experience with, he did have a great deal of experience with ignoring tormentors.

The man calmly asked, "So, Mr. Ewanuschuk, do you mind if I call you Charley?"

Charley gave no response.

The man did not seem fazed by being ignored. "I understand you are not much on talking. I have to say it is somewhat refreshing to meet someone who is not addicted to hearing themselves speak, but we've been told your lawyer is having a hard time getting you to cooperate. Is that correct?"

No response.

With no warning the man smacked the table with his hand. The woman jumped in her seat, and unconsciously, Charley pulled away.

"Sorry, had to see if our communication problem was simply auditory in nature. Do you understand why you are here?"

For half a heartbeat, he almost shook his head, but he caught himself and remained frozen.

"Well, it appears you were staying in a house without the owner's permission, which is a problem. But the bigger problem is that you are a suspect in a murder investigation. Do you understand that?"

No response.

"We believe that you kidnapped a young woman, brutalized her, raped her, and killed her."

Charley realized the man was attempting to aggravate him. He had been treated this way so often he had developed numerous techniques for managing with these situations. Mentally he began listing the names of tractors he used to work on when he was a kid.

"We think you are a perverted psychopath who forced yourself on a young girl because you are unable to get a woman to have sex with you by choice."

He did not hear the man. John Deere. Cockshut. Farmall.

"Are you a pervert, Charley?"

Ford. Versatile. McCormick.

"Are you a virgin, Charley?"

Case. Massey Ferguson. International.

"Do you have trouble performing? Are you impotent?"

Allis Chalmer. Oliver. Moline.

The man apparently ran out of taunting questions and said to his partner, "You try."

The woman in the dark suit whispered back, "We have his

lawyer's consent to talk to him alone, right? I mean we did not even identify ourselves as prosecutors."

"Don't worry about that, just do it."

After a sigh the woman began, "Hi, Charley. I'd like to get to know you better. Where did you grow up?"

This peculiarity did cause Charley to look up. The woman was probably in her late twenties, pretty with long red hair and rosy cheeks. She was smiling at him coyly. He recognized this as flirting. He knew that women did not flirt with him. He immediately lowered his eyes.

"You look to be in good shape. Do you work in construction?"

For ten minutes the woman asked him questions like this, only to get unflinching silence in response. Charley did not need any mind games to ignore her. These words were empty prattle to him.

Eventually, the woman gave up, setting her unused pen down on her unused notepad. "Sorry, he's not breaking for me. Maybe he really is mute."

He heard the man's disgusted snort, "Yeah, he's either really fucked up or too smart for us. I'm going with fucked up."

There was the sound of chairs scraping the floor. As they stood, the man told the woman, "Set up the psych review. And you better make sure the cops don't accidentally dump him in general population until we get him checked. And there should be no record of us being here."

Jenkins was tired but he decided his aching stomach would not tolerate any more coffee. His jubilation from the morning had dissipated by the afternoon. They had left the suburban madam with a suspect in custody and a lead on the bachelor party planner, but both fronts had gone nowhere. Somehow the homeless man had lawyered up before even being arrested. After two hours of working the phones, they learned that the party planner was in Las Vegas for a conference until Tuesday night. They had left messages on the party organizer's cell phone and at his hotel but his assistant was not overly confident he would be checking in anytime soon.

Wilson was storming about the station, trying to find the beat cop who had called the homeless man's lawyer without letting them talk to the suspect first. Jenkins knew this rage was pointless and misplaced as he would not have interrogated a suspect with a lawyer anyway. But he let the young detective vent all the same. It was a difficult lesson to learn that finding the person who committed the crime was not even half of the battle; most of the job was finding and organizing the evidence to prove who committed the crime. Like Wilson, Jenkins had been optimistic that Charley Ewanuschuk would confess as homeless people often lacked the aid of a lawyer and often defaulted to simply telling the truth even when it was not in their best interest. However, Jenkins also knew that, no matter how despondent a person was, it was rare anyone would easily give a confession that would put them in jail for life unless they were faced with a mountain of evidence.

With that in mind, Jenkins had turned his attention to the case report. A case report was a standard file prepared by civilian staff and forensic experts for all major crimes. Opening the Natalie Peterson report, he could not help but wonder how many of these sad files he had read over his career. He had spent most of his life dealing with the tragedies of humanity, his early years being spent attending car accidents and suicides before dealing with domestic violence and bar fights before he graduated to rapes and killings. All of this history of pain and suffering had been devoted to paper, but despite this varied mosaic of unpleasant experiences, every time Jenkins opened a case report, he thought of the first one he had read as a homicide detective.

She had been a young single mother, barely out of her teens, sleep deprived and overwhelmed. Her husband was a long-haul trucker, struggling to make ends meet by spending almost all of his time on the road. The police had been called when a neighbour phoned 911 because they had heard a gunshot. Sometime in the middle of the night, the child had been smothered and the mother had climbed into the bathtub, where she tried to kill herself with her husband's shotgun. It is difficult to aim a rifle at one's own head and the mother had failed to produce a fatal shot, managing only to remove a significant portion of her jaw, cheek, and ear.

The case seemed straightforward. The mother had been left all alone with the colicky baby for over a week. They figured she had lost her patience and silenced the infant. Upon realizing what she had done, she decided to end her own life as well. It was supposed to be a simple investigation, a matter of compiling the evidence to prove what they already knew. But Jenkins's partner at the time was a veteran detective with a severe nicotine addiction and enough experience to know that even seemingly straightforward cases needed to be approached as if they knew nothing.

Despite Jenkins's complaints, his partner made sure they interviewed numerous neighbors and properly examined the evidence from the house. On a second search of the house they had found two empty beer cans in the recycling bin. The husband confirmed that his wife did not drink beer and the cans were not his. Before long they had tracked down the wife's greasy boyfriend, who quickly broke under interrogation and confessed to drunkenly smothering the wailing baby.

The young mother was horribly disfigured, facing months of recovery in the hospital; she was despised by her husband, her entire family had ostracized her, and her child was dead. She was despondent, and Jenkins figured she would not have put up a defence if she had been charged with the baby's murder. The memorized vision of the horrifically scarred and traumatized woman served as a constant reminder of the clear lesson that detectives must question the obvious as much as the improbable.

Bearing that in mind, he opened the Natalie Peterson case report. While he and Wilson had been out talking to witnesses, others had been conducting records searches and making phone calls to get histories on the suspect and the victim. At the same time, forensic experts had reviewed the crime scene and examined the body for evidence. Over the life of an investigation, all of the information was compiled in the case report, which often filled a bookshelf worth of binders. This report, however, was only a handful of pages.

The records search had produced fairly standard information

for Natalie Peterson. Born in Grandview, Manitoba, on April 10, 1989. Mother, Jennifer Peterson; father unknown. Attempts to contact Jennifer Peterson were ongoing. Graduated from high school in Brandon, Manitoba, in 2005. Received an Alberta driving license in December 2005 with a Calgary address. Owner of a 1997 Dodge Neon. Two outstanding parking tickets. Various service jobs at bars throughout the city since 2005 and one job as an attendant at a tanning salon in 2007. One year of night classes in restaurant management at Bow Valley College with no degree received. She had a cell phone. She had a credit card with an outstanding balance of $1,141.22. Her credit rating was substandard. She had an empty savings account and a checking account with a balance of $251.11. Review of the normal social networking internet sites showed that she was single with a number of friends but she did not appear to be overly active in online sharing. She had run a 5k road race in 2007 with a below average finishing time and was listed as an assistant manager on the website for a defunct punk band. A fair bit of information but nothing helpful to Jenkins.

The records search on Charley Ewanuschuk had produced essentially nothing. He had graduated high school in a town called Barlock in central Alberta in 2003. Had received a Calgary Public Library card on November 10, 2004. His birth records were not found, which was odd but not unprecedented. No social insurance number had been issued to him, which was unprecedented in Jenkins's experience. A search of Barlock revealed that it had 5,000 residents but no one with the last name Ewanuschuk. No driver's licence. No car. No tax filings. No credit cards. No internet presence. No arrests. No social assistance.

All they knew was that their suspect had graduated high school in a small town where he apparently had no relatives and then moved to Calgary where, years later, his meagre possessions were found in an abandoned house where a woman's bound body was discovered. And he was now locked up, unwilling to talk.

The forensic analysis confirmed the time of death as early Monday morning. The cause of death was strangulation, which usually indicated a larger, stronger male suspect. But given the small size of the victim and the fact that her hands were restrained, the killer in this case did not have to be large or even male. Plus, the victim's neck was so thin that hand size could not be determined from the markings. The toxicity screen showed the presence of Rohypnol. She was on birth control pills. She had rough, likely non-consensual, intercourse not long before her death but no semen was present. Her arms and legs had bruising that was approximately a day old. She had been struck in the face three to five times contemporary with the time of death. Two fingerprints were found on the woman's sternum. The fingerprints matched those obtained from Charley Ewanuschuk on his arrest.

No items of clothing were found on the body other than the vintage man's dress coat and boots. Her pubic hair, leg hair, and underarm hair had been shaven recently. The handcuffs on the victim's wrists were not intended for law enforcement but were the novelty type sold in adult shops.

The next page contained an inventory of the basement. Six well-read issues of Penthouse from 2009. One sleeping bag. Six blankets. Numerous pieces of cardboard. Nine paperbacks—three from the library, six marked with the name of a used book store. One toothbrush. One half-tube of toothpaste. One bar of soap. One comb. One plastic pail. Two towels stamped with "Red Lion Motel". Two empty malt liquor bottles with a receipt showing that the bottles were purchased for cash at 5:56 p.m. on Sunday evening from the Downtown Liquor Depot. One can of generic peaches. Two cans of generic baked beans. One half-empty box of generic chocolate chip cookies. Three plastic forks. One plastic knife. Two plastic spoons. One roll of paper towel. Two flashlights. Ten generic brand D-size batteries. Two t-shirts. One plaid work shirt. Four pairs of boxer shorts. Three pairs of socks, one pair damp. One pair of damp work gloves, with the left one containing holes.

Not exactly an embarrassment of riches, but compared to many of the homeless people Jenkins had encountered in his career, Charley was not that bad off. He guessed he worked as a day labourer, had some other "cash under the table" job, or was very good at collecting recyclables for return. That would mean he could have saved enough money to acquire roofies and possibly had access to a vehicle. The clean clothes and toiletries meant that he could also go to a bar and not be overly conspicuous. With the way kids dressed to go out to bars these days, Jenkins figured he might even be considered stylish in certain circles.

The crime scene techs only found fingerprints belonging to Charley in the house. Also, no traces of Natalie's blood or hair were found in the basement. Jenkins found this a little disconcerting as it would be strange for such an aggressive attack to occur and there not be any indication left behind, especially since it did not appear that the scene had been cleaned in any way. They did find semen stains on the blankets, but Jenkins knew that was consistent with any young man living anywhere and not evidence of a crime.

Closing the report, Jenkins concluded that the evidence was thin. Regardless, his experience told him that might not matter. If the prosecutor could paint a picture of a young, female victim struggling to make ends meet and then paint the homeless man as a depraved drain on society, a jury could convict him. While he was in the business of getting criminals off the street, Jenkins remembered that deformed mother of the murdered baby who would have been unable to protect herself against an improper charge. He could not send a case to court unless he was certain the right result would be reached. It was likely that Charley Ewanuschuk was the killer, but they needed that elusive smoking gun.

CHAPTER 9

For the thirtieth time in the last hour, Hugh Young refreshed the local news website on his office computer. It was the type of sensational story the media dreamed about, and they were reporting constantly on the murdered young woman—despite the fact that they did not have any information other than she had been beaten, strangled, and found basically naked in handcuffs. Hugh knew that once they figured out what she did for money, the fervor over the story would only increase. And once it was determined what her last job was, it would only be a short period of time before they would link Jason to her and, then, Jason to him. If that happened, Hugh was certain his powerful position in the business community would lead to a full-fledged media frenzy.

Clicking off the website, Hugh sighed. He had sixty-three unread emails about the impending takeover. He was in the middle of selling the company he had slaved seventy hours a week to build, and instead of working on the deal, he was worrying about someone recognizing the whore his idiotic son killed. It was a nightmare made even worse by the fact that the more he thought about it, the more it worried him. Hugh was a man who was used to being able to work through any problem; he was not used to them overwhelming him.

The phone rang. The caller ID told him it was coming from someone at Rainer Hopkins, and he decided to let it go to voicemail. It was probably one of the corporate lawyers wanting to know when he was going to get back to them on some urgent email about the takeover he still had not read. It was five o'clock. Hugh was far from a stickler about not drinking during the day but he was opposed to drinking during the day to relieve stress, so he had forced himself to wait. That wait was over. He got out from behind his wide desk and moved to the wine rack tucked into the corner of his office.

With smooth motions earned through habit, he selected his favorite vintage, uncorked it, poured, and within less than a minute, he was drinking a hearty merlot while watching the rush hour traffic creep through the dark twenty stories below. He could not help but wonder if he would have been happier if he had picked a simpler life, one where you always left work at five o'clock and all you had to worry about was traffic and what the wife was making for dinner. As he grew older, he had begun to feel time slipping away as he repeatedly realized that being a successful businessman meant a life of long days but short years.

There was a soft knock on his open door, and Hugh turned to see his assistant, Amber, her low cut blouse allowing for a healthy view of pale cleavage. Suddenly, Hugh forgot his interest in a simple life. Men with simple lives did not have assistants like Amber. He asked, "Yes Amber?"

The young woman sauntered in on her high heels, holding up a pink message slip. "Urgent phone message for you."

"From who?"

She handed him the slip. "Jacob Poetker."

Hugh immediately stepped back, thrusting the glass of wine at Amber. "Here, take this and close the door behind you."

The abrupt dismissal was not surprised as she was used to her boss' boorish behaviour, and she merely carried away the wine as requested. Panic was striking at Hugh and he actually fumbled at dialing the number on the slip. He calmed himself and managed to get it right on the second try.

"Jacob Poetker speaking."

"Yeah, it's Hugh."

"Thanks for getting back to me, Hugh. I've got some news you might find interesting."

"What the hell is going on?"

"I spoke to a friend of mine who has a friend, who has a friend who knows a guy who works in the police department who is willing to provide a little inside information from time to time."

Hugh was not inclined to fake being impressed by the lawyer's contacts and asked, "What did you find out?"

"They have a suspect in custody and it's not Jason."

Hugh slumped in his chair with relief. He had been trying

force himself not to think of what the outcome would be when Jason was convicted of murder and he was convicted as an accomplice, but it had been impossible to ignore. Nightmare scenarios had played through his mind constantly all day. Now, as he realized this inevitability might not occur, he was surprised to find it was not his physical freedom he was most glad to have back. Instead it was the saving of his reputation and the avoidance of public embarrassment that gave him the most joy. The trial and conviction with the media happily airing the deficiencies of his family would have made him either a laughing stock or a pity case—both of which would have been unbearable. Now that there was a chance they would escape, Hugh was more resolute than ever to ensure that escape happened.

He asked, "Who did they arrest?"

"Not sure on a name but it's a homeless man who was squatting in the basement of the house where Jason left the woman. They've managed to keep him locked up on a trespassing charge. Seems like he's the one that ran to a neighbour to call 911."

"That's not much of a fucking case."

"No, but his fingerprints are the only ones on the body. It sounds like the cops have no other evidence and no other suspects."

"He's not charged yet?"

"No, they'll have to charge him on the murder or let him go though, as a trespassing charge won't allow them to keep him very long."

"So you think they will charge him?"

"I think they would be foolish to do it unless they have more evidence than we know about, but with all the media attention, they will be heavily pressured. So, yes, probably they will charge him unless they find something leading them to someone else."

Hugh was suddenly very curious about the internal workings of the criminal justice system and he asked, "Why do you think it would it be foolish for them to charge him now?"

"First off, we know about Jason. Second off, if they charge the homeless man on weak evidence that won't get a conviction, it will be extremely difficult for them to then later charge another suspect unless they find a smoking gun. Any new defendant will simply point to the failed charge against the homeless man to raise reasonable doubt."

"Ok, assuming they are foolish enough to accuse this hobo, do you think a bullshit charge like that would stick?"

"You mean will they be able to convict the homeless guy? Less than fifty-fifty based on the evidence we know about if he has a lawyer who's not a complete idiot. But I haven't seen the whole report and they are still compiling evidence; if they have anything else that links him to the victim, he's going to be in trouble. Plus it is pretty common for homeless people to not have good lawyers or to not be overly afraid of prison as it means they get a warm bed and hot meals, so he might make a plea deal despite weak evidence against him."

Hugh hated this sort of lawyer-speak where they hedged everything they said to ensure you could never pin them down as being wrong, and he gruffly stated, "Basically, you don't have a fucking clue what will happen."

A comment like that would send most corporate lawyers into an apologetic tail spin, but this criminal lawyer was apparently made of stouter stuff, as he responded in an authoritative tone, "No, I don't have a fucking clue. This is a murder investigation and we are only privy to what limited information I am able to get for you from my contacts. If you want I can stop working to find out what is going on. We'll simply wait for the police to show up with handcuffs. Does that work for you?"

Hugh had to admit that the lawyer had all the leverage here and he would need to keep him on his side. Also, he respected this type of response more than backtracking or grovelling, so he said, "Fine, I hear what you're saying."

With the minor pissing contest settled, the lawyer returned to a more amicable tone. "Look, this is very good news for your son and you. Even if they don't charge this suspect, the mere existence of this squatter means that, unless they find some highly prejudicial evidence, they will have a very hard time convicting you and Jason. If they do get enough to charge Jason, all we need to do is tell a jury about this homeless man coincidentally living in the basement of a construction site where the body happened to be found, and there will be reasonable doubt."

This news did not placate Hugh as much as the lawyer probably figured it would. A conviction was not his only problem. It was not even his biggest problem. The public stigma of being wrapped up in this mess at all caused him the most grief so a trial would be as fatal as a conviction. He asked, "If I'm hearing you right, then the case against the fucking hobo is weak enough that the cops will keep digging around?"

"Well, yes, of course. They will continue the investigation until they are certain they know what happened. What I am saying is that this development makes it highly unlikely they will be able to get a conviction against Jason unless they find something particularly damning. Jason actually got pretty lucky crashing into that particular back yard."

Hugh wanted to yell at the lawyer and tell him that none of that mattered. But he would then have to explain that he was more worried about his reputation than his freedom, and he was too prideful to admit he was so prideful. He hesitated and thought for a moment before saying, "So in order for us to avoid being implicated in all of this, we need the police to be certain this squatter did it or have him confess, that right?"

"That would be the best-case scenario, but the investigation of this other suspect is obviously outside of our hands. All we can do now is make sure that Jason doesn't do anything foolish. If he is approached by the police, he needs to keep silent and then hope that this homeless man's bad luck continues."

Hugh was not the type to sit idly by and blindly hope; his mind was already formulating a plan as he muttered, "Fine, thanks for the information."

*

Based largely on a lifetime of hearing lawyer jokes, Brian had expected to encounter a fair bit of greed and shadiness upon joining the profession. What he had not expected to find was the extreme, almost cultish, devotion amongst lawyers to volunteering. Handling matters *pro bono* was part of it, but even more prevalent was donating time to various causes. This dedication was so total that if an associate in a major Calgary law firm went to his annual review and could not discuss at least one charity he was integrally involved in, the senior partners conducting the review would roundly chastise him. As many had harshly learned, an associate could not claim he was too busy to volunteer because, undoubtedly, the partners would have more billable hours than the associate would and still be involved in a list of causes a mile long. Brian had discovered that lawyers would excuse another lawyer being an asshole, a drunk, an adulterer, an idiot, or a cheat, but they would not abide a lawyer who did not volunteer.

One of the charitable endeavors favoured by the experienced criminal defence bar was to volunteer as advisors for less-experienced lawyers working Legal Aid cases. Brian was exceptionally thankful for this as, while he had been learning, he still had very limited knowledge of criminal law and procedure. After having Charley's file officially assigned to him, he immediately called his favorite advisor to set up a consultation and was invited to come over after five.

Right at five o'clock, Brian arrived at the historical Lancaster Building where Fredrickson and Associates LLP, was located. Despite its crumbling façade and lack of a decent heating system, the old building was a popular downtown address because of its central location and because the elevators went straight down to the Unicorn Pub in the basement. Getting off at the fifth floor, Brian found the door unlocked, but the receptionist was apparently gone for the day, so he walked back through the reception area to Erik Fredrickson's corner office, where he rapped on the door jam.

A broad smile met him as Fredrickson said, "Brian, good to see you. Come on in."

The large office was cramped with piles of documents covering every horizontal surface and a massive desk, which was buried beneath even more paper. The lawyer behind the disheveled mess was in no better shape. He was well over three hundred pounds with a huge head that melded directly into his rounded shoulders without the benefit of a visible neck. His scruffy beard was going from red to grey, his scraggly hair fell over his ears, and his eyeglasses were covered in multiple smudges such that the lenses bordered on opaque.

"Hi Erik, thanks for seeing me on such short notice."

"No problem. You want a Coke?"

"Sure. How are things with you?"

Brian had to move a pile of files and an empty chip bag from the guest chair before sitting as Fredrickson reached beneath his desk and produced two cans of warm Coke. Handing one to Brian, he said, "Things are alright. Too much work to do as usual and my wife's ragging on me to take her on another boring cruise but other than that things are alright. What's going on with you? Have you made that beautiful girlfriend of yours an honest woman?"

"Nope, no ring yet."

"Smart man. People always say that half of all marriages end in divorce. What they leave out is the other half end in death. Basically, there's no good way out."

With a chuckle, he responded, "Thanks for the advice."

"Yeah, well, I wouldn't pass it along to the girlfriend." The rotund lawyer leaned back in his creaky chair. "So we've got a possible murder charge on our hands? Let's hear it."

One of the key reasons Brian liked working with Fredrickson was that he always seemed to be enjoying himself, even when things were going badly. Another reason was that he treated him like an equal, casually working on problems with him rather than dealing with him like a clueless student who needed to be told exactly what to do. If you went to him for advice, you did not receive to-do lists, rather you got an eager partner. Also, as Frederickson liked to tell anyone who would listen, he had been doing defence work through three marriages, two bypass surgeries and one disbarment hearing, so he had seen every oddity the criminal world could throw at a lawyer. Given that experience, he was the perfect fit for the bizarre story Charley had handed him.

Brian tried to explain Charley's strangeness and then told the tale of witnessing the attack from the basement, after which

Fredrickson said with a long sigh, "Pretty weak story."

"Yeah, a bit tough to believe."

"Our guy have a record?"

"He says no."

"No charge yet?"

"Just the section 177," Brian answered, referring to criminal code section for trespassing at night.

"Who's on for the Crown?"

"Clay Matthews."

Fredrickson shook his massive head slightly. "That's bad luck."

Calgary was not that big of a place, so the senior counsellor would have dealt with the senior prosecutor many times. Plus, Brian knew that the members of the defence bar discussed the tendencies of all the prosecutors at great length. Given this, Fredrickson would know all there is to know about Matthews. Curious for information but worried about the answer, Brian asked, "What's his deal?"

"I know Matthews pretty well. I actually articled with him at BGM a thousand years ago."

At this Brian subconsciously looked around the crowded, low-rent space. BGM was the national firm of Block Gladstone & Mellon, one of the most prestigious and well-paying firms in the country. Fredrickson apparently saw this questioning glance around the office, as he said with a smile, "What can I say? Things change. If I recall correctly, you once had a cushy firm job too."

Brian grinned and raised his hands slightly in surrender. "Fair enough. No judgement here. I just want the inside information on our prosecutor friend."

Fredrickson leaned back and sighed, "How do I explain him? He's from the Maritimes; I don't remember exactly where, maybe Halifax. His dad was the dean of some school or something that made his family a big deal in a small place like that. Anyway, he definitely thought he was superior to anyone he was going to encounter out here and wanted to make sure we all knew it too.

Kind of guy that would berate his assistant and harass the mailroom people simply because he could. He would constantly want to know what you were working on so he could make sure he was working on something more important. Always wore a jacket and tie, even on the weekends so everyone knew he was serious. Don't get me wrong, he's sharp and he worked hard but he pissed people off with the constant bragging and complaining about the grunt work we all had to do as students. Basically, he wanted everyone to know he was above photocopying, transcript summaries, and delivering documents. Well, this was back in the day when a place like BGM might hire back about one in three of their articling students to become associates and, when it came time for us to be hired back, he missed the cut.

"At first I was surprised by this as he was definitely smart and ambitious enough to fit in there, but when I talked to some of the higher-up associates they told me the partners figured his ego would be a problem with clients and he'd be trouble with the staff. Anyway, for most students this would be annoying but not a huge problem as lots of firms would gladly take BGM's castoffs, but Matthews had a full-on meltdown. He stormed into a meeting and tore into the hiring partner about what a mistake he was making and how he was so much better than all the students that got hired. They had to have security take him out. Needless to say, his job options were reduced after that display. If I remember right, he disappeared for about a year and then re-appeared at the prosecutor's office."

Brian had seen similar immature egos at the firm he had worked for, so while he found this story interesting, it was not surprising to him. More to the point, he did not know how this information helped him now, so he prodded, "Any read on what he is like now?"

"Well, let's just say that when he re-appeared his smugness was not replaced by humility like one would expect, instead, a massive chip had grown on his shoulder. I think he's always had this need to prove to everyone that he shouldn't have been fired. He only takes cases to trial that he thinks are guaranteed winners and once he goes to trial there is no way he's backing down. I had a file with him go on forever because some alibi evidence for my guy came in after he had already scheduled the trial. Even though Matthews knew he could not win, he kept getting delays and adjournments until he was able to dump it off on a junior prosecutor who took one look at the file and promptly dropped the charges. I'm sure that Matthews dicked around like that so it would not show up on his stats."

Already stressed, Brian's stomach and chest tightened further. Not only would his first serious case be a heavily publicized murder trial, it would be against a ruthless, win-at-all-costs prosecutor. Fredrickson drained his Coke and continued, "Since they've assigned it to Matthews, we have to assume that the murder charge is on the horizon. You've talked to the prosecution already?"

Brian gave an embarrassed smile. "I had to play Matthews a bit to keep Charley out of the general population for a few days. I told him I thought he lacked mental capacity so they needed to do a psych review."

"He bought that?"

"Sort of. I offered to delay the bail hearing if he got the review done and I think he wanted the extra time to strengthen the investigation before deciding on the charge, so he agreed."

"Do you think there's a chance an insanity plea might work?"

"No, Charley's odd and barely speaks but I highly doubt he's actually mentally ill."

"I suppose I should give you the standard speech about not risking your reputation and career for the sake of a single client but you know all that already. And frankly, if the prosecution wants to dick around holding someone on this weak charge bullshit while they prove their real case then I think they can't complain about a little sharp practice on our part." Fredrickson put his elbows on the messy desk as he asked, "What are your thoughts on strategy?"

"Hard to say as we don't know what the evidence is going to be. I sent Charley off with a pen and paper to write out what happened in a letter to me. He said he mailed it the night before he got arrested. Maybe that will give us a better understanding of his side of things."

Fredrickson blurted out a laugh at that. "They still teaching that old trick? We used to do that shit twenty years ago when we thought we had a client who was lying. I think the idea was the client would realize how bad his story sounded when he had to put it on paper, so he'd give up and start telling his lawyer the truth. I didn't think it worked so well; normally they just used the time to make up better lies."

Another junior lawyer had told Brian about the letter idea. Now he felt a little foolish for actually using it, but he still figured it had been worth a shot given Charley's behavior. He answered, "I thought he might give me more details by writing since he doesn't really talk and I wanted to have his story down before he got arrested."

"Hard to get a letter like that in to evidence unless you let this guy testify which, it sounds like, would be a bad idea. Anyway, it's always good to remember that you can't trust your clients, whether they're talking, writing or using smoke signals."

Fredrickson's tone was not harsh or mocking, but nonetheless, Brian wanted to change the topic, "Regardless, I think we need to investigate how the woman got there. Charley lacks the charisma or cash to get a pretty girl interested in coming home with him and I highly doubt he has access to a vehicle to get her there against her will."

"Yeah, that's a good point. We'll need to use that. Hopefully, she's got a boyfriend or regular customer living up there we can point the finger at. Before we get into that, though, what about pre-trial strategy? My guess is that the press is going to be all over this and we might be able to use that to our advantage."

This was the sort of thing not taught in law school that Brian needed to know about. "What do you have in mind?"

"I had a case about twenty years ago where my client beat a mailman with a hammer. It got a lot of news coverage. My guy was a nut case—not criminally insane, but obviously touched. Turns out that he had tried on more than one occasion to have himself committed but the doctors would only give him a cursory checkup before sending him on his way. We got that out to the papers and the mailman beater became the poster boy for the defects of the mental health system. There were a few minor evidentiary problems with the Crown's case and that, coupled with a now-sympathetic accused, led them to settle on favorable terms."

Recalling Charley's dread of jail, Brian said, "I get what you are saying but our guy is petrified of serving time. I doubt he'd agree to any settlement that'd involve time."

"Clients say that all the time. He might change his mind if we can get him a few years instead of life. And if not, then maybe we can find something that will let us work the media message so our guy looks less like a monster preying on pretty young girls and more like a victim himself. There's a whole city of potential jurors out there watching the nightly news." Fredrickson shrugged before adding, "You said he's strange. Maybe there's a good reason why he's strange. A reason that will help his cause."

"Makes sense." Brian would never have thought of such things, but he did see one key problem. "But how do we find out about his past? He's not exactly forthcoming with information."

Fredrickson gave him a smile. "Well, somebody out there somewhere's got to know this guy."

*

The lights were unceremoniously turned off from some remote switch, but pale light still came in from the hall through a small window in the door, making the room more shadow-filled than dark. He had been fingerprinted and photographed. His clothes had been taken and exchanged for a white pair of canvas loafers, a white undershirt, boxer shorts, blue pants, and a matching shirt. The outfit reminded him of coarse pyjamas but he did not mind as it was the first time in recent memory he could recall wearing properly laundered clothes.

After being processed, he had been taken down a hall lined with doors to a cell with two bunk beds and two inmates. One was an old man who seemed confused. The other could not have been more than eighteen and appeared to be drugged. Thankfully, they did not even get out of their beds to acknowledge Charley's presence and neither were physically menacing.

He silently took the bunk above the medicated youth and stared at the ceiling while listening to the old man mutter incomprehensibly to himself. Despite the tolerable situation inside the cell, Charley was unable to relax as he could hear yelling and banging from outside the door. The worst part was being unsure what was going to happen to him next. He did not know if he would be moved to another cell. He was not sure if he would be fed. He did not know how long he would be here. He did not even know where he was, which way was which.

But now, with the lights being turned out, Charley was fairly certain he would at least be safe for the night. He climbed under the blanket and listened to the old man's whispery snores. It was nice to be warm and in a real bed, but he already found that he missed being able to make even the few decisions his previous life allowed him. In his basement he had been able to read by flashlight, drink a beer, or flip through his magazines. Also, when the weather was better, he found he enjoyed going for walks about the wealthy neighborhood in the evenings. The streets were largely empty and he could let his mind wander as he strolled amongst the fine homes without being afraid. As he closed his eyes and tried to fall asleep in the grey cell, he wondered if he would ever have even those sad simple freedoms again.

CHAPTER 10

The familiar face of the police chief came on the TV with a breaking news graphic beneath him. Brian reached for the remote to turn up the volume to hear him say, "…have a person of interest in custody with respect to the Natalie Peterson murder."

An unseen reporter asked, "Have charges been laid?"

"No charges related to the murder have been laid at this time and our investigation is ongoing, but we are confident it will be resolved shortly."

Brian recognized this as the usual comments made when the police thought they had the proper suspect but were organizing the evidence before filing the charge. They had delayed the bail hearing and he figured that before that hearing happened, Charley would be formally charged with murder. Personally, the laying of the charge would mean a significant paycheck for Brian, which would help with the mounting bills, but seeing a case he was involved in being discussed on the news made his stomach tighten with stress. He had run trials before, but the most serious one had been a mugging. He had never defended a murderer before and never tried a case before a jury. And now the whole city would be watching while he did it for the first time.

Another unseen reporter asked, "Can you tell us who the suspect is?"

The police chief gave a wry smile as he answered, "I cannot comment on the individual's identity at this time." He held up his hands as other questions were called out. "Thank you for your time this morning and we will continue to keep you updated."

With that, the press conference was over. Not much information had been provided, but it was pretty obvious to Brian that they had decided Charley was the killer. Brian turned off the TV and moved to put his cereal bowl in the sink. Anna shuffled up behind him in her plush slippers and put her arms around his waist as she asked, "You taking off already?"

"Yeah, the chief of police was just on TV and I think Charley'll be charged pretty soon. I want to get the interviews done so I can be back here tonight in time to get ready."

Anna apparently heard the uneasiness in his voice, as she turned him to look at her. "It'll be ok. You'll work harder than anyone else would and give this poor man the best defence possible."

Brian could not help but smile at her, but he was not sure she was right. He would do everything he could. However, as he was already learning, there was a great deal of strategy and intricacy he was blind to. He was out of his league and was planning to talk to Charley about having him get more senior counsel. But he did not want to take the time to discuss that with Anna now so instead he said, "I'm not even thinking about the trial; I'm not sure Charley can handle general lock. I'm worried something bad will happen before he can even get to court."

Anna asked, "Is there anything you can do to keep him out?"

"A psychologist is meeting with Charley this morning. If they find that he has a mental problem or would be at risk due to incapacity, they can keep him in the infirmary for treatment or in protective custody while he awaits trial. If they say he's ok, then it will only be a matter of hours before he is put in gen pop. And frankly, I doubt him playing mute will be enough to get him special treatment."

Anna seemed surprised by this news. "That's it? There's no plea to be made for a man's safety when he has not even been convicted of anything?"

He drained the last of his coffee and answered as he set the mug in the sink. "Nope. The government is not willing to admit prisons are unsafe for those in custody, so you need to prove that there is a specific threat."

"Well, then I hope the psychologist decides he's a total mental wreck. If the psychologist is meeting with him today, why are you going all the way up to Barlock to find out about his past? Won't anything you find be too late?"

"Yes, for that it won't help, but given the way Charley acts, Fredrickson and I think he may have been abused or mistreated and that might help us cut a deal or soften up a jury." He leaned in and kissed Anna on the cheek before he added, "And on top of that, if I'm about to spend all my waking hours devoted to keeping this guy out of jail, I want to know what he's all about and I'm not going to learn much from talking with him."

*

With the bachelor party planner in Las Vegas and their prime suspect not talking, Jenkins had taken the lull in the investigation as an opportunity to go home early Tuesday night, have a healthy dinner with his wife and get a good night's sleep. He realized these were luxuries while working a homicide, but he also knew enough not to pass up the chance to rest when it presented itself. However, what rejuvenation he had gained from the break was washed away when he awoke to find his voicemail full of panicky messages from Wilson.

He called Wilson as he drove through the early morning traffic to the police station, "Wilson, what's going on?

"Randy, finally. Where the hell have you been?"

"At home, sleeping. What's the big problem?"

"Sleeping? The problem is that the chief has been on my ass all night to charge that Charley guy with the Peterson murder."

"What? We just got the body and the suspect is not going anywhere. Even if a judge lets him out we can keep tabs on him while we sort all of this out. What's the rush?"

"The usual public perception bullshit. Pretty young woman brutally murdered in a rich neighborhood and the press all over it. Chief and his cronies think it'll look good if we get a quick slam dunk."

"But a charge is pointless if we can't make it stick."

"Sure, I told them we only need a bit more time to fill in some gaps. But we've got the guy's fingerprints on the body and a witness that puts him there. They think we've got the right guy and they aren't going to wait around. Honestly, I think they don't want the media to grow tired of the story without us getting credit for catching the guy. Hell, I agree with them that we've got the killer.

We just need to nail it down for trial."

Jenkins silently cursed himself for not sticking it out at the office last night. He had seen this all before and might have been able to temper the fervor. The chief and the other powerbrokers always wanted a quick charge on high-profile cases because they wanted the media to cover the arrest as much as they covered the murder. A young detective like Wilson played right into this as rookies were likely to overstate the strength of their case due to a tendency to believe that the first suspect was always the right suspect, and the general, juvenile inclination to brag.

He sighed, "Ok, well, it is what it is. We probably don't have to make any moves until the bail hearing and we should be able to get it locked down one way or the other by then. If we don't have enough to lay a charge I won't lay it and that's all there is to it. Don't worry, I'll take the heat if the bosses get pissed."

Wilson hesitated for a second before saying, "Actually, I think it is worse than the usual internal bullshit. The Chief was already on the news this morning saying we have a suspect in custody."

This time Jenkins cursed out loud.

*

With a popping sound the lights came on, sending the dimly lit cell into immediate fluorescent brightness. Charley realized he could not see and rapidly pawed about himself in terror until he found his heavy eye glasses under his shoulder. He was essentially blind without them and one of his greatest fears was that he would lose or break them as he had no way to replace them. He had a pulsating headache, and despite the coolness of the cell, he was sweaty with shaky hands. Charley recognized these as signs he had not had a drink in a couple of days.

He was wondering if he would ever get to have a drink again when he heard heavy breathing shockingly close to him. He turned to see a patch of greasy, black hair and two dark eyes staring at him from the edge of the bunk. Instinctively Charley scrambled backwards in the bed, pushing himself against the wall. From there he could see it was the teenager, his medication having apparently worn off. He stared at Charley for a long minute before banging his palms against the bed frame twice and slinking down, out of view while muttering angrily under his breath. Charley had no idea what had upset the young man but he felt extremely vulnerable lying up on the bunk, so he quickly climbed down to get his feet on the ground.

Leaning with his back against the cinderblock wall, he watched the inmate, still talking angrily to himself, repeatedly fold, unfold, and refold his pillowcase. The old man remained under this blanket but his eyes were open, staring straight up blankly. The situation was not as intolerable as other circumstances Charley had endured but the perpetual uncertainty made it highly unnerving. He had no idea if he was trapped in this room with these strange men for a day or a week, or forever. At least if he was on the streets, he could move and try, however vainly, to improve his suffering.

He stood like that, dreading the unknown, for what he thought was probably an hour before a guard arrived and silently delivered three trays with pancakes, one skinny sausage, an orange, and a cup of apple juice. Charley ate his food while standing and watching as the teenager played with his food before wolfing down the dry pancakes and throwing the orange at the toilet. The old man was still staring and had not moved towards his breakfast. The youth eyed the tray and then eyed Charley. With an eerily demented chuckle he slid over and swiped the pancakes off the old man's tray before scurrying back to his bed to eat them out of his hands. Charley knew he should protest this theft from the helpless man, but he was worried about aggravating the obviously unbalanced prisoner, so he merely continued to lean against the wall.

Shortly after breakfast a burly guard walked into the cell and pointed at Charley. "Ewanuschuk, time to go. Hands behind your back."

Uncertain as to what was happening, he hesitated for a brief moment. The large guard sighed, stepped forward, roughly spun him, and expertly pressed him into the wall, holding him there with a knee to the buttocks while deftly cuffing his hands. The crazed inmate cackled and clapped his hands at the excitement. With no further instructions, Charley was marched out of the cell, down the hall lined with doors, and into a narrow, undecorated room with only two plastic chairs and a metal table. He was set down into one of the chairs with his hands behind his back. The guard put a firm hand on his shoulder and said, "Don't cause any trouble. I don't want to have to come in here. And *you* definitely do not want me to have to come in here. Got it?"

With that, the guard left and a hefty woman wearing a purple suit and bright yellow blouse came in, silently taking the chair across from him. She was ignoring him, focussing on some papers, so he took the opportunity to get a look. She was tall and broad but not fat, built more like a football player than a woman. She was wearing a good deal of makeup, had brightly dyed, orange hair and heavy red-framed glasses that made it hard to accurately guess an age. After a few moments, she looked up at him, causing him to immediately look down at his prison-issue canvas shoes.

While familiar fear filled Charley at the proposition of having to sit and talk with a stranger, he again took solace from Brian's advice to simply not respond in any way. He would get through this ordeal the same way he survived yesterday: he would become a statue.

"My name is Patricia Wilde. I am a licensed psychologist hired by the Alberta Corrections Department to determine whether inmates have mental capacity issues or a mental illness which would make having them serve normal time in a penal institution cruel." Her tone was brisk and businesslike with an underlying impression of annoyance. "Do you understand this?"

Charley did not respond.

"Fine. I understand that you are either refusing to talk or unable to talk. I will let you know right now that I have seen this tactic used by inmates before and I will inform you that silent treatment alone will not result in me finding you mentally unable to serve your time in the general population. If you want to make a case that you lack capacity, that will require something further. Is there anything you would like to tell me about yourself that may provide me with an insight into your mental wellbeing or emotional wellbeing."

Unsure what to do, Charley merely remained mute.

"Good, then. I see here that you graduated high school. Obviously you were able to communicate well enough at that time. Do you expect me to believe that in the seven years since you graduated you went from a passable student to some sort of a non-communicative vegetable?"

No response.

She sighed loudly, returned to her papers, and then read out what he assumed was a prepared question, "Have you ever abused a narcotic, including alcohol?"

Charley gave no response. She made a check mark with her pen.

"Are you currently taking any prescription medicines?"

No response. She quickly wrote something.

"Have you ever had serious contemplative thoughts regarding suicide or otherwise harming yourself or another?"

Even though the concept of escape through suicide had been Charley's lifelong companion, he made no response. Another check mark.

"Have you ever been sexually assaulted, physically assaulted, mentally abused, or abused in any manner which you consider to have been traumatizing?"

For an instant he glanced up and opened his lips a sliver. What a ridiculous question. Anger overtook fear and he suddenly wanted to tell this arrogantly rude woman about all the horrible things that had happened to him while living alone on the street. The beatings. The terror. The cold. The robberies. The hunger. The loneliness. The desperation. She could decide if she considered that to be traumatizing. And if she didn't then he could tell her about his earlier years and see if that constituted enough pain to allow him to now stop suffering at the hands of others. But looking in her eyes for a second, he saw they were filled with condescension and his trickle of rage dissipated beneath a wave of embarrassment. He returned his gaze to his prison shoes, saying nothing. She wrote something.

"Ok, then. Well, Mr. Ewanuschuk, I am sure you'll be greatly relieved to know that, based on our discussion where you indicate nothing that would give me cause for concern, you appear to be mentally stable and capable of carrying out your internment without any special treatment."

With that, the woman tore a yellow piece of carbon paper from her notepad, dropped it on his lap, and stepped to the door. The guard opened the door and asked, "What's wrong?"

"Nothing. We're done."

"That fast? Is he that crazy?"

She shrugged. "I don't think so. See you next time."

*

According to his secretary, the bachelor party organizer was back from Vegas and was currently sleeping off his trip at home, so Jenkins and Wilson were on their way to give him an uncomfortable awakening. Technically the man was under no obligation to return their calls, or even speak with them, but when Jenkins contacted someone about a murder investigation, he expected them to call back, and unfortunately for this individual, Jenkins was in an especially foul mood this morning.

"So what's the plan here, boss?" Wilson asked as he cautiously exited off of Deerfoot Trail onto an icy Memorial Drive. Thin snow was falling through the frozen pre-dawn, grey sky. The cold snap had been going on for weeks with no end in sight, making doing anything in the city more difficult.

"Let me do the questioning at first. I want to establish if he saw our suspect at the bar that night. If that leads nowhere, then we'll need to know where Natalie went after the party. That might be tougher to get out of him as we'll probably need him to give up his buddies' names. If he balks, then you bring the angry obstruction of justice rant down on him with a vengeance."

"Sure. What if he full-on refuses to play along?"

Jenkins's stomach ached; he was growing weary of this investigation. He said, "Then fuck it. If we push and he won't cooperate, we street him while we wait on a search warrant for his place."

This was an old school, not quite constitutional tactic that had been outlawed by the department. Basically, the uncooperative witness was immediately forced out of the house on the premise that they needed to search his house for evidence. The witness was free to go, but without a wallet or a cell phone or even shoes, his options were severely limited unless he had a friendly neighbour nearby. What normally happened was the witness would wait in a cop car while they got a search warrant from the courthouse, a process that could take hours. Embarrassed like that in front of the neighbourhood with the impending threat of having his house torn apart hanging over him, the witness would often change his behaviour. It was a risky manoeuvre because if the witness held his ground, his first phone call would be to a lawyer, so getting any type of cooperation after that was very unlikely. Plus, the chance of the police officers involved being sued, or at least reprimanded, was high.

Wilson shook his head slightly but did answer, "Alright, I'm with you."

They pulled up in front of a townhouse development in a trendy neighbourhood just north of downtown and marched briskly through the early morning cold to the door of unit three. There was a doorbell but Wilson banged loudly on the door instead as he called, "David O'Connor, this is the Calgary Police Service."

There was no immediate response, so Wilson pushed the doorbell a few times and then banged on the door louder. "David O'Connor, this is the Calgary Police, open the door."

A voice called out from inside, "Ok, Ok, I'm coming."

A tall, fit man with a messy coif of blonde hair, two days' of beard stubble and bloodshot eyes opened the door wearing nothing but boxer shorts. "Yes, what is it? Is something wrong?"

Jenkins showed his badge and said, "We have some questions for you. Can we come in?"

Without waiting for an answer, Wilson and Jenkins stepped forward, forcing the undressed man back inside. Jenkins recognized the confusion on his face as the look someone with a perpetually guilty conscience makes when they are trying to think of what they did to warrant police attention. He could almost hear the questions rolling through the man's mind: Was it those joints he sold a few months ago at that party? The girl who looked a little too young the morning after Halloween? The laptop he took from the office before he quit last year? He immediately knew this man's first instinct would be to lie at every opportunity.

The townhouse interior was basically a miniaturized version of the suburbia home they had visited yesterday. Dark hardwood floors, granite kitchen counters, beige walls, and new but inexpensive furnishings. Wilson loudly trod into the living area, his snow-covered shoes leaving a trail of water. Jenkins merely leaned against the wall next to the flat screen TV and opened up his note pad as he asked, "You are David O'Connor?"

The young man had put on a brown suit jacket that had been on a hook by the door and now looked especially silly sitting on the couch. He tried to sound unafraid as he answered, "Yes. What is this about?"

Jenkins held up one finger, imploring patience as he scribbled nothingness on the notepad and asked, "Where do you work?"

"I'm self employed as a wine salesman. I work for a bunch of different wineries. Really, if you could tell me—"

Jenkins's finger went back up as there was more scribbling. He figured the longer he let the tension grow, the more uncomfortable the witness would be and the more eager he would be to cooperate simply to get them out of his house. Wilson apparently caught on to this plan. He began looking noisily around the small space in an attempt to increase O'Connor's uneasiness.

"What type of car do you drive?" He didn't care what type of car O'Connor drove but asked anyhow.

"I have a BMW. I really don't see—"

"Do you know a Jessica Standen?" This was a made-up name, the question only being asked to keep the witness guessing why they were there.

"Um, I don't think so. I know a Jessica but I think her last name is Walton or something like that."

Wilson opened a drawer in a side table and began leafing through papers. O'Connor protested meekly to Jenkins, "Hey, man, that's private. Can he just do that?"

He answered with a shrug, "He's doing it, so I guess he can. Have you ever eaten at the restaurant Charcut downtown?"

"Huh? No, I've never been there."

More pointless scribbling. "Too bad, it's pretty good. Have you ever been to Beckham's Bar downtown?"

"Yeah, yeah, I've been there a bunch." He began to stand up. "Look, I really need to get to work—"

Jenkins pounced on this: "I thought you said you were self-employed? Was that a lie?"

O'Connor sunk back into the couch. "No, no, I'm self-employed, I swear."

"Fine. Have you ever paid a woman for sex?"

"What? No, of course not, man. Look is this some sort of prank or something…?"

Without looking up from his writing, Jenkins answered, "Nope, not a prank. Where were you Saturday night?"

There was a hesitation at this. Wilson opened the man's refrigerator and loudly clanked some bottles about. O'Connor, apparently unsure whether he should lie, said, "I was at that Beckham's place."

"What were you doing there?"

"What do you mean? It's a bar. I was drinking with some friends."

"Who were these friends?"

"Look, I don't think that this is any of your business—"

"It was a bachelor party, right?"

O'Connor blanched at this and stared at Jenkins, attempting vainly to figure out how much this detective knew and what he could get away with lying about. Jenkins remained stone faced. By the sounds coming from the kitchen, Wilson was apparently eating an apple and going through the man's silverware drawer. O'Connor glanced towards the kitchen and then back at Jenkins before saying, "Fine, if you want to know about the fucking party, I'll tell you. Nothing illegal happened."

"Good to hear. Who was there?"

"A bunch of us, you know how those things are, people coming and going. It was a lot of Art's buddies from his office that I don't know and some guys we went to school with."

He wanted to push this point but figured this man was going to be reluctant to give his friends' names, either out of a sense of loyalty or because some of them had interesting information about him. Pushing too much might get his back up enough to allow him to find the courage to kick them out. He decided to move on for now. "And you were the one that booked the entertainment?"

O'Connor sat up. "Did one of those girls complain? Is that what this is about? Hey, man, we had fun and all but everything was above board and they were very willing."

Now that he had him worried and talking, he gave the man a way out by asking, "Was there anyone odd at the party? Anyone not invited who was hanging around, watching the girls?"

O'Connor jumped on this life line immediately: "Yeah there was a guy like that. Is that who you're looking for?"

Feeling optimistic, he pulled out the picture of Charley Ewanuschuk and handed it over. "Is this the guy?"

Wilson wandered back into the living room, a half-eaten apple in his hand, eager to see if they were going to put the nail in the coffin. O'Connor scanned the picture and answered, "No, this isn't the guy I was thinking of. Not even close."

Nothing was ever easy. Jenkins took the picture back and asked, "But there was someone hanging around?"

"Yeah, man, some rich dude. About my age I'd guess but

chubby and balding."

"How do you know he was rich?"

"Well, he gave me five hundred cash to join the party. Plus he had a fat ass Rolex on."

"This stranger partied with you guys and the dancers?"

O'Connor paused, apparently trying to recollect the night, before saying, "Only sort of. He didn't really party. If I remember right, he got lap dances from the girls and then he just sat at a table watching."

"Was he still there at the end of the night?"

"Um, I'm not sure. I was really drunk by then and with all the distractions I wasn't really paying attention to him."

Never easy. Jenkins asked, "Ok, do you know how the girls left after the party?"

"No, I don't. Like I said, we were pretty far into it by then."

"What was his name?"

"Didn't get it. At least I don't think he said it."

Flipping to an empty page in his notebook, he held it out to O'Connor as he said, "Alright, we need to get the names and phone numbers of everyone at this party."

The witness leaned back with his hands up. "Whoa, man, look, I'm fine helping out the police and all but a bunch of the guys that were there have wives and kids and shit and they aren't going to look too kindly on me sending the police to their houses to ask about them getting drunk with strippers."

Jenkins nodded to Wilson. He stepped forward, pulled out the picture of Natalie lying on a table in the morgue, and thrust it into the man's face. Glaring at O'Connor, he said, "This is what happened to one of those girls you paid to grope."

Predictable horror filled the man's face as he looked at the dead girl with the bruised eyes, torn cheek, and smashed lips. After a moment he looked up and asked, "Did this happen to her after our party?"

Jenkins merely nodded.

O'Connor took the notepad from Jenkins and began writing names.

CHAPTER 11

Brian was speeding down the highway, hoping his old car would not shake apart, when his cell phone rang. "Hello, Brian speaking."

"Brian, this is Clay Matthews."

"How are you Clay?"

"Fine. I just wanted to let you know that the psychiatrist review of Mr. Ewanuschuk was conducted this morning. He was found mentally sound."

Despite knowing that it had been a long shot for Charley to be kept in special custody, he was still disappointed with the news. He was also worried that the prosecutor had caught on to his trick, so he asked, "Did he actually speak to the psychologist?"

"I don't think so."

That was a relief and also a little puzzling, "Well, how can they find him capable if he didn't say anything? Who was the psychologist?"

"Wilde."

That made sense. Patricia Wilde was far from a criminal's rights advocate. Before being hired by the government, she was famously used by prosecutors as an expert to debunk any pleas of insanity. Charley hadn't stood a chance. Matthews would know this too, so Brian decided to take another shot. "Look, Clay, this guy is seriously messed up. We've got the bail application tomorrow. Can you keep him in the infirmary until then? They'll eat him alive in gen pop. Maybe he'll get out on bail and you can save an innocent man some unnecessary torment."

Matthews sighed loudly. Undoubtedly, he had heard these types of blusterous pleas from defence counsel numerous times before and said, "You know you are not getting bail on this one. We'll only be delaying the inevitable. It was a cute idea to have him stay mute but you lost this one. He's going in."

Brian figured that Matthews was planning on adding the murder charge prior to the bail hearing and there was no way an accused killer with no connections to the community would be released, but the murder charge had not been laid yet, so, trying to sound more confident than he was, he replied, "Hell, I think bail is highly likely. I mean he is only in on trespassing in an empty house and he's got no record. You should be ashamed you held him this long."

The prosecutor was in a bind as he was obviously not ready to lay the information for the murder and could not dispute that holding someone on the minor charge in place now was excessive. With another exaggerated sigh, Matthews answered, "Fine, I'll see if I can delay his transfer until after the bail hearing. But this is just between me and you. I don't need fat ass Wilde in here chewing my head off."

It was not much, but at least Brian had managed to get Charley another night of safety.

*

It was ten in the morning. Even his lazy ass son Jason should be awake, but his call went to voicemail. Hugh had finally come up with a plan that might actually work and he was eager to take some action. He immediately redialled and, finally, on the fourth ring a tired-sounding voice answered, "Hello?"

"You're still in fucking bed? You need to grow up and get a goddamn job."

"Huh?"

"You shiftless moron, wake up and listen."

Hugh had learned enough to know not to impart any sensitive information to Jason, so he merely asked him questions, leaving his purpose unknown. For once, Jason had done the smart thing and did not have what he needed. But in this instance, Jason's memory was remarkably good, making Hugh think he could still make his plan work. Having obtained the details he needed, he hung up and bellowed for Amber to come into his office.

The high school was far from new, but there was no graffiti and no chain link fencing. Brian figured it was probably a nicer place than the massive Calgary high school he had attended, even if this one's parking lot was littered with rusty pickup trucks in various stages of rebuilding.

Charley had been vague about his past during their brief meeting after his arrest. He would only say he had grown up on a farm by the small town of Barlock, graduated high school, and then came to Calgary. When Brian asked him about his family, he merely said that his dad was dead and his mom had left. He had prodded for more but only got ambiguous shrugs in response. Brian had scoured the Barlock phone book and done numerous internet searches to try to find a member of Charley's family, but he had no luck. He even called the chamber of commerce, the newspaper, and the Rotary club attempting to get a lead, but that all went nowhere. Brian had then called the school and explained to a friendly receptionist that he was trying to help one of their former students who was in trouble. She directed him to the vice principal, who directed him to the guidance counsellor. The guidance counsellor remembered Charley and was willing to meet.

Walking past the rows of lockers, Brian smelled a potpourri of fruity teenage girl perfume, well used gym clothes, and long-forgotten lunches mingling with the strong odour of French fries coming from the cafeteria. Homemade posters announced an upcoming dance, a pep rally, and a drama club presentation of *West Side Story*. He stopped to glance inside a trophy case lined with pictures of smiling teams holding trophies. The familiarity of it all took him back to his youth and made him jealous of the kids who got to roam these halls every day with no greater worries than finding gas money and using a fake ID to get beer.

He eventually found a door labelled "Guidance". He knocked but there was no response, so he stepped inside. The space was larger than he had anticipated, with a counter and waiting area like in a dentist's office. Behind the counter, he glimpsed a girl crying in an interior office as a woman patiently rubbed her shoulder. The room was filled with brochures and posters dealing with everything from unwanted pregnancy, to child abuse, to anorexia, to bullying, to suicide, to STDs. Suddenly he was not so jealous of the high school kids.

A man in his forties dressed in a bright red golf shirt with a

Barlock Thunderbirds crest popped up from his chair behind the counter. "Hi, you must be Brian Cox. I'm Keith Stillman."

They shook hands over the counter. "Hi, nice to meet you. Thanks for meeting with me."

"No problem, but I'm not sure how much help I can be." He glanced back at the sobbing girl and then back to Brian before saying, "Why don't we go to my office in the gym; it's more private."

Keith led Brian on a short trip through the halls and into a gymnasium with a black thunderbird painted in the middle of the shining floor. A group of girls dressed in revealing athletic wear were casually playing badminton while another group of girls, dressed mainly in jeans, sat on the bleachers watching. In a lofted area at one end of the gym, a few boys casually lifted weights.

Seeing him taking in the scene, the counsellor laughed as he said, "Typical girls' phys ed class. Half of them come up with excuses so they don't need to do anything and the other half only bother to change so that the guys using the weights can see them in their little shorts. When they need to go outside for class, you're lucky if two out of three of them aren't menstruating."

"Goes both ways I'm sure. I imagine there's less guys lifting weights when the girls' gym class isn't going on."

"Yep, all part of the joy of this thing we call high school."

They stepped into a cramped coaches' office off of the gym that was filled with equipment catalogues, water bottles, rolls of tape, and the good balls being saved for game days. Keith knocked a basketball off of one of the chairs for Brian and then took a seat behind the desk. "Sorry about the mess. Besides being a counsellor, I coach volleyball, which gets me an office but also means I've got to share it with all the other messy coaches." Keith took on a more serious tone as he said, "So, what type of trouble did Mr. Ewanuschuk get himself into that warranted a big city lawyer driving all the way up here?"

This discussion would require Brian to bend the confidentiality requirements, but he doubted Charley would complain. "Well, as I mentioned, Charley has retained me as his lawyer and therefore I need to keep the trouble he is in confidential, but I will tell you that he is in a tough spot and it could mean a very long time in prison."

"Ok, I won't pry. What do you need to know?"

"Frankly, Charley isn't telling me much, so anything you could tell me about his past might be helpful."

Keith leaned back in his chair and thought for a moment before saying, "Ever since you called I've been thinking back about Charley and I have to say that in fifteen years in counselling I've never seen a kid like him. We are grade nine to grade twelve here, so Charley came after he finished grade eight in a tiny town out in the sticks. Often the kids coming in from the rural schools have some issues as they go from being one of twenty students they have known their entire life to being one of five hundred people they have never met, so you expect to see a few adjustment problems."

Worried that he was going to get a dissertation on the challenges of guidance counselling rather than specifics, Brian asked, "Charley was a troublemaker from the get go?"

"Troublemaker is the wrong word. He didn't make the trouble; more like he attracted it." He paused for a second as if he were pondering how to explain before he continued, "I understand that bullies are as much a part of high school as the boys staring at the girls out there but the torment Charley endured was beyond extreme."

"He was bullied?"

"Bullied is not strong enough. No. Charley was tortured."

CHAPTER 12

It had taken three solid hours of Jenkins and Wilson making numerous phone calls to the bachelor party attendees and then making numerous threats to contact wives, but eventually, they got a description of the stranger, and a couple of guys said they thought they saw him talking to Natalie as the party was winding down. All they had was the banal description, but they decided to take a shot and see if their new person of interest was a regular at Beckham's. They also needed to eat lunch.

The downtown bar was busy with businessmen and bankers lingering past the lunch hour over pints of overpriced beer. They sat at a table near the back and ordered Cokes and burgers without looking at the menu. When the waitress returned with their food, Wilson flashed his badge and asked, "We were wondering if we could ask a few questions about a party here Saturday night."

Following the impulse of most service people when confronted by something unusual, the waitress offered to get the manager. Before Jenkins could take a second bite of his burger, a young man in the standard black golf shirt uniform of a bar manager came over to ask, "Is there some sort of problem, officers?"

His mouth full, Jenkins pointed to an empty chair, inviting the man to sit in order to avoid drawing the attention of his other customers before managing to say, "We are looking for a man who was here on Saturday night."

"I'm happy to help but there are a lot of people in here on Saturday nights."

"We understand but we were hoping this man might be a regular."

"Sure, do you have a name?"

Jenkins shook his head as he took out his notepad, "Only a description. About five foot seven. Mousey brown hair but balding. Clean shaven. Not really fat but definitely not thin with a double chin. Aged between twenty-five and thirty."

The manager rubbed his chin and said, "I don't know, that could be a lot of guys."

"On Saturday night he was wearing a dark blazer with an emblem of a bird on the pocket and he had on a massive platinum Rolex watch."

"Platinum? That's silver right? There is a guy like that who's been coming around for the last month or so. He comes in by himself and I tend to notice the loners. He normally just chats up the waitresses, throws some cash around, and then leaves alone."

"What's his name?"

"It's something boring, like John, but it's not John."

"Is there anyone else here who might know this guy?"

"Yeah, I think Lisa had a run-in with him a couple of weeks ago. I only heard the gossip but I guess he gave her a ride home at closing and then he tried to make a move. He was extra persistent and she had to push him off a bit. Apparently the guy apologized by giving her a necklace and she was ok with him coming back around. Give me a second and I'll get her over here."

The two detectives gave each other a quick look, indicating the mutual realization they might have gotten a break, before tucking back into their food.

*

"I'm supposed to lose you for a day or so. If I promise to put you somewhere nice, do you promise to keep your mouth shut about falling through the cracks?"

The guard that came to take Charley from the interview room was a diminutive elderly man with carefully groomed white hair and friendly grin. Charley, unsure what the man was talking about, settled on answering with a slight nod.

"Alright then. I can't put you back in with the other loonies since you are no longer a loony. But we've got a containment cell we use for troublemakers. You'd be all on your own but that might be a nice break after rooming with the crazies. That sound ok?"

After the brief interview with the terse woman, Charley figured he was destined for the horrors of a communal prison cell, so the idea of a night by himself was too good to be true. This realization caused him to pause, wondering if perhaps this was some type of trick. With no answer forthcoming from Charley, the congenial guard continued, "Don't like being locked up all alone? Fair enough. Tell you what, we can grab some books from the library and I'll be able to stop by a couple of times during my shift to keep away the cabin fever. Better?"

Charley nodded.

"Good. What type of books do you like?"

For the first time in two days Charley spoke a whisper, "Mystery."

*

The word "tortured" had focused Brian's attention and he sat forward as he asked the guidance counselor, "What do you mean by tortured?"

"Right from day one he had a target on his back. His appearance made him an obvious choice for bullies. He always wore this floppy engineer's kind of cap and a bulky plaid work jacket no matter the weather. Those super thick glasses that made his eyes bulge out were not exactly flattering. On top of that he had a lanky build and huge feet that made him walk with a sort of shuffling gait."

"Sure, but there must have been other kids that didn't fit in?"

"There were, but what I think gets bullies irate is when there's a kid who doesn't even try to fit in. You know there will be a poor student who may not have the right designer jeans or whatever but they'll find a cheap ball cap or a cool t-shirt or something in order to compensate somewhat. Charley never seemed to make that effort. The cool kids get annoyed by other kids who don't try to emulate the style they work so hard to create.

"Still, it was more than that. They'd all pick on him and he'd take it for a while but at some point he'd snap and push back. Normally bullied kids have learned to turtle and take it until the bullies get bored and move on. But Charley, Charley seemed to refuse to hang his head forever.

"The fact he was big enough to try and fight back didn't

help. It made it seem that picking on him was not all that cruel so the girls wouldn't try to put a stop to the torment like they might if the thugs were tormenting a weaker kid. Actually, I remember him having a bit of a bad habit of staring at the girls too long and he might have even tried to talk to them early on. I think that hurt some of their fragile, teenaged egos. You know, having an unpopular guy think he might have a chance with them. That led to them joining in on the bullying."

Brian was doubtful that this type of general harassment would be of any help so he asked, "Is there anything specific that happened that you can remember?"

"Shit, where do I begin? That first year they all played a game called Charley Tipping where you got points if you managed to trip him or knock him down. I suppose they thought it was funny because he was so clumsy. I learned about that one when he got into trouble for getting to class late all the time. He was sent to talk to me and he explained that he was waiting until the halls were empty to avoid having his feet kicked out from under him. This was one of our first meetings and I found it hard to believe so he pulled down his socks to show me his bruised and swollen ankles. They were black and blue, like someone had been repeatedly beating him with a stick. When I asked who was doing this he told me it was everyone. We managed to step in and stop that but they just moved on to Charley Trimming where they got points if they got a lock of his hair. We stomped that one out pretty quick because he ended up in the hospital getting stitches in his head when he struggled against a group of students with a pair scissors."

This barbaric behaviour shocked Brian and he asked, "Weren't you able to punish any of these little bastards? They are committing repeated assaults."

Stillman shrugged. "It was different even just a handful years ago. Now the police would be involved and kids would be getting expelled or arrested for this kind of shit, but back then all we did was suspend them. I remember that the guy who cut Charley with the scissors was actually a top student, a nerdy type who was doing it on a dare. He got suspended for a week and ended up becoming popular because of it."

"Cut another student, make more friends. That's insane."

"Yeah, I agree, but it was difficult for us to do much. And there were actually a few more severe events like that over the years. But in my mind it was the perpetual nature of it that made it so cruel, day after day of inhumane treatment with barely any letup. I remember one day very clearly: it was the day I realized how horrible this poor kid's life was. It was when Charley was in grade eleven, late in the year so he was probably seventeen by then, and I went into a classroom over the lunch break to get a magazine. He was hiding out in there reading a paperback. As you can imagine, teachers had been sending Charley to me quite regularly and I tried to be a friend so I sat down next to him to eat my sandwiches.

"I've learned that a good way to see if a kid is being neglected is to check his lunch, so early on I had made a point of seeing what Charley was bringing. I'm not sure what all went on at his home but there was obviously a lot of good old-fashioned cooking because his lunches always looked like what turn-of-the-century farmhands would get during harvest. Fat ham sandwiches on thick bread, homemade cookies, containers of hearty soup—basically a feast made from scratch. Anyway, that day in the classroom he was not eating, so I asked him where his lunch was and he sheepishly said, 'I ate it while I was waiting for the bus.'

"My guidance counselor radar kicked in as I thought maybe his parents were only sending lunches as a cover and were not feeding him at home, so I asked if he had breakfast that morning. He answered that it had been waffle day. It definitely sounded like the kid was being fed sufficiently, so I joked something about growing boys being hungry all the time. He looked back at me like I was an idiot and said, 'No, I wasn't hungry right after breakfast. I have to eat my lunch while I'm waiting for the bus or the kids take it.' While this did not really surprise me, it saddened me deeper than any of the other treatment Charley received.

"See, about half our kids come in from farms and that can mean very long bus trips, over an hour one way in a lot of cases, especially during the winter. Normally, once a kid out on a farm turns sixteen, they either get an old truck or have a friend or a sibling who has an old truck who will drive them in. Charley didn't have an old truck and had no friends or siblings so he was stuck riding the bus with a bunch of fourteen-year-olds who tormented him to no end for over an hour a day, twice a day, every day. Early on, Charley struck back at this abuse on a couple of occasions and the bus driver complained, eventually saying he was causing such a disturbance that he would no longer pick him up. He came to me nearly in tears and explained that his parents were furious about him getting kicked off the bus. I told him that I would talk to the bus driver and if he promised not to act up I could get him back on. So every day he had to ride on a bus where his food was stolen and he was harassed for an hour so he could get to a school where the torture continued before he had to ride the bus back home. And he could not even defend himself because the adults forced *him* to behave."

Keith Stillman paused for moment, apparently trying to regain his composure, before saying, "Anyway, I asked him if this lunch theft happened every day. He said that it had happened every day for months, until they broke one of his mom's canning jars and she got mad at him. That's when he came up with the idea of eating it all before the bus arrived and hiding his empty lunch box in the bushes. I tried to get him to tell me who it was, but he said most of the kids on the bus were involved, and by then, he had learned enough to know it would get worse if he got them in trouble. Then he said one more thing that I'll never forget, he said, "Mr. Stillman, they don't even eat the lunch. They just take it and make fun of it and stomp on it or throw it out the window or whatever. It's good food. Why would they waste it like that?'"

The two men sat in silence for a few moments. Brian pondered how awful an existence that would be for an adult, let alone a teenager. He could see why Charley was so shy and afraid, but he figured they would need more than high school bullying to create any effective sympathies.

"Did you ever learn anything about his home life? What was his family like?"

"I don't know much but I do know that it was just him and his parents, and his father was killed when Charley was in grade eleven."

"Killed?"

"Yeah, he was crushed working on some equipment when a jack slipped. Charley was with him when it happened, though."

Brian's eyebrows lifted at that. "Charley saw his father get crushed?"

"Yeah, but I don't think it upset him much. He was back at school within a week."

"Did you ever meet his parents?"

"Met the mother once. I tried to get them both to come in a bunch of times for a conference. It took a number of calls but finally his mother showed up, unannounced and without an appointment." The counselor shook his head with amused recollection, "I got paged to the office and a tall, birdlike lady in her fifties with thick glasses and a homemade sweater on was waiting there. The instant I saw her I immediately knew that she was Charley's mother. We spoke for over an hour—well, she spoke. Let's just say that Charley's quiet nature is not genetic but a learned trait as I'm sure he barely got to speak at home."

"What was your impression of her?"

"To be frank, she was not the smartest person and might be considered manic. It was impossible to get through to her about him not fitting in. A lot of parents don't understand what high school is like for their kids but Charley's mom was extra sheltered and extra thick. Hell, it took a lot of work just to convince her not to march down to the class he was in and confront him about not fitting in right then and there in front of everyone."

"You never met the father?"

"Never met him but I saw him once. One afternoon some jocks had taped Charley up and left him in a girls' bathroom. By the time he escaped he had missed the bus. I was coaching a practice and let him use my phone to call home for a ride. It was freezing out and I offered to let him wait inside the gym to be picked up, but he waited outside, saying he did not want to make his dad look for him. When I left the practice an hour or so later, he was still out there. I was beginning to think that I would have to drive him home myself when a rusty pickup truck slid into the parking lot. Charley slipped on the ice running to the truck and this old man in coveralls got out of the cab. I couldn't hear what was said but it was fairly clear that he was angry and scolding Charley pretty good."

Thinking perhaps there was a possibility that his client had been abused, Brian asked, "Did he miss much school?"

"Well, as you can imagine we get a fair bit of truancy around here so that the boys can work on the farms, especially in the spring and fall. Charley's family had a decent-sized farm and also ran a used machinery business, so his dad kept him home whenever he needed an extra pair of hands to work in the fields or to fix on equipment. Technically he had too many absences, but I figured he was probably safer and happier beating on rusty old tractors then he would be hiding out from his tormentors here."

"Anything else you can tell me about his home life?"

Keith thought for a minute before shrugging and saying, "No, sorry, as you know Charley's not much of a talker. The mother talked a lot but told me little, and like I said, I never met the father before he died."

The thought of the long drive back to Calgary having gained nothing but a greater sense of pity for his client prompted Brian to ask, "Is there anyone else who might have more information? Another teacher or a family member?"

"Don't think any teachers knew him better than I did. And I'm pretty sure the family was only his parents and they're gone now. I remember talking with the other teachers about Charley and his parents a fair bit and no one seemed to know anything about them other than the fact that they had the used tractor business and the mother was seen around town acting strangely. It is extremely rare in a town this size to have a family that no one knows about, but that seems to be the case here."

"No other students or a cousin or someone I might be able to speak with?"

He thought for a moment before answering, "It's a long shot but there was one kid. He was a midget, or a dwarf or whatever you are supposed to call them. He had a bunch of birth defects and was always sick or recovering from an operation or getting treatment so he was absent a lot, but when he was around he would hide out with Charley in the library playing chess."

"Charley played chess?"

"I don't know if he was any good but they did play together."

"Ok, I'm willing to try anything. Is this student still in town?"

"Yeah, he actually became a fairly successful computer consultant, setting up networks and programs and stuff for local businesses. His name is Shamus Burnes. He's got an office on main street, next to the old hotel."

CHAPTER 13

While Calgary has over a million residents, a search of the Department of Motor Vehicles showed, thankfully, only three late model green Jaguars with two doors. The waitress from Beckham's who had gotten the aggressive ride home from the man who had apparently left the party with Natalie Peterson knew him only as Jay, but she did know he drove a vintage green sports car with a silver cat hood ornament. One of the registered Jaguars was owned by a little old lady named Olga, who swore it had not left the garage since the late eighties. Another was registered to an antique car restorer who had his in pieces. The last was registered to Young Exploration Corp. Finding it odd that an oil and gas company owned a sports car, Jenkins and Wilson dug a little deeper. A corporate search showed that a man named Hugh Young was the President and CEO of Young Exploration, which was not overly helpful, but after more online searching, they discovered a newspaper article stating that he had a son named Jason. They pulled a copy of Jason Young's license. The picture matched the description provided by the partygoers and he lived two blocks from where the body had been found. The optimism that Jenkins had yesterday about the case was returning as the gap between the known and unknown was closing.

Apparently Wilson was also excited as he hurried Jenkins out of the office, exclaiming, "Come on old man, one more interview and we've got this one in the bag."

Jenkins pulled on his coat, "We're not done yet. We have no idea what this guy is going to tell us, if he tells us anything."

"I'm not buying your pessimism today. This Jay's going to tell us he drove the girl back to his place, they did what adults do and then she left. My guess is she'd head for Centre Street to try and find a cab; that would have her walking right past Charley's basement of depravity. Or maybe Chuck was doing a little peeping and saw her leave. Either way, in an hour we'll be able to put suspect with victim."

Even though he thought Wilson was right, Jenkins had been doing this for far too long to make definitive findings until all the evidence was in. Still, he had to admit he was feeling good about how this was coming together. One of the biggest questions was how their homeless suspect got a pretty woman from a crowded downtown bar to the crime scene. Now it looked like Jason Young could be the answer to that question.

As they walked out of the station he clapped Wilson on the shoulder and said, "Ok, I don't want to get ahead of ourselves, but hopefully this guy will tell us the story we need."

*

Barlock's main street was not exactly a bastion of commercial activity. It spanned two blocks and contained a hardware store, a rundown hotel, a church, a dentist's office, a library, a denture clinic, an insurance brokerage, and, for some reason, two large pharmacies. Brian found the office of Burned Out Computing squeezed between the denture clinic and one of the pharmacies. An electronic chime sounded as he stepped through the door and a voice in the back called out, "One second, please. Grab a seat."

There were two messy desks, a couple of filing cabinets, a long shelf filled with random electronics, and some mismatched guest chairs spread out on a much-worn carpet. Brian sat in the sturdiest-looking chair and waited, oddly hopeful he might hear a devastatingly traumatic story about his client. After a minute he heard a clanking followed by a man on aluminum crutches stumbling into the office.

He was not even five feet tall with an overly large, misshapen head covered in a mess of reddish hair. Using the crutches, he was swinging his stunted, crooked legs forward with each quasi step. As he rounded the desk he said, "Hello there. Sorry for keeping you waiting, my forty-yard dash time is not quite up to snuff."

Brian stood up and handed over a business card. "No problem. My name is Brian Cox."

"Shamus Burnes. Nice to meet you." Shamus awkwardly fell into a chair. "What can I do for you today?"

"I'm representing someone who I believe was a friend of

yours in high school and I was hoping you could give me a little information."

"Well, I think you may have been misinformed. Despite my good looks I was not exactly Mr. Popular in high school. I'm not sure any of my high school alums would refer to me as a friend."

Brian had to smile at this as he clarified, "I suppose 'friend' may have been an exaggeration. I was speaking with Kevin Stillman, the guidance counselor over at the school, and he said you may have spent some time with Charley Ewanuschuk?"

Shamus pondered the business card for a moment and then asked plainly, "So what did Charley do?"

"Sorry, he's my client and I can't disclose details."

Shamus looked again at the business card. "Calgary, eh? Long way for a lawyer to come to talk to people who barely knew their client. Must be something serious."

"It's serious."

The man seemed to think for the briefest moment before apparently putting together the stories in the news with this strange visit, "He the one who killed that naked girl they found handcuffed in the snow?"

Realizing he was dealing with a fairly sharp individual, Brian answered with a slight, telling grin, "I can't comment on that."

"Ok, we'll leave it at him being in serious trouble. What can I tell you?"

"Frankly, anything you can recall about Charley might be helpful as I'm trying to get a sense of his past and he's not being overly talkative."

"Must be five o'clock somewhere." Shamus pointed at a bar fridge hidden beside the shelf. "You wanna grab us a couple of beers? I'd get them myself but by the time I make it back we could both be dead of thirst."

A beer was not a bad idea, so Brian retrieved two cans. He handed one to his host before settling back into the worn-out chair and cracking open his own can. They both took a long first drink before Brian asked, "So, you remember Charley?"

Shamus scoffed out a laugh through his beer. "Hard to forget a guy like that. He was the most awkward, gangly, google-eyed, clumsy kid you could possibly imagine. And the poor bastard got berated and battered by every student in that school for four years."

"The guidance counselor used the word tortured."

"Yeah, torture would be about right. I should say though that I didn't spend that much time at the school." He lifted a crutch. "I was born with the health of a ninety-year-old so I spent a lot of my school years in and out of the hospital or at home recovering from whatever the treatment of the day was. I got picked on a fair bit due to my appearance and small size but I think I was too pathetic to be much of a fun target. Hell, sometimes my mouth would get me into trouble and the only thing that saved me was that beating up a cripple is frowned upon. Charley on the other hand could never seem to stay off the assholes' radar.

"I obviously wasn't much for sports or chasing girls and Charley just wanted to stay out of sight, so I taught him chess and, when I was around, we would play in the library at lunch. Students weren't supposed to use the library for hanging out, but we kept quiet and the librarian was willing to take pity on the handicapped kid. When I wasn't around, I think he either hid out in empty classrooms or would wander the streets around the school, hoping to be ignored."

Brian blurted out without thinking, "You felt sorry for him?"

"Of course I did. Normal guys like you can't comprehend what it is like to be bullied and picked on every day. To even come close to understanding you have to imagine if you were him. You'd get up every day and ride a school bus filled with immature juvenile delinquents who each enjoy nothing more than tormenting and humiliating you in order to prove to the other idiots how cool they are. The horrible ride would take you to a place where you face having your meager belongings destroyed, being continually embarrassed, and facing the constant potential for a beating. That's bad enough but you have to remember, you are only a teenager and everywhere you look other kids are laughing with friends, kissing girls, talking about massive parties, and playing sports while you are only trying to get through the day without being publicly ridiculed or injured. Hell, everyone is saying these are supposed to be the best days of your life and you cry yourself to sleep every night because you can't wait for them to be over.

"On top of that, because you're young and stupid you've been brainwashed into thinking there's hope. Maybe tomorrow someone will talk to you on the bus instead of tripping you. Maybe next week you'll make a friend to eat lunch with instead of having to wander around all lunch hour alone. Maybe next year things will be different and you'll be included in something, anything. Every morning he would get on that fucking yellow bus and have to relearn that it was never going to get better. I may not have had a great time in high school but I was not tortured like that. So, yeah, I felt sorry for him."

Brian realized he had been avoiding this contemplation, hiding behind the guise of lawyerly indifference, but now, confronted straight on by the thought, he was immensely saddened by how Charley had been treated. Now the man-child was sitting in a jail cell, waiting for whatever fresh hell was about to be piled upon him. He took a drink and forced himself to push the sympathy and worry aside so he could think rationally. Despite the horrendous treatment, having a brutal high school experience would not be enough to help Charley, so he decided to explore another angle. "Did you ever meet his parents?"

Shamus gave a bit of a nod and a sigh. "I did. They definitely did not help out Charley's cause."

"How do you mean?"

"I went over to his place for his sixteenth birthday party. His dad was the standard grumpy old farmer type and ignored us. His mom seemed out of it and rambled on about the food most of the time. They seemed to live in a secluded time warp. Walking into their house you would have thought it was the 1950s. They had a TV but it only got two fuzzy channels and there was no computer or video games to be seen. Their nearest neighbour was five miles away and, given the way they reacted to me being there, I think visitors were rare. Entertainment in the Ewanuschuk house seemed to be limited to chores, reading books, more chores and, maybe, an occasional card game when the weather was too bad to do chores. Charley spent all of his free time working, either in the fields or fixing those rust piles his dad tried to sell as useable. Now that I think about it, his dad had two full sections of land and his newest piece of machinery was twenty years old the day he bought it, which means they must have been working almost around the clock for the two of them to get a crop on and off on their own."

"Did you ever suspect that perhaps there was something more malicious occurring at home besides his parents' being out of touch and working him too much?"

"Can't ever say what happens in someone else's home but I don't think so. Like I said I was only there for his birthday party. Well, it was not much of a party. It was me, Charley, and a couple of teachers' kids. You probably don't know this, but teachers make their kids go to the unpopular parties. My birthdays were littered with teachers' kids. Anyway, there was not much to do out there, but we did shoot an old shot gun at magpies and his mom made us sundaes. It was boring and his dad was absent for most of the time, but there was not the tension I would expect to feel in an abusive home."

Hearing this, Brian wondered if anyone else had ever been disappointed to learn a child had not been abused.

*

Charley awoke with a start from a familiar nightmare where he endlessly wandered the empty streets of the city in the middle of a frozen night carrying a large ring of keys, looking for something but never able to remember what he was looking for. It took a moment for him to realize he was in a cell, lying on a cot under bright, fluorescent lights. He could hear some sort of commotion occurring nearby and he instinctively scrambled to his feet before he recalled he was alone in the room.

Thankfully, as he stood in the cell, the noise in the hallway died down quickly after some authoritative yelling. Charley picked up the book he had fallen asleep reading and laid back on the cot. Yesterday the elderly guard had brought him two novels and a spaghetti dinner with extra dessert, and had checked in on him numerous times. History had made him wary of kindness, but at this moment he was content. Years on the streets made him accustomed to not knowing what would happen next. He had learned that if things were going well he should enjoy them because it would not last and another enjoyable moment might never arrive. For now he would happily read a book until the lights went out and then he would sleep in a warm, safe bed with no thought towards what the inevitable morning might bring. Because even though he never had a reason to assume that anything but deeper hardships were coming, Charley knew that to ensure being miserable, one only needed to continually expect misery.

CHAPTER 14

Jason Young's driver license led Jenkins and Wilson to a monstrosity of a house above the river bank overlooking downtown. The area had become trendy for the new rich over the last ten years or so. It was becoming very hard to build a new house in the city's traditionally wealthy neighbourhoods as a new build required tearing down a pre-existing expensive home. Up here on the ridge, though, the existing homes were relatively cheap, simple dwellings on wide lots with breathtaking cityscapes, mature landscaping, and short commutes. As a result, massive mansions now loomed over the few remaining pre-war bungalows that had survived the influx of development.

The detectives walked up the long drive to the columned porch, but Jenkins noticed that the huge front window was lit up and had no curtains so he motioned to Wilson and they detoured to take a look inside. The living room was a wide, empty expanse of parquet hardwood flooring with only a big recliner and massive flat screen TV for furnishings. Some sort of army video game was being played by a pudgy man sitting in the leather chair with a half-eaten pizza on the floor next to him. Jenkins figured the man was probably in his late twenties but was dressed like a teenager in basketball shorts, a hooded sweatshirt, and bare feet.

Wilson looked at Jenkins, but he could only shrug in response as he had no idea why this man was apparently living like a college student in a multimillion dollar house without furniture. With the voyeurism done, they knocked on the door. When the man answered, Wilson immediately shoved his badge in his face. "Calgary Police. Are you Jason Young?"

The chubby man only stared mutely at them, so Wilson pushed inside as he said, "We have some questions for you about Saturday night."

Jenkins was carefully watching Jason's reaction and he saw him visibly blanch as he muttered out, "Um, oh well, uh, I'm sort of busy right now…"

"Yeah, we saw you were just about to level up on your little arcade game there."

Jason's voice got higher pitched as he complained, "You were watching me? You can't be peeping in windows. That's illegal."

"Fine, call the police. While we're waiting for them to get here we can talk about your date with Natalie Peterson."

Jenkins would have preferred to not let Young know the purpose of their interview right away, but they also had to be concerned when dealing with someone of means that if they took too long the subject would get smart and call in a lawyer who would promptly put an end to any meaningful discussion. The technique they had settled on was a blitz of intimidation in order to overwhelm Jason into talking about the incident right away. Jenkins slammed the door closed behind him so the witness was standing between the two detectives who were glaring down at him.

"Um, I'm not sure what you are talking about, so..."

Wilson quickly pressed his finger into the soft man's chest, "Ok, Jason, you want to play it that way, I'll explain to you what happened. You have no friends so you bought your way into a stranger's bachelor party, hired one of the strippers to come home with you, things got a little rough and she ended up dead. You put her naked body in that fancy Jaguar that your daddy bought for you and dumped her at a construction site to be buried under the snow."

"No, no, that's not what happened, not what happened at all."

Jenkins leaned in close and said, "Alright, Jason, then you tell us how it happened."

The man glanced widely back and forth between the two detectives as if looking for help. Seeing that no one was going to save him, he opened his lips as if he was about to answer, then touched a finger to his chin but did not speak. Jenkins, through years of interrogation experience, recognized this as a sign a witness was preparing to lie, the mouth impatiently waiting for the brain to concoct a believable story. Then, as if this minor pause in the pressure allowed him to realize or remember something, his opened lips slowly evolved into a grin.

"Actually, I don't think I need to tell you anything." He brushed past Wilson and plucked a business card off a side table.

Jenkins knew what was coming even before Jason Young thrust out the card and smugly said, "If you have questions you can call my lawyer. He's with the firm of Rainer Hopkins. Now if you'll excuse me, as I said, I'm busy."

*

Brian and Shamus had spent the better part of another beer talking about Charley's family. According to the rumour mill, which had run despite having very thin information to grind, after Charley's father died his mother quickly married a man from their church. This opportunistic suitor apparently had little interest in farming and no interest in being a stepfather. Within a year of the matrimonies the farm and used tractor business were sold for an estimated seven figures, the newlyweds moved to a warmer climate, and Charley disappeared.

It was getting late but Brian wanted to follow up on something the guidance counselor had mentioned before leaving, so he asked, "What about girls? The counselor mentioned that Charley might have stared too much."

"Shit, you so old you don't remember high school? We all stared at the girls, even the hopeless guys like me who couldn't get laid in a whorehouse dressed in hundred dollar bills."

"Fair enough but I was wondering if maybe Charley was more lecherous than the rest."

Shamus' grinned. "You're not sure if he did it or not, are you?"

Brian thought about giving the spiel about innocent until proven guilty and doing everything to give Charley the fullest defence possible no matter what he thought. But looking at the sharp eyed Shamus, he figured he would not be impressed by such technicalities, so instead he stowed the legal jargon and answered frankly, "I don't have a clue. You think I'd come all the way up here to take shots in the dark if I knew what the hell happened?"

"What, you didn't come to Barlock for the culture? We've

got a MacDonald's now, you know?"

"Unfortunately I've got to be back in Calgary for a bail hearing tomorrow so I won't have a lot of time to take in the sights."

"Okay, so your question was whether Charley ever overdid it with the girls?"

Brian nodded.

"Intellectually Charley was a long way from being a genius but he was probably pretty close to average if not smarter than average. Socially, though, he was closer to an eight-year-old than an eighteen-year-old. It's tough enough for anyone in high school to try and figure out girls but for a guy like Charley, with no friends, no siblings, very out-of-touch parents and no access to basic popular culture references, it was beyond impossible." Shamus took a drink before continuing, "Yeah, he stared too much at the girls but it wasn't perverted. More like a kid looking at a strange animal in a zoo—he doesn't know what it is but it gets his full amazed attention. I suppose it would be fair to say that it would not be hard to believe that a guy like that, I mean someone filled with unknown and unsatisfied urges, might get into trouble over a woman."

This concerned Brian, but while he was afraid to hear the answer, he still asked, "Can you recall any specific incidents where he got in trouble over girls?"

"No, there was nothing like that," Shamus said, looking down at his beer can with a ponderously sad expression, "but there was a prank pulled on him. Beginning of grade twelve this older girl transferred in from a school in the city. She must have been over twenty. Not sure why she was so late in graduating but I would not be surprised to learn that it was because she was in either a penal facility or a maternity ward. Her name was actually Barbie, if you can believe that. Anyway, she was hot in a trashy sort of way—tall, big blonde hair, lots of makeup, tight jeans, and flirtatious as hell. I think at first she loved all the attention she was getting from the excited farm boys, but I think she quickly got bored of their fumbling. Apparently she figured that Charley would be good for some entertainment.

"You know how some memories stick? I'm not talking

about the things you'd expect to remember like graduations or a first fuck or whatever but those odd memories of mundane events that come back crystal clear when you are on a long drive or walking the dog. One of those memories for me is of Charley and me sitting in the library over lunch. We were playing chess. He sucked at chess so I'd let him take a couple of pieces before I'd start paying attention and I even remember that he was winning when it happened. Barbie had gotten in trouble for something and was in the library doing detention. I noticed that Charley kept looking over my shoulder at her. I whispered to him that it was not smart to stare but he didn't stop. Before long she came over and I was cringing, waiting for a barrage of insults but instead she simply said something about Charley being a good chess player.

"Confused, I looked up at her and she was playing with her blonde hair with a flirtatious look in her eyes. She was wearing one of those shirts with the really wide neck they had back then, the kind that always look like they were about to slip over their shoulders and fall the floor, and she leaned forwarded so her shirt flopped down and we could both see her lacy red bra. I only took a glimpse so as not to get caught looking but Charley was transfixed. She had to notice—hell he was practically sticking his nose in there—but she didn't do anything, just let him stare. After he got a good long look, she gave him a peck on his cheek before wiping the smear of red lipstick off and saying, 'A good luck kiss,' before sauntering away.

"See, any normal kid would've realized in an instant that she was playing with him. But not Charley. He bit, hook line and sinker. I was in the hospital for a while after that and when I got back to school he was beaming. He told me about how Barbie talked with him every day. She even ate lunch with him one day in the cafeteria. He had been going to that school for over three years and that was the first time he had actually eaten his lunch in the cafeteria. Needless to say, he was overwhelmed with the idea that he not only had a friend, but a girlfriend, a hot girlfriend at that. That juvenile hope I mentioned, waking up every day thinking that things would change, that probably blinded him as he clearly believed the horror was over. A fucking afterschool movie come to life."

Brian could see where this was going and his stomach tensed

at the idea. "She was jerking him around for her amusement?

Shamus drained his beer and set the can down. "Worse than that. She told him that she wanted to meet up with him behind the gym. Hell, I don't even think Charley knew what that meant but even a man raised by wolves knows he wants to be alone with a woman so he went back there with her. She kissed him and then told him to drop his pants. He was wearing old man boxer shorts and was obviously keen to continue. I'm not sure what the end plan was because a couple of the usual assholes that she had hiding behind the equipment shed with a video camera started laughing. Charley had numerous bad experiences with people jumping out at him so he tried to pull up his pants while running away, which he was not coordinated enough to do. He ended up on the ground, looking up at Barbie while she had a good laugh at him. This was before uploading videos to the internet was really an option, but the cool kids still showed it every chance they got.

"I even saw it once when some guys played it in the AV room. Charley was lying there in his underwear, suddenly realizing that the girl he thought was going to rescue him from his lonely hell had only paid attention to him in order to ridicule him. He didn't come to school after that for days. I remember because I was worried he might have dropped out or maybe even done himself in. I called his house to check. The idea of Charley getting a call was apparently unbelievable as I had to explain numerous times to his mom that I wanted to talk to him. When she finally put him on I asked if he was quitting school and he muttered that he couldn't quit because he was too close. Sure enough he showed up the next week and continued shuffling down the halls while enduring the increased barrage of jeers."

Brian looked out the window to see that the sun had set and snow was falling. While the trip had been interesting, he suddenly felt tired as he realized the information would not help Charley and he had a long drive back. He sat his can on the desk and stood, "Well, thanks for your time and the beer. I better get on the road."

"Sure, hopefully some of this will be some help to Charley."

"Frankly, I'm hoping we won't even need the information,

but thanks nonetheless. I never would have gotten Charley to tell me half of what I've learned today."

As Brian moved to the door Shamus said, "Thinking back now, he was always quiet but he did talk some when I first met him. After his dad died, I remember, he quieted up even more, which I suppose makes sense, but then he really went silent after Barbie. It was more than just being silent. His quietness changed, he was always sort of shy or unsure before but after that his muteness became something different. I'm not sure if he was embarrassed or ashamed or what."

Looking back at Shamus, he spoke without thinking, "Maybe, after all of that, he wanted to disappear, wanting nothing but to be ignored by everyone."

CHAPTER 15

Jenkins appreciated that the chief of police did not have an easy job, but at the same time the man seemed to enjoy over-complicating matters. Wilson and Jenkins had explained to the chief that they were confident they knew how Natalie Peterson had been transported to the neighbourhood where her body was found, but the owner of the vehicle was refusing to cooperate. Jenkins was certain that if they spent another day or two looking into the matter they would be able to find someone who put Jason Young and Natalie Peterson together on the night she disappeared. From there they could get a search warrant for Young's house, which would likely lead to evidence placing her in the home. Facing that evidence, Jenkins figured Young would have no choice but to explain what had happened or risk being charged himself. Once Young started cooperating, they would be able to determine how Natalie Peterson ended up at the construction site.

Regardless of Jenkins having this sensible investigation plan that would lead to more certainty, the chief was adamant that they already had the right suspect in custody and he was to be charged now. The media was clambering over this case now but something else might come along and steal away their attention. The chief congratulated them on the good job they had done catching the killer and explained that they should get the public recognition for their work.

The chief foolishly figured that after the charges were laid against Ewanuschuk they could still go back and get Young to talk. He tried to tell him that Young had top-notch legal advisors who would immediately realize that, since they had charged someone else with the murder, Jason was not at risk and all he would get by talking to the police was embarrassment. Despite Jenkins loudly making this argument, the chief persisted that they had enough to lay the charge now and that was what was going to happen.

He stormed out of the office and was fuming at his desk. For twenty years he had been forced to deal with a bureaucracy that was more concerned with statistics and public perception than actually doing the job properly, and for twenty years he had managed to get things done despite this system. But now, the idea of having the last investigation of his career undermined for the sake of media attention irritated him to new heights. He was seriously contemplating speeding up his retirement plans when his phone rang, providing him with a reprieve from having to decide. "Yeah, this is Jenkins."

"Hi, Randall, this is Cheryl at dispatch. We received a call from an individual with information on the Natalie Peterson case. The caller hung up pretty quick without giving a full name but I thought you might want to hear it."

He was immediately doubtful that this would be any help. Murder cases always got a large number of call-ins. Normally it was wannabe cops trying to help by pointing out ludicrously irrelevant things they had noticed from the reports in the news or it was crazies expounding about vague conspiracy theories. The ones that didn't leave a name were often in the latter category. Still, there was no harm in listening; in fact, it might be amusing and he could use a laugh.

"Sure, send it on up, Cheryl, thanks."

All calls to the police station were digitally taped and converted into computer files. Cheryl emailed the file to him so he could listen to it on his computer:

"Calgary Police Service."

"Yes, I have some information on the Natalie Peterson killing."

"Ok, sir, what is your name?"

"Steve."

"Steve who?"

"Look, I'm not stupid and I'm only going to tell you my first name. Now I know you have Charley in jail on this. I was working with Charley the other day and he told me that he took a pair of her underwear as a souvenir. He said he hid them in a duct in the basement where he was squatting. He was saying that no one would find them until they finished

building the house and turned the furnace on for the first time. This Charley's crazy and he should not be out walking the streets."

"Ok, please stay on the line to talk to one of the detectives on the case so he can take your statement."

"No, you just tell the detectives they need to search heating vents in the basement. They'll find the dead girl's panties and then you can get this nut job off the streets."

Jenkins listened to it again. And then again. It was intriguing. There were enough specifics in the message that he thought it might have some merit. The man seemed rational and he did not ask for anything other than that they go and look. He decided that it would be worth checking out mainly because finding the victim's underwear in the basement would make him confident in charging their suspect, which would let him avoid having to stand up to the chief. He hollered for Wilson to find some crime scene techs.

*

"Don't worry, the roads are pretty good and I'm not tired." Brian had called home to let Anna know he was on his way but that it would be late before he made it home.

"I don't like you driving by yourself when it's snowing but at least you have winter tires on."

He felt a twinge of guilt. He had told Anna he went to get winter tires put on his car, but when he found out it would cost two hundred dollars, he opted to pay down the credit card bill instead. Deciding that hurtling down an icy highway in the dark was not the place to have an argument over trust in a relationship, Brian chose to ignore that point and instead said, "Heard some interesting stories but nothing that I think is very helpful from a legal standpoint."

"Interesting like what?"

With his phone on hands-free mode, Brian spent a good thirty minutes telling the snow-filled blackness beyond his windshield about the horrible treatment Charley had been forced to endure. Anna let him tell the long story uninterrupted but for a few muttered comments of disgusted disbelief. When he was finally done, she asked, "What about his family? Where were they in all of this?'

He explained how Charley's parents were secluded and not in touch with what was occurring. He then told of how Charley's father had been killed in an accident and before long he had been abandoned by his mother.

Anna asked, "He manages to graduate despite all of that suffering and all he gets by way of reward is being put on a bus by his crazy mother, who sells the farm and runs off with some new guy? And none of that helps him now?"

"Not really. Definitely not enough for a defence of insanity. Maybe it will help create some sympathy with the jury or with the judge on sentencing but if we need to play that card he's already screwed."

"What happens now?"

"Tomorrow he likely gets charged with murder, I meet with him before the bail hearing and explain he needs to plead not guilty and we push for a trial as soon as possible because I'm worried about how he'll manage."

"You mean because they'll hold him in jail until the trial?"

"Yeah, he's got no community ties, no way to pay a bond, and my little mental capacity trick failed so he'll be locked up in the remand center."

"How long to get to trial?"

"At least six months, even with me pushing."

"They can hold him in jail for half a year without trial? Based on what you told me that will be tantamount to hell for this guy."

"It'd be hell for anyone. For Charley I'm worried it could be permanently disabling. But there's nothing I can do about that now, so it's not my biggest worry."

"What's your biggest worry?"

"Clay Matthews seemed confident they were going to lay the information for murder tomorrow. Prosecutors like to bat a thousand so they generally don't place a charge with the sort of weak circumstantial evidence we know about. My biggest worry is they have a smoking gun I don't know about because Charley's not telling me everything."

After saying goodnight to Anna, Brian was left alone with only his car's straining engine noise. Normally he would subconsciously reach for the radio to find some musical distraction. Now, though, he did not want to be distracted as his mind pondered what he had been told about the sad young man who was now his client.

Brian had been popular in high school. Brian had been popular his whole life. Looking back now he realized that, while he did not think he had been cruel to anyone, he definitely had not been friendly to those he had seen as beneath him. As the miles passed, a flood of remorse began to course through him. The faces of those he had easily mistreated passed before him in an endless parade. The college roommate who had been too shy to say anything about Brian not paying his fair share from time to time. That associate at the firm he could always get to take the garbage files he wanted to avoid. The drunken girl at that resort in Mexico. His kindly great aunt whom he always knew he could turn to for a quick hundred bucks. The girlfriend who was so desperate to have a boyfriend she would do anything for him.

Now that he knew about Charley, Brian knew that all of those he had mistreated were people who had deserved kindness and gotten coldness instead. None of his transgressions were overly egregious, but the cumulative effect of recalling all of his poor behaviour pressed on his chest as he realized there was nothing he could ever do to correct the past wrongs. While he had already planned to help Charley, he now needed to help him. He wanted the fee, and a part of him, at least, wanted the recognition and challenge that would come from running the murder trial, but perhaps the best thing for Charley would be for him to get a more seasoned lawyer.

*

The crime scene technicians were obviously not pleased with having to go back to the freezing basement, but one look at Jenkins's face convinced them not to complain. Jenkins and Wilson stood in the stairway, impatiently watching the technicians tediously setting up flood lights and meticulously arranging video cameras before finally beginning to search the ducts. After setting up all the equipment, it took less than two minutes of actually searching before a technician, with his gloved hand in an open vent, called out, "I've got something here."

He pulled out a pair of tiny, black lace underwear, and Wilson immediately clapped Jenkins on the back and said, "We've got 'im."

Jenkins knew that most cases needed a break in order to be solved. Some of his most difficult files had been closed when he had stumbled over damaging evidence left behind by unintelligent criminals or when someone unknown called out of the blue to tell him what he needed to know. Standing in the dank basement, it appeared to him that this case had gotten its break, and while he still had some concerns over how Charley came into contact with Natalie, he was now confident he was their guy.

"Looks like it, but we need to prove that they are hers. Get some good pictures; we are going to pay another visit to our party boy right now."

During the drive to O'Connor's townhouse, Wilson chatted away about how lucky they had been to get that call and how useless the crime scene technicians were for not having checked the heating vents initially. Jenkins merely nodded, inwardly glad that they appeared able to put this case to bed but not willing to let the younger detective see him jump to conclusions.

When they arrived, he banged on the townhouse's door, eager to get the answer he was expecting. After a moment Daniel O'Connor answered the door. He was barefoot, dressed in designer jeans and an untucked dress shirt, holding a heavy tumbler of icy whiskey. He was the very model of a youthful businessman casually relaxing after work. However, upon realizing who was there, obvious fear crossed O'Connor's face. Before anyone could speak, Jenkins heard an impatient woman's voice call out from inside, "Who is it?"

O'Connor called back into the house, "Um, census takers. I'll be right there." Looking back to them, he whispered, "I've told you all I know already."

"One more question."

Glancing back over his shoulder, he asked, "Do we need to do this right now?"

Jenkins shoved a digital camera in his face and asked, "Is this the underwear Natalie Peterson was wearing at the bachelor party."

O'Connor looked quickly at the picture before distractedly saying, "Yeah, yeah, those are them."

Annoyed by this lack of focus, he thrust the picture back into the man's face. "This is important. Are you sure?"

"Yes, I'm fucking sure. She didn't have them on long, but I got pretty close to them and I remember the little bow and the weird lace."

"Were any pictures taken at the party?"

"No cameras are allowed at parties like that but I'm sure they are them, ok?"

Jenkins turned away without answering. Walking to the car, trailed by a mist of frozen breath, he told Wilson, "Type up the information against Charles Ewanuschuk. Charge murder, first degree due to forcible confinement. I'll swear it before the justice of the peace first thing tomorrow morning."

*

Another small room. This one had two chairs, a tiny table, and, like all of the other small rooms, it had no windows. He had been put in here and told to wait for his lawyer.

After a few minutes Brian, looking a little harried, came in and sat down, "Ok Charley, we don't have much time but we need to talk about a couple of things."

Charley was still nervous around Brian but he was able to answer, "Ok."

"First, you are now facing a murder charge which is obviously very serious. I need to explain that I am very new at criminal defence work and have never had a murder case before. Because of all of the media attention that this is getting there may be very expensive, senior lawyers out there who will be willing to take over your case. Do you understand that?"

Having been abandoned before he thought he understood what was happening and said, "You don't want to help me anymore."

Brian shook his head and said, "No, that's not it. I want to help you. I'm just thinking that there may be someone out there who is more qualified to help you. Do you want to try and get a more senior lawyer to represent you?"

The idea of meeting with another lawyer was untenable to Charley and he liked how Brian talked to him. He referred to them as a "we" and they had joked together. He looked up for a brief moment and whispered, "No."

He could not tell if the lawyer was relieved by this answer or not as Brian hesitated, looking at him as if he was pondering if he should push this point or not before he continued talking. "Ok. The second thing we need to discuss is your plea. We are going to have to enter a plea of guilty or not guilty. At this stage there is no point in pleading guilty, so we should enter a plea of not guilty. Do you agree with that?"

Charley nodded.

*

Sweating in his one passable suit, exhausted from having gotten home late from Barlock and then being too stressed to sleep, Brian nervously addressed the court, "My Lady, we were only told of this murder charge this morning. I cannot possibly be expected to have developed a proper bail application in that short a period of time."

Without looking up from her papers the judge said, "Mr. Cox, I understand your position but I am not sure what delaying this hearing by a day will do. According to the Crown your client has no address, no employment, no family, and cannot even produce a piece of identification. Can you refute any of that?"

Brian was neither glad nor upset when he learned that the judge assigned to Charley's case was Vivian Rothborg. She was a former law professor and highly respected member of the bench. She knew the rules extremely well but was also smart enough to not allow technicalities to overrule common sense, which Brian appreciated as he was sure his inexperience would lead to a few procedural blunders. However, she was also not the type of judge to provide too much sympathy to the accused based on their past troubles, which made the information he had gotten in Barlock less likely to be helpful if it came to sentencing.

Faced with this question, he had no choice but to answer the judge truthfully, "No my Lady, I cannot refute those claims."

"Then whether I decide today or tomorrow or next week the answer is going to be the same. The accused will be remanded without bail. Mr. Cox, how does your client plead?"

"Not guilty."

"Are you prepared to discuss scheduling today?"

Clay Matthews jumped to his feet behind the prosecutor's table to interrupt, just as Brian had hoped he would. "Yes, my Lady. The Crown would like to proceed as quickly as possible to a trial, and given the heinous nature of this crime and our clear evidence, we are prepared to meet any dates the court sees fit."

This statement was an obvious bit of grandstanding for the numerous reporters in the gallery. Justice Rothborg gave Mathews a long look over her reading glasses. This was a silent statement that judges used as a way of letting a lawyer know that his behaviour was not appreciated without having a formal reprimand show up on the transcript.

After the minor reprieve she turned her attention to Brian, probably assuming she was going to hear him complain that the prosecutor was skipping over the preliminary inquiry stage. A preliminary inquiry was a hearing at which the prosecutor presented the basics of the case and the judge would then determine if there was enough evidence to warrant a trial. The hearing was basically a sham as the threshold was very low, and if a prosecutor was willing to charge someone, he always made sure there was enough evidence to warrant a trial. Still, the inquiry was useful to defense lawyers as it allowed them to get a sense of what the prosecution was planning for trial. And even if Brian was not going to complain about this procedural leap-frogging, surely he would give the normal song and dance about needing as much time as possible to prepare given the seriousness of the accusations against his client. Instead he responded, "Given that my client is innocent I do not believe he should spend one more day locked up than is absolutely necessary, so we too would like to have the trial as soon as possible."

As he spoke, he watched Matthews and received a small amount of satisfaction at the look of worry crossing his face. Rothborg continued eagerly, "Great. I've just had a trial settle and have got a week-long opening in five months starting May 3rd. Will that work?"

With a very open schedule, Brian was able to answer immediately, "Certainly, thank you ma'am."

Despite his little speech, there was no way that Matthews could have suspected that the trial would be in only five months and there was definitely no way that a busy senior prosecutor would have an opening that soon nor the time to prepare that quickly. He flipped frantically through his calendar, probably trying to find a reasonable excuse as to why he could not meet that deadline, but with all the reporters in attendance, no matter what he said now it would be reported that he had been the one to delay the trial. After a few moments, his shoulders slumped and he responded, "I will need to move a few things around, but I should be able to make that work."

With a slight smirk, as she also realized Matthews had painted himself into a corner, the judge stated, "The court appreciates that, Mr. Matthews. The clerk will be in touch to schedule the preliminary inquiry and set out other required dates. If there are no other matters—" she paused to see if either lawyer was going to raise a point and, when neither did, she concluded, "Court adjourned."

He had to grab Charley, who had been sitting next to him and staring at the floor through the whole process, to prod him to stand with everyone else. The bailiff came over to lead Charley out. Charley looked up at him, and even through the thick glasses, the panic and desperation were clear. He could think of nothing reassuring to say, so the bailiff took Charley's elbow and gently pulled him away.

Brian fell back down into his chair. He had just scheduled his first murder trial. A murder trial where his client might well be innocent.

PART TWO
CHAPTER 16

A sharp blow to the shoulder shocked Charley back awake. He stumbled to keep his feet. Experience had taught him not to reach out with his hands or he would be punished, so he kept his arms down, letting his face hit the cement wall in order to regain his balance before returning to stand at rigid attention in the corner of his cell. His cellmate cackled quietly behind him, "No sleeping, Chuck. Nice use of your face though."

He knew it was the middle of the night as the cell was only lit with greyish light coming in from the hall. The shrieking cramps in his legs and lower back pleaded with Charley to sit but he couldn't. For weeks now this had been the favourite game of his cellmate, forcing Charley to stand in the corner all night without moving. The demented man rarely slept and would sit on the edge of his bunk for hours playing solitaire in the dim light, watching Charley carefully out of the corner of his eye. If he moved or slumped at all he would whip him with a long wire made out of a smuggled coat hanger. One time Charley made the mistake of leaning against the wall and he had been strangled to the point of unconsciousness. Another time, after three nights in a row of this treatment, he had collapsed from exhaustion and had awoken to the crazed man pummelling him.

He had considered attacking his tormentor. Charley was larger but his cellmate was more powerfully built, and judging by the scars on his face and body, the man was no stranger to fighting. He did not fear being killed, but over the months, Brian had gone to a great deal of work preparing for the trial, and he did not want his only friend's effort to go to waste. He had thought about complaining to guards, but he had learned long ago that reporting mistreatment more often than not only made things worse, so he remained silent.

Unable to escape the abuse, Charley tried to use his normal mental techniques for ignoring torment, but the pain was too great and he could not force his exhausted mind into distraction. All he could do was stare through the grey dimness at the cinderblock wall and silently plead for morning to come.

*

The trip to Houston had not gone as well as Hugh had hoped and now, despite the late hour, he was stuck in a long line at customs. The sale of his company had been completed on schedule, but as numerous business reporters had pointed out, the purchase price had been significantly lower than what had been expected. He figured that the gossip on the street would be that Hugh had gotten beaten at the negotiation table. What had actually happened was that a piece of damaging information had slipped through in the due diligence process. The Korean purchasers had learned that Young Exploration had a large number of indirectly owned dry gas wells which they had not properly abandoned. This was the type of liability that Hugh would normally be able to keep buried, but with the chaos surrounding Jason and the murder, he had not managed the process closely enough. The mistake was costly not just because the value of the company was reduced, but because Hugh could not allow the fact that he had doctored his books to become public knowledge or he could face regulatory scrutiny. The Koreans easily used this leverage to beat the purchase price down.

Young Exploration was supposed to be his last company, the crowning jewel on a thirty-year career. Now, however, with the sale being touted as a bust, he found that he could not walk away. Retirement would have to wait. He had gone to Houston to purchase some shale gas rights to vend into a new startup, but Hugh had rushed the deal, and looking back, he was certain he had overpaid.

Waiting in the unmoving line, he checked his voicemail. There were two messages from Jason. With the trial approaching, his son was getting nervous about testifying and was looking to Hugh to find a way for him to get out of it. Jason could not comprehend that sometimes there were obligations which could not be avoided. Hugh erased Jason's messages and put the phone away. Jacob Poetker had spent numerous billable hours prepping Jason on his testimony, and that would have to suffice.

Hugh had to admit that he was surprised with the generally

competent way his son had handled himself this far. The police had interviewed him at length, and with Poetker's help, he had managed to stick to the story that he had picked up Natalie Peterson at the bar, brought her home, drank with her, had sex with her, paid her two hundred and forty dollars, and then she left. Jacob had thought it would be smart to mention that he had paid her as it made the story more believable, given the disparity in attractiveness and the fact that people were not inclined to lie about paying for sex. Jason also managed to convey that he was very regretful he had let the woman leave by herself—without sounding too guilty—by saying he was too intoxicated drive and she was adamant that she had to go despite the hour. Jason had even been asked by the police to confirm that the pair of underwear they found in the basement was what she had been wearing that night, which made Hugh confident that the police were looking at the homeless man as their only suspect.

Regardless, he could not rest easily until he heard the judge pronounce someone else guilty for this mess. Putting on his familiar fake smile, he handed his passport over to the custom agent.

*

The conference room in the prosecutor's office was littered with binders, coffee cups, and note pads. As much as he hated this part of the job, Jenkins took solace in the fact that this would be the last time he would need to suffer through trial preparation. He had put in his retirement papers two months ago, his desk was cleared off, and the Natalie Peterson murder would be his last case.

Clay Matthews, his jacket off and tie loosened, stood up to stretch as he said, "Alright, that's all the questions we'll be asking you. It's pretty straightforward and I think you've got it down cold."

Jenkins merely nodded. Prosecutors always came across as condescending in these preparation meetings. They never said it outright, but it was made clear they believed they were the only ones who could possibly understand all the intricacies, strategies, and technicalities of a criminal trial. There was a definitive pecking order in the justice system, with prosecutors at the top, and they did not want people to forget it. Jenkins had long ago learned that once a detective laid an information against a suspect the case was out of his hands as the prosecutor took over responsibility for getting the conviction. At that point, advice from lowly cops is not accepted, and the detective's role reverted to that of mere evidence, not that much different than a fingerprint.

It was coming up on nine at night. Jenkins would never understand why prosecutors waited to the last possible minute to take care of these things. It was not like they didn't know this trial was coming for the last five months. Matthews settled back into his chair and said, "Ok, let's move on and run through some of the questions we think the defence is going to ask you on cross."

Not that long ago, the thought of being crossed examined on one of his files made Jenkins nervous. But for over twenty years now, defence lawyers had been questioning every tiny imperfection in his work and he had survived each of those tests handily, so testifying no longer worried him. For over an hour, they went through the questions he could expect. The cross examination would likely focus on there not being any witnesses to put the woman with the accused, about finding none of the victim's blood or hair in the basement, and so forth. Finally, Matthews said, "I figure that besides just poking holes in our case, they'll try and point the finger at Jason Young as a possible alternative suspect to create reasonable doubt. You interviewed Young?"

"Yes. We tried to talk to him at his home before charging Ewanuschuk but Young requested counsel, so we met with him and his lawyer a couple of days later. That's when he told us the story that's in the file."

Matthews, playing the role of defence counsel, immediately jumped on this: "Story? You don't believe him?"

Jenkins sighed. He would not miss the dramatic theatrics by lawyers over simple word choices. While he did not think that Young had lied about any key points in his interview, Jenkins did not fully trust him. For one it had been clear from the outset that he had carefully practiced what to say as his answers had been too concise to be impromptu. Plus, it was odd for a perfectly innocent witness to have a very high-priced lawyer holding his hand at an interview. Even more odd was that the grown man had his powerful businessman father wait outside the interview room for him for three hours in the middle of the day. Jason's father, Hugh Young, had even accosted the detectives afterward to explain that if they slander his son with any bogus charges, he would sue them personally, thoroughly, and repeatedly. Despite these oddities, Young's answers had not faltered significantly under pressure, so Jenkins chalked up the high-priced lawyer, the anxiously waiting parent, and the practiced answers to Young being the spoiled son of a rich family who was trying to avoid scandal and, possibly, a nuisance lawsuit by the victim's relatives.

Jenkins answered Matthews with frustration clear in his tone, "I believe the important parts of what he told us but I think he is probably sugarcoating his behaviour a bit for the newspapers."

"Ok, well, let's leave that last part out of our testimony."

Another annoyance. Prosecutors liked to refer to police testimony as *our* testimony, as if they were sitting on the stand with the detective. Jenkins responded, "Sure, we'll do that. Anything else?"

Matthews, apparently ambivalent to Jenkins's chilled tone, looked at his notes as he said, "The defence got an order to have Young's car examined for damage. Nothing was found. Can you think of any reason why they would look for damage on his car?"

This surprised Jenkins. "No. Young told us that he drove Natalie from the bar to his house and then she left on foot. There was no reason to check his car. Why'd they say they want to see it?"

Matthews looked back down at his notes and casually answered, "Don't worry about it. If you don't know, then you don't know."

This dismissal annoyed Jenkins so he added, "I'm not asking for my testimony. I'm asking because I want to make sure we didn't miss anything in our investigation."

Matthews looked intensely at Jenkins and said pointedly, "Don't worry about it."

Jenkins had seen this attitude before. Once a competitive prosecutor like Matthews got a case, all he worried about was getting a conviction. It became a game to him—a serious game, but a game nonetheless. He would move the various pieces of evidence like chess pieces, play to the perceived sympathies of the jury, and try to ignore anything that might hurt the chances for a conviction. People often thought that the reason prosecutors were so driven to win was because of career ambitions or public attention, but Jenkins had seen the inner workings of the prosecutors' office and he figured it was internal competition that truly drove them. Since the Crown got to pick the cases that went to trial, they were expected to win, and almost always, they did. So if a prosecutor lost, it was cause for embarrassment and ribbing amongst their colleagues, especially if they lost a case that was not considered troublesome.

Matthews stared at Jenkins for a moment, wordlessly daring him to question him before he coldly said, "That's all I've got. Thanks for sticking around late tonight."

Jenkins had originally planned to head home for a solid eight hours of sleep but now he could not ignore the twisting sensation in his stomach. Something was wrong. Defence lawyers did not waste time and money getting experts to look for evidence without a reason, and seasoned prosecutors like Matthews did not get their backs up unless an issue made them nervous.

CHAPER 17

The waitress walked them to Fredrickson's usual table. Over the last few months, Brian had learned that Fredrickson knew the best restaurants in town and had a usual table at all of them. The lawyers were settled into a corner booth, and Fredrickson immediately placed an order of Indian food for both of them. Brian began opening his briefcase, planning to go through his cross-examination questions one more time, but Fredrickson held up his hand and said, "No paper tonight. Let's talk it through."

"Talk through my cross of the detective?"

"Nah, you've got all of that set. Let's just talk about the case."

This was a surprise, as they had discussed the general trial strategy *ad nauseam* over the months and now, on the eve of trial, he was more concerned with the specifics of getting through tomorrow. "What part do you want to discuss?"

Fredrickson leaned back in the booth and asked, "What are we worried about?"

The answer to that was all too easy. Brian had been worried when the authorities laid the murder charge that they had a smoking gun he was unaware of, and when the discovery had been provided by the prosecutors, they revealed a double-barrelled smoking gun: Charley's fingerprints were on the body and a pair of Natalie Peterson's underwear had been hidden in the basement. With a sigh, Brian answered, "The fingerprints and the underwear."

Fredrickson began pulling pieces of buttery flat bread from a basket as he said, "The fingerprints are bad but manageable. Charley told you he touched her chest to see if she had a heartbeat and you can get that point in through the doctor. That should be believable enough for the jury if they don't want to convict him. The hidden underwear, however, is a whole different ball game."

"Charley says he doesn't know how they got in the basement."

"You believe him on that?"

Brian had received the letter he had asked Charley to write

the night he had first come into the Legal Aid office. The language was simple but clear, providing a basic chronology of the night. Brian had read the letter at least once every day for the last five months and could recount each word from memory. Charley had worked all day shovelling snow, been dropped off at the day labourer corner, and then purchased six cheeseburgers and two bottles of malt liquor. He then walked the two miles to the abandoned house where he drank the malt liquor and fell asleep. He was awoken by a noise outside, and he looked out of a dryer vent hole into the yard. From there he was able to see a green sports car stuck in the alley. A short, heavy man got out of the car. Then a woman bolted from the car with her hands tied behind her back. The man chased her, caught her, and pulled her down where Charley could not see them. Then a light came on across the alley and the driver fled. Afraid, Charley huddled in his blankets, drunk and unsure what to do next. He managed to gain some composure and went outside where he found Natalie Peterson in the snow. He touched her chest and felt no heartbeat so he figured she was dead. Charley ran across the alley to get help. As he was returning to the basement, a pickup truck with two men arrived. One man was very big with long hair and the other was small with a shaved head. They towed the car out of the ditch and drove both vehicles away. He went back into the basement to get his things but heard sirens and ran away before he could collect anything. The letter did not mention the victim's underwear.

Brian answered with a shrug, "I don't know if I believe him or not."

Fredrickson seemed to guess what he was thinking and gave him a grin through a mouthful of bread, "Those silly client letters can make sorting out what to do a bit tricky, can't they?"

When Brian told Fredrickson about the letter at their first meeting, he had gotten a laugh for a response. However, when the senior lawyer had read Charley's simple words, he had to admit that, even as cynical as his years dealing with criminals had made him, he found the story believable. Despite this believability, Fredrickson seemed to take joy in pointing out to his protégé that just because a client wrote something believable, that did not mean they could use the information in court. Because of this they had to strategize as if they did not know what had been written. It was a mental exercise Brian was having a hard time accepting.

"Fair enough. I suppose we need to assume Charley put them there as we have no other presentable explanation."

Fredrickson shook his head. "I'd love to try and throw out a good old fashioned 'the police planted the evidence' defence."

They had discussed this planted evidence strategy at great length. The logic was simple: if Charley didn't put the underwear there, then someone else had to. The problem was that at the time the underwear was found, only the cops knew that there was a squatter in the basement who was available for framing. That meant they would have to argue that the police planted the evidence, which obviously lacked credibility. It had been decided that blindly slinging mud at the police would only make the defence look desperate and would put added focus on the underwear. They had opted instead to draw the jury's attention to the fact that the underwear was only found during a later search of the basement, let them draw the inference that it was possible they were planted, and leave it at that.

Fredrickson continued as a waitress set down their food, "Ok, so the hidden panties are our biggest problem. Does the prosecution have any problems?"

"Jason Young is the prosecution's biggest problem."

Fredrickson pointed a fork with some butter chicken impaled on it at Brian as he said, "Yep, there's your straw man."

Brian pondered the Crown's problem. Young was the only son of a wealthy, powerful family and had been given everything. Charley was the only son of a hardworking, troubled family and had been given nothing. Now the blessed man might be seen as using the battered man to cover for his indiscretions.

Every day, seven days a week, for the past five months, Brian had gone to the remand center for at least two hours—not because he was able to get useful information from his client, but because he was worried for his safety. Brian had learned from one of the friendlier guards that Charley was, predictably, at the very bottom of the prison food chain. It was suspected that he was being heavily tormented and assaulted by his cellmate, who was a lifetime criminal that took any opportunity to cause trouble for the pure entertainment of it. However, Charley would not report any of this abuse, so the guards could do little. In a vain attempt to help Charley, he had set up the daily meetings in order give him a brief break from the horror. Most days Charley merely sat and ate the snacks Brian bought him out of the vending machine while Brian worked. Some days, though, they would play chess badly. On very rare occasions, they would talk.

Through these few, stilted conversations, Brian figured he got all the information he could from his quasi-mute client. Charley said he was sure that the car in the ditch was a green sports car. Also, his vague description of the driver matched Jason Young. Green was an odd color for a car and it was even rarer for someone to be foolish enough to be driving a sports car in the winter in Calgary. It had to have been Jason Young's Jaguar. At first Brian thought the fact that the car Charley claimed to have seen matched the car in which Natalie Peterson had apparently left the bar lent serious credence to Charley's story. But he soon realized it was likely that Charley, since he was living in the same neighbourhood, had seen Young and his car before and he might have even seen him come home with Peterson that night. And actually, the more he thought, the more he figured that if he were the prosecutor he would argue that Charley spent his nights sneaking about the wealthy homes, had seen Natalie arrive at Young's house, and had stalked her from there. Such a story not only made sense, it would scare the jurors.

Regardless of that argument, Brian believed his client, and he did not think that the frightened young man he had spent the last five months with did anything that night but hide in the basement like he said. That meant there had to be holes in the story Jason Young was telling the police. He would need to find and attack those holes to make Young out as the villain.

*

Instead of going home after his tedious meeting with Matthews, Jenkins had gotten a copy of the transcript of the hearing where the defence counsel requested an order to examine Jason Young's car for damage. He had hoped that the prosecutor was right and this was simply a case of a desperate accused trying to raise reasonable doubt by pointing to the last person to be seen with the victim. Unfortunately, reading the transcript had raised more questions than it answered.

At the hearing, Matthews had been difficult and he managed to get the rookie defence lawyer to tell more than he probably should have. They stated they were potentially proposing an alternative supposition for the crime that involved Mr. Young keeping the victim at his home until Sunday night. When he tried to move her in the middle of that stormy Sunday night, he crashed his car in a ditch, at which time the victim escaped from the car only to be caught by Mr. Young, who killed her in the backyard where Mr. Ewanuschuk discovered the body. If this alternative were true then Young's car may have signs of a crash. Despite the senior prosecutor being uncooperative, the request was very fair and the order was granted requiring Jason Young to turn over the car for examination.

The fact that the alternate explanation by the defence had Young holding the girl until Sunday night struck a chord for Jenkins. He had always found it problematic that their understanding of the crime supposed that Natalie had been held in the basement for over a day, yet the crime scene technicians had not found any sign of her being there—no hairs, no blood, no fingerprints. He knew it was possible; she could have been kept tied up in one spot, on a blanket or sheet and then Ewanuschuk could have thrown that all away. He doubted that though; the basement did not look cleaned, plus Jenkins had investigated a lot of crimes and this one did not seem to be borne of planning and intelligence. Maybe Ewanuschuk had held her and got lucky that no sign of her was found. Jenkins had seen far stranger. But Jenkins did not think Ewanuschuk was the lucky type.

Looking around the dim, empty office, Jenkins wondered if perhaps he was over-thinking this because it was his last case. They had found the victim's underwear in the accused's heating vent. That evidence should overwhelm any concerns. Jenkins tossed the hearing transcript in his recycling bin and headed home.

*

Fredrickson climbed into his massive town car, which was illegally parked right front of the restaurant to ensure he would not need to walk more than a few feet. As he got settled he said, "You'll do fine tomorrow Brian. You know this one down cold."

"Thanks. Maybe I'll get lucky and pull out an acquittal. Even a blind squirrel finds a nut once in a while."

"Don't kid yourself. Mother Nature would never tolerate a blind squirrel. A blind squirrel trying to find a nut breaks its back falling from the tree and then a cat comes along to eat him. I definitely think you can get an acquittal but it won't be because of luck; it will be because of all the hard work you've put in getting ready." With that he closed the car door and sped off down the street.

When Fredrickson had insisted on this late dinner, Brian had been perturbed at the idea of wasting time going out the night before the trial, but now, watching the huge car disappear, he realized what the whole evening had been about. His briefcase had remained closed all evening as they casually discussed the various elements of the case, dissecting problems, predicting surprises he might face and considering possible angles to exploit or avoid. By the end of the very lengthy meal, Brian realized that he knew the file inside and out such that he would be able to adapt on the fly to anything that came up. Walking home through the refreshing spring night air, Brian felt far more confident than when he had arrived, more confident than he had in the last five months, right when he needed the confidence most.

*

Laying in his bunk, Charley was straining to hear. The cell was cast in the pale light that passed for dark in the remand center. Finally he heard the cherished sound of soft snoring from the bunk below. That sound meant he was safe until morning, as his demented cellmate apparently would not be up to any of his tricks tonight.

As the snores deepened, Charley checked off another day. For almost five months now he had been enduring the constant nightmare of prison. He forced himself to not think more than one sunset ahead and faced each day as its own isolated horror. To look any distance into the future would cause him to realize the totality of the grief he was facing and such a realization would result in crippling desperation. According to Brian, the trial would begin tomorrow and would last about a week. He had already decided he could hold out through the trial for Brian's sake but he would not endure prison any longer than that.

Charley curled up on the thin mattress. His cellmate had long ago taken his blanket and pillow, so he was cold and uncomfortable, but he was used to being cold and uncomfortable. He did not try to fall asleep right away. This might be the only moment of peace for some time, so he would try to make it last as long as possible. Almost done counting down these days of suffering caused him, for the first time in years, to reminisce over his day-by-day life.

He refused to let his mind linger on memories of the constant humiliation of school. But while his home life had generally been unpleasant, there were a few things he missed and allowed himself to recall. Depending on the season, most nights Charley would get off the school bus, eat a quick snack, put on his overalls and move right into tearing down machinery for sale or doing field work. He did not mind the work. Bouncing over endless acres of dirt in a tractor was uncomfortable, especially since his father did not believe in air conditioning, but on clear nights he could listen to the radio and, most importantly, he was left alone with his daydreams. Despite the perpetually skinned knuckles, tearing down old equipment was also tolerable. It normally involved working with his dad who had a harsh temper and talked very little, but when he did speak, he spoke to him as a man rather than a child, and no one else did that.

After nightfall, when the work was finally done, the three of them would eat dinner together. His mother spent almost all of her waking hours on food preparation, so the meals were always hearty and tasty. If his mom was in one of her outgoing moods, she would chatter non-stop about random subjects while Charley and his dad ate their fill. If she was in one of her sullen moods, they would all eat in silence. Most nights his dad would go to bed right after supper, his mom would carefully do the dishes while listening to gospel radio and Charley would sit in his room doing homework or reading.

Saturday was the one night of the week that was different. If there was a hockey game on one of the two channels their TV got, they would sit in the living room after dinner. His dad would watch while slowly drinking a beer, his mother would knit between serving snacks, and Charley would merely sit between the two of them on their ancient couch. If there were no sports on, they would sit at the kitchen table and play three-handed cribbage. There was never much, if any, conversation, but at least he was spending time with someone. Lying on his prison cot, feeling a million miles away from everyone, it was those simple Saturday nights that Charley let his mind recall.

CHAPTER 18

It is required, for some ancient reason stretching back to England, that in Canadian court proceedings where verbal evidence is being given, the lawyers must dress in black gowns. Brian's gowns were a gift from his mother for passing the bar and were the polyester type that did not breathe well. The odd garment coupled with the intense stress had caused Brian to have sweated through his shirt before the proceedings had even been called to order. Still, he was somewhat thankful for the antiquated tradition, as he did not have enough suits to be properly attired for a weeklong trial.

On top of being stressed, Brian could also not help but feel immensely alone. At the prosecution table, Matthews was talking with detective Jenkins and a junior prosecutor while two assistants organized documents behind them. He figured they were discussing strategy and determining ways to take advantage of his inexperience. Alone at the defence table, he was pretending to review his notes while sitting next to Charley who was, of course, staring silently at the floor.

The media coverage had died down when it was learned that the accused was a mute homeless man rather than some wealthy resident of the upscale neighbourhood where the body had been found. However, the gallery was nearly full with reporters and interested members of the public for the opening day of trial because any murder case in Calgary warranted attention. Brian was hoping that the number of spectators would dwindle once the prosecution's opening statement was done and the tedium of evidence presentation began, as he did not need an audience witnessing his mistakes.

Finally, the small door at the front of the courtroom abruptly opened. The clerk jumped to her feet and called the court to order as Justice Vivian Rothborg entered. As people shuffled back down into their seats, Rothborg addressed the crowd, "I see we have more than our usual number of spectators for today's activities. I would remind all of you that this is a court of law and ask that you remain quiet throughout the proceedings." She then turned her attention to the clerk. "Madam clerk, please read out the case."

The clerk recited, "Docket number 8894632, Regina versus Charles Ewanuschuk, one count of murder pursuant to section 229 of the Criminal Code of Canada, such murder being in the first degree pursuant to section 231(5) of the Criminal Code of Canada."

The trespassing charge had been dropped, likely to keep it from distracting the jury. Any murder involving forcible confinement, such as a handcuffed victim, is first degree murder under the Code. This meant that if Charley was found guilty, he would automatically be sentenced to life in prison.

Rothborg prompted, "Mr. Matthews?"

Matthews stood and introduced himself, "Clay Matthews for the Crown, My Lady."

Brian managed to keep his voice steady as he rose and introduced himself, "Brian Cox for the defence."

Rothborg continued, "Any motions or other matters to address before bringing in the jury?"

Both lawyers said no and Rothborg instructed the bailiff to get the jury. Thinking that a judge would be more able to apply the concept of innocent until proven guilty and overcome the preconceived notion that any homeless man who has been arrested likely committed a crime, Brian had applied to have the trial by judge alone. However, in murder cases, the prosecution must consent to such an application, and Matthews was not foolish enough to give up the chance to put the picture of a strange vagrant killing a pretty young victim before a jury. So Charley was forced to take his chances with a jury even though no one on it could be considered his peer.

Everyone watched as the twelve jurors they had selected last week from the random array of one hundred citizens filed into the box and took their seats. Brian figured it was not a bad jury, but it was not a great jury. He had tried, based on advice from Fredrickson, to get educated, liberal-minded people who would be more sympathetic to a homeless person and more likely to question the fairness of the criminal justice system. Matthews had appeared to favour working-class people or parents with children near the victim's age. Through both sides using their twenty peremptory challenges, the result had been a wash. The jury was comprised of seven women and five men with a total of four professionals, four retirees, and four non-professionals. Of the twelve, five had children or grandchildren in their late teens or early twenties.

Rothborg gave them the standard instructions and carefully explained the process before saying, "Mr. Matthews, your opening statement please."

The seasoned prosecutor stepped up to the podium and spoke with a confident tone borne from decades of addressing juries: "Thank you. Ladies and gentlemen of the jury, I will keep this brief as the matter before you is quite simple and the evidence against the accused very clear. The prosecution will show you that Ms. Peterson left a residence on foot at 3:30 a.m. on Sunday, December 5th, 2010, with the intention of going home. However, she was accosted before she could complete her trip. We will show that Ms. Peterson's likely path led her past a certain abandoned house under construction. This shell of a house was where the accused was living in the basement as a squatter and where Ms. Peterson's beaten, lifeless body was found approximately twenty-four hours after she had tried to go home. A witness will place the accused at the scene of the crime contemporaneously with the time of Ms. Peterson violent death. You will be shown evidence that the victim was restrained with handcuffs and badly beaten before being choked to death. We will then present forensic analysis proving that two fingerprints belonging to the accused were found on the body of the victim. Finally, we will show that the victim's underwear she was wearing on the night of her disappearance was found hidden in the basement among the accused's belongings."

At that point Matthews paused, allowing the jury to soak in the import of this damning last sentence, before continuing, "Based on this indisputable evidence, we contend that you will have no difficulty finding, beyond a reasonable doubt, that the accused confined and murdered Ms. Peterson. Those are my submissions, thank you."

With that Matthews sat back down at the prosecutor's table. Brian could sense the disappointment from the reporters in the gallery as the opening statement lacked fanfare and surprises. Brian figured this straightforward opening statement was a consequence of Matthews believing they had such a strong case that playing on emotions would only serve to detract from the evidence. The prosecution would likely save the point that Charley was a deviant vagrant who did not contribute to society and the victim was a hardworking young waitress merely trying to make a living for herself for the closing statement so that any desire for revenge would be at the forefront of the jurors' minds when they began deliberating.

The lawyers waited while the judge took some notes before looking back up. "Thank you, Mr. Matthews. Mr. Cox, would you care to make your statement at this time?"

Defence counsel has the option of making their opening statement immediately following the prosecution's opening or waiting until after the prosecution had closed its case. This tactical decision is not a simple one to make. There is a benefit to casting doubt over the prosecution's assertions from the get go so that all of their evidence will be viewed by the jury with suspicion rather than being seen as the only possible explanation. On the other hand, there is also a benefit to waiting so that anything particularly harmful raised by the prosecution can be addressed directly. In this case Brian had decided to wait, if for no other reason than he wanted to get his legs under him before making a crucial address to the jury. Brian stood and answered quickly, "We will defer until after the prosecution has closed its case, My Lady."

"Moving right along then. Mr. Matthews, please call your first witness."

"If it pleases the Court, the Crown calls Detective Randall Jenkins."

Brian watched as the hefty detective moved to the witness stand. He was wearing the standard, unimpressed look of a veteran police officer being interrupted from his real work to have to testify. Brian had asked around to get an impression of the detective and the response from the defence bar members had been consistent: Jenkins was an astute investigator who was fair and did not make procedural errors. This had not been what Brian wanted to hear as

Charley's best chance was a sloppy investigation that they could punch holes in. However, he had also learned that this was Jenkins's last case before retiring, so Brian was hoping the detective had been a little lazy on this one.

After Jenkins was sworn in and Matthews had him introduce himself, the veteran prosecutor and detective fell into a practiced routine of questions and answers whereby the necessary evidence rolled out seamlessly for the jury. Watching this display as he scribbled notes, vainly looking for any inconsistencies or procedural breaches he could attack, Brian realized that perhaps the true reason for Matthews' succinct opening was that he wanted the jury to view the prosecution as the upstanding professionals dominating the courtroom. This would make the defence look desperate and floundering by comparison. Watching the jurors take in the choreographed scene while feeling his own stomach churn with nervousness, Brian was worried this strategy was working perfectly.

*

As Matthews took a break from lobbing him softball questions to get a document, Jenkins took a drink of water and scanned the gallery as he calmly waited. There was a collection of poorly dressed reporters alongside the elderly courthouse spectators who came daily for the free entertainment. Intermingled amongst the media and the regulars were a few lawyers who were probably just checking in on the proceedings to pass time between their own appearances in other courtrooms. Near the back, close to the door, Jenkins's eye caught a man with a coif of silvery hair leaning over an attractive blonde woman in a stylish suit with a notepad on her lap. As the man stood up and left, Jenkins realized that it had been Jacob Poetker, the lawyer that had accompanied Jason Young at his interview.

As Matthews returned to his questioning, Jenkins watched the young blonde woman begin to furiously take notes. She was the only person in the gallery keeping notes on the rather benign points of his testimony. Jenkins would be willing to bet that she was an articling student in Poetker's office who had been tasked with the job of reporting back to the partner on what was happening in the trial on an ongoing basis. While Jenkins did not think there was any sort of conflict with having a witness' lawyer watching the proceedings, it was odd for someone who was merely a witness to pay a very expensive law firm to audit a trial. Although he was fairly certain this was what was occurring, he had no idea as to why it was happening. Matthews interrupted his train of thought, "Detective, can you please answer the question?"

Jenkins snapped his gaze from the young woman, "Oh, sorry, could you please repeat the question?"

This lack of focus earned Jenkins a harsh glare from Matthews as he re-asked about the positioning of the body. Jenkins stopped pondering Jason Young and returned his attention to his testimony.

*

Having read almost every courtroom thriller in the public library, Charley was well acquainted with trials and he had serious doubts about his chances with a jury. He had learned that people's reaction to encountering a homeless person was always a combination of pity and disgust. All that varied was the relative amounts of each. Some people seemed to be almost all pity while others seemed to be all disgust, with most being an odd mixture of both. In his experience, the disgust generally outweighed the pity, so a jury of twelve people would likely not be sympathetic towards him. Even if a juror was not disgusted, he or she might not be too worried about ruining a life they pitied.

However, now, sitting at the wide oak table, the focus of the crowded courtroom, Charley was less concerned with the jury's eventual verdict and more concerned about all of the eyes watching him. Brian had told him to concentrate on the testimony being given to see if he could find anything they could use as an inconsistency, and Charley wanted to help, but with all the stranger attention on him, he was having a hard time listening. As he often did in stressful situations, he tried to use his trick of mentally disassembling agricultural equipment to distract himself, but this failed to stem his desire to stand up and run away. Knowing that he could not physically flee, he decided to allow his mind to take refuge in its favourite daydream.

It was a fantasy he had harboured since high school. He now knew it was juvenile, impossible, and ridiculous, so when he caught himself playing it out in his head, he tried to force himself to stop. However, sometimes because of either fatigue or drink or fear, his resolve would waiver and his imagination would take over. Today he needed the distraction of the fabricated future so, staring at the tabletop, he reached for the familiar strings of the story, letting it weave itself together.

Over the years, there had been many factual variations but the gist remained constant. Charley would save a woman from a danger; sometimes it would be a random attacker, an abusive husband, or simply an accident. Even his imagination would not be so vain as to have the rescued woman fall immediately in love with him, but they would become friends and over time that friendship would turn into Charley's vague understanding of a romance. They would then decide to run away together. Depending on how desperate he was feeling, this would either involve finding a remote cabin somewhere in the hills where they would raise their own food and always be left alone or, if he was not overly despondent, they would move to a small farm where they would have sporadic contact with friendly neighbours. No matter how it played out, the end of the dream always focussed in on quiet winter nights spent sitting under quilts after a hearty dinner.

Back when he was younger, the woman in the dream was always a girl from school. Not the prettiest girl because that was too farfetched, but a pretty enough girl because it was a fantasy, after all. Over the years his memories of the girls in his classes had faded such that they were only vague impressions, but he had no interactions with any other women that he could replace the ghosts of the past with, so his unconscious created fictional mates out of these remembered wisps.

Before long, he was happily walking through ankle-deep snow on a crisp, sunny day with two fat rabbits and a rifle over his shoulder as a petite woman with long black hair stood in the doorway of their cozy cabin waving at his return with a welcoming smile across her face. Before he could reach the cabin, he was cruelly brought back to reality. Brian had grabbed his elbow and was lifting him to his feet as he whispered, "Come on Charley, stand up. Ten minute recess."

Charley stumbled to his feet without looking up. He was embarrassed for not paying attention. And, even though no one knew he had been doing it, he was embarrassed at his futile, adolescent fantasizing.

CHAPTER 19

For over three hours, Matthews had Detective Jenkins move through the investigation for the jury. Natalie Peterson's body had been found in the backyard of the half-built house. She had been handcuffed, undressed but for a coat and boots. Her body showed signs of recent mistreatment. Inside the basement of the house, they had found blankets, empty liquor bottles, food, some furnishings, and clothing, along with a collection of books and pornographic magazines. As this listing occurred, Brian noticed the jurors looking at Charley, apparently checking to see if he would have any reaction, but he merely stared resolutely at the table top. From there, Jenkins explained that they had used the library books to identify the man who had been living in the basement as the accused, who was later arrested leaving a shelter downtown. Throughout this process, Brian had objected a couple of times on the basis of speculation and once claiming hearsay. The objections had been sustained, but like jazz musicians who had played together for years, Matthews merely reworded the questions and Jenkins knew what he had to change in his response to get the evidence in. As a result, rather than breaking their rhythm or scoring points for the defence, the objections served to reinforce for the jury that the prosecution were the professionals and the defence was the amateur.

After the lunch recess, Matthews continued his questioning of Jenkins and asked, "Was anything else of interest discovered in the basement?"

Technically this was a leading question which was not allowed, but Brian figured there was not much point in objecting. Jenkins answered, "Yes, after the initial crime scene review was completed, we received a call indicating that the accused had—"

Brian, anticipating this was coming and not wanting the jury to hear any more, got to his feet quickly and said, "Objection, hearsay."

Matthews immediately asked, "Sidebar, My Lady?"

Rothborg waved the two lawyers up so they could consult without the jury hearing. Matthews explained, "The person who called the police station only identified himself as Steven and the call was from a pay phone. As a result the prosecution is unable to present the caller as a witness, but we do have the tape recording we could enter as—"

Brian interjected, "My Lady, clearly, entering into evidence a recording of a phone call when we do not even know who is talking and cannot cross examine the speaker is highly prejudicial hearsay and cannot be allowed."

"My Lady, as I mentioned, the declarant is unavailable to testify and as such we can rely on the exception to the hearsay rule of declaration against interest—"

Rothborg interrupted Matthews by raising her hand. "Mr. Matthews, I can't blame you for trying but the exception is not applicable here. There's no way the tape is coming in unless you can present the caller for cross examination."

Matthews, knowing he was fighting an impossible battle, gave a slight nod. "I understand My Lady. We will not reference the phone call."

"Fine, please continue your examination."

Matthews returned his attention to Jenkins, who had been patiently waiting. "Detective Jenkins, please explain what else was found in the basement."

"We found a pair of women's underwear hidden in a heating duct."

There were no murmurs in the gallery as this information had come out in the preliminary inquiry, but Brian either felt or imagined an ominous silence fall over the room, allowing the damning statement to hang in the air. After a moment, Matthews stated, "Thank you detective. No further questions."

Rothborg turned to Brian, "Mr. Cox, any questions on cross?"

"Yes, My Lady." Trying to look much calmer than he felt, Brian stepped to the podium. "Detective, you mentioned a number of things you found in the basement. I would like to discuss things you did not find. Did you find any of Ms. Peterson's fingerprints in the basement?"

"No."

"None?"

Matthews jumped up. "Objection, asked and answered."

"Sustained."

Brian had hoped that Matthews would give him some leeway, but it appeared that was not going to be the case. He continued, "Did you find any of her hairs in the basement?"

"No."

"Did you find anything that placed Ms. Peterson in the basement at all?"

The detective coldly asked, "Other than her underwear?"

Three questions in and Brian had already had a misstep. He paused for a second before continuing, "We will get to that point, but first can you confirm that no forensic evidence indicating Ms. Peterson's presence in the basement was found?"

"That's correct."

"In your experience, would it be strange that a person could be held in a location for an extended period of time without there being some sign of them being there?"

A shrug from the detective. "Sure."

"In your opinion, did it appear that the scene had been cleaned at all?"

The detective flipped through his notes briefly before answering, "There were no definitive signs that the scene had been cleaned."

"So it is possible that Ms. Peterson was never in the basement?"

Another shrug. "Anything is possible."

Brian considered complaining about the extra commentary being made by the witness, but he decided he had made his point clearly enough. "Fine, let's talk about this mysterious underwear. You have investigated numerous crimes; would it be fair to say that evidence can be moved to confuse or impede an investigation?"

Jenkins appeared to ponder this before answering, "That would be fair."

"Good. So does the existence of an article of clothing in a location mean that the owner of that article had been there?"

"No, not necessarily, but it is indicative—"

Having learned that one of the largest advantages a trial lawyer has is his ability to lead a witness when cross examining them, Brian figured it was time to use this advantage and interrupted in his best cold lawyer scolding tone, "A simple yes or no will be sufficient Mr. Jenkins. Does the existence of an article of clothing in a location mean that the owner of that article had been there?"

"No."

"The underwear was not found on your first examination of the basement, is that correct?"

"Yes."

"It was Monday when you originally searched the basement, is that correct?"

"Yes."

"And the underwear was found on Thursday night, is that correct?"

"Yes, we received a call—"

"Again, detective, please only answer the question asked with a yes or no. So it is possible that the reason you did not find the underwear on Monday was that it was not there at that time?"

"Yes."

"Thank you. So it is possible that between your original search on Monday and the search on Thursday someone put the underwear in the basement?"

Jenkins, an obvious pro at giving testimony, sighed in order to show his disgust for this ludicrous line of questioning before saying, "Yes, it's possible."

*

In Jenkins's opinion the young defence lawyer was not great, but he was better than many he had come across. Getting the vague admission that the underwear was possibly planted was weak as the jury would not buy that idea, but there was not much else they could do with such damning evidence. At least, however, he had given the jury a way out of convicting the accused if they wanted to take it. The defence lawyer had also managed to get Jenkins to admit that the fingerprint could have been left on the body post-mortem if someone had attempted to check for vital signs. Regardless, when the cross examination finished, Jenkins was confident that the Crown's case had held up well.

The judge turned to Matthews and asked, "Any rebuttal?"

"A couple of quick questions, My Lady."

Jenkins had now been on the stand for hours; his stomach was bothering him and he needed a bathroom. Matthews would have considered the comfort of another witness, but not the comfort of a police officer. He was merely a piece of evidence. Spending endless hours in an uncomfortable witness chair answering lawyers' never-ending questions was added to Jenkins's mental list of annoying things he would not miss in retirement.

"Detective Jenkins, I just want to go back to something my friend raised regarding the underwear. You stated that they were not found on Monday when you commenced your investigation, but rather they were found three days later. By the Thursday night, who was aware that a suspect had possibly been living in the basement?"

The question confused Jenkins so he asked, "You want me to list off who was involved with the crime scene?"

"No, no. Just give us a sense of who had access to the information, whether it was public knowledge or not at the time."

It dawned on him what the prosecutor was aiming at and he answered, "Only the police, the crime scene techs that worked on the case, and perhaps the coroner would have been aware that someone had been living in the house. The information was not made public."

"So no one outside of the police service would know that

there was any point in planting the underwear in the basement?"

"Like I said, it was not public information, but cops talk like anyone else, to their wives or buddies or whomever, so it would be possible that outside people would have been told."

"Fine, but it would be unlikely that anyone outside that relatively small group would have the requisite knowledge such that they would know that the planting of the underwear in the basement would be an effective way to frame someone for the murder of Ms. Peterson?"

The defence lawyer objected. Matthews, having made his point, withdrew the question and the re-direct was over. They had managed to quell the notion that someone was framing Ewanuschuk by putting the underwear in the basement, but the questioning did pique Jenkins's interest regarding something else.

*

An electronic chime announced the arrival of the awaited email from Poetker. Hugh Young, sitting at the Italian marble-topped island in his dimly lit kitchen, pushed his dinner plate aside and pulled his laptop over. He checked his watch, six fifty-eight. Goddamn lawyers. Hugh had been told that he would get the trial summaries before seven each night, and of course, the lawyers had taken every last minute.

It felt odd to be home at such an early hour, but with his new company only getting started and his mind flooded with thoughts of the trial, he found it difficult to find proper distraction in the empty office. At least Hugh was alone in the house. His wife was in Cannes at some fashion show or film festival or something. He had given Maria, the housekeeper, the night off, which meant that she was watching game shows in her apartment over the garage. The fact that she was sitting out there irked Hugh for a couple of reasons. For one, she was Jason's former nanny who had been hired when he was born so that the cherished infant would never want for attention. When Hugh had suggested they let the woman go once Jason started school, his wife protested loudly, mainly because she did not like the idea of returning to cooking and cleaning. Hugh had not cared enough to fight back and the flesh-and-blood reminder of his child's spoiled upbringing had remained in his employ for twenty-five years and counting. The second reason he was annoyed was more contemporary. Her presence out back meant that if he wanted to hire an escort for some companionship tonight, he would have to go to a hotel room to avoid detection, which was an extra hassle he did not feel like enduring.

Hugh refilled his wine glass with hearty merlot and settled into the lamb skin recliner in his study with the laptop. He opened the attached memo. The beginning of the trial summary was fairly banal as the prosecution appeared to do an effective job of setting out the basics of the crime scene. The cross examination interested Hugh more because the defence counsel tried to plant the idea that the underwear had been placed in the basement by some unknown person for the police to find. Even to Hugh's inexperienced mind, this tactic seemed desperate and fanciful, especially when the prosecutor pointed out that when the underwear was found no one but the police knew that the homeless man even existed.

The rest of the summary was fairly straightforward. There was some testimony showing that that handcuffs were cheap and common. Then, an expert testified about the Rohypnol found in the victim's system, explaining that it was affordable and fairly readily available. Apparently the prosecution wanted to show that these items could easily be acquired by anyone, including the impoverished. With that, the trial was recessed until tomorrow morning.

It appeared that the homeless man would take the fall for his son's stupidity. Of course that would only happen so long as Jason could keep his story straight when he testified tomorrow. At that worrisome thought, Hugh took a long drink.

CHAPTER 20

Sitting in the trial with all those eyes on him was horribly uncomfortable, but Charley would have gladly stayed there forever if it meant he could avoid one night of the torments awaiting him in prison. Upon being returned from the courthouse, Charley was taken directly to the dining hall. He had learned that if he took his tray of food back to a table the other men would take whatever they wanted, often leaving him with nothing. As a solution, he employed a similar tactic he used in high school. He would delay as long as possible in the line as he carried his tray with one hand so he could rapidly stuff some of his food into his mouth with the other hand. This was messy, brought embarrassing scolding from the guards, and elicited anger from the inmates hoping for an extra serving, but the only other option he could think of was starvation.

    This evening, he was slowly trying to find spot to sit while balancing the orange tray on one hand and eating a handful of pasta with the other when he heard the shrill voice of his demented cellmate call out, "There be the stripper killer, boys."

    A murmur rose through the crowded dining hall, growing into a cacophony of jeers, which Charley, to his horror, realized were directed at him. The guards hollered angrily and the noise reduced back to the usual din. When he took his seat at one of the long tables, the man next to him—an older inmate he had seen before and took to be a scared loner like himself—poked him in the side with his thumb and whispered without looking up from his food, "Careful, word got out about your trial and your fucked-up roommate's been doing a good job of making sure they all know who killed the hot, young stripper. He spent all day riling them up. A few of these bastards might be looking to put a beating on you for entertainment's sake."

    Looking furtively around, Charley saw he was being glared at and he appeared to be the topic of many conversations. Not wanting to aggravate anyone any further, he rapidly turned his attention to his dinner but before he could lift his fork, the fat inmate across the table from him slowly pulled his tray away, calmly replacing it with his empty one. With a malicious grin that showed more than a few missing teeth, the man deliberately plucked up a single pea and placed it on the empty tray now in front of Charley as he sneered, "Enjoy your supper, that's all lady killers get."

Despite not having any food to eat, Charley was required to sit at the crowded table as violent criminals finished their meals while discussing his demise. Finally, the guards ordered the dining hall cleared and they were led out. The next two hours before lights out were free time. Most inmates would congregate in the common room to watch TV or play cards. Normally, this was a tolerable time of day as his cellmate was out of the cell, so he could lie on his bunk and read in peace.

Tonight, though, he wished he could be locked up even if it meant more time with the demented man. He was too scared to read so he merely stared at the ceiling, listening for any odd noises from the common room. After only a few minutes he heard the sounds of an argument turning into a minor scuffle. This was not unusual as there were often fights over what channel to watch or someone cheating at cards, but it went on for quite some time, which was strange. Concern caused Charley to swing his legs over the side of his bunk to look out the door. As soon as his feet cleared the bed they were grabbed and he was hauled off.

The crash to the cement floor knocked the wind out of him. He was disorientated, but he definitely felt the first solid blow smash into his cheek. He tried to curl up to protect himself but someone stepped on his ankles pinning his legs to the floor. All he could do was cover his face with his arms as he was pummelled. Lying there, trapped in the small space between the bunk bed and the wall, Charley heard the men jovially cursing him between kicks and punches.

"Whatta ya got against strippers?"

"My sister was a stripper."

"Didn't ya wanta pay for the dance, asshole?"

"There ain't enough hot women in the world gettin' naked for you to be out there killin'em."

Above the comments, Charley heard the distinct cackle of his cellmate. Even through the pain and fear, that absurd cackle came through. Suddenly the thought of one more immature deviant laughing at his torment caused an unusual rage to pour forth. Another comment. A kick. That cackle again. A pair of punches. Another comment and a louder cackle. Anger. It was thin at first but it widened to the point of overwhelming Charley. He twisted roughly on to his side, causing the person standing on his legs to stumble off and allowing Charley to slide back from his attackers and scramble to his feet.

There were three men crammed into the entrance of the narrow cell and, without thought, Charley swung wildly. He was able to whip his long arms with the power of a body formed by a life of physical labour so his large, bony hand struck with the force of an iron ball at the end of a flail. Normally his inaccurate, ungraceful blows caused more humour than damage as they generally missed badly and toppled him off balance. But with all these targets in such a small space, he could not have missed if he tried. His first right-handed hook caught one man with a satisfying crunch square in the jaw, causing him to totter backwards. The falling inmate grabbed blindly about to try and stay up, but instead he ended up pulling the man next to him down with him. Charley's second punch glanced off the remaining attacker's shoulder before thudding into his neck. It was a weaker, left handed cross but it stunned the man long enough for Charley to connect again with a wild right haymaker.

Before the attackers could regain themselves, guards swarmed the cell, grabbing inmates indiscriminately. Charley, the anger having dissolved into his usual state of fear, was standing meekly next to his bunk and got taken last. As the guard cuffed Charley's hands behind his back he asked, "This is your cell, right? These guys come in here to start trouble?"

Charley nodded.

"I'll take you to the infirmary and then it probably should be protective custody until your trial is over."

As he was taken from his cell in front of the onlookers gathered in the common room, he looked up for just long enough to catch the eye of his cellmate. The man was a deviant who wanted nothing more than to cause suffering. Nonetheless, albeit far too late, the monster had accidently gotten Charley exactly what he wanted.

*

"It was about four in the morning. I had gotten up to answer a call of nature."

The elderly man from across the alley was testifying. He was in his late seventies, but unfortunately, Brian thought he was not coming across as doddering. Instead, the retired investment banker, neatly dressed in a nice three-piece suit with the hint of a British accent, was coming across as charming and composed.

Matthews asked, "What happened next?"

An embarrassed grin from the witness, "My plumbing is not as robust as it once was so I was in the loo for a fair bit of time. Thankfully I keep a novel in there for such occurrences."

After some minor chuckles from the gallery, Matthews prodded him along, "And then?"

"There was a knocking at my door. I was concerned but figured that robbers don't usually knock, so I went downstairs after arming myself with my trusty nine iron. A young fellow was standing on my back porch. I did not want to open the door so we spoke through the window at first, but he seemed more scared than scary so I opened the door. I cannot recall word-for-word what was said, but it was something along the lines that I should call 911 because there was a dead woman across the alleyway."

Brian knew that this testimony was coming and had spent numerous hours with Fredrickson deciding how to handle it. They had considered making a number of objections to try and throw off the rhythm of the testimony but the evidence was so straightforward they figured this would backfire. Instead they decided they would only attack on cross. But now, since he doubted he would be able to dent the credibility of such a solid witness, Brian figured he would take the long shot of getting Charley's statement to the neighbour ruled inadmissible. Brian reluctantly got to his feet. "Objection, My Lady, the alleged statement is hearsay."

Matthews responded with an exasperated tone, "My Lady, this is not hearsay as the statement is not offered in evidence to prove the facts contained in the statement. The witness is merely stating what he heard. The prosecution is not seeking to use the statement to prove there was a 911 call or a dead body. The fact that the police found a dead body shortly after receiving a 911 call is proof enough of that. "

Rothborg looked at Brian for his response. He realized his impetuous objection had allowed Matthews to clearly reiterate that a dead body was found where Charley had told the neighbour it would be found. With this mistake laid bare before him, he only managed to shake his head slightly and slunk back down next to Charley. Another amateur error.

With no counter argument from the defence, the judge shrugged and said, "The objection is overruled. Please continue Mr. Matthews."

"Thank you, My Lady." Turning back to the witness, Matthews asked, "What happened next?"

"Well, the strange man ran off so I called 911 as he had suggested and told the lady on the phone what had occurred. I didn't want to go out into the dark alone but after a few minutes I heard the sirens and saw the police lights in the alley, so I got dressed and walked over to explain that I was the one who had called."

"Please, describe the man who came to your back door that night."

"No need to describe him, you can see him for yourself sitting right there. But without all those nasty bruises."

The old man pointed to Charley, who did not even lift his gaze to meet the accusation. With that Matthews got the record to reflect that the witness had indicated the accused and then stopped his questioning, smartly leaving the damning identification hanging in air. Brian put up a valiant effort on cross examination, pointing out that it was dark, the witness had just awoken and that his eyesight might not be as good as it once was. But the jury could see plainly enough that Charley, with his gangly figure, angular face, and thick glasses, was not the type of person that an eyewitness would be mistaken about seeing. The damage had been done. There could be no doubt that Charley was at the crime scene when the murder occurred.

*

Listening to the recording of the anonymous call informing them about the underwear in the basement Jenkins's stomach began to ache. The defence's questions about how the underwear had found its way to the basement had made him curious. On its face the phone call seemed fine, but when he listened to it under the guise that it might be fraudulent, specific statements stood out as odd. For one thing, the person calling himself Steve said Charley was in "jail," which was not a commonly used term by those associated with the homeless. They normally called it remand or the pen or lockup. Plus, Jenkins doubted that a day labourer would refer to anyone as a "detective". Maybe "officer" but more likely "cop", "the police", or maybe even "the pigs". More importantly, the anonymous caller knew Charley was in custody. Charley had been arrested on the Tuesday morning. The call came in that Thursday evening. The only person that Charley had contacted was his lawyer.

Jenkins knew that rumours and gossip from the remand center often made their way to the street quickly, but not that quickly. He figured it was possible someone could have seen the arrest outside the homeless shelter, but it happened too early in the morning for there to be many people about. And, thinking about the awkward, silent young man sitting in the courtroom and the basement filled with books, Jenkins's detective senses told him that Charley was not popular enough that word of his arrest would interest many.

Regardless, the only sensible explanation for the underwear being in the basement was the squatter hiding them there. But Jenkins had encountered many things in his career that required nonsensical explanations. Again, his instincts had him worrying that he had overlooked a gap. He could not ignore this feeling a second time.

Flipping through the file, he realized they had made a rookie mistake. They had been so happy that the critical piece of evidence had fallen into their laps that they had not completely followed up. Instead they jumped to the easy conclusion because it was helpful to their case. They only had two people, Jason Young and Dan O'Connor, confirm that the underwear matched what the victim was wearing on the Saturday night. If the homeless man had not already been under arrest, those two men would have been their best suspects. He could think of no probable way that O'Connor could have known that there was a homeless guy in the basement waiting to be framed. He supposed that Young, since he lived in the neighborhood, could have known Charley was living there, but he was well hidden in the basement and Young did not strike Jenkins as the observant type. Still, just because Jenkins doubted that these men knew Charley was there, that did not mean that was the case.

It was too late to talk to Matthews, as the lunch break was about to end. Nonetheless, he figured this was an important enough problem for him to go to the courtroom and wait for a recess. It would not be fun telling the prosecutor that he needed to dig deeper into the key piece of evidence mid-trial, but he could not let it go.

CHAPTER 21

After the neighbour's testimony, Matthews called Jason Young to the stand. The prosecutor moved him through his testimony succinctly and turned the witness over to Brian. He had prepared, practiced, and then prepared some more for this cross examination, and like an actor about to take the stage, he wanted to ensure he was composed before rehearsal became live, so he took a long moment to go through his notes. This also let the obviously nervous man sweat in front of the crowded courtroom before Brian began, "Mr. Young, you drive a green Jaguar is that correct?"

The rather random question seemed to surprise Jason Young as he stuttered out an answer, "Um, yes, yes I do."

"Where was that car on the night in question?"

"Well, I drove it to the bar and then back to my house where I parked it in the garage."

"I meant the Sunday night when Ms. Peterson body was found."

"Oh, it was in my garage."

"And it stayed in the garage all night? You didn't run an errand or lend the car to someone?"

Young rubbed his chin as if pondering, "No, no, I'm pretty sure it was in the garage all that night."

"Have you ever driven that car in the alley behind the house where Ms. Peterson's body was found?"

More chin rubbing was followed by a hesitant answer: "Um, maybe, I mean, it is close to my place so I may have gone down there before, I suppose."

Using his best scolding lawyer face, Brian glared at the witness. "You suppose? Have you or have you not driven down that alley?"

"Sure, I mean, yes."

"Ok, you've been down that alley before. Do you recall driving your green Jaguar down that alley on the Sunday night in question at about four in the morning?"

Brian had no way to show that the car had been there unless he put Charley on the stand, which he was not willing to do. However, Jason Young did not know this, so perhaps a bluff might work. The confused concern that crossed the witness' face lead Brian to suspect even more strongly that Charley was telling the truth about seeing the car there that night. Young glanced over at the prosecutor's table, apparently seeking help, which Matthews could not give him. He then seemed to scan the gallery for an instant.

Standard trial strategy dictated that Brian should prod the witness to answer in order to draw attention to the fact the witness was stalling but one quick look at how the jurors were quizzically viewing Young during this obvious delay led him to decide that the longer it took to answer this simple question, the better. Finally, after not finding any relief from the prosecution or the gallery, Young leaned back slightly and shook his head as he stammered out, "Nah, no, I don't think I drove down that alley that night. Maybe another night or something, but no, I don't think I was down there that night."

"Mr. Young, this is a very important point so I want to get a clear answer." Despite *saying* he wanted a clear answer, there was no way Brian was going to ask the question clearly as he wanted more confused stammering. "Now, that night it was snowing heavily out and your car is not exactly equipped for the snow so I doubt you would have chosen to use the unplowed alley without reason, therefore, I would expect you would be able to remember if you went down there that night or not. So, did you drive down that alley on the night in question?"

This prolonged question brought Matthews to his feet, "My Lady, for one that question has been asked and answered. For another, Mr. Cox is clearly testifying rather than asking questions of the witness."

Rothborg replied, "The objection is overruled. The witness can answer but Mr. Cox let's keep the preambles to a minimum."

"Of course, My Lady. Mr. Young, please answer the question."

"Um, well, it was a long time ago, but no, I don't think I was down there that night."

"You don't think so. Does that mean that maybe you were in the alley that night?"

Again he looked at the prosecutor before answering, "No, I'm pretty sure I wasn't down there."

"Ok, let's talk about the Saturday night. Did you drive down that alley on your way home from the bar?"

Young shifted his weight to his right, away from Brian, and answered again in an unsure stammer, "Well, um, I guess I don't remember exactly, you see we had been drinking—"

Brian could not believe his luck and interrupted quickly before the witness could clean up his answer, "Ok, let's leave it at you don't remember and discuss this drinking. How much did you have to drink at the bar?"

"Maybe about six or seven drinks over the course of the night."

Brian's extensive experience with drunk driving cases suddenly became relevant, "Did you eat anything at the bar during this time?"

"Yes."

"What did you eat?"

Apparently somewhat proud that he actually remembered some information, Young said confidently, "I had the chicken fingers with fries."

"Great, and how long were you at the bar?"

"About three hours."

"How much do you weigh, Mr. Young?"

"About one eighty."

The man's double chin showed this was clearly a lie but it was a lie that helped, so he let it go and asked, "Do you drink fairly often? More than once a week?"

"Sure."

"Ok, so you had a meal and seven drinks in three hours and you are telling me you, a man of average weight who drinks regularly, were too drunk to remember how you got home. Is that correct?"

Young shifted his weight backwards again, "Well, it was quite a while ago. Maybe I had more to drink than that. It's hard to remember."

"But you can remember exactly what you ate?"

This only got an uneasy shrug from Young. Brian was on a roll and did not want to slow things down to have him actually answer so he pressed forward. "Ok, so one way or another you managed to drive yourself and Ms. Peterson back to your place, but you could not remember how you made it home. Once home you had more to drink, is that correct?"

"Uh, yes."

"How much did you drink?"

"Um, like I said, it was a long time ago and I don't recall exactly."

"Can you give the court a guess?"

"Well, we probably each had a beer or two."

Brian pressed on. "So, the two of you drank, then engaged in intercourse and right after that she collects her money and wants to leave immediately, is that correct?"

"Well, maybe not immediately…"

"You have this beautiful young woman in your house but as soon as she gets your cash she heads for the door. Did that anger you?"

A coy smile actually crossed the witness' lips. "No, not really, I mean, I had gotten what I wanted by that point."

Matthews cursed under his breath and Rothborg shook her head, either in disgust or in disbelief at this man's stupidity. Brian continued, "Fine, in total how long was she at your house?"

"Not sure, I'd guess an hour or so."

"And even though, as you so politely put it, 'you got what you wanted', when she tried to leave you were not willing to drive her home?"

"As I said, I was too drunk to drive. I would've driven her if I could. I offered to let her stay over until I sobered up but she wanted to go right then—"

Brian interrupted, "I'm sure she did."

That got Matthews up. "Still with the commentary, My Lady."

Rothborg only glared slightly at Brian over her glasses rather than actually reprimanding him, so he merely nodded before continuing, "So we are to believe that, despite you being too drunk to remember the trip, you decided you were sober enough to drive the pretty girl to your house from the bar. But when she wanted to leave, even though you only had two more beers over an hour, suddenly you became law abiding and decided you were unable to drive her home. Is that right?"

"Well, yes, sort of, I mean, that's what happened."

Brian sensed that Young was sufficiently confused by what Brian was trying to do so he decided to change directions and asked, "In both 2008 and 2009 you were convicted of marijuana possession. Have you ever purchased other illegal narcotics?"

Matthews, apparently desperate to break this up, stood and objected, "My Lady, Mr. Young's drug use is irrelevant."

This time it was Brian's turn to sound smug, "My Lady, beyond going to this witness' credibility, I will also show relevancy shortly."

"Overruled, please continue, Mr. Cox."

"Mr. Young, have you ever purchased illegal narcotics other than marijuana?"

Thankfully, Matthew's interruption did not make Young any smarter, as he answered, "Um, sure."

"What drugs have you bought?"

"Well, nothing too hard, mainly ecstasy, shrooms, and oxy."

"Oxy? So you know a drug dealer who can provide pills?"

"Sure, I suppose."

"You could contact a drug dealer who could provide you with roofies?"

Brian could almost feel Matthews' glare from behind him as the prosecutor was willing his witness to say he did not know. Instead Young answered, "I don't know, I suppose he could, I mean, he can get you whatever you want."

Despite trying to hold it back, a small smile flashed on Brian's face before he moved on to discuss what Jason was doing attending a bachelor party where he knew no one.

*

Jenkins had been in the back of the courtroom for most of Jason Young's testimony. The direct testimony had been wooden, but at least it served its purpose of getting it on the record how Natalie Peterson had ended up in that neighbourhood. His answers under cross examination, however, had been a disaster.

It had gone on all afternoon as the defence counsel kept plucking at all the loose threads coming from Young's testimony. When the battering was finally done the judge recessed for the day. After watching the poor display on the stand, Jenkins was feeling even more uneasy about the case. It was clear that Young was lying, and while it was very possible that he was one of those individuals who always lied, it was more likely he was covering something up.

Matthews, looking a little pale, was angrily packing up his papers when Jenkins came up to him. "Clay, we've gotta talk."

The prosecutor did not even look up from the table as he answered, "Not now Jenkins. We just got our asses handed to us and I've got to come up with a way to salvage this mess. If you haven't noticed, this slam-dunk case you brought me has now become a stone-cold loser."

"That's what we've got to talk about."

Done packing up his papers, Matthews grumbled, "Fine, walk with me back to my office."

Moving briskly through the courthouse halls with a junior prosecutor trailing behind, her high heels clicking out a rapid staccato on the tiles, Jenkins explained that he wanted to talk to some other people about the underwear they found. That stopped Matthews in his tracks. He waved at his junior for her to keep going before rounding on Jenkins and saying through gritted teeth, "Shit, first my key witness makes a fool of himself on the stand and then you tell me you've got a problem with my key piece of evidence. Next you're going to tell me you charged the wrong fucking guy?"

"No, I think we've got the right guy but I listened again to that anonymous call we got telling us to look in the basement again and it seems off."

"Off?"

"It doesn't sound like a usual day laborer and he knew we had our suspect in jail. How could he know that?"

"Fuck, Jenkins, it really is time for you to retire. Shit gets around with the homeless. Your caller probably had a grudge against our guy and was waiting for an opportunity to screw him."

Jenkins could feel his anger rising but he managed to quell it and say calmly, "Still seems like it's worth looking into. And since you mentioned it, that display on the witness stand has me thinking that Young is covering something up, and it would not be improper for us to find out what that something is."

"No. Look, don't do anything. We already have a disaster on our hands. If you go messing around it will only raise more bullshit that we can't explain."

Jenkins opened his mouth to respond but Matthews lifted a finger at him as if he were shushing a troublesome child before he continued, "I have enough problems right now without having to deal with having to disclose your last minute flights of fancy. If you wanted to dig around you had your chance back before you made this my case. Go back to your desk, put up your feet, and play computer solitaire or surf porn or fucking nap until your last day. I don't care what you do but do not mess with my trial or I'll make sure your fat ass never sees dime one of your pension."

With that, the prosecutor stormed off leaving Jenkins standing alone in the hallway as people cast glances at the poor man who had been so harshly scolded. Watching the arrogant prick walk away, it took Jenkins all of two seconds to decide what he was going to do.

*

Instead of an email with the daily summary of the trial, Hugh Young got a phone call from Jacob Poetker. Hugh, who had been anxiously waiting news of how Jason had done on the stand, knew getting a phone call could not be a good sign. He picked up his phone and gruffly asked, "What happened?"

Poetker, not expecting any small talk, answered, "The evidence in chief went fine. But the defence counsel started their examination strangely and for some reason Jason seemed to completely forget the advice we gave him to answer with 'I don't remember' or 'I don't know' if he got into any sort of trouble."

Hugh rubbed his forehead. It had been so simple yet it was far too complicated for his idiot son. He took a deep breath and said, "Without all the fucking lawyer speak and ass covering, tell me how goddamn bad it was."

Poetker answered, "Fucking bad."

He then went on to explain how the defence counsel easily beat up Jason. By the end of the summary, it was clear that Jason had given the defence a perfect place to point at for showing reasonable doubt. And in Poetker's opinion, if the finding at this trial was not guilty, the cops would have no option but to further investigate Jason's involvement in the murder.

For a brief moment Hugh stewed in his rage, but having dealt with innumerable business crises, he knew that placing fault and doling out punishment was better left for after the crisis had passed. Right now they needed a solution and they needed to find it quick, which required calm thinking. He asked, "What now?"

"Frankly, there's not much we can do. We are stuck with the record being what it is now. I'm sure the prosecutor will want to talk to Jason tonight to figure out what he can present on rebuttal to try and refute what the defence was able to do."

"He's going to put my idiot son back up on the stand?"

"Maybe. If he thinks he can show the jury some evidence that shows Jason could not be the killer."

Whether there was a hint or not, Hugh took an implication. He hung up the phone. Once again he would have to stick his neck out.

CHAPTER 22

Normally they only came to the pub on Monday nights, when domestic draft was on sale and the appetizers were two for one. But tonight they were celebrating.

Anna asked over the music, "So, now you think this Jason guy did it?"

Brian wanted to explain to her that what he thought didn't matter, that it was the fact that he had gotten the jury to at least wonder if Young might be the killer that mattered. However, he knew that re-explaining this technicality would come off as condescending so he merely said, "Not sure. I do think something more happened that weekend than what we are being told, but we might never know for certain."

This apparently stunned Anna. "Doesn't that bother you? I mean, all this work and time and stress and you might not ever know what actually happened?"

He could have pointed out that for criminal defence lawyers, not knowing, while possibly making it harder professionally, made it easier personally. With this case, if Brian knew for certain that Charley was the killer, he would have to deal with the moral dilemma of helping a murderer go free. On the other hand, if he knew for certain that Charley had nothing to do with the murder he would have to deal with the pressure of an innocent client possibly going to jail for life. The ambiguity of not knowing served as a protective covering. Regardless, this was a celebration and he did not feel like sullying it with discussions of morality and ethics, so he merely shrugged as he answered simply, "Not really. I guess sometimes ignorance is bliss."

Anna was smart enough not to push. "What happens now?"

"Not sure. Matthews will probably have some rebuttal questions for Jason Young."

"By the sounds of it you shredded him. What can he do to salvage his mess?"

"I never asked what Young was actually doing on the Sunday night when Peterson was killed so I imagine he'll explore that."

"Why didn't you ask him?"

"The cops never asked him in his interview so I didn't know what he would say. With everything else going so well, I didn't want to risk asking a question I didn't know the answer to. It's hard to pick holes in a story under cross examination if you haven't heard the story you are attacking."

"You're thinking that Matthews will put this guy back up to have him give an alibi story and then you'll pick it apart?"

"That's my plan, assuming of course that he has an alibi to present. He lives by himself and was hanging out at a stranger's bachelor party, so I'm guessing he spends a fair bit of time alone. If he doesn't have a solid alibi to present, then Matthews would be smart not to offer any rebuttal and move on, which I'm also fine with."

Anna gave him a sly grin and asked, "If he's got no alibi would that make you think Young is the killer like Charley said?"

Brian knew that, through his stories, she had become a fan of Charley, seeing him as the product of mistreatment rather than as a potential criminal. Brian smiled back, "I don't know, maybe, but you have to see this Jason guy. It's not that he's merely stupid. He does not appear to understand how people interact at all. Even though he's in this serious situation he seems to be approaching it like an immature high school kid. It's hard to imagine someone like that coming up with a plan to frame Charley and then actually pulling it off."

"Maybe someone's helping him out."

As Anna, enjoying having her boyfriend back for at least one night, ordered more beer from the waitress, Brian pondered her idea. Young's testimony in chief had been heavily coached and he had an expensive lawyer from Rainer Hopkins at his police interview. Clearly he was getting assistance. From his pre-trial research, he knew Jason Young was from a wealthy family where the father had made many fortunes selling oil and gas companies. Given this, he supposed there would be ample resources and motivation to help out the prodigal son. Regardless, it made no sense that they would take the risk of framing Charley once he had already been arrested. Even if Charley got off, there was no way they could then convict Young. There would be tonnes of reasonable doubt simply because another suspect had been tried. Why go to the trouble of trying to frame someone who was already providing you with a get out of jail free card?

All of this was making Brian's already tired head hurt. He was supposed to be relaxing, so he asked, "Wanna play pool? Loser sleeps with the winner?"

Jumping out of her seat, the slightly drunk Anna quipped, "Ahh, a bet with no losers. I'm in."

*

Stepping out of the car into the cool night air, Jenkins took a deep breath as he looked up at the old apartment building. For the last few weeks, he had found himself contemplating what things he would miss and not miss when he retired from police work. He figured he would miss the camaraderie with his coworkers, the mental puzzles, and the satisfaction of putting dangerous criminals away. One thing he knew he would not miss was knocking on doors to interrupt people's lives with questions about murdered friends.

His partner, Wilson, was now running his own cases so Jenkins was alone, which was good because it meant he did not need to explain why he was reopening an investigation mid-trial and why they could not tell the prosecutor what they were doing. After climbing the stairs and catching his breath, Jenkins could hear music playing inside the apartment, so he knocked.

From behind the door a woman called out angrily, "Mr. Card, the music is not loud and I know you are coming up here just to stare at my tits so piss off."

Jenkins knocked again and stated, "It's not Mr. Card. I just need a moment of your time, Ms. Tatum."

After a minute the door, held by the chain, opened a crack and Shelia Tatum's pink-striped hair and makeup-encircled eyes came into view. Upon realizing who was at her door, she sighed and closed the door. Jenkins thought he had wasted his time, but the door re-opened with the chain removed and she waved him in.

"I thought you had the guy who killed Natalie?"

Jenkins stepped inside the interestingly decorated apartment, took a seat on the couch, and set his file on the coffee table. Shelia was dressed in a tight man's dress shirt and cut-off jeans, which Jenkins figured were meant to appear casual but were offset by heavily applied makeup and shiny boots that ran up to her knees. He would never understand youth fashion and was fine with that defect in his knowledge.

"You're right. We are currently trying a suspect. However, a minor concern has arisen regarding the veracity of some of the evidence."

Shelia remained standing as she said, "Look, I've told you everything I know and frankly, I'm just about to head out and I don't really want to rehash this all over again."

Jenkins hesitated. He had been uneasy about taking this step as it would be crossing a line he could not uncross. But now, looking up at this frightened young woman who was trying to appear tough, he decided he needed to know what had truly happened to Natalie Peterson that night—if for no other reason than he did not want any other girls to be found dead in the snow.

"I understand that and I apologize for the intrusion. To be honest, I'm not completely sure why I'm here. There is enough evidence to put away our suspect for good and that should be sufficient but, well, I have some concerns. And I'm retiring this is my last case, and I can't walk away when there are doubts in my mind about what happened that night."

"You don't think this guy on trial did it?"

"He likely did it but I also think the man who left with her from the bar may have been more involved than he is letting on. I don't like leaving guys like that thinking they can get away with doing improper things. It makes them even more dangerous in the future."

Shelia moved towards the couch. "The weirdo from the

bachelor party? He's the one that left the bar with Natalie, right?"

"Yes, his name is Jason Young. He testified today and, well, let's say his story was not all that convincing."

"So if this Jason didn't kill Natalie, what do you think he did?"

"I don't know. Maybe he only kicked her out of his house when she was drunk and helpless. Maybe he drugged her. Maybe he raped her."

Fear and disgust flashed across Shelia's face, and Jenkins figured she did not want to hear about the horrors that faced women in her business. Her stony resolve quickly returned and she said, "Look, there's a lot of fucked up guys out there. I can't be wasting my time helping you chase down every pervert in the city."

He silently opened the file on the coffee table and spread pictures over the coffee table. There were a number showing the abuse inflicted on Peterson's body that he laid out slowly, then on top of these he laid the photo of her face showing her closed, swollen eyes. Next he took out an enlargement of Jason Young's driver's licence photo. The man appeared soft, unassuming, and banal.

"This is Jason Young. He could be anyone, the man next door, the guy who does your taxes or bags your groceries or drives your cab home. No one would suspect him of being violent, but I think he hurt your friend for his enjoyment. I need your help ensuring he never does something like this again."

It seemed that Shelia did not want to show she had been influenced by this dramatic approach, as she merely slumped down on to the couch. But she then asked, "What do you want to know?"

"Can you remember anything from that night that made you think that there was something off about him?"

For fifteen minutes they discussed Young's actions that night. Shelia's memory was hazy. She really only remembered that he had been relatively polite for a pervert at a bachelor party and that he had tipped well. As Jenkins had feared, she could tell him nothing new or helpful.

More so he could provide a semi-defensible explanation for why he had come to talk to her, Jenkins handed her the evidence picture of the underwear and asked, "Do these look familiar to you?"

"Were these Nat's?"

"We found those hidden at the crime scene. We have two witnesses identifying them as what Natalie was wearing at the bachelor party."

Shelia stared at the picture quizzically for a few moments before pointing at the tag barely visible in the photo and answering, "They look like her gear but these are Le Perla. They'd cost like forty bucks a pair—more even. I'd have thought Natalie's were just knock offs."

"You don't think these were hers?"

"I don't know. I know she had a pair like this but I don't think Natalie would spend forty bucks on panties. But who knows, I mean maybe she had a sugar daddy buy them for her or something." She put the picture down but continued to look at it as she said, "Still, it would be odd for her not to tell me if someone bought her those."

*

For over an hour, Charley had been pleasantly immersed in the reality avoidance that came with reading. The protective custody area of the remand center proved not to be the solitary confinement which Charley had been hoping for, but it was an extreme improvement over his previous situation. Instead of a large cell block with forty-eight inmates locked up in pairs, the segregated area held only ten prisoners, elderly or ill men deemed too fragile for the rigors of the general population.

All the men here slept in a dormitory-style room, which should have bothered Charley, but the freedom from his previous cellmate outweighed any unease over being around so many strangers. Charley had taken a bunk in a far corner and promptly ignored his roommates, who, much to his relief, seemed content to ignore him. Plus, the men did not have to go to the dining hall to eat, instead their meals were given to them in the segregated unit. This meant that, for the first time in months, Charley had been able to actually eat his food.

Before lights out, a guard interrupted Charley's peaceful reading and took him to the infirmary. A doctor silently checked on Charley's injuries before giving him a painkiller and a sedative to ensure he could sleep with the cracked ribs. Having endured far worse, he had essentially forgotten about the pain, but he could not find the words to tell the severe-looking doctor that he did not want the medicine.

Back on his bunk, he found that he could no longer focus on the words in his book, so he carefully tucked his glasses inside his pillow case and closed his eyes. The constant threats of prison had helped Charley resist the temptation to fall into his fantasies, but now his medicated consciousness quickly moved to wallow in the familiar dream of saving a pretty girl. As he drifted away, the hint of a crooked smile touched Charley's lips.

*

Loud music came through the phone and Hugh hoped that Julius Garner was not in some bar in Mexico. "Garner, its Hugh. I've got a job for you and MacKenzie. You guys in town?"

Jules Garner and Trenton Mackenzie were the men Hugh had called to pull Jason's car out of the alley. The pair were former oil field workers, Jules a drilling supervisor and MacKenzie a truck driver. About seven years ago they caught Young's attention when a gas well in British Columbia blew, killing two derrick hands. It was odd for a gas well to blow given the amount of safety equipment that was involved, and the story caused Hugh to recall that he had heard an equipment salesman bragging that he had sold used blow out preventers only a month before the accident. It only took a few phone calls for Hugh to quietly put the pieces together.

Through his investigation he determined that Jules and MacKenzie had created a lucrative side business for themselves where they would swap out new equipment being delivered to job sites with used equipment and then sell the new equipment for a profit. The system was fairly ingenious and complicated as it involved a wide range of individuals. They had apparently done this for years without getting caught until greed caused them to replace one piece of equipment they should have left alone.

Intrigued by their entrepreneurial spirit, Hugh opted not to turn them in. Instead he blackmailed them into coming to work for him as secret consultants of a sort. He paid them well for the work they did to keep them relatively happy, but if they ever stepped out of line, he did not hesitate to remind them that there was no statute of limitations for felony murder.

As usual, Jules' voice was toneless as he answered, "We're in town."

At first Hugh had thought about handling this problem on his own, but he figured his involvement would bring too much public scrutiny given his stature in the community. Next he had considered using an escort given the testimony Jason had already provided, but Hugh did not like the idea of a random whore having leverage over him. He did not like having anyone else involved but it was necessary, and he found it more palpable to know that he could completely bury any men who had dirt on him. That was why he had ultimately decided to call Garner and MacKenzie.

"Can you be at my house in an hour?"

"This a paying job?"

"Aren't they all?"

"We'll be there."

With that the phone went dead. Hugh called Jason and relayed to him, in the simplest terms possible, what he was supposed to do.

CHAPTER 23

Clay Matthews looked exhausted. His skin was grey and his eyelids were drooping to the point that Brian wondered if he had slept at all last night. The sight of the harried prosecutor made Brian inwardly smile, as for the first time it seemed like the mighty machinery of the prosecution was fallible.

They were sitting in the chambers of Justice Rothborg half an hour before the trial was set to start at the urgent request of Matthews. He did not know what the issue was and Matthews, rubbing the bridge of his nose slowly as he stared at the carpet, had not been willing to tell him what was going on. It was not unusual for counsel to raise procedural issues with the judge outside of the courtroom, but Brian was highly concerned regardless.

He looked around the small office in an attempt to remain calm while waiting. In law school he had imagined sitting in judges' chambers with wood panelled walls lined with leather-bound law books, padded club chairs, and bars discretely holding brandy decanters. Instead he had learned that judge's chambers were merely offices. Simple, functional furniture filled the small space, and they were sitting on standard office chairs that could be found in any conference room in the city. Instead of bookcases filled with legal tomes, a sleek computer monitor sat on the desk. Brian was forced to realize that the application of justice was handled as a bureaucracy, merely another department of the government.

Rothborg walked in carrying a travel mug of coffee in one hand and a pile of papers in the other. "Morning, gentlemen. I guess we are getting an early start on this today."

The men lifted their asses from their seats, pretending to stand before settling back down as she sat behind the desk. A nameless court reporter quickly set up her equipment in the corner of the room and when she gave Rothborg a nod that she was ready, the judge said formally, "It's eight thirty three in the morning on May 5, 2011, and we are meeting on Docket number 8894632. Present are Justice Rothborg, counsel for the defence Brian Cox, and Crown prosecutor Clay Matthews. Mr. Matthews, this is your application."

"Yes, My Lady. I actually have two matters to discuss this morning. First, the prosecution would like to amend its witness list to add two more witnesses—"

Brian interrupted using his best exasperated lawyer voice, "My Lady, we had no prior indication that the prosecution was seeking to add new witnesses at this late date—"

Rothborg lifted a hand, "Ok, ok, Mr. Cox. It is too early in the morning for dramatics. Let's hear out Mr. Matthews before we get overly excited."

Matthews continued, "We submit that the cross examination of Mr. Young yesterday by the defence created an implication for the jury that perhaps Mr. Young was culpable with respect to this crime. This constitutes a positive defence being put forth which we have a right to refute."

Brian had not even considered the fact that his battering of Young on the stand would constitute a positive defence, and now the unknown ramifications of that legal distinction worried him. He was not sure what he should do but he needed to say something, so he stated, "Regardless, My Lady, the prosecution cannot merely change its disclosed evidence to fit one of its own witness's testimony."

As was the custom, the two lawyers argued with one another by addressing their comments to the judge. It was like two siblings arguing about who should get the last piece of cake by pointing out to a parent all the flaws of the other child. Matthews contended that the new witnesses were to provide rebuttal to information gleaned from the cross examination, which was acceptable under the rules since the defence had essentially provided an alternate view of the crime. Brian countered that it was information from the prosecution's own witness that was being rebutted and that did not allow them to re-introduce new evidence.

They bickered these points for fifteen minutes before Rothborg put a stop to it. "Alright, I am going to allow these new witnesses but only to the extent that they rebut points raised by defence counsel's cross examination of Mr. Young. You step outside of that scope by one inch, Mr. Matthews, and I will give a stern instruction to the jury to disregard these new witnesses in their entirety."

While he was not sure Charley would survive in prison long enough to see the appeal process through, Brian figured this ruling may at least provide them with grounds if they were needed, so he said, "My Lady, I would like to state my objection to this finding for the record."

Rothborg stated, "So noted. Mr. Matthews, what is your second issue?"

Matthews rubbed the bridge of his nose more before continuing, "Some additional evidence has come to the attention of the prosecution which we feel needs to be disclosed to the defence at this time."

The prosecution is required to disclose all information they have to the defence prior to the trial. Even with his lack of experience, Brian knew it was odd for new evidence to be disclosed mid-trial and it could be a sufficient breach of procedure to result in a mistrial. Brian protested, "First new witnesses, now new evidence. This is making a mockery out of the disclosure process—"

Matthews interrupted, handing a paper to the judge, then thrusting a copy in front of Brian and saying, "Save your breath. I wouldn't disclose it if I didn't have to. I received this late last night."

The document was a photocopy of a single page of investigator notes dated yesterday. Detective Jenkins had visited Shelia Tatum again. The notes showed that the conversation appeared to be a fairly banal re-enactment of her previous interview by the police. Until the last line where Shelia questioned whether the expensive underwear actually belonged to Peterson.

Brian could feel Rothborg looking to him for a response, but his mind was swimming so he pretended to be reading in order to buy himself some time to think. This evidence was good for Charley but it only raised credibility concerns, it did not provide enough certainty to allow the jury to entirely disregard the underwear. He needed time to investigate further, but he did not like the idea of giving Matthews more time to formulate his rebuttal to Jason

Young's terrible testimony. He briefly considered moving for a mistrial but then they would only get better prepared and re-try Charley. Finally he stated, "My Lady, given this morning's events, I would like to have Mr. Matthews present his rebuttal witnesses to Mr. Young's testimony this morning and then I would seek to have a one-day recess in order for us to further examine this newly disclosed evidence from Ms. Tatum."

Matthews protested, "My Lady, the defence cannot have their cake and eat it too. If they want a recess, I am fine with that but there is no reason for that recess not to commence immediately—"

Rothborg held up her hand and interrupted, "Mr. Matthews, you are the one pushing the rules here. I think you should be glad Mr. Cox is not asking for a mistrial. I will allow the rebuttal testimony this morning followed by a recess of one business day, which will give the defence the weekend to absorb what you are dumping on them at this late date. Unless some more procedural oddities have been created, let us get to the courtroom."

As Brian walked out of the judge's chambers behind Matthews, he could hear him muttering under his breath about incompetent detectives.

*

Having been roundly chastised last night when he gave Matthews his notes from the unauthorized interview of Shelia Tatum, Jenkins wanted to avoid running into the irate prosecutor. He waited until the trial started before sneaking in to take a spot in the back row of the gallery. Matthews' re-direct examination of Jason Young was already in progress and proceeding briskly.

Mathews asked, "At what time did you finish playing cards?"

Jason Young responded woodenly, "Three in the morning."

Jenkins did not know what they were talking about, but he guessed that an alibi for Jason Young on the night of the murder was being presented. Matthews continued, "And they both left your home at that time?"

"Yes."

"What did you do then?"

"Went to sleep."

"And what time did you sleep until?"

"Until noon."

"Thank you. No further questions."

Both the prosecutor and the witness appeared tired but they seemed to have their routine down pat. Jenkins was willing to bet they had been up until the wee hours, locked in some windowless conference room going over Young's testimony *ad nauseam* to ensure there would be no more mistakes.

Rothborg turned to the defence counsel, "Re-cross Mr. Cox?"

Given how well things had gone with the original cross, Jenkins was not surprised to see the defence lawyer eagerly hop to his feet, "Yes, My Lady, thank you."

"Mr. Young, have you played cards with these gentlemen before?"

"Yes."

"How many times?"

"Twelve times."

"You are certain of that number?"

"Yes."

"When was the last time you played together?"

"Four weeks ago."

For almost an hour the defence counsel peppered Young with questions. What games were played? How much was wagered? Who sat where? What snacks were eaten? And so on as he tried to find any sort of crack in the story that he could pick at. It didn't work. It was obvious to Jenkins that, after his previous debacle, the witness had learned to keep his answers short and straightforward with no uncertainty or embellishment.

Jenkins noticed that Young kept glancing into the gallery.

He had seen the look of a witness trying to get help from a person in the audience numerous times, but this was not that look. It was more of a frightful checking to make sure he was not angering someone. It reminded him of a child giving a performance in front of overly involved parents with the kid constantly checking with them for approval. Since he was hiding from Matthews way in the back, Jenkins could not tell whom exactly the witness was looking at, but his curiosity was piqued.

When the defence counsel finally gave up, Matthews stood and announced the calling of Julius Garner as a re-direct witness. Jenkins had never heard the name before. His last trial was turning out to be the strangest of his career.

A bear of a man wearing an ill-fitting suit was escorted into the courtroom by a bailiff and led to the witness stand. Someone unfamiliar with the trial watching Julius Garner scowling at the gallery as he was sworn in probably would have assumed he was the accused. He was massive but he did not appear soft. Jenkins figured he was the type of man who had spent much of his life doing physical work fuelled by a diet of steak, potatoes, and beer which led to his hulking form. But it was not Garner's imposing physical presence that set off Jenkins's policeman's intuition; it was the way the man glared at everyone as if he was attempting to intimidate the room. Normally, witnesses are nervous or at least uncertain, but this man looked wholly confrontational.

Matthews seemed uneasy questioning this beast and he moved through the process as rapidly as possible. In a manner of minutes he managed to get the obviously rehearsed testimony from Garner. He had spent the Sunday night in question with Young and another man, Trenton MacKenzie, playing cards at Young's house. He had won over a thousand dollars, but at three in the morning, Young was out of money so Garner and Mackenzie left. At no point did he see or hear anything suspicious in the house.

Defence counsel put up a valiant effort in cross examination, but for the most part, he only got useless answers delivered with an icy glare. Cox did point out that it was odd for a blue collar man like Garner to be socializing with a rich loner. However, this point was diffused when Garner simply responded, "Yeah, that kid is a loser but I got bills to pay. If I can make a grand off of him sitting around playing cards and drinking his beer for a night I'll take that deal seven days a week."

Next Matthews called Trenton MacKenzie to the stand, and a short, wiry man with a badly tied tie and a clean-shaven head was led into the courtroom as Garner was led out. On the surface, MacKenzie seemed more nervous than Garner as his eyes darted about and he seemed to shift with extra energy, but Jenkins figured it was less nerves and more a case of the man being cagey. It was as if he was searching for something to steal or an escape route rather than being concerned by all the eyes on him.

MacKenzie's answers to Matthews' questions were almost identical to the answers given by Garner, except this witness had only won eight hundred dollars off of Young. Again Cox attempted to poke holes in the testimony, but again he was stymied. While he was not buying the story, Jenkins had to admit that Jason Young had managed to establish a fairly believable alibi for the night of the murder.

Instead of carrying on with the trial as expected, the judge called a recess until Monday morning. No explanation was given as to why they were taking a break, but Jenkins guessed it had something to do with his last-minute interview with Shelia Tatum. The recollection of what he had done and the fury it had invoked in Matthews reminded him that he should get going before the prosecutor saw him there. Still, he lingered for just long enough to catch a glimpse of the man Young had been looking to during his testimony as the crowd stood to leave. He recognized him as the man who had waited while they interviewed Jason, his father, Hugh Young. While he figured it was unusual for a parent to watch his adult son testify, it was at least understandable. The fact that this powerful business man, however, stayed and took the time to watch the testimony of two alibi witnesses was yet another oddity in a long list of oddities.

CHAPTER 24

When the first alibi witness had testified, Charley wasn't sure, but he thought it might somehow be the large man who had driven the truck into the alley to pull out the sports car. When the second, smaller witness testified, Charley was certain that the two men testifying for the prosecution were the same men he saw that night. Confusion struck at him. He knew that this was important and he should tell Brian, but when he looked over at the lawyer he was busily writing notes and paying careful attention to the testimony. Charley could not force himself to interrupt.

Finally, when Brian got up to ask his questions, he took the opportunity to write on Brian's notepad, "I need to tell you something."

When the questioning was over and Brian saw the note he looked at Charley, who gave a slight nod before looking back down at his lap. Then the judge dismissed the court. He was taken to an interview room.

After Charley waited for few minutes, the lawyer walked into the small room, tossing his brief case in the corner as he asked, "What do you need to tell me?"

"Those two men."

Brian flopped down in the chair across the table, "What men, Charley?"

The tone was not harsh but it was clear Brian was exasperated, and this made Charley even more nervous. "The two men, the two men that were witnesses."

"Julius Garner and Trenton MacKenzie?"

Charley had not paid attention to the names, but he assumed Brian was right so he nodded.

"Ok, what about them?"

"They were in the alley that night."

Brian leaned forward over the table, causing him to instinctively lean away, "What do you mean they were in the alley?"

"They were the ones with the truck and the chain that took

the car away."

For a long moment Brian merely sat there, apparently trying to comprehend the information as Charley worried he would call him a liar. Then the lawyer retrieved his brief case and pulled out the letter Charley had written. Despite it seeming like he had written the letter a lifetime ago, Charley could still remember how he had described the two men who had come to get the car out of the ditch: one was big with long hair; one was small with a bald head. Brian looked up from the letter and said, "Damn Charley, why didn't you tell me this in the courtroom? I could have asked them about it. That might have thrown them off."

He had no intelligent response so he simply shrugged.

Another long pause. He waited for Brian to erupt at him for being so stupid. But no eruption came, instead the lawyer only sighed, "Shit, it definitely seems someone is working hard to make sure you go down for this." After a moment he said more clearly, "Well, I doubt there was much I could do with the information anyhow. Those two seemed sharp enough, bold enough, and coached enough not to admit they had gone anywhere near that alley. We probably would have only looked foolish."

With that, he patted him on the shoulder and moved towards the door, saying, "Sorry Charley, looks like we need to go back to the drawing board."

*

Stepping out of the courthouse and into the spring air, exhausted from having been up all night repeatedly going over what Jason, Garner, and MacKenzie would say on the stand, Hugh took a deep breath and let the relief of this all being behind him wash over him. The testimony of Garner and McKenzie had not been spectacular, but he figured it was sufficient to deflect any finger pointing towards Jason. However, as he turned the corner into the parking lot, he saw Garner and McKenzie leaning causally against his car. His relief was instantly replaced by rage. Cursing to himself he hurried over.

"You fucking idiots, do you really think it's smart for us to be having a goddamn meeting right outside the courthouse?" Hugh growled through gritted teeth, trying to keep his voice low despite his anger.

Garner calmly stepped up and looked down at him, "You owe us for that in there."

He forced himself not to back away from the intimidating man, "I know, I know. Have I ever fucking stiffed you before?"

"No, but we were thinking that your price might be low for all the risk we're taking on this."

Yet again Hugh realized nothing was ever easy. He had already paid each of them five thousand dollars for their late night tow truck driving and had agreed to pay them each another twenty thousand dollars for their doctored testimony. As he was already in for fifty thousand dollars to these thugs he was not keen to renegotiate, but he did not like the idea of haggling over the price of perjured testimony in the courthouse parking lot.

"Ok, we can talk but not here. Get in the car and we'll go for a drive."

Garner made a point of pausing to watch two police officers walk past before he looked back down at Hugh and said, "No. We want forty grand each."

This brazen, aggressive style had been one of the things that had attracted Hugh to hiring Garner and he knew the man would not give up easily, so he pointedly asked, "Do I need to remind you that there is no statute of limitations for felony murder?"

This brought an unnerving smile to Garner's face as he answered, "Way I see it now we are pretty close to even on who can tell the cops about the other's activities. Wanna bet on which one of us would fare better in the joint?"

Looking up at the menacing man Hugh thought he was probably bluffing, but the risk was so high there was no way he could call it. "Alright, I'll do thirty thousand each."

"Tonight."

"Tonight. The bench. Six o'clock."

A curt nod from the beast and it was done as he walked

away with McKenzie trailing after him.

*

The reception area for the offices of Fredrickson Law LLP, was filled by a motley group of individuals seeking legal advice. Two apparent Hell's Angels were staring at a woman wearing short shorts, thigh high boots, and a tube top over obviously fake breasts. An overly thin man was loudly discussing a drug deal on his cell phone. And a child of about four was running amok with no apparent parental supervision. Brian told the harried receptionist why he was there and then leaned awkwardly against the wall until a woman with numerous piercings and a tattoo covering most of her neck walked out from the back and the receptionist told him to go in.

Not looking back as the hooker and the drug dealer began arguing about how each of them were supposed to be next, Brian made his way back to Fredrickson's office. He was eagerly greeted by the round lawyer behind the messy desk. "Brian, shouldn't you be in court? What happened?"

Brian had talked to Fredrickson at least twice a day during the trial to keep him apprised so he only needed to fill him on the morning's activities. He told him about the meeting in the judge's chambers, the report about Shelia Tatum doubting that the underwear belonged to Peterson, the rehearsed alibi testimony, and finally, about how Charley thought the men who testified were the tow truck drivers.

Fredrickson shook his wide head and let out a low whistle before saying, "Wow, you sure got a doozy for your first murder trial. I suppose you see the problems as well as I do?"

"Yeah, we know all of this bullshit is going on but we have no proof or any way to get it before jury."

"Right. You did a good job by getting the recess, buying us some time to consider options. What do you think about next steps?"

"I don't know what to do. I wish we could get Charley's evidence in but he'll be worse than useless on the stand. The judge seems to be on our side now. Maybe I could make some sort of an application that Charley is unable to assist in his own defence and attempt to get his testimony in through a video deposition or some other method."

"I doubt she'd let that go this late in the game. This trial is already enough of a mess. Even if we did get his evidence in that way, the jury'll just see the accused making a bunch of self-serving statements with no back up."

"You're right. Honestly, I don't even know if he would be able to answer questions on video. We'll have to do this without Charley telling the court what he knows."

They discussed how Brian would need to call Shelia Tatum to make the jury more suspicious to the veracity of the underwear evidence. They also considered the idea of re-calling Detective Jenkins to determine why he was still asking questions about the underwear. The whole time they had been talking, Fredrickson's phone had been ringing constantly and twice his receptionist had yelled down the hall in vain attempts to get his attention. The lawyer seemed immune to this chaos but eventually he looked at his watch and said, "Sorry Brian, I better get back to it before those bikers out there decide to burn the place down."

"No problem, thanks for your time."

"Glad to try and help, although this case is so strange I'm not sure how much help I'm able to give."

"Yeah, as you can see, I'm in a bit over my head on this one."

Fredrickson laughed at this and waved around his office covered in paper as he replied, "Son, look at this place, I've been in over my head for thirty years. Welcome to the criminal defence bar."

*

Despite knowing the prosecutor would not be receptive, Jenkins had tried to talk to Matthews about the fact that he now was concerned that Hugh Young might be manipulating the trial. As predicted, Matthews was livid at this suggestion. What he had not predicted was how adamant Matthews was that Jenkins no longer interfered with the case. Within minutes of being ordered out of Matthews' office, Jenkins was called by the police chief and told that he had been informed that any further unauthorized investigation based on unfounded suspicions would likely result in a mistrial. The chief figured Jenkins was over-thinking the case because his work load had dissipated on the eve of his retirement, and he was not about to have the fanciful ponderings of a bored mind result in a murderer going free. The orders were clear: Jenkins was off the file. The underlying threat was more subtle but present nonetheless: if he did anything further, his ability to retire with a full pension would be jeopardized by a professional misconduct hearing.

He knew the smartest thing to do was to leave the case alone and spend the last week before his retirement reading magazines and going for long lunches. But Jenkins did not like the idea that some rich businessman might be sending a homeless man to jail to save his spoiled son. He also knew that perpetually wondering if the verdict in the last case of his long career had been tainted would overwhelm any pleasant memories and soil any sense of pride he had in his work as a cop. Plus, he hated long lunches almost as much as he hated arrogant prosecutors willing to imprison the wrong citizen as long as it meant avoiding the embarrassment of losing a trial. Jenkins logged onto his computer and began looking into the life of Hugh Young.

*

After leaving the chaos of Fredrickson's office, Brian headed home, made a pot of coffee, and spread his papers over the kitchen table, hoping vainly that he would see some angle that would allow him to use all of this new information. He was on his third cup of coffee but no closer to finding the elusive angle when Anna got home from school. Her eyes lit up when she saw him home and she happily asked, "Hey, why are you home so early? They drop the charges?"

He stood up and gave Anna a hug, welcoming her home. "No, but we are recessed until Monday."

"Really, why?"

"It was an interesting morning, to say the least."

He explained while she quietly listened, and when he finished she said, "What a mess. Sounds like the prosecution has made a dog's breakfast out of this. Can they really bring in evidence and witnesses this late in the trial?"

Brian shrugged. "I probably could get a mistrial but I doubt the judge would grant a mistrial with prejudice and Matthews is not the type to give up so they would simply regroup and re-try Charley. That would give them time to fill in all these gaps and would likely mean more time in custody for Charley waiting for a new trial."

Anna had apparently learned not to complain about the unfairness of the system and instead asked, "What about the girl who doesn't think the underwear belonged to the victim?"

"It is strange that it came up so late but I doubt it will sway anything. They have two guys saying that they were what Peterson was wearing, plus they were found where she was killed. This Shelia girl can't be positive they were not the victim's." Brian took a sip of the cold coffee before continuing, "And I was thinking about it this afternoon: if the real killer planted them in order to frame Charley, why would he use a fake pair? The killer should have the actual pair she was wearing."

"Who knows? If someone is crazy enough to kill a girl maybe the psycho would not want to let go of his cherished souvenir."

"Maybe, but I'm sure if I attack the validity of the underwear, the prosecution will have a field day making the claim of planted evidence sound ridiculous unless we have something more concrete to present."

Anna shuffled through the mess of papers strewn on the table until she found the photograph of the underwear. She looked at picture as she said, "You know I'd bet there's only a few stores in town that sell high-end stuff like this."

Catching her gist, he asked, "You think a clerk is going to remember selling a specific pair of panties five months ago?"

"If this Jason Young guy is as odd as you make him sound, then maybe he creeped out the sales girl. Women remember getting creeped out. You're recessed until Monday. You want to sit around here for three days wallowing in how screwed you are?"

It was a long shot but Anna was right: he did not want to continue to stew over the same problems he had been stewing over for months, so he said with a sigh, "Alright, I guess I'm going shopping."

Anna moved towards the bedroom, calling back over her shoulder, "Let me change and I'll go with you. You'll need help figuring out what stores to try and you'll seem less weird if you have a woman with you."

Brian knew it was odd for his girlfriend to be helping him on a murder case, but this was far from normal legal work and the task would be less painful with her along. He doubted Anna would take no for an answer anyhow.

Predictably, there were no records of warrants or arrests related to Hugh Young. Online searches led to business information, which was not overly helpful. If this was a normal investigation, Jenkins would head over to the man's house and try to ask him a few pointed questions, but this was not a normal investigation. A businessman like Young would immediately call his expensive lawyer, who would scream police harassment, and before his looking around had even begun, Jenkins would be hauled back before the police chief.

Instead he decided to go about getting at Hugh Young in a more roundabout way: by focussing on Garner and MacKenzie. Their lengthy records showed both of them being arrested for minor infractions, normally involving the over-consumption of alcohol. A DMV search showed that Garner and MacKenzie both drove Ford F-150s, but the addresses given were post office boxes rather than residential addresses. A review of the various police reports revealed that the bar they normally terrorized was Poco Loco's downtown, a seedy watering hole that he recalled as a problem spot from back in his uniformed patrol days. He decided it was worth taking a shot and paying the grimy bar a visit.

*

Hugh did not consider himself to be a sentimental man, but as he aged, he found himself recalling his past more and more often. Sitting on the bench in the peaceful Prince's Island Park, he recalled that this was where he would eat his lunch when he first started working in the city. Back then he was broke and friendless; he did not want anyone in the office seeing him eating his sad bologna sandwiches by himself, so he retreated to the solitude of the park on the edge of downtown for his lunch breaks. This was also where he closed his first deal, the deal that allowed him to move beyond bologna lunches.

It was over thirty years ago. He had made it through college where he learned all there was to know about reading seismic surveys. His degree got him a job at a survey company in Calgary where he worked with geologists reviewing logs and pinpointing drill locations. This was in the days before computer analysis, which meant he was spending fourteen-hour days pouring over reams of data. It was there that he saw the fortunes people could make by simply drilling where he told them to drill.

The plan came to him while he was working alone on a Sunday. He had spent the day reviewing an impressive survey of the northwest corner of a quarter section of land near Lacombe that showed a highly prospective hydrocarbon reservoir. Later that night, however, he was reviewing a survey that appeared completely dry, even though it was only a mile from the rich site. The exploration rights to the one piece of land were worth millions while the rights to other were worthless. Hugh still remembered pouring himself another cup of coffee, they had those ugly, bumpy brownish-green mugs popular in the seventies. They were the same cups his parents had.

That night, tired and frustrated, the sight and feel of the familiar cup reminded him of home. Normally, Hugh shirked memories of his childhood but, for some reason, that night he allowed one recollection to come through. His father, not one for giving advice, was talking to his mother about an unpopular cousin who had accomplished something. Hugh did not recall the specifics but he clearly remembered the statement, "Success happens by overcoming obstacles or because all the obstacles have been removed for you."

As a child, Hugh had not truly understood at first but as he learned of the world, he pieced it together. The cousin had achieved because her powerful parents had made sure she would succeed and his father placed no value on her inherited success. No one had removed any obstacles for Hugh but, that night, he realized he was all by himself in the office with very valuable information. More importantly, he was the only one who knew the information even existed. It dawned on him that his father had been wrong, you did not need to overcome obstacles or have them removed, perhaps you could simply circumvent them.

From that point, it was merely a matter of changing the log numbers on the surveys so the expensive land became the worthless land and vice versa. The rights to the good land would be thought worthless and be abandoned back to the Crown, who would then put it back up for sale at the next government auction where it would be lowly valued. Obviously, when the exploration company drilled into what they had been told was a deep oil reservoir and got nothing it would reflect badly on the survey company, but no one would be able to fault Hugh specifically as his analysis of the fraudulently labelled log would be confirmed by any other geologist's review.

A week later, Hugh met with his uncle on the park bench. His uncle, who made his living selling insurance, had quietly incorporated a new corporation innocuously called Northern Lights Oil and Gas and used a line of credit to provide the new corporation the funds needed to buy the exploration rights and drill one well. Hugh gave him the land location and his uncle gave him the trust agreement showing that Hugh was the beneficial owner of fifty percent of the new company. They had the well drilled that winter, and to the surprise of everyone but him and his uncle, the unheard of company hit a gusher.

Before that year was out, Northern Lights Oil and Gas had, miraculously, made two more significant finds on land they had bought for extremely little. After that initial run, Hugh left the survey company before anyone could put together what he was up to. Soon thereafter, his uncle decided, with Hugh's encouragement, to take a payout and retire to Arizona. As a result, at the age of twenty-four, Hugh found himself owning and running a highly successful oil company.

    His reminiscing abruptly ended as he saw Garner and MacKenzie striding over the bridge into the park. The sight of them brought him back from the victories of the past to the uncomfortable present. The two men approached the bench and when they were a few steps away, he stood up, leaving two envelopes thick with cash on the cement bench. Now sixty thousand dollars lighter, he silently walked past Garner and MacKenzie out of the park.

*

By the time the stores were getting ready to close, Brian and Anna had gone through half a tank of gas and one food court dinner while visiting high-end lingerie shops all over the city. There was only one place left on the list they had compiled off the internet, a boutique called Belle's Ball tucked away in the corner of a strip mall on a trendy section of 17th Avenue.

    Despite the narrow floor space, the store was not crowded as only a few luxury items were on display. Before they could take three steps inside, a middle aged woman who was heavily adorned in gaudy jewellery and appeared overly tanned for spring in Calgary scurried from behind the counter, asking, "Hello, can I help you?"

    Following the script they had perfected through their numerous stops, Brian handed over his business card and said, "My name is Brian Cox. I'm the defence counsel in a criminal trial. This is my associate, Anna. We are trying to determine if a piece of evidence relevant to the trial was bought in your store."

    The woman looked at the card. So far the responses to this introduction had been pretty evenly split between the clerk being eager to help, probably happy to have some excitement in her work day, or the clerk refusing to help, probably concerned that this odd request would get her in trouble. With the clinking of jewellery, the woman looked back up and asked, "What is the trial about?"

    At this question, Brian knew she was going to help without any painful arm-twisting, so he gave her a straightforward answer. "It's a murder trial and one of the pieces of evidence is a pair of underwear."

Anna dutifully handed over the picture and the clerk put on a pair of glasses that hung from her neck on a chain as she muttered, "Oh, my, a murder?"

"Yes, a young woman was killed about five months ago. There is some question as to whether she was wearing the underwear in that picture at the time of her abduction."

"Oh, ok," she carefully reviewed the photo. "Well, yes, we did sell those back then. They were part of a specialty bra and panty set. They were not very popular and I believe we only sold a few sets. Let me check the computer."

They were led to the counter where the woman typed for a few moments before saying, "Yes, yes. We sold a set on December 9th."

Brian's pulse quickened as he asked, "Do your records show who made the purchase?"

"No, it was a cash payment for that set plus a teddy." A quizzical look crossed her face as she tapped the computer screen with a long finger nail, "Wait a moment, I remember this sale."

Anna stepped forward, obviously excited that their detective work was paying off, and asked, "Was the buyer a man?"

"No, it was to a young woman. Very attractive. Probably in her early twenties. Long black hair. She was dressed in business attire. I remember this sale because she was extremely specific about the panties she wanted and seemed very relieved that we had them, but then she came back the next day to return the bra from the set along with the teddy."

Brian asked, "She wanted to return everything but the panties?"

"Yes. As you can imagine we generally don't take items back for hygiene reasons. But when I asked her why she wanted to return them, she was apologetic and shyly told me that she realized she could not afford them. I thought, perhaps, a gentleman friend had left her. Anyway, I didn't think that any of the items had been worn. I clearly recall that when I told her I could not take the bra back as it was part of a set she seemed upset. I felt sorry for her so I changed my mind and offered to buy it back at half price which she eagerly accepted."

Anna showed the clerk a picture of Jason Young and hopefully asked, "Are you sure this man was not with the woman?"

"No, I'm pretty sure she was alone both times she came in."

"Did you get her name?"

The clerk furrowed her brow and looked at the computer screen, "It was a cash purchase so we have nothing on the system."

"Do you remember any information that might help us track her down?"

She glared at the screen as if the answer would magically appear before shaking her head and answering, "It was quite some time ago. I don't think so. I remember fairly well what she looked like and that she seemed like a nice girl who was perhaps a bit down on her luck—that's all, though."

Brian asked, "Is there any way you can tell if the pair we have is the same pair this woman bought? Like a serial number or something?"

"No. They are a designer brand so they are not labelled like mass produced items."

After thanking the clerk for her help, Anna and Brian left. Anna was clearly enthusiastic that they had obtained at least some information. While he did not say anything, Brian was not sure how helpful this would be without being able to connect the purchase by the unknown woman to the evidence found in the basement. With Shelia Tatum testifying that she doubted that Peterson owned designer underwear and the clerk testifying that a pair had been bought shortly after the killing, Brian might be able to further hurt the credibility of the prosecution's key piece of evidence. However, he doubted damaging the credibility of the evidence would be enough.

*

Parked across the wide street, Jenkins had a good view of the debauchery occurring in the parking lot of Poco Loco's. In the two hours he had been there, he had seen three obvious drug deals, a fight between two homeless men, and one charge of soliciting a prostitute being consummated in the back of a pickup truck. Jenkins added attending these types of locales to the list of things he would not miss when he retired.

As he began thinking about quitting and heading home to bed, Jenkins saw a black Ford pickup speed into the parking lot. He watched as the unmistakable bulk of Julius Garner got out of the driver's side and the smaller figure of Trenton MacKenzie slipped out of the passenger's door. The two men strode into the bar. It appeared Jenkins's work day was not over.

Stepping inside, the detective was accosted by the intertwined smells of deep fried food, unwashed bodies, and half a century of stale cigarette smoke. The space was filled with a dozen dirty tables holding patrons representing what Jenkins knew to be the entire spectrum of desperate people, from the downright desolate hoping someone will buy them a glass of draft to wannabe entrepreneurs trying to impress the easily impressed with stories of fanciful business ventures. Four video lottery machines had entranced four players into mindlessly pouring money into them. A redheaded woman in a short skirt who Jenkins figured to be a hooker was flirtatiously playing pool with a drunk young man, probably attempting to get him so interested that he would not think to say no when she finally revealed it would cost him. A fat man in a rumpled suit was loudly telling an elderly man, who appeared to be asleep, about some masterful real estate scheme he had come up with. All in all, Jenkins recognized it as a standard night in the city's underbelly.

Jenkins inconspicuously sat on a stool near the end of the sticky bar where he could watch the two men from the corner of his eye as they settled in at a large table. It became immediately obvious that the two alibi witnesses were regulars at the dingy bar. Without a word, the tired-looking waitress quickly brought over a jug of beer while a couple of the bar flies came over to join them.

Garner and MacKenzie let it be known that they were there to celebrate and the party picked up as the other patrons learned they were flush with cash. Rounds of drinks were bought, the music was turned up, and the prostitute from the pool table abandoned her mark to focus her attention on Garner.

Jenkins had planned to try to start an informal conversation with the men, but now it was unlikely he would be able to penetrate the crowd of partiers. He leaned over and asked the wizened bartender, "Is it always like this in here?"

He nodded at Garner and MacKenzie. "When those two find a pay day it is."

"What do they do?"

"Don't know and don't want to know."

Jenkins nursed a bottle of beer for an hour, trying to discreetly listen in hopes the source of the money would be revealed, but no intelligible conversation was being conducted. Giving up, he paid for his drink and headed to the door. As he walked past the jubilation, he saw Garner pull out a thick wad of bills from his jeans and peel off a hundred dollar bill, which he laid on the waitress's tray before calling for another round. The alibi witnesses had definitely found a pay day on the very same day they had testified to protect a rich man's son. Coincidences kept piling up.

CHAPTER 25

The pleasant, elderly guard who had first hidden Charley away before his bail hearing mainly worked in the protective custody area and was delivering mail. He unexpectedly walked over to Charley and tossed a letter onto his lap. "Mail for you."

Picking up the envelope by one corner, he looked at it as if it were about to explode. The guard laughed, "It's just a letter son. I don't think you need to be afraid of it."

Without thinking, Charley asked, "Who is it from?"

The elderly guard looked down at the letter and answered, "The return address says it's from M. Ewanuschuk in Jacksonville, Florida. That your dad?"

"Mother." The word slipped from his lips as a whisper.

"Well, there you go. It's always nice to get a letter from your mom."

The guard walked away, leaving Charley sitting numbly on his prison bunk holding the letter. He had not heard from his mother since he had been told to leave home eight years ago. In his first couple of years in Calgary, when he became particularly desperate, he had gathered enough courage to go into the public library a few times to use the computers to find contact information for her in order to try to get some help. Each time, though, he found nothing useful and had to return to the streets feeling more lost and alone than ever before. After the third attempt he decided he would never try to find her again, having learned the painful lesson that hope was a luxury he could not afford. Now, however, he was looking at her name and address and that trickle of hope that he would be getting help forced its way back into his hardened consciousness.

The envelope had already been slit open by the prison officials so Charley only had to slip out the single sheet of loose leaf paper. The letter, written in his mother's blocky hand writing, was remarkably brief:

Dear Charles,

Emma Mortenson (I do the email with her) told me that she saw about you on the news. I hope you did not do what they say you did. Either way I am glad your father is not alive to see what has happened.

We have a condo in Florida with a pool. It is very nice. The weather is warm but it might rain later this week. Last week we went to Miami with a bus tour group from The Church and we saw whales.

I will pray for you as only Jesus can judge.

The letter was an example of his mother's usual ramblings, and it took him a second to contemplate the nonsensical writing. He supposed that the proper response would be a sense of nostalgia at finally hearing from his mother or even sadness, but instead rage filled him. He was being tortured in prison, on trial for his life, and his mother, who had said nothing to him in years, was writing about weather and whales. She had put him in this position by selling the family farm out from under him and abandoning him to the torments of a solitary life. And now, the only help he would get were her useless prayers. The rage was so powerful that he felt physical pain at not being able to act upon it. He had wanted so very little from his mother and instead he had gotten worse than nothing. After years alone he had finally come to terms with the fact that he would never get anything from her and now, for no reason, she had decided to finally write him to let him know she was still not going to help.

The powerful rage coursing through him reminded him of a day a lifetime ago. For his entire life Charley could not recall ever asking his father for anything, but at the beginning of grade twelve he desperately wanted to get his driver's license so he could stop riding the school bus. Their farm was littered with old trucks, so it would be no problem getting one of them road worthy, but even though he had been driving since he was eleven, he did not know the various traffic rules well enough to pass the driving test. When he saw an ad at school saying that a driving school was offering lunchtime classes, it seemed like a perfect solution, except the program cost three hundred dollars.

For two weeks Charley had been waiting for an opportunity to ask for the money and he thought it had come when they got an offer on an old tractor that had been sitting in the yard for years. His father had thrown out his back and was laid up. In order to sell the rusty tractor they would need to get it running again, so Charley took the task upon himself. For five long, frustrating days he fought with the ceased engine until it finally sputtered to life.

When he brought his dad the purchaser's check for six thousand dollars, the old man merely grunted but he had to be pleased. Mustering all of his courage, Charley asked him for the three hundred dollars so he could take the class and get his license. With no hesitation his father dismissed him with some distractedly mumbled words, "You don't need no government license to drive on the farm."

He watched as his father, with no emotion on his weathered face, slipped the check into his shirt pocket and walked away with the creaky, limping steps of an old man. It was at that moment that Charley, for the first time, saw him for what he was. He had always seen him not as a person but only as the godlike personification of the idea of fatherhood, an entity that did not exist but for the fact that he was his father. Seeing him coldly take the money and waddle away, he realized that the old man was only that, a person. A person like all others. A person that ate and shit and snored when he slept. A simple, uncaring, miser of a person who had done nothing to earn respect or fear.

It was a few days later; they were working on a rusted out hay baler. His father had never been big on safety and Charley knew the ancient jack they were using had been repaired with an ill-fitting bolt. The slightest nudge to the right spot would send the heavy machinery crashing down.

Returning his attention back to the current situation, Charley watched an elderly inmate with dementia play one of his endless games of solitaire—the worn out deck of cards was missing the ten of diamonds and the four of clubs—when he decided he needed to get out of jail so that he could see his mother one last time.

*

With the lingerie shopping trip done, Brian was unsure what to do next so he was spending his Friday evening in the poker room. He had tried to work on his closing statement at home as the draft he prepared weeks ago was woefully out of date with all that had happened. However, now that there was a real chance of getting Charley off, panic over holding his client's life in his inexperienced, uncertain hands froze his pen. He had been pacing about the apartment, so Anna suggested going to find some distraction to clear his head. The rhythmic clicking of chips, the routine of the game, and the pointless banter of the players helped him relax enough that he could think about the case without worrying about ramifications.

The prosecution's case had not played out as perfectly as it had been detailed in Matthews' opening statement, but the basic proof of the crime was still there. That meant that the defence's case would need to be sufficient to tip the balance in Charley's favour. Brian would call his own expert on crime scene analysis, who would explain that it was highly unlikely a woman could be attacked in a room and there be no sign of her being there or there being remnants of a thorough cleaning. A trauma specialist would be called to testify that it was possible that Charley's fingerprints were on the body because he had been checking for vital signs. He would then call the 911 operator who received the call and get her to testify that the caller calmly told her that a young man told him there was a body across the alley. All of this was an attempt to make it appear that, rather than killing Peterson, Charley had only had the bad luck of finding the corpse. He then did what every good citizen would do and informed the authorities in the only manner available to him before fleeing to avoid getting in trouble for squatting. This evidence was all important as it provided a possible rationale for the jury to rely on if they decided to let Charley go, but in order for it to be truly useful he would have to convince the jury they wanted to let Charley go.

Without thinking about it, Brian called a ten-dollar bet with a nine-ten of spades and watched distractedly as the flop came king-five-eight. The big decision he was facing was whether to stick with the original plan of ignoring the existence of underwear or now, with more uncertainty surrounding the evidence, to try to completely discredit the idea that Charley put them in the basement.

A young man in a Saskatchewan Roughrider's jersey and cheap sunglasses bet twenty-five dollars under the gun. Brian called and the other players folded, leaving him heads up with the guy in the jersey. He would talk with Shelia Tatum over the weekend to see what she was able to testify to. If she seemed competent, he could call her in order to cast doubt that the underwear was not the victim's.

The dealer flipped over the jack of diamonds on the turn.

There was also the store clerk. He could call her to show the jury that there was at least another source of the underwear. Maybe he could leave them with the impression that it was highly coincidental that a matching garment had been purchased a couple of days following the murder. That was all they had. Brian knew it was not enough.

The guy in the jersey bet fifty dollars and Brian distractedly called.

Fredrickson had often told him that there was no second-place prize awarded in trials. He knew he could either ignore the underwear and lose with a whimper or take a run at making the underwear appear planted and likely lose while giving Charley a fighting chance. However, if he took that chance, Brian would look foolish. The members of the defence bar and all the prosecutors would think of him as the crazy guy who argued that an unknown person framed his homeless client. He would not get any meaningful referrals from his colleagues and he would not get any cooperation from the prosecutors going forward. His career as a serious defence lawyer, a career he now had to admit that he really wanted, would end before it had a chance to begin.

The dealer flipped over the seven of hearts. Roughrider jersey bet another fifty dollars. Brian almost folded without thinking but then checked his hole cards again. He had riverred a straight. He pushed all in and got the instant call.

As he flipped over his cards and listened to his opponent loudly curse him as a donkey, he doubted that he had the intelligence or wisdom necessary to do the job of convincing the jury to believe this strange story. But as he stacked his newfound chips, Brian realized the job was his nonetheless, so he had no choice but to take the only chance his client had and hope for some good luck.

*

Jenkins figured a bribe had been paid to the alibi witnesses, but he would need a warrant in order to get at Hugh Young's financial records. Even with the records, he knew he would not find anything; men like Hugh Young had funds tucked away in places that would never show up on any paper trail. Thankfully, this time Jenkins had neither the authority nor the time to follow protocol. He decided instead he would pay an informal, early-morning visit on Trenton MacKenzie, as he appeared to be less formidable than Garner.

After a few off-the-record phone calls, he had managed to get MacKenzie's address. It was a tiny, one-bedroom shack in a poorer neighbourhood deep in the northeast. Driving by the house, Jenkins noted that the lawn had not been tended in some time and the roof needed a new set of shingles, yet an expensive pickup filled the narrow driveway. He circled around the block and drove slowly down the alley to get a look into the back yard. A trailer held two dirt bikes and there was a snowmobile partially covered by a blue tarp. The home was shabby but MacKenzie had managed to find money to buy all the costly toys. Jenkins knew this was a sign of someone making most of their income in under-the-table cash which they did not want to be traced back to them.

Parking down the street, Jenkins walked to the front door and listened for a moment. He heard nothing, no one moving around and no radio or TV playing. Rather than knock, he decided to walk around to the back.

A dirty side window lacked curtains, and unfortunately for him, Jenkins was able to clearly see into a bedroom. A mattress without sheets rested on the floor, which was littered with empty beer cans and an overturned bong. On the mattress was a sight that turned even the veteran homicide detective's stomach. Mackenzie's diminutive, malnourished frame was being spooned by a large, naked woman. The woman, lying sprawled on her side with Mackenzie's curled form under one beefy arm, appeared to be in her late forties and had a belly that remind Jenkins of a bag half filled with milk. Her breasts sprawled over stomach like a pair of old gym socks. Thankfully, pendulous flab covered all but a few dark pubic hairs that were creeping along her blue-veined, cellulite-pocked thighs. Looking at the scene, Jenkins wished he had a camera as he was certain one picture of this sight could end drug and alcohol abuse entirely.

Continuing around to the back of the house, he stepped carefully onto the rotted deck and looked in the kitchen window. More beer cans along with various other clutter filled the room. Amongst the mess something caught his eye. On the counter, only a few feet from the door, sat a man's wallet, a set of keys, and a cell phone. He would not be able to get a warrant for phone records but maybe he would not need one.

The door was locked but the window was open, and he was able to reach through it to unlock the door. Forcing himself not to think of what might happen if he were caught breaking into a witness' house, Jenkins plucked the phone off the counter and slipped it into his jacket.

He was almost back out the door when he heard someone behind him say, "Good morning?"

Jenkins wheeled to see the rotund woman, now wearing overly tight jeans with a utilitarian, beige bra holding in her elongated breasts. She did not seem angry so Jenkins merely responded, "Morning."

She looked around the kitchen as she asked, "You Trent's roommate?"

"Um, yeah. You a friend of his?"

She looked under a dirty dish towel on the counter as she laughed a bit. "Sure. We met last night. Have you seen a red blouse around here?"

Jenkins pointed at some shiny red cloth crumpled in a corner. She scooped it up from the grimy linoleum. As she buttoned up her wrinkled shirt she noticed that Jenkins was leaving and asked, "Oh, would you be able to give me a lift downtown? I gotta get home before my kids get up."

"Oh, no sorry, I can't. No car." He pointed to the keys on the counter and added, "Why don't you take Trent's truck. He'll probably be out for hours yet. You can just bring it back later."

She looked a little surprised by that and asked, "Really? You don't think he'd mind."

"Nah, I'm sure he'll be happy to see you later today."

"Alright, if you think it's ok."

With that Jenkins darted through the back door and walked briskly away.

*

Friday morning Brian awoke earlier than normal. Last night he had stayed later at the poker room then he had intended, and he was feeling twinges of guilt for relaxing while Charley was in jail. Plus, now that he had decided to fully pursue the idea that the underwear had been planted, he had a good deal of work to do. He was writing questions for the lingerie store clerk when there was a knock on the apartment door.

The front door buzzer had not gone off, so it must be a neighbour, probably the elderly man next door who was always looking for his cat that had died two years ago. However, when he opened the door Brian found Detective Jenkins standing there.

Confusion struck at him first, followed quickly by concern for Charley's wellbeing. "Detective? Did something happen to my client?"

"Your client is fine." The large man gave Brian a long look before he finally continued, "But, I think we should talk."

It was a serious breach of ethics for Brian to talk to a prosecution witness without Matthews' consent. "Detective, you know I can't talk to you—"

Jenkins lifted a finger and said coldly, "All of this is completely off the record."

For what felt like the millionth time in the last five months, Brian felt like he did not have a clue what he was doing. He could not imagine a request like this was normal murder trial procedure, but it was actually the unusual nature of the request that made him think it was worthwhile to accept. Unless something unusual happened, Charley would be found guilty. Brian stepped to the side and let the detective in.

CHAPTER 26

Jenkins took a seat at the kitchen table as Brian moved to hide his papers and asked, "Can I get you a cup of coffee?"

The polite offer from a defence lawyer surprised Jenkins, but he answered, "Sure. Black is fine."

The lawyer set a mug in front of him before taking a seat. The table had been put into a corner to save room and the two men had to sit with their knees almost touching so they both leaned back with their drinks to gain some space. He had carefully looked through the phone he stole from MacKenzie. The list of calls was not overly helpful, but there was a text message from the evening after Jason Young's damaging testimony that said, "*Urgent job from HY. $$$ Meet now at PL."*

"This is Trenton MacKenzie's cell phone." He pushed a few buttons and slid the phone with the message on the screen across the table before continuing, "That's a text message he received the night after you made Jason Young look foolish on the stand."

Brian Cox appeared apprehensive at taking such an odd piece of evidence directly from the police, but his curiosity must have outweighed his concern as he looked at the phone. After a moment he slid it back and asked, "Who's HY?"

"I think it's Jason's father, Hugh Young. He's some sort of a player in the junior oil company sphere, definitely rich enough to pay—"

A cute blonde woman in a bathrobe walked out from the hall and asked, "Hello?"

Brian stammered out, "Oh, Anna, this is, well, this is…He's here to discuss Charley's case."

Jenkins stood awkwardly in the small space and shook the young woman's hand as he said, "Sorry for barging in so early. We shouldn't be too long."

She flashed a pleasant smile. "No problem. Let me just grab a cup of coffee and I'll get out of your way."

Silence filled the kitchen while they waited for the woman to leave. Jenkins had spent the night pondering this next move. The text message largely convinced him that Hugh Young was manipulating the trial, but without some context it was not going to be all that effective in court, never mind the difficulties of getting the stolen evidence admitted. He had considered taking the phone to Matthews, figuring that the existence of the new evidence might allow him to look past his zeal for a conviction and consider what was truly occurring. However, based on Matthews' past reactions, he decided there was a better chance the prosecutor would throw the book at him for stealing the evidence and then throw the phone in the garbage.

This made Jenkins realize that, even if he found a smoking gun over the weekend, he would still have the same issue with getting Matthews to act properly. The trial was re-commencing on Monday and it was very possible that it would conclude on Tuesday. If any of the risky steps he was taking now were going to be of any use, he was going to have to get the defence lawyer involved right away so whatever he found could be used.

Regardless, Jenkins did not take the decision of talking with Brian Cox lightly. Thirty years of police work had ingrained in him a deep mistrust of defence lawyers and anything associated with them. But based only on his instincts, he decided the kid would not use this attempt to help as a way to attack the prosecution or garner headlines like a more experienced defence lawyer might.

When the girlfriend left the kitchen, Brian, his mind probably full of questions, immediately asked, "How'd you get the phone?"

"Let's just say no one knows I have it."

Coming to the conclusion that he was involved in something clearly unethical and likely illegal, the young lawyer gingerly slid phone back across the table and said, "If there is some sort of witness buying going on then you should be talking to your bosses, not to me. Why are you here?"

Jenkins was actually glad to hear this question. His biggest concern had been that Cox would throw him out and call the judge to tell her the trial had been compromised by a rogue cop. At least if he was asking questions, Jenkins had a chance to explain. He said, "I'm retiring. This is my last case. I want it to end right. The prosecutor is hell bent on getting a conviction based on the original evidence I gave him. In his mind he has a solid suspect in custody so is not interested in listening to new theories at this point. Hell, I'm not sure your client isn't the right guy but I'm concerned there is more going on here than we know about."

"I'm supposed to believe you're switching sides in the final days of your career?"

"I don't see it as switching sides. I've always wanted to make sure that only the guilty are convicted. Due to the bizarre circumstances of this case, I think coming to you might be the best way to make sure that happens." He could see Cox remained uncertain so he continued, "Look, it's simple: I can't get the people who are supposed to care about these things to listen so I'm coming to you. You can either decide that I'm somehow out to fuck over your client, when frankly he is already being fucked over, or you can take my help. Think about it: I'm the only one with my ass in the wind here."

The young lawyer hesitated for a heartbeat and then let out a long tired sigh before he asked, "Ok, what do you think happened?"

*

He knew it was smart to be wary of Trojans bearing gifts, but Brian could see no downside to at least hearing the detective out. He had always figured that if the long shot lucky break he had been hoping for came, it would come in the form of a surprise witness showing up, the jurors seeing how suspicious the case appeared, or Jason Young breaking down and confessing. But maybe it would come in the form of a cop on his doorstep. Regardless, his risk was negligible. If what Jenkins said was useful, he would consider the implications of using the information at that point, and if what he said made him uneasy at all, he would talk to Fredrickson and they could decide together whether to talk to the judge or pretend this meeting never happened.

The hefty detective leaned back, making the flea market

chair under him creak as he answered, "I don't know what happened that night but I do think the Youngs are trying to fix the outcome of the trial and I can't imagine they would take the risk of doing that without something significant to gain."

Realizing that the detective might be able to confirm if Charley's story in the letter was true, he asked, "We are completely off the record here?"

Jenkins smiled as he said, "I'm sure as hell not going to tell anyone we talked. In fact if this discussion ever comes up, I'm completely denying ever being within a hundred feet of you."

He pulled the letter from its usual place atop his file and slid it over to Jenkins, "My client wrote this the night before you arrested him."

Jenkins scanned the letter before saying, "Well, this makes the picture a lot clearer."

"Yeah, but I can't get it in as evidence, and even if I could, would anyone believe that story?"

"Probably not, but if you would've let us talk to your client we might have started looking at Young a long time ago and then we wouldn't be in this mess."

"Would you have looked at Young or would you have used Charley's unbelievable story to prove he was there that night and then concocted this bizarre tale to cover his trail?"

A reflective moment before Jenkins answered, "Honestly, I don't know."

"And you've seen my client. I can't put him on the stand. It's likely he would remain mute and if he didn't Matthews would eat him alive." He pointed to the relevant sentence on the paper, "After he saw them testify, Charley thought Garner and MacKenzie were the ones that showed up to tow out the Jaguar."

Jenkins picked up MacKenzie's phone and began scrolling. After a moment he handed it to Brian and said, "No tell-tale text message, but on December 6, 2010, MacKenzie received a call at 3:48 a.m."

"Can you tell who made the call?"

Jenkins pulled out his own cell phone and dialled as he said, "Maybe." He listened for a second before continuing, "Disconnected. Whoever is contacting MacKenzie is smarter than him."

"Even without knowing the caller, this could be enough if I can piece it all together for the jury."

Jenkins did not look convinced and asked, "What did your client tell you about how the girl's underwear ended up in the heating vent?"

"Nothing; he doesn't know anything about them."

"Do you think he would tell you if he did know about them?"

Despite his numerous debates about the technicalities of this point with Fredrickson, Brian now felt confident the letter was the truth and answered quickly, "Yes, I think he would."

"I went back and re-listened to the anonymous call we got telling us to look in the heating ducts and it sounds strange, not the language I would expect from a day labourer. That's why I went and talked to that Tatum girl again."

Brian had to smile as he saw pieces coming together, "Last night I went to some lingerie stores and found a clerk who remembers that a woman bought a pair like the ones you found. They were bought earlier on the same day you found a matching pair in that vent."

"That's interesting but it could be coincidence."

"Doubtful. I went to about a dozen stores and I now know way too much about those panties. They only were sold in Calgary as part of an expensive designer set. I bet in that whole month there were only a couple of sets sold in the city. And the clerk at the store remembered the sale. The purchaser was very specific about what she wanted. She bought a couple of other things as well but then, the next day, she returned everything but the panties."

Jenkins nodded. "Alright, sounds like a solid lead but you

said it was a woman who bought them. Did you get a name for our buyer?"

Brian shook his head. "No, she paid cash. The clerk was able to give us a decent description but no name."

"What was the description?"

"Early twenties. Very attractive. Black hair. Dressed in business attire."

"Definitely not Hugh's wife and I doubt Jason has ever had a girlfriend—"

Without warning Anna popped back into the kitchen from the hallway where she had apparently been eavesdropping. She exclaimed excitedly, "She's his assistant!"

Jenkins shot Brian a look questioning how he could so foolishly let his girlfriend listen in on their secret conversation. He only shrugged slightly in response. He figured Anna was overhearing them, as the apartment was so small that anything said anywhere was heard throughout, but he did not care because even if she wasn't listening he would have recounted the discussion with her anyway.

Brian asked her, "You think the buyer is Hugh Young's assistant?"

"You told me he's a big-time business type, right? I doubt he would be able to leave his office in the middle of the day to hunt down a pair of panties without people asking questions. It makes sense that he would send his assistant and it makes sense that the father of Jason Young would have a young hottie for an assistant doing his dirty work."

Jenkins nodded, "Could be. If he is half as creepy as his son, his assistant might have gotten so many slimy assignments that this one would not even seem out of the ordinary."

Anna, her excitement at solving the riddle apparent, continued, "Yeah, and if she has been his assistant for a while there could be some loyalty there, or at least financial motivation for her to keep his creepiness quiet so he might not have worried about sending her."

Brian felt foolish for not having guessed this. In his time at the law firm, he had seen numerous examples of senior partners whose assistants blindly adhered to their every whim, no matter how unprofessional or ridiculous the requests. He said, "That sounds reasonable to me. I suppose Jason could know a homeless man was living there, and with his father's help, he could probably come up with the plan to frame him by planting the underwear. But I still have an unanswered question: why did they need to buy the underwear? If Jason Young abducted Natalie Peterson, he would have been able to use the actual underwear she was wearing to frame Charley."

"Hard to say." Jenkins glanced apologetically at Anna before adding, "Maybe they were worried Jason's DNA would be found on her pair. Or maybe he threw them out after he dumped the body. Trust me, it's not odd for evidence to disappear. Frankly, I think we should focus on connecting this purchaser you found to the Youngs; if we do that they'll have to be the ones doing the explaining."

"Ok, we have a decent theory but no proof. What do we do with that?"

Jenkins got to his feet as he answered, "Give me the morning to find out about Hugh Young's assistant back in December to see if she matches the description and then let's meet back up. Do you know the donair place in Eau Claire Market?"

Brian answered, "Yeah, it's awful."

"Which means it's normally empty. Meet me there at one o'clock."

*

As everyone who had ever worked on a business deal with him could attest, one of Hugh Young's favourite angry mantras to yell whenever he was told his unreasonable timetables were unreasonable was "Time kills all deals." Knowing that delays were deadly, Hugh had been worried when he got the summary from Poetker saying the trial was recessed until Monday. He felt that since the alibi witnesses had held up, the case was going his way, and soon the nightmare would be over. Now he was being forced to wait in the dark even longer, and the longer he waited the more he was able to think of possible problems that might arise.

Doubting that the lawyer would have any extra information but needing to do something, Hugh called Jacob Poetker. "Jacob, it's Hugh Young. Any idea why this trial is being delayed?"

"Hi, Hugh. Actually, we have been hearing some rumors—"

"Rumors? What rumors?"

"Well, look, this is just courthouse gossip so you have to take it with a grain of salt. But the word going around is that the detective on the case has gone rogue and keeps digging around on his own which is giving the prosecutor fits."

"What does digging around mean?"

"Not sure. That's all we've heard. Basically, the defence bar is enjoying the rumor that a cop is making life difficult for Clay Matthews."

For a few minutes, Hugh had tried to get the lawyer to speculate. However, Poetker refused to play along, so he had to end the call having learned only the troubling information that a detective was still investigating. He was unsure what that meant for him, but as usual, his largest source of concern was Jason doing something stupid. The more he pondered, the more Hugh figured it would be best if his son was out of town for a while. Hugh dialled his number and Jason answered on the fourth ring, "Hi Dad, what's going on?"

"It's time to take a trip."

It took Jason a second to comprehend what was being said, but then he sounded excited as he asked, "Ok sure, where do you want to go?"

"Not us. Just you. I don't care where you go but get out of the country until this fucking, never-ending trial is over."

"Oh, ok, if you think that is the best idea…"

"I do. Get going today."

"Sure, sure. But, well, I'm not certain I can really afford a trip right now; my credit card is…"

Hugh let out a loud sigh, "Fine, I'll put some cash in your account right now. Take your phone but only answer if I call you. If anyone else tries to get a hold of you ignore them and call me and I'll tell you what to do. You got that?"

"Yeah, I got it."

"Go today and stay gone for at least a week."

*

When Jenkins arrived at one o'clock, Brian Cox, looking more than a little nervous, was already sitting at a table in the donair shop. The place was nearly empty, with only two men in cab driver uniforms drinking coffee in the corner. Regardless of Cox nervously waiting, he took his time and ordered lunch before sitting down. "Your sleuthing girlfriend couldn't make it?"

The lawyer did not catch the slight jab and responded without humor, "She had to go to class. What did you find out?"

Jenkins unwrapped his donair and took a bite, it truly was awful. "Well, when she's done school, she should join the police force. Hugh Young had an assistant back in December that matches the clerk's description."

"That's good. Isn't it?"

As he chewed a mouthful of slimy lettuce, Jenkins realized that one thing he would miss about the law enforcement world was young lawyers. They had to act serious and confident because they were lawyers. They had made it through law school, got called to the bar and everything. But they actually knew nothing about how the world operated, which often put them in the humorous predicament of playing the ignorant expert, and Jenkins enjoyed watching them splash about in that mess. At least this kid was less arrogant than normal and seemed to understand that, despite his law degree, he actually knew nothing.

Jenkins answered, "Yeah, it's good. Seems like we might be on the right path. Now you have to go and talk to her."

"Me?"

"Sure, I'm guessing you aren't looking for a mistrial but

want an outright acquittal?"

"Right."

"Well, then I can't very well go up to her flashing my badge while gathering evidence for the defence. Hell, if I want to retire above the poverty line, I can't have her telling anyone that."

Brian seemed to ponder this for a moment before saying, "I guess I can talk to her. I can't see why she won't want to cooperate. An innocent man is on trial for a murder he didn't commit."

Jenkins had to force himself not laugh as his mouth was full of tasteless meat. "Of course, members of the public always want to come into court and testify about their involvement in covering up a crime. Should be easy."

CHAPTER 27

"Her name is Amber Watkins."

Brian was sitting in Jenkins's unmarked car outside a massive office building downtown. Watching the crowd of homebound workers walking by, he asked, "How'd you find that out?"

"It was harder than usual. Normally, I would simply ask around the office and see if anyone knew anyone that had worked at Young Exploration, but now I can't really explain the reason behind my request if anyone asked. So instead I had to go online. The company got taken over a few months ago but their website is still up and listed five members of the management team. I was able to get a hold of the former Chief Operating Officer. I told him that I was a friend of Hugh Young's and he told me that he used to have a good assistant but I didn't get her name and now I couldn't get a hold of Hugh. This guy remembered the young woman very well. He gave me her name and the temp agency where they found her."

"How do you know she's working here now?"

Jenkins shrugged as if it was so simple it did not warrant talking about. "I called the temp agency, said that Amber Watkins had not shown up for work this morning. The lady on the phone was very apologetic. I asked what address they had given Amber, she told me and that brought us here."

"Nice, we've already gotten her in trouble and we haven't even talked to her yet?"

"Nah, once I got the address I played it up that I was mistaken and thought that she was going to our other office."

"Alright, so what's the plan?"

"We wait until she leaves work and then follow her."

Brian disliked the idea of stalking a witness so he asked, "We can't just call her or go to her house and wait?"

"Unlisted."

"Don't cops have access to all sorts of records?"

"We do but thanks to pain-in-the-ass defence lawyers

making bogus claims about due process, in order to do the necessary search I need to follow a protocol which involves giving a duty officer a written request. I don't exactly have a lot of valid reasons to be requesting searches."

"Ok, then how do we recognize her?"

Jenkins handed over three pictures of an attractive brunette, and before Brian could ask how he got them, he said, "I can still search the internet. Facebook."

Brian was extremely nervous but he wanted to seem calm since the detective appeared completely unfazed, so he tried to regain some control. "Good, we can sit here and watch the door and then we'll follow her right home. Seems easy."

Jenkins shook his head. "No, you need to go watch the other door. You'll be the guy on foot."

So much for taking any element of control. "Why do I need to go on foot?"

"She's a temp. She won't be able to afford parking downtown. If she takes the train we can't follow by car. Even if she takes a bus it's hard to follow because it stops too often. You need to shadow her."

"Shadowing seems more like police work."

"There's no way I'm letting you drive a police car, and frankly, I don't feel like walking."

After exchanging cell phone numbers with Jenkins, Brian stepped out of the car and walked around the corner so he could see the building's other door. It was nearing four o'clock and the sidewalk was already filling with office workers getting an early start on the weekend. Clutching the pictures, he loitered by the door but soon felt conspicuous, so he wandered up and down the block a few times before leaning against a pillar while pretending to intently read something on his cell phone.

*

Shortly after four-thirty, Jenkins spotted Amber Watkins leaving the office building. She was neatly dressed in the standard office attire of a black skirt over black nylons with a grey jacket. Despite the business clothes, she wore sneakers and carried a bag that probably held her uncomfortable work shoes. He called Brian and curtly said, "She just left heading south. She's in a grey jacket and carrying a green tote bag."

Almost immediately he saw Brian speed walking around the corner before stopping to obviously scan the street. It was apparent the lawyer was not going to have a career in spy craft. Brian saw Amber and scurried after her, his cell phone clutched to his ear, "Ok, I see her. I think she's heading to the trains."

"Alright, stay with her but try not to get arrested for stalking before you can talk to her."

*

Brian was glad for the crowded sidewalks as he could blend in with the commuters. After five blocks they made it to a busy train platform, and he had to force himself past two angry ladies to make sure he got on the same car as Amber.

Standing behind her in the packed train, Brian could safely get a good look at Amber. She was in her early twenties, dark hair pulled back in a ponytail and only a hint of makeup to accent her full lips and pale cheeks. Undoubtedly she was attractive; many of the male, and some of the female, passengers were openly staring at her, but she seemed not to notice. When the train took a sharp turn, he noticed how a man standing near Amber held his ground, letting her sway into him, at which point he took the opportunity to clutch her in an attempt to keep her from falling, which she was in no danger of doing. It was a veteran move of a public transportation creep but Amber merely stepped away from the pervert. Brian figured the groping was probably as common an annoyance on her daily commute as hitting two red lights in a row.

As the train left downtown Brian called Jenkins, "We are on the northwest bound train."

"Ok, I'll do my best to keep up but you'll probably have to follow her on your own once she gets off."

"What if she gets into a car?"

"If you can, stop her and try to talk to her right there. If you can't talk to her then get a license plate. I may be able to trick a rookie on patrol to run the number and get me the address on it."

The idea of having the awkward conversation with this woman after confronting her in a parking lot made Brian nervous, but he managed to answer, "Alright, I'll try."

For over an hour the train lurched its way through the city, dropping off downtown office workers as they went. Finally, with the car nearly empty, Amber moved to get off at the second last stop of the line. Trying to appear casual, he followed as she crossed the parking lot to a bus stop. Hoping she would not notice that the same man from outside the office building was now at the same bus stop as her, Brian stood well away and called in to Jenkins, speaking in a hushed tone, "We got off at Dalhousie Station. Now we're waiting for a bus. Looks like it's going to be Route 37."

"Good. I should be able to catch up soon."

After a ten minute wait, the Route 37 bus arrived. Amber got on at the front so Brian, not familiar with bus etiquette, forced his way on through the back door which earned him curses from those trying to depart. They travelled a circuitous route through residential neighbourhoods for thirty minutes before Amber pulled the cord. She was the only other passenger getting off at the stop so when she started walking left, he went right to avoid being obvious. When he got to the corner, he turned and was happy to see her moving briskly down the sidewalk. He crossed the street and then walked back down the block on the other side of the street from Amber, staying a good fifty yards behind her.

They travelled this way for two blocks before she turned up the driveway to a white bungalow with faded stucco and peeling, green trim. Surprisingly, she went to the front door and rang the bell. Frustration struck at Brian as he thought that, after all of this, she was not even going home.

An angry-looking woman with a cigarette dangling from her lips opened the door, allowing a cloud of smoke from inside to escape. Even from across the road, Brian could hear a cacophony of children's noises coming from the house, including at least one loudly crying baby. Amber handed over some cash to the displeased matron as a girl of about four or five came running out of the house and almost tackled Amber as she bent to hug the child. The old lady disappeared back inside without uttering a word.

With the girl holding her hand and skipping alongside her, Amber turned back towards the way she had come from. It soon became clear that she was headed back to the bus stop where they had gotten off. Unsure what to do next, Brian called Jenkins with panic tinting his voice. "She's picked up a little girl and is getting back on the bus—I think so anyway. She'll see me—I mean, I think she'll realize I'm following her."

"Calm down. Remember you are just following a witness. If she sees you then she sees you, it's not the end of the world. I doubt she's armed."

Brian realized he had gotten caught up in the cloak and dagger, forgetting the rather pedestrian purpose of what he was doing. "You're right. I got a bit carried away."

"No problem, it happens. Where are you?"

Brian had to look at the street signs to give him the address as he was hopelessly turned around.

Jenkins didn't even have to hesitate to think before saying, "Ok, I'm not that far away. How far is she from the bus stop?"

"Couple of blocks, she's going a lot slower now because of the kid."

"Good. Let's switch jobs. I'll park across the street from the bus stop and get on with Amber. You get in the car and I'll call you with directions when I can. No lights, no sirens, and stay off the radio."

*

Standing beside Amber at the bus stop, Jenkins was able to overhear the little girl excitedly telling her about how some boy at the babysitter's kept trying to kiss her. However, by the time the bus arrived and they took their seats, the girl's excitement seemed to have faded as she promptly fell asleep. It was past six o'clock. An hour and a half since Amber had left work and they were still not home—a hellish commute that would be even worse in winter when the roads were covered in ice and snow.

Eventually, Amber, now carrying the sleeping child along with the girl's stuffed backpack and her own bag, got off the bus and walked to a ragged house. She went to a side door which he figured led to a basement suite, unlocked two locks, and went inside. A second later the basement windows lit up. They had found her house. Well, he had found the house. The lawyer was apparently very lost despite Jenkins providing him with numerous location updates. Jenkins continued walking past the house, hoping Brian would show up before he had to do too many laps of the block.

*

The call display on his phone read "Bilderberg Gardens." Hugh recognized it as the name of the luxury hotel in Amsterdam he frequented. It was near the red light district, yet lavish and discreet. He picked up the phone. "Hugh Young speaking."

"Good evening, Mr. Young, my name is Hans De Vries. I am calling from the Bilderberg Garden Hotel in Amsterdam."

The man had a heavy Dutch accent but his English was perfect. "Yes?"

"Sorry to disturb you but I am here with a gentleman named Jason Young who has a female guest and they would like to check into the hotel. However, he does not have a reservation. Given the late hour we would normally not accommodate such a request but he said he is your son."

Of course. Only Jason would be stupid enough to travel halfway around the world, not think to make a hotel reservation, pick up a hooker right from the airport, and then try to check into a luxury hotel at two in the morning. Hugh was actually shocked the idiot had been smart enough to make it out of the country. His first inclination was to ask to be put on the phone with his son so he could yell at him for being so dumb, but instead he took a deep breath and decided it was not worth the hassle.

"Yes, he is my son. I would appreciate it if you could find him a room."

"Very well, Mr. Young. Thank you and sorry for the bother."

*

The neighbourhood was a maze of curving streets and cul de sacs, but eventually, Brian managed to find Jenkins. As the detective took his seat behind the wheel, he expressed how confused he was by someone getting that lost in their own town. Brian did not say anything as he did not want to irritate the man any further, but he did not think it was that strange given he had never been anywhere near this part of the city before.

"Ok, so I go in and talk to her now?" Brian asked, partly dreading the conversation and partly wanting this night to be over.

"I'd wait a bit. She just got home, has to feed the kid and get her to bed. She'll probably be more receptive if she doesn't have to discuss all of this in front of the girl, plus I've learned mothers usually open the door if someone keeps knocking when their kid's sleeping."

"You don't think she'll let me in?"

"A young, good looking woman, apparently living alone with her daughter in a basement. It's possible she won't be overly receptive to a stranger knocking at her door wanting to talk about panties."

Annoyance at all of this strained his voice, "So after all of this I might not even be able to talk to her."

Jenkins slowly turned his massive form in the car seat, looked at him, and said with a sigh, "This is not some law exam on how to interview a willing witness in a fancy conference room. This is knocking on someone's door at night and getting them to talk to you about something they don't want to talk about. You need to think of how you can convince her to do that. And before you start talking about the rule of law and citizens doing the right thing, let me remind you that this woman just worked all day doing boring administrative shit for very little pay and then spent almost two hours being leered at on trains and buses in order to get her and her daughter home to some crappy basement apartment in a sketchy neighborhood. So my guess is she's got more important things to worry about than her civic duty."

CHAPTER 28

Brian checked his watch. They had been sitting in the car for two hours, almost entirely in silence. Tonight was anything but normal, but if it were a normal Friday night, he would most likely be sitting on the couch with Anna, sharing a bottle of cheap wine, while playfully arguing over what movie to watch or merely discussing their days. Amber Watkins had spent all day working in an office surrounded by strangers and was now spending Friday night in a basement apartment, alone with a young child. He said, "I think she's lonely."

Jenkins seemed to think about this comment for a minute before agreeing, "Yeah, she might be. Do you think you can befriend her?"

Thinking back to his first encounter with Charley, Brian thought that perhaps he could at least get the lonely woman to trust him enough to let him in so he answered, "Possibly."

"I think we'd actually be better off is she is more bitter than lonely."

"Why's that?"

"Well, if she holds a grudge maybe she'll be motivated to screw over her ex-boss."

"I suppose, but it'd have to be a pretty nasty grudge."

"I don't know, I've seen people flip on one another for fairly trivial things. And I imagine old Hugh spent a lot of time pinching her ass and staring at her tits and now she's back at the temp agency, so I'm guessing she's not a big fan."

"Ok, maybe I can try to use that."

"First you have to get in the door."

He reluctantly opened the car door, "Right."

The lawn had not been mowed and the driveway was cracked. The upstairs appeared to be vacant with sheets hung in the windows rather than curtains, no lights were on, and there was a significant amount of junk mail piled on the porch. He made his way to the side of the house where there was a metal door next to a mail box with a number two on it but no name. There was no doorbell so he was forced to knock. No answer. He knocked louder. No answer.

At this point he would have left, glad to have avoided the awkward conversation, except he could not return to face Jenkins without having at least tried. He knocked again and yelled at the metal, "My name is Brian Cox. I'm a lawyer and I would like to ask you some questions."

He felt ridiculous, yelling at a closed door, but he could not think of anything else to do. He was about to yell again when he heard a noise. Looking down he saw Amber Watkins peering up at him from a slightly opened basement window next to the door. There was fear in her eyes as she whispered, "My daughter is sleeping and I don't know you. Please go away or I will need to call the police."

"I'm sorry for bothering you, I really am, but I need to talk to you about one of your former bosses, Hugh Young."

Her brow furrowed. "Are you some sort of sexual harassment lawyer?"

"No, I'm actually a criminal lawyer, and to be frank, I think he is framing my client. You might be able to help keep an innocent man from going to jail."

"Sorry but I don't know anything about any crimes. I just answered his phone and did the photocopying." She stepped back and started to slide the window closed.

The mistake immediately became obvious. Jenkins had been right. The mention of a crime scared her off. He should have pretended to be suing Young. Before the window shut, Brian called down, "Please, it will only take a moment. I think he is framing my client. An innocent man is going to go to jail for life because of Hugh Young's lies."

Still not moving towards the door, she seemed to ponder this before she quietly asked, "What would you need me to do?"

He had decided to keep things general at first and said, "I only need to talk to you about your time working for Young and what he was like. We are quite desperate and are hoping you might help us understand what he was up to a few months ago."

"This might get him in trouble?"

"It might. Yes."

"And your client, he's innocent but Mr. Young is setting him up somehow?"

"We believe so, yes. But we need help proving it."

She glanced back into the basement before asking, "Do you have some ID or something?"

Quickly, Brian produced a business card along with his Law Society card and awkwardly handed it down to her through the window. She scanned it for a second and then looked at Brian for a quizzical moment before asking, "Brian Cox? You were in the news? The girl who got killed and left in a backyard around Christmas."

"That's right."

"This is about that?"

"Yes."

"You think that Hugh Young might have something to do with her getting killed?"

"Him or his son, we don't know exactly—"

She interrupted, "His son? Jason?"

"That's right."

She looked behind and then back up at the window, "I guess I should talk to you. But only for a bit and we need to stay quiet."

*

Seeing the side door open and the young lawyer disappear, Jenkins was relieved. Hopefully all the career risk he had taken would not be for nothing. In a move as familiar as tying his shoe, he pulled his cell phone out of his jacket and called his wife to tell her he would be late getting home. As he waited for her to answer, Jenkins realized that this might be the last time he would need to make this habitual call and a small knot caught in the bottom of his throat.

*

Amber led Brian down a narrow cement staircase into the basement. The space was cramped, the ceiling not much over six feet. The apartment seemed to be comprised of a kitchenette, a living room dominated by a couch pointed at an old fashioned TV, and an ad hoc bedroom created out of bookcases and screens surrounding a double bed pushed into one corner next to a furnace and water heater. Despite the lack of space, it was well organized with things neatly stored out of the way except for a few toys on the floor. The coffee table held a children's bowl with some macaroni and cheese beside an empty chocolate pudding cup.

"We normally have a more balanced dinner but it's Friday," Amber spoke with that low tone that parents use when children are sleeping nearby, not really a whisper but not a full voice either.

As he sat on the couch, Brian used the same tone to nervously say, "Yeah, we are the same way with Fridays at my place."

Amber, now dressed in a sweat shirt and jeans with her hair pulled back, sat on a vinyl kitchen chair beside the couch. For an awkward moment, Brian could not think of what to say so they merely avoided eye contact before she asked, "So, you are defending the homeless guy who killed the girl?"

"Well, yes, but I don't think he actually killed her."

"Who killed her then?"

"I'm not sure, but I think Hugh Young is covering something up. Probably something to do with his son Jason as he was the last person to be seen with the victim." Brian did not want to discuss the underwear too soon as he figured that might end the interview before it began so he said, "Were getting ahead of ourselves, though. Can you tell me what it was it like working at Hugh's company?"

Amber seemed a little confused by this change in topic, but she answered, "It paid well—at least better than temping. But it was not a great place to work. Mr. Young had a horrible temper. He'd yell a lot and even throw stuff if things were going especially bad.

People often had to work late or on the weekends to meet his crazy demands."

"Sounds rough."

"Well, to be fair he never actually yelled at me and he would let me go early if I needed to pick up my daughter." She shifted in her seat before continuing, "Look, I know why I was there. I came over as a temp and Mr. Young liked me so they kept me around. He'd flirt with me and I'd flirt back a bit to keep him happy."

She wasn't bragging about the attraction, merely stating a fact. Brian was unsure how to deal with having this type of conversation with a stranger, but he blundered forward, "Were you his personal assistant as well?"

She gave him a cold look and said, "I'm not sure what you mean by that."

He felt himself blush as he realized this had come out wrong and he stammered, "Sorry, that's not what I meant. I'm not here to judge or anything in any way…"

His visible embarrassment seemed to put Amber at ease as she lifted her hand a little to stop his stammering and said, "I wasn't his mistress if that was what you were asking, but I needed the paycheck. If that meant letting my skirt hike up when I crossed my legs or brushing up against him in the elevator, that's the way the world works sometimes."

"I get that. What I was trying to ask was if he ever asked you to do anything you found overly personal?"

She shook her head, "No, he was pretty careful about being too obvious. One of the other women in the office told me that he was familiar with where the line was as he had gotten in trouble before, lawsuit kind of trouble. He'd stare, make subtle comments, and maybe stand a little too close but he never actually propositioned me."

Worried he would make another foolish misstep, Brian decided to take the plunge and said, "That's not really what I meant. One of the pieces of evidence that the prosecution has is a pair of underwear they are claiming belonged to the victim—"

Instantly realizing what was coming, she said, "Wait. That's what those were for? All I did was go and buy what I was told to buy."

"I understand that but I think part of what you bought for him were planted at the crime scene—"

She interrupted again, "Look, I'm sorry, I don't know...You should go."

Brian leaned forward, his elbows on his knees. "I'll go if you want but if you just bought the underwear and gave them to Hugh Young you won't get in trouble and you could stop a horrendous injustice."

Amber stood up and said, "I'm sorry about what happened to that girl, really, I am, but I can't afford any trouble. Please, just go."

He did not want to defy her but he moved slowly to buy some time as he tried to come up with a better way to explain that what she knew could save an innocent man's life. As he moved reluctantly to the door, he heard a squeak of a voice from behind him, "Mommy, is this a bad man?"

Looking back he saw the young girl, wearing an oversized t-shirt for a nightshirt and fearfully clutching a yellow blanket. With the supernatural speed of a mother with a scared child, Amber crossed the space and picked up her daughter in one motion. "No, don't be worried, honey. This man had some questions about mommy's work but he's leaving now."

The girl looked quizzically at the visitor with her head cocked to the side. Brian smiled and the fear left her eyes as she asked shyly, "Do you want to see my pictures?"

Amber answered for him, "Oh, I don't think so, Sophie. It's late, you should be asleep and Mr. Cox has to get going."

"Ahh, Mommy. It will be fast. No one ever comes over and I never get to show anyone."

Seeing a chance to prolong his stay, Brian intervened, "I'll take a look. I bet they're good and I could use some new art for my office. You don't charge too much do you, Sophie?"

*

Charley was so enraged by his mother's taunting letter that he had been unable to engage in his only methods of reality escape: reading and sleeping. As the never-ending minutes slowly ticked by, his fury grew. For all the years he suffered on the streets, the image of his mother had become one of his few enjoyable memories. Now, with too much time to think and the horrible letter haunting his thoughts, he had been forced to realize that the image he had kept in his mind was wrong. In reality she was an unpleasant woman who had not understood how to raise a child and did not care enough to learn.

In the quiet of protective custody, he recalled smacks with a wooden spoon for no intelligible reason, embarrassing trips to stores where she would loudly argue with clerks about nonsense, and unending rants about how he was an awful child. Piecing together his childhood, he realized his early years were spent either wandering the farmyard alone or sequestered in his room for endless hours, as he had learned that it was best to avoid his mother as much as possible. By the time he was ten or eleven, his days became filled with nothing but chores, fieldwork, and fixing antiquated machinery.

Worse than the neglect and harassment of his childhood had been the way she had acted after his father died. Within a week of the funeral, a man from her church had become a regular visitor at their house. Within two months they were engaged and within a year he had convinced her to sell the farm and machinery business that Charley had spent his youth working on. His new stepfather easily persuaded his mother that Charley needed to make his own way in the world. With no discussion, they placed him on the bus to Calgary and excitedly made frantic plans to use the newfound fortune to move to a warmer climate without him.

Distracted by this influx of tormenting memories, Charley forgot where he was as he moved through the daily prison routine. He had not noticed when one of the mentally unbalanced men in protective custody sat near him at one of the small tables the men used for meals. Normally, he would have simply changed seats, knowing that the unpredictable nature of this inmate could cause a problem. The man took his sandwich and, without thought, Charley grabbed the man's wrist and glared at him through his thick glasses. The thieving prisoner was not large or thuggish, but even in protective custody, there were eyes on them now so he could not back down from someone as weak as Charley or he could become a target. The brawl was a clumsy and brief affair as guards moved in to easily break it up.

With his involvement in multiple altercations, the guards had lost any sense of empathy. There was no soft bed in the infirmary this time; instead he was quickly checked for serious wounds, told he was being put into administrative disassociation, and tossed in a solitary cell with no furnishings where he could do nothing but sit and ponder his growing anger.

*

Brian had been given an enthusiastic art showing. The pictures were numerous and they all involved at least one horse. Sophie reminded Brian of his nieces when they had been the same age. He had spent many holidays discussing the numerous attributes of horses and was well versed in the lingo. As a result, by the time Amber ordered Sophie back to bed he had bought a colourful drawing of what she claimed was a unicorn for four dollars and been invited to her birthday party in three months.

"Thanks for that, she doesn't get to talk to enough adults." Amber gave the tiny apartment a small wave. "We don't entertain too often."

"No problem, she's a sweet kid. You must be doing a good job." He continued his bluff and moved slowly towards the stairs. "I better go; seems like I've got a lot of investigating to do this weekend."

Amber sunk back down on the vinyl chair and asked, "Are you sure I won't get in trouble for telling you about the lingerie? Did I do something wrong? Legally, I mean."

She suddenly looked very tired for her age, her shoulders now slumping forward under the weight of another unpredicted worry. A large part of Brian wanted to reassure her that she had done nothing wrong as he felt guilty for bringing her another burden. However, he knew Charley would not survive in jail. He needed the information she had and scaring her might be the only way to get it. "Look Amber, I'm not a cop, or even a prosecutor, so I can't get you in trouble. Why don't you tell me exactly what happened and then I can let you know if I see any issues?"

She grinned at him. "You really think I'm that easy?"

"I took a shot." Brian grinned back. "I'm a lawyer with an innocent client on trial for murder. I've got to take every shot I can."

"Do you actually think Hugh Young used the underwear I bought to cover up the fact that he was involved in killing this young girl? He had a bad temper and was an asshole but a lot of businessmen are like that. I don't think he would kill someone. Jason, on the other hand…"

With that, her voice faded off as she pulled her legs under herself and began fiddling with the cuff of her jeans, so he prodded, "You knew Jason?"

"Sort of. He had a desk at the office but was only there once in a while." Amber kept her eyes on her frayed jeans as she continued, "This might be hard to explain to a man and you might think I'm talking nonsense, but I think most women learn from the day they grow breasts how to quickly read a man's intentions. Working in any downtown office, most women get their fair share of inappropriate looks or whatever but I work as a temp. This means I normally go to smaller companies that are more likely to be old boys' clubs with no such thing as workplace polices or human resources departments. And each day I'm going in as something new, something fresh for the bored perverts to entertain themselves with. Because of this I think I have developed a pretty good radar for when a creep is just a harmless loser who tries to glimpse down your blouse or if he might be a problem."

"And you thought Jason might be a problem?"

She nodded, "Yeah, but worse than that. By a problem, I just meant a guy who went beyond the nervous looking and actually did something, like asked you out or pushed up on you at the photocopier. Normally this is not a big deal, it leads to some awkwardness as you have to turn them down or push them off, but that type of thing most women can deal with. Jason was on a whole different level.

"He either didn't care about what anyone thought or did not realize that people might think badly of his actions. Most guys, if you catch them staring, they look away or, if they're cocky enough, they might smile back at you but that's it. Jason would keep staring as if he didn't care if you caught him or not. A really confident guy in an office might come up and flirt a bit but they generally give up fairly quick if you're not responsive. But Jason never seemed to get the hint and kept at it. Twice he asked me, well actually told me, to go for drinks with him after work and both times I told him I couldn't. The first time, I gave him the usual line about having to get my daughter from daycare but he still kept pestering like a child who wants a toy. The second time, I told him I had to go to the airport to pick up an imaginary boyfriend and he told me he would pay to have a limo drive him home."

"So what did you do?"

She looked up and let the corner of her mouth curl up with the twinge of a smile, "I knew that Hugh had no patience for his son, so I told Jason that if he kept hounding me I would have to tell his dad on him."

Brian laughed at that, "How'd that go over?"

"Worked like a charm. He tripped over his words back pedaling. After that I didn't see him around as much."

She hesitated and returned to fingering the cuff of her pants before she continued, "I did see him one more time that bothered me though. There was a big party for the closing of the takeover of the company in January. I wasn't going to go but Hugh asked me personally and I was hoping for a good reference from him. Anyway, I managed to get Sophie a sleepover play date for that night, got dressed up, and went. The first part of the night was actually nice. They had booked a ballroom at the Sheraton; there was a fancy dinner and people made funny speeches.

"Most of the employees had left, the main party was winding down, and I was going to go home, but one of the higher-ups said that some people were heading to the hotel lounge for a nightcap and that I should come. I had no kid to get home to, I hadn't been out in forever, and I had drunk too much wine so I went. As I should have predicted, I ended up sitting right next to Hugh Young, whose wife had apparently gone home. This seemed ok at first—I mean the whole reason I went to the party was to make sure he remembered me, so when I felt his hand on my knee I didn't move it.

"It was awkward but manageable until Jason showed up. He was obviously drunk and possibly high on something as he stumbled to our table slurring apologies about being too late for the dinner. Following behind him was a girl in a tiny, silver dress covered in sequins. She looked coked up, and while she was trying to look older, I'd bet she was barely out of high school.

"Hugh was furious and loudly chastised Jason in front of everyone for missing the dinner and about how inappropriate it was to bring some teenaged tart to an office event. Most disturbing though was, as he was yelling, I felt Hugh's hand moving up my thigh. When he was done screaming, Jason slinked out of the bar. I quickly excused myself and slipped out of the bar. As I was getting into a cab I saw Jason loading the girl into the passenger seat of his car. He had to basically carry her into the seat, she was so out of it. It was awful to see. I knew I should do something but I did nothing and they drove off."

CHAPTER 29

Two steps, turn, four steps, turn, two steps, one step, around the toilet, two steps, turn. The cell was tiny with no windows and the lights were left off for long periods. Brian had come to visit three times over the weekend, but those were the only times Charley had been let out since the skirmish on Friday. He now guessed it was some time on Sunday night.

He had thought that solitary would be enjoyable, but with no stimulus of any kind Charley's waking hours became filled with obsessing over his mother, and with each dark minute, his need to see her and tell her of all the suffering she had caused him multiplied. After a lifetime of merely surviving, he now had a greater goal. Suddenly he wanted nothing but to get out of jail so he could confront her.

*

Reporters liked to listen to opening statements because they served as helpful summaries, so Jenkins was not surprised that the courtroom was crowded with media on Monday morning. He took his usual spot near the back, hoping to avoid any interaction with Matthews, as Brian stepped up to the podium to deliver the defence's opening.

"Good morning. I will be brief."

Jenkins thought the young lawyer sounded a little nervous but not too bad as he laid out what he was going to present to the jury. Most of it was predictable, innocuous information, but Brian soon got to the interesting part: "Finally, we will present evidence that the underwear found in the basement did not belong to the victim."

This got the bored reporters to sit up. Jenkins guessed most of them figured the inexperienced lawyer was promising evidence he could not deliver. However, any reference to police misconduct or negligence regarding evidence handling would make for good stories, regardless of whether the claims were true or not. As Clay Matthews turned to look at Brian, Jenkins could see a triumphant grin crossing the prosecutor's face. Matthews was probably figuring that this was a desperate move by an over-ambitious lawyer, and when this desperate attempt failed it would deflect attention from the holes in his case. Things were about to get enjoyable.

Brian continued, "We will call a store clerk as a witness who will state a woman bought the underwear in question from her three days after the victim was killed. Further, we will call that purchaser, who will testify that she was instructed to purchase the lingerie by her employer, who happens to be the father of Jason Young—"

Matthews, apparently realizing his triumph was being stolen, popped up on his feet to interrupt, "My Lady, we have the defence's list of witnesses and there is no woman—"

Rothborg scowled, "Mr. Matthews, this is Mr. Cox's opening statement and not a time for you to bring up procedural matters. You know better than that."

Before Matthews could say anything, Cox intervened, "That's fine My Lady. We can address this matter now. I'm sure the jury will be able to comprehend my opening statement despite this interruption."

"Fine." Rothborg waved the lawyers up to the bench.

The lawyers moved up to the bench to debate whatever it was that lawyers debate. Members of the gallery took the opportunity to discuss this development in whispers, but they all held their seats, wanting to see what was going to happen next. Except one young woman near the front, who stood and scurried past him on her way out the door. It was the articling student from Rainmaker Hopkins he had spotted taking notes during his own testimony.

*

Rothborg looked at both lawyers, "I must say gentlemen that I am getting very impatient with all of the procedural discrepancies in this mess of a trial. Now, Mr. Cox, what is this about undisclosed witnesses?"

Sweat was trickling down Brian's back. He could not lose this point. Brian had spent most of Sunday preparing for this conference. He had done extensive research, spoken at length with Fredrickson, and had strong arguments ready.

"Ma'am, as you are aware, there is no absolute duty on the defence to provide disclosure to the prosecution, and the witness list we provided was given only as a procedural matter at the request of the court. Our ability to present a full defence should not be hampered by our agreement to provide the list. Further, the witnesses we are calling only came to our attention after the prosecution provided us with the last-minute report of the interview of Shelia Tatum. To not allow the defence to adapt to this new information would be highly prejudicial. Why give us the knowledge but prevent us from acting on it?" Brian handed up a thick pile of paper to Rothborg and handed a copy to Matthews. "There is a number of compelling precedents where the defence has been allowed to call undisclosed witness in order to refute…"

Rothborg did not even look at Brian's carefully prepared brief, but instead asked him, "These new witnesses were discovered as a result of the last-minute report?"

"Um, yes."

"Fine. They are in."

Matthews said, "My Lady, I must object."

"Object away. But you dropped this information on the defence mid-trial. They are making a valiant effort to move this case forward. If you didn't want surprises, you should have had your house in order before bringing these charges into my courtroom."

Matthews managed to keep from showing any sign of disgust as he replied, "If that is the finding of the court, then I must ask for an adjournment so that we can get information on the witnesses and prepare for cross."

Rothborg looked at Brian, "Mr. Cox?"

"We do not believe an adjournment is necessary or appropriate. The evidence to be provided is very straightforward…"

Again Rothborg seemed eager to punish the prosecution for their earlier procedural mishaps as she quickly agreed, "Fine, no adjournment."

*

The blonde articling student had her cell phone out of her pocket before she was two steps from the door. Jenkins's curiosity caused him to follow her out of the courtroom. He pulled out his own phone, planning on pretending to be taking a call as he eavesdropped, but she did not even notice him. One of the benefits of being old and out of shape.

"Jacob, it's Allison. I'm over here at the Ewanuschuk trial and you told me to call if anything unusual happened."

A pause to listen before she said, "Well, I think so. The defence counsel was making their opening statement and he said they were going to present evidence that the underwear they found in the basement was not the victim's."

Another pause and then the articling student used her best fake expert tone to respond, "Yes, that's exactly what I thought, simply a desperate ploy. However, the defence further stated that they would be calling a clerk to say that the underwear was bought a few days after the killing. They would then call the purchaser, who would say she was told to buy the underwear by Jason Young's father."

A cringe crossed the student's face. Jenkins guessed her boss had loudly cursed into the phone. The cringe turned into a smile as the partner apparently regained control and thanked his spy. The student put away the phone and turned to return to the trial, realizing for the first time that the detective was standing awkwardly close behind her. He gave her a nice smile but she merely rolled her eyes as she hurriedly stepped past.

*

The breakfast meeting was going badly. It seemed that all of Hugh's meetings were going badly lately. His new start-up needed outside funding, but given the mediocre gas claims he had bought he could not even get a discussion with any investment bankers, so instead, he was buying breakfast for two venture capitalists in shiny suits. They were saying all the right things but seemed far more interested in their twenty-dollar omelettes. Hugh felt the vibration of his phone in his pocket but ignored it as he spoke about his track record in getting good returns for investors. The phone had barely stopped before it began vibrating again.

As he excused himself from the table, he wondered if his guests would even notice his absence as they shovelled in the free food. He answered the phone, "Hugh Young."

"Hugh, it's Jacob Poetker. A problem came up at the trial."

CHAPTER 30

The phone call about the trial had panicked Hugh. He had tried to meet with Poetker immediately but had been told he would have to wait until the afternoon. When he arrived at the law firm, he noted that this time the meeting was not in the main boardroom but in a small side room and there were no muffins or coffee waiting for him.

"So is there any merit to this claim the defence is making about you having an employee buy this lingerie?"

Jacob Poetker had not offered any small talk and his abrupt question had an exasperated tone which Hugh did not appreciate. However, he had larger concerns than a smug lawyer, so he merely answered, "Yeah, I got an assistant to buy the underwear. I didn't like the idea of sitting on our hands waiting for the cops to show up with cuffs, so I got a proactive."

Poetker shook his head and asked, "You did what? I don't understand."

He sighed as if the lawyer's question was ridiculous before he explained, "After you told me about the hobo living in the basement, I called Jason to see if he had any of the girl's things. Of course, when it turned out to be the wrong fucking thing to do, Jason had actually done something smart and ditched all of her stuff. However, my idiot son is apparently a savant when it comes to stripper panties. He remembered every detail about what she was wearing that night, so I sent my assistant out to find a duplicate pair."

"And you had her plant these in the basement?"

"No, I did that myself. I went late and snuck in through a window. I put them into a heating duct through an open vent. Probably didn't even take three minutes. I wore gloves and I'm sure no one saw me so they can't be traced back to me."

Hugh did not want this arrogant lawyer to know, but planting the evidence had not been as simple as he let on. He had driven up the hill late at night and parked a block away from the house. It was bitterly cold and he had to walk through the deep snow in the dark alley to avoid being seen. Having learned long ago that a man in a nice suit would be able to explain away almost any strange behaviour and be believed, he had opted not to change for this adventure, so his feet were frozen in his dress shoes and the frigid wind immediately cut through his thin dress coat.

After his intense career, he did not think anything could make him nervous anymore, but by the time he reached the backyard his heart was racing with the fear of being caught sneaking into a crime scene with a pair of panties in his pocket. For a moment he strongly considered going past and forgetting this plan but there were no lights on anywhere and his breathing was the only sound in the sleeping neighbourhood, so he figured he would have no better chance. Regardless, he caught himself constantly jumping at imagined threats as he crept through the yard.

The basement windows were boarded up and buried in snow. It took what seemed like an eternity of clawing through the ice to find a piece of plywood that was slightly loose followed by another eternity for his frozen fingers to pry it open wide enough to get through. He had never been athletic or coordinated and his entry was ungraceful to say the least as he crashed through the window to the dusty cement floor with a loud curse. Laying in a wet heap on the freezing floor in the pitch black, he strained to hear if anyone was coming, pleading that no one heard him call out. After five terrible minutes of silence, he decided it was safe and he pulled out his small flashlight.

He scanned the space. It was a cement cave of shadows filled with nothing but skeletal stud walls without drywall. At first he thought this could all be for nothing as he could not see any spot where he could hide the underwear such that it would be believable that the police missed finding them. Then he spotted the ducts running near the ceiling. He hastily moved to the nearest vent and crammed the evidence inside.

It took him a number of tries to get his soft body up to the window, but finally, panic at the thought of being trapped in the basement gave him enough of a rush to allow his arms to pull him through into the yard. Hugh knew he should not run as it would attract attention, but it took a great effort to force himself not to sprint to his car. Watching in his rear view mirror for flashing lights the whole way home, Hugh's heart did not stop racing until his garage door closed behind him.

      Poetker tore the page from the pad where he had been taking notes and loudly ripped the yellow paper into tiny pieces. The lawyer then took off his glasses before saying, "And then you called the police to tell them to go and look for them?"

      "Yeah, but I used a pay phone. It can't be traced back to me."

      "And you did all of this because I told you that they had arrested the man living in the basement even though I advised you to do nothing?"

      Hugh did not like being spoken to in this condescending manner, especially by someone he was paying an hourly rate, so he glared at Poetker and coldly explained, "You weren't fucking doing anything so I had to make sure the cops had enough to convict the homeless guy."

      Poetker did not seemed fazed by Hugh's attempt at intimidation as he glared back for a moment before calmly asking, "What do you think now? Maybe doing nothing was not such a fucking bad strategy?"

*

For her testimony, Shelia Tatum had pulled her hair back in a ponytail, which minimized the pink streaks. She was dressed in dark jeans with only one small rip, shiny boots, and a bright blue blazer. The perfect picture of Goth formal. She was sworn in and Brian walked her through her friendship with Natalie Peterson. Once it had been established that she was close with Natalie, Brian asked, "Can you tell us about Natalie's clothes shopping habits?"

      "Sure, I shopped with her a lot. She liked clothes and had good style but did not have much money so she looked for bargains."

      "What about lingerie?"

      "It was especially important to get good deals on gear."

"Sorry, gear?"

"Yeah, that's what we called underwear. It was a cost of doing business. But you didn't want to spend too much money on it."

Brian could hear the reporters behind him waking up now that the testimony was turning towards stripping, and he hoped this meant the jury was also paying attention as he asked, "Why was that?"

"It normally didn't stay on very long so why waste cash on it? And it often got ripped or some pervert would steal it or you'd lose it in the fray. You're lucky if a thong lasts two or three gigs." She spoke plainly, obviously not enjoying having this discussion in public but not wanting to show her embarrassment.

"What would be the most you'd spend on underwear?"

"On stuff I'd wear on the job? I'd keep it under ten bucks a pair for sure, closer to five dollars most of the time."

"And in your experience, Ms. Peterson had the same lingerie shopping habits as you?'

Matthews popped up, "Objection, leading."

Rothborg said, "Sustained."

"Sorry, I will re-phrase. Ms. Tatum, can you discuss what you understood Ms. Peterson's shopping habits to be regarding the cost of underwear she'd wear for work?"

"Same as mine. She'd keep it cheap—unlikely that she'd pay more than ten bucks a pair."

"Thank you, Ms. Tatum, Mr. Matthews is going to ask you some questions now."

Matthews moved slowly to the podium, took a couple of minutes to shuffle his notes, and then said, "Ms. Tatum, I would like to revisit the history of your alleged friendship with Ms. Peterson."

Hearing this comment, it dawned on Brian that the prosecutor had been taking his time all day, stretching out his questioning and requesting recesses. He had made a serious tactical mistake by not addressing the planted evidence first and protecting the element of surprise. He had stuck to the usual mantra of trial organization of finishing with your strongest point. Matthews had realized he was doing this and delayed the process to allow him a night to try and deal with the new evidence. He had planned to call the store clerk next and finish with Amber. Amber had not wanted to take any time off of work so he was supposed to text her when her turn to testify was coming up so she could hurry over from her office. But it was becoming clear that Matthews was going to run out the clock.

There was nothing he could do about the error now. He hoped that it would not be fatal. He forced the mistake from his mind so he could focus on the task at hand.

*

Poetker was adamant that he had properly advised Hugh to do nothing and everything would be fine. He was not going to get involved any further in trying to undo the mess Hugh had created. Hugh figured the lawyer was worried about his own skin since he had been the one to find out that the police had arrested the homeless man to begin with. In an attempt to retain some dignity, Hugh stormed out of the law firm before he was told to leave.

Unsure what to do next, he called Garner, thinking that perhaps he could get the brute to apply a little pressure on Amber to make her reconsider testifying. But as he and Garner discussed a plan, Hugh decided he had involved too many unintelligent people already. More oafish involvement now would only dig his hole deeper. He would need to deal with this unpleasantness on his own. He told Garner to forget about Amber, but before hanging up, he told him to get lost for a few days and to take MacKenzie with him. Better that they were not available for questioning or deal making if things went badly.

While he knew he needed to talk to Amber, Hugh had no idea how to get to her. A phone call, even from a pay phone, would leave a record, plus he could be more persuasive in person. Based on what Poetker had told him about the defence's opening statement, he was hopeful Amber would not be testifying until this afternoon. He did not know if she would be at the courthouse waiting for her turn to testify or if she would arrive later. If she was already in the courthouse he was screwed, but if she had to travel there he had a chance.

It had taken more calls than he predicted for Hugh to locate Amber Watkins, another sign of his slipping influence in the business community. However, he had been able to learn that she was back at the temp agency and he had managed to get her current work assignment and a home address under the guise of having some tax documents for her.

A quick trip to drive by her house showed that she was not there. His last chance was that she was at her office. He would have to stake out the building and hope that he could intercept her before she got to the courthouse. Having the conversation on a busy downtown street was problematic, but he was desperate.

*

For almost two hours, Matthews tediously and slowly explored the relationship between the two women and their shopping habits. Beyond using the questions to waste time, the prosecutor also seemed to be trying to aggravate Tatum into losing her composure. As a result, Brian had to object to some irrelevant and harassing questions but that only served to further prolong the process. Finally, Matthews checked his watch, apparently decided he had wasted enough time and finally moved to the point he wanted to make by asking, "Ms. Tatum, were you familiar with all of Ms. Peterson's underwear?"

"Well, no, but—"

"Just a yes or no, please. Did customers ever buy you or the other girls gifts?"

"Yes." Tatum managed to make the single word sound sarcastic, and Brian hoped she would be able to retain her self-control.

"Have you or any of the other girls received lingerie as a gift?"

"Sure."

"So it is possible that someone bought the panties in

question for Ms. Wood?"

"Yes, but like I said, she would never have worn expensive gear to work a party—"

Tatum had tried to rush out the words but Matthews expertly interrupted before she could say any more, "Thank you, those are all my questions."

Judge Rothborg asked Brian, "Any redirect?"

The point had been made that Natalie's friend believed that she would not wear expensive underwear to a bachelor party, so there was no point in any further questions, "No, My Lady."

Matthews jumped up, "My Lady, given the time, I would ask that we recess for the day rather than commence new witness testimony we will not be able to complete."

It was not quite five but it was too late for Brian to call another witness, so he could only nod when Rothborg looked his way. She then replied, "Fine. See you back here tomorrow at nine. Court adjourned."

*

Jenkins could not understand why Brian had allowed the trial to recess for the day without having called Amber Watkins. With all the external pressure being exerted on this case it was ludicrous to give the Youngs and Matthews the night to find a way to refute this new evidence. Now, Jenkins's instincts told him it was only a matter of time before Hugh Young or one of his lackeys would pay Amber a visit.

He had tried to get a support team for developing a witness-tampering case but had failed. Hugh Young was an upstanding member of the community, which made the higher ups less than enthusiastic to put together the rapid response needed, especially since they would be investigating a crime that had not been committed yet. Regardless, Jenkins thought he could overcome the institutionalized fear the department had of confronting the rich and powerful, given that it involved a murder, but as soon as he had to admit that the investigation involved a defence witness in the Peterson trial, he was immediately and totally stonewalled. Word had obviously gotten around that the prosecutors' office was livid because he had derailed the case.

However, he had a few favours he could still call in, which was why, while he was parked down the street from Amber's house, his old partner Stephen Wilson was wearing out his shoes doing laps of her office building. Jenkins's phone chirped and he picked it up. "What have you got Steve?"

"Your witness just left work and boarded the Northwest train. She got more than her fair share of long looks from numerous males along the way but no one tried to talk to her."

"Thanks Steve. I'll take it from here."

"You sure you don't need anything else?"

He knew it was likely going to be a long night and that he could use the extra eyes, but he did not want to get the young detective in trouble for helping him so he let the offer go, "I'm good, get back to your own cases."

"Alright, old man, be careful out there."

Taking a long drink of his coffee, Jenkins reclined in the car seat and got comfortable for what he hoped would be his last stakeout.

*

When five o'clock had come and gone, Hugh was certain that Amber had already testified. It had taken four tries for Hugh to get through to Poetker, but the lawyer eventually talked to him, and to his great relief, confirmed that Amber had not testified before the trial was recessed for the day. This confused Hugh, but while he did not understand why it had happened, he was glad for finally getting some good luck. Hopefully he could manage to confront the woman when she was alone.

He considered waiting right at her house but somehow that piss-ant defence lawyer had found out about Amber buying the panties, which meant he needed to be careful, more careful than he had been so far. He would need to make sure she was not being watched before he approached her. While he worked so late that rush hour traffic was never a concern for him, he had often overheard underlings complain about how taking the crowded trains was the only real option for getting in and out of downtown. This made him fairly certain that Amber would be taking the train home.

A review of the route map revealed that Amber was most likely to get off at the Dalhousie station in order to get home. Hugh had immediately driven there and was waiting when the train pulled in. A dozen people scattered from the train and he spotted Amber moving among them. Most of the group wandered off to cars waiting in the parking lot, while a few, including Amber, moved towards the bus stop.

Hugh scanned the group waiting to board the buses. There were only four loud teenagers, three middle aged secretaries, and a man in rumpled suit. None of them were paying any special attention to her. He started the car and got ready to follow the bus.

*

When the trial had recessed for the day, Brian had requested that he be allowed to meet with Charley as usual, so instead of going back to his solitary cell, Charley was taken to the client meeting room. He was slowly eating the pretzels Brian had bought for him from the vending machine. Normally he would simply focus on the snacks and the joy of being safe for a few hours, but today was different.

Throughout the day in court, Charley had continued to fantasize about finding his mother. He was not sure how he was going to get to her or what he was going to say to her, but he needed to see her, to let her know what she had done to him. First, though, he needed to get out.

Before he made the decision to confront his mother, he had not really cared if he was found guilty. Being freed would mean escape from the torment of prison, but it would also mean a return to lonely suffering on the streets. He had been hoping for a finding of not guilty only because that meant Brian, a person whom he now considered to be a friend, would be successful. Now, however, he wanted to be let out for his own reason.

He leaned over the table, looked at the papers, and asked, "Who is Amber Watkins?"

Brian looked up, confused shock on his face. This was the first question about the case Charley had ever asked. The lawyer merely stared, and for a moment, Charley thought Brian was going to get mad at him. For months the two men had been sitting together for endless hours in windowless rooms, and for all that time he had been unable to properly discuss the matter that had thrust their lives together. Now, on the eve of the last day of the trial, Charley was finally speaking. It would be understandable if Brian were to lose his temper with him, but instead the lawyer eventually grinned and said, "She's the person that's going to get you out of prison."

CHAPTER 31

Following the bus proved more difficult than Hugh had thought it would be as pulling over every time the bus stopped would have drawn attention. Thankfully, the route ran through a residential area, so he was able to circle back or park ahead of the bus until it passed him in an attempt to mask his actions. Now, as Hugh drove past the stopped bus, he was surprised to see Amber stepping out onto the sidewalk. They were still far from the address the temp agency had given him as her home, but Amber was walking towards his car. The street was empty. He should act now.

Hugh did not want to frighten her off, so he got out of the car when she was a hundred feet away. When she glimpsed a man on the sidewalk she lowered her head, preparing to ignore the stranger as he passed, but she apparently noticed he was not moving and looked up to determine if she was walking into a threat. As soon as she recognized Hugh she stopped.

Raising his hands in a sign of peace, he called out, "Hi Amber, I only want to talk for a couple of minutes."

She quickly looked around, probably trying to decide if she could run away or not. Seeing she had nowhere to go, she answered, "Sorry Mr. Young, I can't talk to you right now; I need to get my daughter from her daycare."

"I understand; this will only take a moment," Hugh gestured to his car, "I could give you a lift and we could talk on the way?"

She shook her head. Of course she was not going to get in the car with him. Hugh was used to dealing with frightened women, but this time he fought the instinct to step forward and intimidate her into doing what he wanted as that might send her to police. Instead he kept his distance and said, "I understand this is an awkward situation but I think we can both benefit here."

Amber took another look around for an escape route as Hugh continued, "I'm not mad. I know that you had to answer the questions. I feel awful—I should never have gotten you involved in this mess. I'm simply here to give you some incentive for helping me out of this jam."

"I'm sorry, Mr. Young, I really am, but I've already told the lawyer everything and the woman at the store remembers me. If I back out now I'll get in trouble."

"I doubt it." Hugh began to move forward slowly, as if he were approaching a wild animal, and in his most grandfatherly tone he said, "The defence lawyer will not be able to contradict you because he can't testify. And the woman at the store could be mistaken. Hell it was months ago and she deals with a lot of customers."

"I'm not comfortable lying—"

"Sure, of course, no one wants you to lie but perhaps you could become forgetful." Hugh had managed to get only a few steps from her and he reached both hands into his suit jacket pockets. "For the right price, of course."

He pulled out a thick envelope. He had strategically left the flap open so she could see the brown bills inside. She merely looked dumbly at the envelope so he pressed on, "Five grand cash right now for simply considering to help me. Another twenty thousand dollars after you testify that you don't remember me having you buy the underwear."

The young woman stared at the envelope with her tired eyes as Hugh silently willed her to take it. For the longest time she did not move. Worried that his first plan was not going to work, he was about to pull the knife he was clenching in his other pocket, deciding that she needed to be scared into complying. Just as his hand moved, thankfully, her hand reached for the money.

*

Sitting up as Amber and her daughter came walking down the street, Jenkins glanced at the clock. It was too early for them to be home. Wilson had said that Amber had left work at the same time as when they had followed her on Friday, but now she was home well over half an hour earlier. Something had happened to change their commute. He started up his unmarked car and drove past them.

A large Mercedes sedan was waiting at a stop sign two blocks away. In the lower-class neighbourhood the luxury vehicle stood out like a sore thumb. As he closed in he could see that he had been right: the driver was Hugh Young.

His first instinct was to flip on his siren and lights and pull over the sedan. But he realized he had not real reason to pull him over. All he had was suspicion that he had contacted a witness. It might be smarter to be patient, follow him, see where he went next. Also he could see if the young lawyer could get any information from the woman before he confronted Young.

*

The examination questions for the store clerk and Amber Watkins had basically written themselves, but Brian was obsessively going over them Monday night to ensure he did not miss anything when his phone rang.

"Hello?"

"Cox, this is Randy Jenkins. I think we have a problem with Watkins."

Over the weekend Brian had spent a fair bit of time with Amber, first convincing her that testifying was the proper thing to do and then going over her proposed testimony. He had gotten the impression that her life was focussed solely on making ends meet, doing what was needed in order to pay for her and her daughter's frugal lifestyle. Despite her outwardly confident appearance, she was actually quite shy but she had shown a sharp, humorous wit once she got to know him. Over their meetings he had come to empathize with her difficult situation, which he was making worse, and he was greatly impressed by how she kept her humor and pleasantness despite her problems, so this abrupt call caused worry to grip Brian's stomach. Perhaps his foolish mistake of not getting her testimony in today was not only a tactical trial error but had put her in danger.

"What do you mean? What happened?"

"Calm down, she's fine. But I was staking out her house, in case anyone came by to try and talk with her since you didn't bother to get her to testify today. She came home with only the kid but was well ahead of schedule. I took a drive down the street and stumbled upon none other than Mr. Hugh Young."

The relief that Amber was not hurt was immediately replaced by the concern that he had lost his star witness. Brian asked, "You think he talked to her?"

"Of course. I think he met her at the train or the bus or somewhere along that nightmare commute and gave her a ride. He's smarter than us apparently, smart enough not to be seen right at her house so he dropped her off a block or two away."

Brian was doubtful that the woman he had gotten to know would change her mind about testifying so he said, "Ok, well, he talked to her but that doesn't mean she's not going to testify."

Jenkins sighed, "She'll testify. She has to get up there now but my guess is Young convinced her to have a remarkable memory lapse or a complete story change."

"I don't know, I talked to her a lot this weekend and she seemed adamant about making this right."

"That was before she was either handed a pile of cash or had her daughter's wellbeing threatened or both. If he hadn't got what he wanted I doubt he would have driven her home. I'd bet the bank she's flipped."

At first, this made Brian think that the case was lost but then he pondered for a moment and thought that he still might be able to pull it off. He replied, "That's a problem but we still have the clerk's testimony and she'll say she remembers Amber buying the underwear. Then I call Amber and she looks foolish denying that she bought them. The jury will put it together."

Anger coated Jenkins's response. "Do they teach naïve in law school? Matthews will chew up the old lady clerk on cross to the point that she won't be able to say she can remember her own name, which will look like the truth when Amber gets up there and denies ever being in the store. Then they call Hugh Young, who will look impressive as hell on the stand in his three-piece suit as he says he has no idea where this conspiracy theory about planted underwear comes from. A guy like that will hold up easily under your cross exam. In the end, all of this looks like some hare-brained ploy by the defence."

Frustrated yet again by his lack of experience and desperate for any kind of help, Brian asked, "Ok, what do I do then?"

"Well, counselor, this is your case but if it were me, I'd get my ass in front of Amber Watkins right now and use some of that persuasive speech making you defence lawyers are supposed to be experts at. And if you can't persuade her nicely, I'd threaten every type of perjury and obstruction of justice charge you can make up or your client is going away for a very long time. Call me when you are done with her and I'll see what I can get off of Young."

*

Merging on to Crowchild Drive, Hugh was beginning to relax. It was the look on Amber's face when he said "twenty thousand dollars" that made him confident she would ensure her testimony did not hurt him. It was the look of a person on death row receiving a pardon.

Like he did before entering into any transaction, Hugh had done his due diligence. An online search had found Amber's Facebook page. She was not very active on the site, but Hugh was still able to learn that she was twenty-four, single, and had a pre-school-aged daughter. A couple of phone calls and he had a credit report that showed she was divorced and had declared bankruptcy, but since then, had somehow managed to stay out of debt. Hugh hoped to see some crippling loans, but even without debt, he knew how much she would be earning and she would be struggling mightily to pay her bills. He weighed her desperation against her probable sense of duty and settled on the twenty five thousand dollars as an appropriate first offer.

Her reaction made him think that he had weighed her desperation too lightly and had overpaid, but that was fine as he would have been willing to pay far, far more to keep his reputation intact. Hell, he had been willing to threaten the woman and her child with grievous harm if it came to that. Turning south towards home, Hugh was glad that the meeting had gone well and he was not turning north towards the airport. His packed suitcase was in the trunk with his passport. A red eye flight to anywhere far away had been the plan if Amber had refused his offer.

Now he could begin to think about a press statement. The media was reporting that his name had come up in the trial, so he would need to address the matter publicly. The statement would be brief. Something along the lines that his son had made mistakes in his life but that neither he nor his son had anything to do with this tragedy, that this was merely a desperate ploy by the defence to protect the true killer. If he played this right, he could come out looking good.

CHAPTER 32

The sun was setting when Brian's car sputtered to a stop in front of Amber's house. Stepping out into the cool spring air, he was struck by the odd stillness of the street. They were in the middle of the city but were too far from any main thoroughfare for there to be traffic noise, and it was not the type of neighbourhood where people talked across driveways or kids roamed the streets on their bikes. He walked briskly to the metal side door and knocked as he called towards the basement window, "Amber, it's Brian. I need to talk to you."

There was a long delay before she came to the window, forcing him to look down at her as she coldly said, "I'm sorry Brian, I can't talk to you right now. You should have called before coming all the way out here."

The formal way she spoke and the guilt on her face made it clear that Jenkins had been right. She was going to change her testimony. Amber moved to close the window, but he called down, "I know you talked to Hugh Young today."

She looked up at him, apparently trying to figure out how he knew about the meeting. Brian did not want to upset her, but an innocent man's freedom was on the line and he had to put that ahead of her emotions. He said, "You could be in trouble, Amber. I want to let you know what could happen if you fabricate testimony. You can do whatever you want but you should get all the information first. I brought this mess on you and I don't want you to end up getting hurt because of it."

Worry flashed across her face but she did not move, so Brian pressed on, "Think about who you are smarter to trust, me or Hugh Young?"

That got her to open the door. As he stepped inside Sophie charged up the stairs on all fours like a monkey in pyjamas before clasping her arms around his knees. He barely had time to kick off his shoes before the girl excitedly led him by the hand down the stairs while chattering about all of the new pictures she had. With complex thoughts about how to deal with Amber rolling through his mind, he had to sit through a half-hour art show before Amber asked her daughter to go into the bedroom and work on a new picture for Brian so they could talk.

Amber took her spot on the vinyl chair next to the TV, tucking her thin legs beneath her. Wearing plaid cotton pants and a worn out sweatshirt with her hair pulled back and no makeup, Amber looked like a high school student, but her face showed her tired concern.

"How do you know Mr. Young talked to me?" she asked sternly, using a loud whisper so Sophie would not hear.

"The cops were watching your house, worried that he might come to threaten you. They got suspicious when you made it home early and then found Young a couple of blocks away."

"So the police know?"

Only Jenkins knew and he had no proof but Brian answered, "Yes."

Amber looked past him to where her daughter was sitting on the apartment's only bed intently drawing before looking back and asking, "Am I in trouble?"

This direct question was a problem. If she held up on the stand there would be no indication that any crime had been committed. Even if questions about the veracity of the testimony arose, it was unlikely that they would be able to prosecute for perjury unless she or Hugh Young did something foolish. Regardless, with Amber filled with worry, eagerly awaiting his answer and likely to believe whatever he said, the lie would be easy.

Brian always figured that the main reason people thought lawyers were corrupt and deceitful was because lawyers were instilled with a high level of trust simply by the nature of their profession. A person listened to a lawyer because they had to rely on his expertise and not because the lawyer had earned their trust through past action. This made it an easy trust to betray.

Amber was chewing nervously on her bottom lip and playing with the cuff of her pants as she waited to hear if she was in trouble. He could hear Sophie humming to herself as she happily coloured. This tiny family had done nothing but struggle, and if he told Amber that she was facing criminal charges he would be betraying them. Even though it could greatly help his client he couldn't do it.

"Look, Amber I could tell you that they will throw you in jail and take Sophie away if you get up there tomorrow and lie, but I don't think they will. I doubt they have enough to warrant charging you with anything. They might suspect perjury but unless you or Young do something stupid they won't be able to prove any of those suspicions."

The lip chewing stopped and in a small voice, she simply said, "Thanks. And thanks for telling me the truth."

"What are you going to do?"

Her wet eyes seemed to be pleading with him to understand as she sadly answered, "I'm going to do what I've always done: I'm going to do what's best for my daughter."

With that she stood, indicating that it was time for Brian to go. He had failed and Charley would end up hanging himself with a prison sheet because of it. He could not give up so easy, he opened his mouth to try and convince Amber to do the right thing even though he knew the sanctimonious words would fall on deaf ears. "Look—"

Before he could form a sentence, Sophie scurried out of the makeshift bedroom, proudly thrusting an indecipherable picture. "Here. It's you and me and mommy on a horse."

"Oh, that's very nice, Sophie. Thanks." He reached into his pocket to pay the child. "I think this one is worth even more than the last one."

She shook her head emphatically, sending her dark curls in all directions, as she happily screeched, "Noooo, it's a gift. You don't get paid for a gift."

Sophie hugged him around the knees as he muttered his thanks. Then, as Brian and Amber silently watched, she skipped back to the bedroom explaining in a sing-song voice that she had to get her teddy bear ready for bed.

Putting the picture in his briefcase, Brian said, "Sweet kid."

As he moved to leave, Amber touched his elbow and said, "Tell me about your client."

*

Without warning, the light in the barren, solitary cell went out, sending Charley's tiny world into darkness. It did not matter. He remained sitting in the corner, his eyes closed.

With no distractions, the free-flowing imaginations of confronting his mother filled his mind. He only took breaks from these fantasies to recall her letter and remember various hardships from his youth. Sometimes in the dreams he would merely scold her for abandoning him before turning away and leaving her stunned. Sometimes she would immediately apologize upon seeing him and invite him into her home. Sometimes—most times actually—his temper would boil up and the meeting would devolve into violence.

In the deprivation of the darkness, it became even more difficult than usual for Charley to control his fantasizing and maintain any understanding of reality.

*

It dawned on Brian that this was it. This was the closing argument on why Charley Ewanuschuk should go free. It would not be made to a jury of twelve people in a courtroom, but to one person in a basement apartment. It would not involve legal nuisances like reasonable doubt and burdens of proof, but it would simply be a telling of the story of the life he was trying to save.

Sitting forward on the well-used couch, he put his elbows on his knees and lowered his head. The room and situation was so odd that maintaining eye contact while he spoke would have been distracting. Instead, when he began speaking in a slightly hushed voice, he kept his gaze on the worn carpet. "When he first came into the Legal Aid office, he seemed completely terrified even though it was only me and him. He barely speaks, even now after we've spent months together, he can go days without uttering a word to me. His extreme shyness and bizarre muteness intrigued me from the beginning. I could not get him to tell me anything about himself so I took a trip to the small town where he grew up.

"I was hoping to talk to his family, but his father was killed in an accident when Charley was sixteen and his mother moved away with her new husband years ago. I was unable to find any other relations but I did talk to his high school guidance counsellor and a classmate. They told me his parents were highly out of touch, his mother seemed to be manic while his elderly father seemed wholly disinterested in his son other than as a source of free farm labour. The pair was completely unable to raise a teenager, so he was sent to the battlefield of high school not just woefully unprepared by his parents, but actually hindered by their persistent strangeness. On top of that he is physically odd: gangly with thick glasses. As you can imagine, he did not stand a chance surrounded by predatory students who immediately targeted him.

"The counselor referred to it as three years of continual torture. They stole his food daily. They played school-wide games focused on his humiliation. They faked friendships to build him up so they could more effectively tear him down. If he was lucky he might get through a day only being embarrassed and tormented. If he was unlucky he would be beaten, mortified, and robbed. Imagine having to go to a place every day of your life where you could not walk down the hall without being publicly mocked or tripped or punched. He did this for three years when he was still growing up.

"He could have quit school and avoided the torture but the classmate I spoke with thought he did not want to waste all that suffering by walking away empty handed. So Charley persevered and graduated. Unfortunately, his reward was having his mother force him from the only home he ever knew. He ended up alone in a city when he had never been anywhere larger than a one-stoplight town. As he had no money and no contacts, he, predictably, became homeless.

"I know enough to know that living on the streets is horrible but I can't even imagine what it would be like for someone as unsocialized as Charley. He's too shy and awkward to order a cup of coffee let alone fend for himself. He's not stupid though. He was smart enough to somehow survive despite his poor upbringing, and he wisely realized the opportunity to take shelter in the basement of a half-built house.

"Charley was willing to talk to me a little about his life once he moved into that basement. No heat, no water, and no electricity, but it was a safe, private place where he could find some peace. It is hard to tell, as he speaks so sparingly, but I think he was proud of it, sort of like a college kid with his first apartment. Having a refuge allowed him to work consistently as a day labourer and I think he had a good chance to get a steady job and off the streets until..." Brian hesitated, not sure how he should mention the murder.

Amber, her feet tucked underneath her, had been playing with the hem of her pyjama bottoms while he talked but he could tell that she was listening intently. Now, without looking up, she interjected, "Until the girl was killed."

"Yes, one more turn of horrific luck for Charley. Based on what he has told me and the evidence we've uncovered, I'm confident that Jason Young held Natalie Peterson at his house and was driving her somewhere that night. However, he crashed his car in the alley. Peterson then managed to briefly escape only to be caught and killed in the backyard." He decided to keep the focus away from the killing and on his troubled client so he added, "Despite his numerous oddities, the thing that has struck me the most about how remarkable Charley is, is that never once has he complained about the unfairness of his life. He first was dealt woefully incompetent parents who basically used him as a slave and then was forced to endure the very worse brutality of strangers. And when he seems to finally be overcoming all of that, he is framed for a murder. Even when it recently became clear that he was not getting a fair trial, he has not complained. He has always been mistreated, he expects to be mistreated so he cannot understand that being mistreated is wrong. I think he has been mistreated enough for one lifetime."

There was a long pause as Brian was out of things to say, so he let his speech sink in for Amber who was looking down at her lap. All he could do was hope that Charley's sad story would be enough to convince her not to add more mistreatment. Finally, she looked up. She was not crying but her soft eyes were glistening as she said in a pleading tone, "Honestly, I knew there was something wrong... Mr. Young was far too specific and he didn't seem lecherous or playful about the lingerie shopping. It was a serious matter. You have to understand that it was not supposed to be this way."

CHAPTER 33

On his drive home, Hugh checked his voicemail. He had three messages from Clay Matthews, practically begging to be called back. He figured dodging the prosecutor would look suspicious. Hugh's call was answered on the first ring.

"Matthews speaking."

"This is Hugh Young returning your calls."

"Oh, good. Thanks for getting back to me. I imagine you've heard that your name was raised by the defence counsel in their opening statement—"

"Yes. What's going on in that kangaroo court you're running?"

Matthews apparently chose to ignore the rude question, as he asked, "I have to know if there was any attempt to tamper with evidence either by you or anyone else that you are aware of?"

Hugh could only shake his head in disbelief. This lawyer was so daft that he actually thought he was going to openly confess to a serious crime. Hugh let his frustration touch his voice as he responded, "Of course not. My son has been extremely cooperative with you and your fucked up process. I have no idea where this accusation is coming from."

"Fine. Is there any reason you can think of as to why this former assistant of yours might testify that you had her buy this lingerie that was found at the crime scene?"

Now this was making sense to Hugh. The prosecutor was not looking for the truth, he was merely going through the motions of asking the questions so he could claim he had asked them and had been told there was no wrongdoing. He quickly decided it would behoove him to work with this prosecutor as their motives, the conviction of the homeless man, were apparently aligned.

"I am very surprised by all of this. In fact, I doubt that she will testify. I expect this is all a stunt being put up by the defence." Hugh figured that, on the slim chance Amber failed to properly fabricate her testimony as planned, he should take the opportunity to discredit her as much as possible so he added, "I treated all of my employees fairly and ensured they were well compensated. However, as I am sure you can appreciate, it's difficult to keep everyone happy all of the time. My company was sold in January and a lot of the senior people made a great deal of money, while, as is usual in these cases, the administrative staff received only severance packages. Amber had not been working with us very long and her buyout was fairly small."

"So you think that her motivation here is dissatisfaction over her payout?"

"Maybe. She also called me a few times after the buyout. I didn't talk to her but in her voice messages she said that she wanted to discuss getting a reference. I never called her back."

The prosecutor seemed eager to learn more as he asked, "Ok, was there any reason you did not want to give her a reference? Did she have any sort of problems that made her a bad employee?"

"I assume we can talk about these things in confidence and as men?"

"Certainly."

"Amber is a hot piece of ass and she knows it. Nice to have around for obvious reasons but she's a walking sexual harassment suit. I've been around and am smart enough to avoid such pitfalls but I was afraid of unleashing her on any of my associates. That's why I didn't call her back."

"I highly doubt we will need you to testify but would you be available to come to the courtroom tomorrow in case we need you to refute this woman's claims?"

Hugh was confident that he would not be needed to testify since Amber was in his pocket, so he had no problem with this request. "Sure."

This seemed to calm the worried prosecutor only slightly. He continued to ask questions, but Hugh's patience with the interrogation waned as he neared his house. He told Matthews he was not going to waste more of his time on this trivial matter.

*

At least Amber was talking, so Brian blindly prodded her along. "I think I do understand. From time to time we are all put in situations where we don't like any choice available."

She wiped her eyes with her sleeve and continued in a more composed manner, "You must think I'm horrible. A single mom living in this awful basement suite that pushes up on old men and runs their perverted errands to pay her bills."

With no idea how to respond to this, Brian could only mutter, "Oh, no, I'm sure you only did what you needed to do…"

Tears overflowed and wet her cheeks as she continued softly as if talking to herself, "Life was not supposed to go like this. I grew up in a little town in Ontario. My parents were hardworking, devote churchgoers. Even though they were furious with the idea, I got married right out of high school to Paul. He was a hockey player. A goalie. He played Junior A and had a season in the WHL as a backup. He never made it past that level and after it ended, well, he had a hard time not being the hockey star.

"I tried to understand, I tried to be supportive, but we were always broke. At least while he was playing he had some income and some structure. When he got cut from the team that went away. Whenever I brought up the idea of him getting a job he'd get mad and say that he was training for a comeback. Training meant he was hanging out at the gym; no teams were actually interested. He did become a ringer for hire for beer leagues, intramural teams or whatever. They'd pay him forty bucks a game, but more often than not, that money and more got spent at the bar after the games while he basked in the praise of his teammates who had real jobs. Before long he was playing and drinking every night of the week. If I complained he would explode, arguing that I was the one that told him to get a job. The bills kept piling up but we were young and I figured soon he would grow out of the hockey player thing."

Amber paused and glanced back to the bed, where Sophie had fallen asleep gripping her teddy bear. A tiny grin slipped in beneath the tears before she looked back down. "I got pregnant when I was twenty. At first I was scared but the news seemed to mature Paul. He got a job at a sporting goods store and started coming home most nights right after his hockey games. When Sophie was born it was good for a while. We were still broke but we were making ends meet. It was a grind but we were managing. Then Paul lost a bunch of money he borrowed on some real estate investment scheme that he was sure would make us rich. He started staying out drinking again and he got fired from the store. We had a big fight one night and, in the morning, he was simply gone.

"My first reaction when I realized he was not coming back was not sadness or anger but relief. He was a bigger drag than a help so I figured me and Sophie would be better off on our own. Then the bill collectors started calling. Paul had run up debts all over without me knowing. Credit cards I had never heard of. A student line of credit even though he never went to school. He even owed money to the store he had worked at because he bought things on credit. It was as unbelievable as it was overwhelming. With nowhere to turn I called my parents to see if they could help.

"We had not really talked much after I married Paul. I think my mom was actually glad to see it all falling apart for me so that she could say I told you so. Late that night my dad showed up and handed me an envelope with a thousand dollars in it. He told me not to tell my mother and not to ask for anything more. I cried for three days straight after that. I wanted to give up. But when Sophie ran out of diapers. I realized I had to stop crying. I couldn't give up. I pulled myself together and went to one of those free debt counsellors. With their help I declared bankruptcy, got out from under Paul's debt and me and Sophie have been living paycheck to paycheck ever since.

"So, when Mr. Young handed me three hundred dollars just to buy him some underwear, I took it without asking any questions." She looked over at a spot where the overlapping throw rugs ran out and the bare concrete of the floor showed. "And now, well, I know it's not a fortune but the kind of money he is saying he'll give me, it would change our lives. Get us out of this cave and into an actual home where Sophie could have her own bed, maybe even her own room. I could put her in a real day care and save something for her education. I can't say no to that."

*

He still had not heard from Brian, and Hugh Young had only driven home. If the pompous businessman made it inside, Jenkins would have no chance of getting him to talk. Out here, in the driveway, he at least had the very slim hope that the stares of the neighbors would worry Young into cooperating somewhat. As Young drove into the garage, Jenkins, acting on impulse, quickly pulled in right behind so the overhead door would not close. He chirped his siren and flashed his lights.

He merely sat to watch as Hugh Young scurried out of his sedan and nervously looked back at him. He had no evidence and no basis for an arrest, but he found the overt panic covering the arrogant man's face so rewarding he figured that even if he got nothing from the conversation, the trip had been worthwhile. Taking his time, he climbed out of the car and stretched his heavy body, feeling his spine creak back into place as his knees whined under his weight. He decided that his retirement would definitely not include endless hours in a car seat and should probably involve some sort of exercise program.

"You have no fucking right to be on my property—"

Jenkins ignored the blustering and strode right up, forcing him back against his car. "Shut up. I know you contacted Amber Watkins this evening—"

The sensation was sharp, intense, and immediate but his mind did not acknowledge the sensation as an injury. It was not until he felt the wet warmness on his legs and looked down to see the blood that he realized he was hurt. Young's fist was clutching the hilt of the knife he had buried deep in Jenkins's belly. Looking up at Young's eyes he did not see anger but instead he sensed terror, a child who had done something awful he knew he could not take back.

He fumbled for his sidearm, but before he could draw the gun, Young grabbed his hand, pinning it against his side. He tried to struggle but he was suddenly weak and his arm would not move. His legs went numb as the world went black and he crumpled to the cement floor.

Lying there, knowing he was bleeding to death, his thoughts drifted to his wife. For a couple of weeks now she had quietly made it known that she really wanted to go to a new movie that was out about ballerinas, but he had put it off. Such a simple thing, taking your wife to a movie, and he had not done it, would never do it. The guilt made him remember her happiness at his decision to finally retire. She was glad solely because she would have him to do things with again and now, after waiting so patiently for so long, she would forever be denied that basic want.

*

Moving numbly, Hugh hurried to the detective's car and drove it into the garage so he could close the door. With the door closed, hiding the horror, he slumped against the wall, staring at the corpse in the spreading pool of blood.

He could not believe what he done—it had happened in an instant. Seeing the cop, he'd been struck by the realization that this meddler was going to ruin his plan and, worse, expose him to the world as nothing but a criminal who planted a pair of panties to frame a hobo to hide his son's depravity. He would be an immediate and total laughing stock. Before he could stop himself, he had buried the knife into the man's stomach.

For a number of minutes he stayed sitting on the floor, thoughts pouring over panicked thoughts. A normal man would be doomed but he would not accept that fate for himself. He would stay calm and think this though, no more rash actions. Poetker had told him that he had heard the detective was acting on his own, so maybe no one would know where he was. He would find a place to leave the police car with the body in a bad neighborhood, somewhere the cops would think the detective had merely come across the wrong person at the wrong time, and then he would very carefully cover his tracks. He could get through this so long as he thought every step through calmly and properly. He knew he was smarter than the foolish criminals who got caught.

*

Brian trudged into the apartment. He was frustrated, tired, and angry. The detective had been ordering him about and now, when he needed to talk to him, he could not get him on the phone to discuss what he had found out. Actually, he had to admit to himself that his anger was deeper than Jenkins not calling back—he was finally fed up with the whole miserable process.

He had explained to Anna why he was going to speak with Amber, so she met him at the door, eager to find out what had happened, "How'd it go?"

His answer came out more curtly than he meant it to. "Not sure. But Young definitely got to her."

"You think she's going to lie."

"Yeah."

They walked into the kitchen where Anna had wine waiting. He took a glass, leaned against the counter in his usual spot, and drank deeply. Anna sat in one of the chairs and twirled the wine in her glass. She asked, "What did he do to get her to change her story?"

"Paid her off. I don't know how much."

"She's willing to risk going to jail for some cash?"

Brian shrugged. "I probably should have pressured her more. Scared her about the chance of getting convicted of perjury. But I couldn't. She's not doing this out of greed or malice, She's simply desperate."

After a long drink, he relaxed somewhat and he was able to recap the discussion. His first futile attempts followed by the little girl giving him the picture, the telling of Charley's life story, and then Amber's own sad story.

"After all of that Amber was pretty upset. I tried to get her to tell me what her plan was but she said she was too tired to talk anymore and politely ordered me to leave. I had no choice but to go and have no idea what she's going to say tomorrow, but I doubt it will be good."

"Can't you go and tell the judge or the prosecutor about all this tampering?"

"I can but I've got no proof so I doubt the judge will do anything. Matthews appears so dead set on getting a conviction he probably wouldn't do anything even if we had proof."

"What about the detective, can't he help?"

"I don't know, I can't even get him on the phone." He drained his glass. "Doubt it would matter though, not really anything he can do. Have to play the hand I'm dealt."

"Sounds like tomorrow's going to be interesting."

"For sure. Unfortunately the interesting part is going to be me looking like a fool." Brian set his empty glass down. "And frankly, I'm fine with that because I'm too fucking tired of thinking about this mess to come up with a new plan."

Anna knew well enough not to try and get him to talk. Instead she moved in front of him and wrapped her arms around his waist, setting her head against his chest. They stood like that for a moment, Brian forcing his mind to stop thinking as he enjoyed the simple pleasure of holding her. Without lifting her head, Anna quietly spoke in his shirt, "Do you want to hear a joke?"

He chuckled slightly, "Sure."

"What's the difference between God and a lawyer?"

"I don't know."

"God doesn't think he's a lawyer." Anna leaned back and looked up at Brian. "You've done your best, did everything you could, everything that anyone could have done and more. You'll do your best tomorrow and whatever happens after that is out of your hands."

CHAPTER 34

After spending a sleepless night stressing, Brian was leaving the apartment to head to the courthouse when his Blackberry rang.

"Hello?"

"Hey Brian, it's Fredrickson. Ready for the last day?"

Before going to bed, Brian had tried a number of more times to get a hold of Jenkins, but he never answered his phone. Picking up, he had hoped it would be the detective but he was also glad to have the chance to talk with Fredrickson before heading into court. He had told him about Amber Watkins but had to be vague due to Jenkins's involvement. The advisor had been understandably curious about the appearance of such miraculous evidence at the eleventh hour, but lawyers learned quickly that some things were not available for discussion, and it was considered rude to pressure another lawyer about such matters. All Brian had to say was that he could not tell him how he came to find the witness, and Fredrickson never raised the issue again as they moved onto contemplating how to use the new evidence at trial.

"Actually, we encountered a setback."

He could not explain how he knew Amber had talked to Hugh Young as that would reveal Jenkins' involvement. However, he told Fredrickson everything else about her being paid to change her testimony. He explained that he had met with her last night to try to convince her to tell the truth but that he had failed. There was a pause. Then Fredrickson let out a hearty laugh. In his intensely exasperated state, this irritated Brian to his core, but before he could say anything, Fredrickson spoke through his chuckles, "You have to be setting the record for most fucked up first murder trial ever. Hell, if you survive this, you'll have a story to tell for years, and every member of the defence bar will have to buy you a drink—and no cheap shit either."

The jovial comment faded the annoyance and actually cheered Brian. He realized that, while he may have made some mistakes, he was facing unusual circumstances that even the most senior of lawyers would have struggled with. A grin actually crossed his lips as he asked, "So what the hell do I do today?"

"Tough to say. I mean every trial lawyer has had a witness change their story on them but normally you don't get a head's up like this. What were you planning?"

Brian had been thinking about this all night, so he was able to answer rapidly, "I'll call the store clerk. Have her identify Amber as having bought the underwear like we planned. I need to call Amber as I mentioned her in my opening. But I don't need to ask her if she bought the underwear for Hugh Young. I could get her to say she worked for Young at the time and let the jury draw their own conclusion. Matthews will probably ask the question on cross and she'll lie then but it will look better if she tells him she didn't buy the underwear for Young rather than her telling me that and tainting her whole testimony."

"Makes sense, and Matthews is likely in the dark on this so he might not even risk pushing the point by asking her whether she bought the underwear for Young."

Brian took some hope from this idea, "You think?"

"Maybe, if he doesn't know what she's going to say then he might not want to take the chance. Of course that would mean he thinks he can win without getting her to deny your blatantly unasked question."

Realizing Fredrickson was merely leading him to the conclusion he was playing it too safe, Brian said, "Alright, I get it."

"Well, there's no point in aiming for second place in a murder trial. Do you think you have enough to win if you don't ask her straight out?"

Brian was growing weary of discussing this same issue over and over but he knew Fredrickson was right. "No. The underwear will sink Charley unless we can give the jury a clear explanation for it being there. Problem is I'm sure Matthews will make hay out of whatever I can put forward now. I'm tempted to get out of the way and take our chances playing on the jury's sympathy."

"Let me try to put it to you this way: If some psycho put a gun to your head and said you had to fuck an animal but you can pick the animal, what would you do?"

"Honestly, I've never considered that particular question."

"Well, I'd tell the asshole I want a walrus. Why? Because fuck *him*—sure you're screwed but now the asshole has to go and get a goddamn walrus."

This made Brian chuckle despite himself. "Alright, fair enough, but how does your bestiality preference help me in this particular mess."

"What I'm saying is there's no point in doing the work for the prosecution just because we're in a tough spot. We ask the question, if she lies, she lies. You push her on those lies because that's what defence lawyers do and, at least, you make that prick Matthews earn his salary."

*

In his younger years he been able to work through the night with no repercussions, but this morning the lack of rest was pulling heavily on Hugh Young. For over an hour he had waited down the street in his car, teetering on the edge of panic, ready to flee the instant he saw police arriving at his house looking for the detective. When they did not arrive, Hugh figured Poetker had been right and the detective had been acting on his own, so no one knew he had come to his house. He had a chance to escape the nightmare without having to go hide in some jungle while the whole city gossiped about his demise.

It had taken all night to clean, re-clean, and then scrub the garage and get rid of the corpse, the knife, his bloody clothes, and the patrol car. While the tasks had not been physically demanding, it had taken an enormous amount of will power not to think about the horrific nature of his actions. In those darkest hours, he could not help but contemplate all the innumerable small things that led to this massive disaster. If only the detective had let him get inside the house, where he could have ignored him. If only the cop would have kept his distance instead of rushing him. If only he had not had the damn knife in his pocket. In order to retain some semblance of composure Hugh focussed his rage on Jason, pondering how to punish the fool when he returned.

Now it was time to leave for the courthouse. It took all of his determination to simply dress in his favorite dark suit. He wanted nothing more than to get in his car to drive somewhere far away where he could hide in peace, but he knew not showing up for the trial after he told the prosecutor he was going to be there would appear strange. Any strangeness might draw unwanted attention. Normalcy and calm would be his shield. He tied his tie.

Arriving at the courthouse, Hugh saw a television reporter taping an introduction on the steps. For obvious reasons, he had forgotten about the idea of drafting a press statement. But, seeing the reporter, he decided a little public recognition that he was the person being mistreated was still desirable.

All it took was introducing himself to the reporter and he had his small press conference assembled. There was only one television camera, but he had been assured that the footage would be picked up by all of the stations, and at the site of someone important-looking being interviewed, other reporters with tape recorders had gathered, along with a photographer who began rapidly taking pictures. Given all of this attention, Young was confident his message would be prominently shown.

He stood up straight in an attempt to not look exhausted as he delivered his statement, "Allegations have been made at this trial regarding improper actions by my son and, recently, by myself. I admit that my son has made misjudgements in his life but he has committed no crime. Regardless, my wife and I are working diligently to ensure that he gets the help and support he needs to live a better life in the future. While I have stood by my son in this difficult time as any caring father would, this recent assertion that I somehow tampered with evidence is simply a misguided ploy by the defence to obscure the truth so that the accused, the man responsible for this tragedy, will be freed. I am confident that the former employee of mine, which the defence is planning to call as a witness, will not play along with their games. Her honest testimony will show I did nothing improper."

With that, he abruptly turned away from the reporters and strode into the courthouse.

*

Sitting at the defence table, staring at his lap as usual, Charley could feel the increased excitement in the courtroom. By the sounds of rustling and murmuring voices, he knew the gallery was filling up behind him. Brian was furiously reviewing his papers. The prosecutor was berating the young lawyer next to him.

Brian had explained to him that the underwear the police found in his basement was not actually the girl's but had been planted there. However, Brian was now having trouble getting truthful testimony about them. Charley knew he should feel a sense of outrage at the fact that he was being framed and people were not telling the truth when his life was on the line, but he always expected mistreatment so now it failed to anger him. He glanced up at the clock, one minute to nine. This was likely the last day of the trial, which meant his ordeal was going to come to an end, one way or another. The judge walked in and Charley shuffled to his feet.

*

The lingerie store clerk's name was Dolores Coopersmith and she sat primly on the edge of the witness's chair as she spelled it out for the court reporter. Brian, trying to calm his racing heart, stepped to the podium, "Good morning, Ms. Coopersmith. Please tell the court where you work?"

The woman leaned close to the microphone and answered, "I am a manager at Belle's Ball on 17th Avenue."

"What does your store sell?"

"High-end lingerie."

He handed her the underwear in its plastic evidence bag. "Does your store sell these?"

The woman put on the glasses that hung from her neck on a chain and took a moment to examine the exhibit before answering, "Yes, we used to. They were part of a designer bra and panties set we carried up until a couple of months ago."

"Can you tell us about this underwear?"

The woman became at ease now that she was in her area of expertise. "Certainly. They were made by a company called Le Perla and are from their winter 2010 collection. They were not very popular, I think because most woman who purchase such expensive items are not interested in the booty short model as it is seen as slightly juvenile, especially given the little bow in the front."

"What did the set cost?"

"Initially we priced the set at $99.00 but they did not sell very well, so we reduced the price to $79.00."

"Would you consider these to be a common item for sale in the city?"

Matthews got to his feet. "My Lady, objection. The question is leading and calls for speculation on the part of the witness."

Rothborg did not even look up before answering, "Sustained."

Brian had anticipated the possibility of an objection and had his other line of questioning ready: "What other stores in the city sell this item?"

"As far as I know there is only one other store that sells the Le Perla collection in the city. They may have offered this item."

"Ms. Coopersmith, can you tell us about any sales of this set that you can recall?"

"Yes, I recall selling that particular set to a young woman on December 9th, along with a couple of other items."

"Why are you able to recall that particular sale?"

"The next day she came back and returned all of the items except for the panties. We don't normally allow people to return items for hygienic reasons, but the garments were clearly not worn and the woman seemed desperate so I decided to help her out. I took back the clothes but I could only give her a refund for the bra as it was part of a set and she was not returning the panties."

"Can you describe the woman that made that purchase?"

He was glad when the witness did not hesitate but pointed immediately as she answered, "Yes, actually she is sitting right there next to the little girl."

Everyone turned to look at Amber, who was sitting in the

second row with Sophie, who was happily scribbling in a notepad. Amber blushed slightly at the attention but managed to hold her gaze stoically forward. Sophie, sensing the eyes suddenly on her, looked up from the paper and actually gave a small wave.

"My Lady, we would ask that the record show that the witness has identified Ms. Amber Watkins."

Rothborg looked at Amber and asked, "Are you Amber Watkins?"

Amber nodded to the judge.

"So ordered."

Brian picked up his papers. "Thank you, Ms. Coopersmith. Mr. Matthews may have some questions for you now."

Content with the clear direct testimony, Brian nervously watched the prosecution's cross examination. Matthews went through how many sales the clerk conducted and how that meant she met many attractive young women on a daily basis. From there Matthews was able to harass her into admitting that she could be mistaken that Amber Watkins was the purchaser. All in all, Brian thought the clerk's testimony had held up, but if Amber emphatically said that she had not made the purchase, the jury would have no problem believing that the clerk was wrong.

With the cross exam over, Brian got up and called Amber Watkins to the stand. He then watched as she reassured her daughter before getting up and walking towards the stand, her green tote bag under her arm. The only sound in the room was the clicking of her heels on the floor as she strode up the aisle.

CHAPTER 35

He was normally immune to such things, but the increased stirring about the room piqued even Charley's curiosity. He looked up. The woman being sworn in was stunning and he stared openly. She seemed accustom to attention, appearing oblivious to all the eyes on her. However, Charley knew what fear looked like as he had spent a lifetime being afraid, and he was able to glimpse fear beneath the façade of indifference. Surprisingly, he felt sorry for the stranger, for putting her through this ordeal, even if she was about to lie in order put him in jail.

As she sat on the witness stand, the woman's eyes fell on him. His natural impulse was to hide by dropping his gaze but the strangeness of her look held him. At first it seemed to be the usual confusion at his bizarre appearance, but then it transformed into a look he was not familiar with. It was close to the pity he was used to seeing when he was on the streets but it was different—it was more than that, or maybe less than that. It had no hint of the normal taint of disdain. It was the briefest of a moment but in the moment he thought, perhaps this woman actually empathized with him.

*

"Good morning, Miss Watkins. By way of introduction please tell us what you do for a living and where you worked in December of last year."

Brian realized that Amber was not listening. She was looking past him. He glanced behind him and realized she was staring at Charley. Oddly, his client did not immediately lower his gaze. The two of them were sharing a look.

The moment lasted for only a few heartbeats but to Brian it seemed longer. Then Charley looked down at his lap and Amber seemed to recall where she was, nervously asking, "Sorry, could you repeat the question?"

"Please tell us what you do for a living and where you worked in December of last year."

"I am an administrative assistant. Last December I was working at a company called Young Exploration."

Brian had planned to develop a history, show the jury how long she had worked there, what her duties had been and so forth in order to let her get comfortable testifying before bringing up the key point. But he had noticed that shared looked with Charley. Hoping she was feeling pangs of guilt, he decided to move right in before they could fade, "What was your job there?"

"I was an assistant to the CEO."

"The CEO was whom?"

"Hugh Young."

"Did Mr. Young ever ask you to purchase a specific pair of women's underwear for him?"

The question hung in the air as the whole room seemed to hold its breath. Amber fingered the hem of her skirt where it lied above her knee. She looked past him but this time not towards Charley. He did not need to turn to know she was looking at where Sophie was sitting alone in the gallery. He asked again, "Did Mr. Young have you purchase a pair of women's underwear for him?"

Finally she took a deep breath and answered, her voice coming out first as a weak whisper, "Yes." Then, more strongly, "Yes, he did."

Despite his hope, the words still stunned Brian and he merely stood as murmurs filled the courtroom. However, excited relief quickly replaced the shock and he managed to prompt her, wanting to get it all out before anything else could go wrong, "When and how did that request occur?"

"On December 9th. He gave me a very specific description of what he wanted me to buy. He gave me money. I don't recall how much it was at first but then I... well, I sort of flirted with him, saying something along the lines that it might not be enough for me to get anything for myself. He then gave me all the money in his wallet, almost three hundred dollars. It took a lot of looking but I found what he had asked for at the store the last witness works at. Then, I also bought a teddy that was on sale in case Mr. Young asked to see what I had spent his money on."

"What happened next?"

"I returned to the office and gave him the panties. I pulled the teddy out of the bag a little bit, to show him a glimpse of what I bought myself so he would not ask for the change. Thankfully he did not seem interested in that at all so I left. The next day I went back to the store on my lunch break and the clerk was kind enough to let me return the other items."

Brian handed her the evidence bag with the panties. "Are these what you bought and then gave to Mr. Young?"

She looked at them closely before handing the bag back and saying, "I think so, yes."

As Brian returned to the podium she continued, "I honestly didn't know what they were for. I needed the job and I couldn't just disobey him. And, well, three hundred dollars is an awful lot of money to us."

Brian glanced at the jury. They were all paying rapt attention. Since she had decided to be truthful, he considered asking about the bribery attempt by Young, but if she did not play along it could undo some of the good they had garnered. Her testimony was more than enough; they had an explanation for the underwear. He smiled a silent thanks to Amber. She looked back with no smile but nodded slightly, as if she were accepting his gratitude. He said, "That is all from me, Ms. Watkins."

*

Smart phones being used by reporters to get the dramatic news out with their thumbs lit up the gallery. Panic fought despair for the right to overwhelm Hugh. Every part of him wanted to flee but he was forced to sit and watch his demise play out.

The judge spoke: "Mr. Matthews, please begin your cross examination."

The prosecutor was manically scribbling notes. Hugh realized with dismay that his last chance of escaping this disaster was a lawyer who was too inept to be in private practice. Panic was winning the fight over despair.

The prosecutor moved slowly to the podium and scanned his notes for another long minute. He seemed lost, but when he began the questioning the lawyer sounded surprisingly composed and formidable.

"Ms. Watkins, you are still employed at Young Exploration, correct?"

"Um, no, it no longer—"

"A simple yes or no will be sufficient, Ms. Watkins. Did you quit?"

"Um, no, but—"

"Again, Ms. Watkins, a simple yes or no will be sufficient."

Hugh was slightly impressed. The prosecutor had managed to create the impression she had been fired rather than laid off as part of the takeover. Maybe he had a chance yet.

"Have you tried to contact Mr. Young since your departure?"

"Yes."

"You tried to contact him a number of times to ask for an employment reference, correct?"

"Yes."

"Have you managed to speak to him since your departure?"

"Yes."

Hugh silently cursed. The idiot was going to walk the bitch right into telling everyone about the bribe. The fucking bribe was his salvation only minutes ago and now it was going to ruin him.

"You did speak to him about getting a reference?"

Amber shook her head, "No."

There was a long pause as the prosecutor appeared to ponder whether he wanted to continue down this line of questioning or not as he obviously did not know what they had spoken about. Hugh silently pleaded that the fool would give up. His plea was not heard.

The prosecutor reluctantly asked, "When did you talk to him?"

"Last night. He stopped me on the street right after I got off the bus on my way to pick up my daughter."

Hugh shifted as he felt all the eyes in the crowded room turn on to him. It was over.

*

It took a great deal of effort for Brian to not laugh out loud. The prosecutor was pretending to flip through his notes in order to buy time but he had no options. Matthews was an officer of the court and he had a duty to ensure that the case he was presenting was not fraudulent. If he did not pursue this line of questioning the judge would likely intervene to determine if the witness had been tampered with. He had to follow through on the matter even though he knew it would likely sink his case.

Finally, setting down his useless notes, Matthews asked, "Ok, well, Ms. Watkins. What did you discuss with Mr. Young last night?"

"He gave me five thousand dollars in cash and told me he would pay me another twenty thousand dollars if I testified that I did not remember buying the lingerie for him."

Brian was starting to stand to ask for sidebar to discuss the implications of this revelation but Matthews, apparently hoping this claim was so outlandish that it must have been made up, immediately pushed forward, "You say that Mr. Young gave you five thousand dollars in cash. I imagine, then, that you have the ability to prove to the court that you received this money?"

Amber picked up her green tote bag that she had set down beside her and fumbled inside as she talked, "Yes, actually I can do that now if you like. I was afraid to leave so much money lying around my apartment so I brought it with me."

She produced a thick, white envelope and set it gingerly on the rail of the witness stand.

CHAPTER 36

Like everyone else in the courtroom, Brian could only stare at the envelope sitting on the witness stand. It was thick, unmarked, and slightly worn. The perfect picture of bribery.

Justice Rothborg, realizing the murder trial had now devolved into something else entirely, quickly moved to regain control. "Ladies and gentlemen of the jury, I am going to ask the bailiff to escort you to the deliberations room for a moment while we sort this out."

It took a few minutes for the jury to clear the room but the judge's harsh gaze kept everyone from making a sound. As soon as the door closed behind the jury both Matthews and Brian began talking at once. Rothborg raised her hands against their babble. "Gentlemen, hush."

Brian, realizing that he had already won and could only hurt his position at this point, happily sat back in his seat, but Matthews' arrogance was not going to let him go quietly. "My Lady, I must object to the interruption of my cross examination—"

"Seriously? You should be thanking me for stopping you. Sit down."

Matthews opened his mouth but appeared to come to his senses before saying anything. He sunk into his chair as Rothborg turned her attention to Amber and asked calmly, "Ms. Watkins, am I understanding you correctly that Mr. Hugh Young stopped you on the street last night and offered to pay you to falsify your testimony?"

Amber looked up at the judge, "Yes, ma'am. He gave me this cash and told me that I would receive another twenty thousand dollars if I testified that I did not recall buying the underwear for him."

"But despite this payment, the testimony you gave today was truthful?"

She looked down and fingered the hem of her skirt as she said, "Last night I had decided to lie for the money. I was awake most of the night practicing what I would say. I wasn't proud about the decision—I know it is not a fortune, but that much money would be life changing for me and my daughter." Amber looked up to where Charley was sitting as she continued, "This morning, though, seeing that poor man sitting there I decided that I couldn't help send him to prison. Every time I spent the money I would remember his face and know that someone even less fortunate than me had to go to jail because of my lies. Also, seeing my daughter watching me testify, I realized I would have to explain to her why our lives had changed. I can't lie to her but I also knew I couldn't tell her what I did, so I changed my mind and testified truthfully. Mr. Young asked me to buy that underwear for him and I did. I'm sorry for all the grief that has caused."

Rothborg replied with a nod, "Thank you, Miss Watkins. Your integrity and your honesty are to be applauded."

Next the judge turned to Matthews, who was running his hand through his hair as he stared at the tabletop, and asked, "Does the Crown perhaps have a motion to make at this time?"

Slowly the prosecutor moved to the podium and said, "My Lady, perhaps we could have a recess to contemplate this startling revelation."

Looking over her glasses, Rothborg said, "Do you really expect me to grant a recess and send Mr. Ewanuschuk back to remand for another night?"

With a sigh, Matthews finally accepted defeat as he said, "The Crown moves to have the charge against Mr. Ewanuschuk dismissed at this time."

Rothborg simply glared at the senior prosecutor and he continued, "The charges are to be dropped without prejudice, My Lady."

"Any objection to this, Mr. Cox?"

Brian happily popped to his feet. "No, My Lady."

"All charges are dismissed on a without prejudice basis. Mr. Ewanuschuk you are free to go."

He had heard the judge say that he was free to go, but he had been taken by police van back to a holding cell at the remand center. As he sat and waited for whatever was coming next, Charley worried that this had all been some cruel hoax and they were now going to throw him into an even worse prison. However, before long, a guard came and took him to an office. It was a normal office with a desk and a bald man in a rumpled suit. There were no bars or screens on the window and Charley was not handcuffed. The man behind the desk pointed to the empty chair. Charley sat as the guard left. He realized that he really was being let go.

The bureaucrat, appearing bored, slid some papers across the desk along with a pen and said, "These are your release papers; please sign at the bottom."

Charley, eager to please, scrawled his name on the line and the papers were taken back.

The man slid an envelope and another paper across the desk. "This is the check for your net pay."

He knew that each day inside a prisoner was given a small sum of money which they could use to buy things at the remand center store. Charley, however, never ventured to the store as it would have involved unnecessary contact with inmates, plus he figured that whatever he bought would only be stolen from him anyhow. He took out the light blue government check and read: Payable to Charley Ewanuschuk, $518.63.

The man pointed at the paper he had put on the desk and said, "Sign at the bottom there acknowledging receipt."

Charley, numbed by the fortune he had been handed, scrawled his name again and clutched the envelope tightly as the man pulled back the receipt.

Next the man handed him a paper bag, "Here are the items that were with you upon your arrest. Do you need me to list them?"

He shook his head and the man slid another paper in front of him. "Ok, sign here."

Charley signed.

"That's it. Take a right outside this door and then left down the wide hallway and you're out of here."

He walked out of the office, holding the paper bag and envelope tight against his chest. Once outside in the spring air he merely stood on the cement steps, not sure where to go next. He was happily surprised to find that he was actually savouring having the ability to decide. Although he had not thought he would care, he was truly glad to have his freedom back.

*

His right wrist was cuffed to the metal table or Hugh would have attacked Jacob Poetker. He had been arrested as he tried to leave the courthouse and then was roughly fingerprinted, his belt and shoelaces were removed, and his mug shot was taken as if he were a common thug. When the infuriating processing was done, he had then been chained to this table and told to wait for his lawyer. For over an hour he had been left there, stewing in his own fury before Poetker finally showed up. And then all Hugh got was excuses and half-answers.

"Look, as I said Hugh it's not that easy. The bail procedure is going to take—"

"Fuck, I don't care about all that shit; just get me the hell out of here."

Poetker leaned back and said, "Maybe, if you are willing to offer up Jason for the murder, we can cut some sort of deal."

Hugh shook his head. "Jason is in Amsterdam."

"Will he come back if you ask him to?"

Hugh pondered this for a second. He could not tell him about his arrest, but it would take at least a day for him to get back and over that time surely he would hear the news. Knowing he was back to being a murder suspect again, he would stay gone. Jason was dumb but not that dumb. In fact, if he realized Hugh was in trouble, Jason might enjoy the thought of screwing over his father by staying away. He answered, "I doubt it."

"What about the two other guys you had testify? It won't be as good but maybe we can offer the prosecution something on them."

Hugh shook his head again, realizing that, in order to protect himself, he had actually gotten everyone but him out of harm's way. "I sent them off too. They're probably in Vegas or Mexico by now. Once this hits the papers I'm guessing they'll completely disappear."

"Ok, so you're the one guy they've got holding the bag on all of this. That is going to make it tough to cut any sort of deal—"

The handcuff chain rattled loudly as he banged his fist on the battered table and yelled, "This is fucking ridiculous! I don't want a goddamn deal! I want to walk out of here so I can tell the reporters out there that this was all a big fuckup. Now get your lazy lawyer ass to work and get that fucking done."

When the rant was over, Poetker calmly folded his hands on the table and quietly said, "Stop talking and listen carefully. I told you from the very beginning of this disaster to do nothing and it would blow over. Very good advice and so simple even a slow-witted child could have followed it. You were too arrogant to listen. Now you are going to go to jail because of that arrogance."

The lawyer wrote largely across his notepad, tossing it on the table as he stood and began walking out. "That's the phone number for Legal Aid. Maybe someone there is kind enough or desperate enough to help out an asshole like you."

Gathering his senses, Hugh turned in his seat to try to persuade the man to stay and help him, but before he could speak the heavy door crashed open. A young man in a cheap suit burst in, holding up a badge to Poetker as he moved briskly past him. "Don't worry counsellor, your client doesn't have to say a word. I'll do all the talking."

Before either Hugh or Poetker could react, the police officer slammed a plastic bag with a notebook in it onto the metal table. "Mr. Young, I'm Detective Steven Wilson. My former partner, Randall Jenkins, was found murdered this morning. Every detective keeps notes on their activities but whoever killed him apparently did not know that as they failed to take his notebook from his jacket."

Hugh started to speak but the detective stuck a finger in his face. "Don't say a fucking word. The last note in the book says that

Jenkins followed you to your house last night. Right now I've got a team of technicians going over your house with fine tooth combs while half the cops in the city are interviewing your neighbors."

The detective moved to the door but before he left he turned back and said, "You know, in a way you were lucky. Randy Jenkins was the best detective on the force and he would have been assigned to any case involving a cop killing. He'd have an idiot like you in cuffs for this in a matter of hours. In another way, though, you got very unlucky because he took the time to teach me well and I plan to use all of those lessons to make sure you spend the rest of your life in a deep, dark hole with very unpleasant roommates."

*

The Legal Aid office was an odd place to have a party but, on this occasion, it seemed fitting. The celebration had begun shortly after the charges had been dropped and it was still going strong hours later. Brian, enjoying his first stress-free moments in months, was drunkenly listening to one of the volunteers explain how they could use Charley's case to increase awareness and help fundraising. As the enthusiastic woman talked, Brian surveyed the scene around him.

Beer cans, plastic glasses, and paper plates holding pizza crusts covered most of the flat surfaces. A slightly off-tune radio was providing music. Most of the guests were Legal Aid volunteers or staff who spent their days dealing with misery, unfairness, and defeat. They were clearly taking full advantage of the opportunity to revel in the rare triumph.

A senior advisor had her head on a desk and was softly snoring while a junior lawyer was making out with a middle-aged assistant behind a cubicle partition. Fredrickson was holding court in one corner, loudly telling war stories through mouthfuls of pizza. Anna and Amber were sitting on a desk, sharing wine-soaked stories as Sophie, overwhelmed by the gluttony of office supplies at her disposal, was frantically drawing away between them. Laughing to himself, Brian had to admit it was one of his favourite days ever.

*

After watching a number of customers come and go from the check cashing store, Charley had managed to cash the government check with only minimal interaction with the clerk behind the glass. With that done he had made his way across downtown to the bus depot. Again with minimal interaction with a person behind a pane of glass, he had managed to purchase a bus ticket to Jacksonville.

The trip would take a week and involved changing buses eight times, and he would need to somehow cross the U.S. border. The journey made Charley extremely nervous, but after surviving the constant barrage of inhumanity in prison, he figured he could handle anything. And confronting his mother had become a constant, pressing need he could not ignore despite his concerns.

His first bus was scheduled to leave in eight hours. His plan was to eat dinner out of the vending machines in the station and then find a quiet corner to pass the night. However, as he settled down on a bench and opened a bag of chips, he was reminded of the kindness Brian had shown him over all of these months. All of the hours they spent together, the lawyer working away while he slowly ate snacks or the two of them playing chess or talking. Brian was his friend, his only friend. He could not recall the last time he had any concern over the feelings of another person, yet the idea of merely leaving without thanking him struck him as wrong.

*

The party showed no signs of winding down and Brian was getting more pizza when Anna waved at him to come up to the waiting room. Anna and Amber, having become fast friends as the celebration had progressed, had made a makeshift bed out of coats for Sophie near the front of the office, as far from the rowdiness as possible, and were watching her sleep while continuing their chatting.

He put his arm around Anna and asked, "What can I do for you?"

She pointed out the large window. "We think that's Charley out there?"

Her words had a slight slur to them that made Brian smile as he peered out the dark window and asked, "The man of the hour?"

"Yeah, he walked past a couple of times and now he's just standing on the other side of the street."

He peered through the glass and could make out a lanky figure standing between two streetlights. He moved to go outside as Anna nagged him to be careful. The beer made Brian oblivious to the threats of the bad neighbourhood and he loudly called out as he stepped out of the office, "Hey, Charley, that you? Come on in and have a beer. It's your party."

The figure in the shadows looked like a horse with a bug in its ear as it vigorously shook its head. It was definitely Charley. Brian jogged across the street.

"What are you doing out here? Come on inside, we're celebrating. I'm sure everyone would love to meet you."

"Um, no, I can't. But I wanted to…"

Charley removed his glasses and tried to wipe them on his shirt. For the first time Brian realized it was misting, that sort of spring drizzle you could stand in all day without really getting wet. Drying the glasses was futile so they were left off as he said, "I wanted to thank you."

Brian could not recall ever seeing Charley without his glasses on. He looked much younger, almost boyish. He clapped him on the shoulder, "Sure, you're welcome. I mean, I actually owe you. You gave me a chance to successfully defend an innocent man for my first serious case. Now come on inside, I think there's some food left…"

Charley shook his head again and, without the glasses, the fear in his eyes was plain. Brian realized that, while he had survived being framed for murder and all the torments of prison, Charley's paralyzing shyness remained. He moved to the street, calling back, "Ok, why don't I bring you out something? There's beer and pizza. That sound alright?"

*

He had wanted to say that he did not need any food but Brian darted away before Charley could form the words. He watched as the lawyer ran across the damp street and into the office to perform another act of kindness for him. After a few moments, Brian reappeared carrying a plate covered with pizza and two cans of beer still in their six pack ring.

"Here you go. Sorry, there is only vegetarian left. The girls always order it and then eat all the pepperoni."

Charley silently took the paper plate, still not sure how to respond to generosity. Brian opened the beers and handed him one. Brian held up his beer but Charley did not understand what he was doing. Brian clinked his can against his. Such a simple thing, drinking a beer with someone, but Charley realized that in all of his life he had never done it.

"Here's to the proper working of justice. It was messy, but the system got it right in the end as the innocent went free." Brian leaned against the wet brick wall behind them before continuing what Charley recognized as a slightly drunken speech. "You know, you spend all this time in school and you constantly hear about how it's better to have ten guilty men go free than to have one innocent man be wrongly imprisoned and so on. But until you see it all playing out or meet someone unfairly charged, well, you know better than me…"

Brian let the rambling sentence die unfinished in the mist as he took a drink and, suddenly, Charley's simple moment of joy eroded beneath a powerful pang of guilt. He had only had one friend, one person who cared at all for him, in all of his life. And that friend had worked tirelessly for him, treated him like an equal, and asked for nothing in return.

Without thinking he muttered, "I'm sorry."

Brian took another casual drink before asking, "For what?"

"I'm sorry." Charley wanted to tell him but he was scared. There was no way he could make Brian understand, so he decided to flee. He set the full beer can and the untouched food on the wet street, turned, and walked away.

*

For some reason, Charley suddenly set his plate and beer on the pavement and hurried away. Standing in the thin rain, Brian pondered this latest instance of oddness from his client. He had apparently come to apologize but he did not say for what. For a heartbeat, the thought that perhaps his client was not wholly innocent re-entered his mind, but watching Charley shuffling away through the rain and knowing how he disliked imposing on people, Brian told himself that the apology was likely only for the trouble he thought he had caused him.

However, as he crossed the street to head back to the party it hit his drunken mind like a hammer. The letter. He had memorized every word in Charley's letter. It said the woman had her hands cuffed behind her. With the oversized coat, there was no way Charley could have seen her hands when he was in the basement watching her run towards him. She was on her back with her hands behind her when he checked to see if she was dead. Why did he say her hands were cuffed? It would have been more likely to assume her hands were tied.

Doubt wedged its way into his drunken consciousness. The conversations with Charley were few and far between, so now, in the dark street, the recollection from months ago still came sharply to Brian. The first time they met in the Legal Aid office Charley had said she had been bleeding badly. Corpses do not bleed; they definitely do not bleed badly.

A bizarre, lonely man. A beautiful, naked woman. If Charley found her alive, alone and chained in the darkness, what was he likely to have done?

Many scenarios rolled through his mind as he watched Charley reach the corner. Regardless of his new-found doubts Brian knew there was nothing he could do, nothing he should do. It was over. The murder charges had been withdrawn with prejudice such that double jeopardy precluded Charley ever being tried again. Charley turned the corner and, as the poor man moved out of sight, Brian was left to take thin refuge in not knowing if the justice system had failed or worked.

Walking slowly back to the party, he looked through the barred window of the office and saw Anna and Amber happily talking amongst the celebrating legal aid workers. Reaching for the heavy door he forced a smile onto his face. The uncertainty would remain with him and him alone.

*

Charley watched the pre-dawn skyline of Calgary disappear out the bus window. He was nervous about the trip but he felt relief at leaving the city. He was escaping. He did not know anything about the place he was escaping to, but at least this ordeal was done.

As the city disappeared, Charley's only regret was that he was leaving behind the only friend he had ever made. Thinking of Brian caused guilt to well back up. He had wanted to tell him but he knew he would not understand. Brian could not understand. He did not know about the dream. He thought about trying to explain but how could he explain that an adolescent fantasy he had sought refuge in had become a part of him. And even worse, that in the middle of that stormy night, he had thought that this unbelievable dream was actually coming true.

Brian would not believe that when he picked the groggy and hurt woman up out of the snow he was only going to bring her inside in order to protect and help her. There was no way to tell him how utterly confused he felt when the woman came to and did not look at him with the adoration he expected but instead began to struggle. He had only wanted to reassure her, to comfort her and let her know that he wanted to help but the words would not come. Then she screamed. Only wanting to stop the noise before a neighbor heard, he had covered her mouth with his large hands. But he could not tell her he was not going to harm her and she fought harder so he held harder until she stopped moving.

He could never explain what he had done, and now, as the bus flew further down the highway, he knew he never would. It was done and over. Leaning back in the seat, Charley closed his eyes, letting the threads of the familiar daydream ravel themselves together yet again so the pleasant distraction would fade away his memories.

Made in the USA
Charleston, SC
16 July 2015